Samurai Honor

Dan... ...amed in his mind. Tonomori began running, dod... ...to the left, to the right.... A shot rang out from ... ...him. The bullet crinkled through a pane on th... ...le doors. Tonomori went through them at a jun... ...ugh the shards, feet first, rolling and skidding ... ...marble, then running, taking stairs three at a t... ...By all the gods that ever were, let me not be too late!

Diana, ...to crawl to safety under the bed, felt a fleshy ... ...rab her ankle. She cried out as Lucia began pulling. Her thin nightgown caught on something sharp, ripping. Now both ankles were grasped. Diana tried to hold onto the carpet, a bedpost, but Lucia's grip was much too strong. The nightgown tore away completely.

The door splintered open, and Diana felt Lucia's weight snatched from her aching legs, saw Tonomori seize the woman by the throat. Steel flickered yellowly. "Diana-san ..." Tonomori's heart was racing, but with relief he saw her move. Diana shuddered. "Kill her, Tonomori-san!" she ordered harshly. "Kill her!"

DAIMYŌ

William Morell

Created by the producers of
Wagons West, White Indian, The
Australians, Rakehell Dynasty, and
The Kent Family Chronicles Series.

Executive Producer: Lyle Kenyon Engel

PINNACLE BOOKS **NEW YORK**

To Amanda

DAIMYO

Copyright © 1983 by Book Creations, Inc.

An original Pinnacle Books edition, published for the first time anywhere.

Produced by Book Creations, Inc. Lyle Kenyon Engel, Executive Producer

First printing, June, 1983

ISBN: 0-523-42048-X

Cover illustration by Norm Eastman

Printed in the United States of America

PINNACLE BOOKS, INC.
1430 Broadway
New York, New York 10018

DAIMYO

SASHIMONO (BANNER)

NAGINATA (SPEAR WITH CURVED HEAD)

ARQUEBUS

KABUTO (HELMET)

NODOWA (GORGET)

MEMPO (IRON MASK)

SODE (SHOULDER GUARD)

TSUBA (SWORD GUARD)

KOTE (ARMORED SLEEVE)

TACHI (LONG SWORD)

DAI-SHŌ (MATCHED PAIR OF SWORDS)

DŌ (CHEST ARMOR)

TANTO (SHORT SWORD)

OBI (SASH)

KUSAZURI (ARMORED SKIRT)

WAR FAN

HAIDATE (LOIN GUARD)

SHURIKEN (THROWING KNIFE)

SUNEATE (SHIN GUARD)

KUTSU (SHOES)

✳ A SAMURAI ✳

© BOOK CREATIONS INC. 1983

RON TOELKE '83

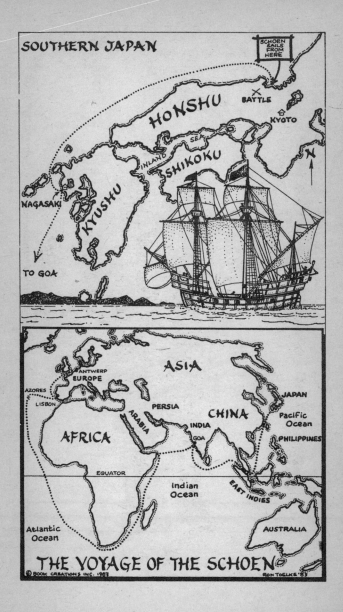

SOUTHERN JAPAN

SCHOEN SAILS FROM HERE

HONSHU

BATTLE

KYOTO

INLAND SEA

SHIKOKU

N

KYUSHU

NAGASAKI

TO GOA

THE VOYAGE OF THE SCHOEN

ASIA

ANTWERP
EUROPE

AZORES

LISBON

PERSIA

ARABIA

JAPAN

CHINA

Pacific
Ocean

INDIA

AFRICA

GOA

PHILIPPINES

EQUATOR

Indian
Ocean

EAST
INDIES

Atlantic
Ocean

AUSTRALIA

© BOOK CREATIONS INC. 1983

RON TOELKE '83

To Amanda

Prologue

It is sixteenth-century Japan, the Age of Battles. The emperor reigns serenely but impotently in his golden pavilion at Kyoto in the heart of the main island of Honshu and in the eye of the gathering storm.

The shogun, military ruler of Japan in the emperor's name, has grown weak and ineffective. Taking advantage of this situation, feudal barons called *daimyo* now rule their ancient holdings as independent kingdoms while waging continuous warfare on each other with the aid of their samurai, the elite warrior class which has dominated the Floating Kingdom for the past five hundred years.

From this chaos, one of the barons will slaughter his way into power as the new shogun and rule all of Japan to begin the cycle all over again. But which one?

And the barons and their samurai face yet another danger. Ships from the other side of the world, as seemingly far away as the moon, have touched on Japanese shores. The strange men in these ships have introduced guns into the land of the gods. With alarming frequency, the guns have been sounding their bitter voices above the havoc of battle, becoming the ultimate threat to the way of Bushido, the code of the samurai who depend only on their precious swords as the true way of the warrior.

On the fertile Kinai plain near the central east coast of Honshu, *Baron Atsuhira* prepares to launch a war of con-

1

quest against his western neighbor, the equally powerful daimyo, *Lord Betsuo*. If he succeeds, Atsuhira intends to consolidate the central mainland beneath his banner of the twin hawks and make the emperor his virtual prisoner. In control of much of Japan's richest agricultural lands, and with the emperor forced to espouse his cause, Atsuhira believes that other daimyos will rally behind him.

With solid backing, Atsuhira intends to push northward and overthrow the shogun. Once in power, Atsuhira will destroy the growing threat of the foreign ships. But first, Atsuhira must deal with Lord Betsuo. . . .

Chapter One

With the rising sun at his back, the young samurai strutted across the small bridge spanning a shallow river. To his right, an archer was wheezing his last, a death rattle in his throat from the arrow piercing his chest. The samurai paid no notice. Behind him was the proud army of the Atsuhira clan, eight thousand strong, twin hawk banners flying, mounted samurai in the vanguard drawn up in battle formation, waiting for the moment to scream into action.

"Atsuhira no Kanemitsu, champion of champions, challenges a samurai of equal rank to mortal combat!" The blue-and-white lacings of his armor reflected the colors of the Atsuhira clan. He wore no helmet, only the full *mempo* steel face mask depicting an old man, a counterpoint to his youth but not to his experience. Kanemitsu, of high rank and a renowned and ambitious swordsman, held his fighting *tachi*, the two-handed killing sword, at the ready and unsheathed.

He confronted boldly six thousand warriors of the Betsuo clan, their green-and-gold colors scattered along a thousand-yard front, a glimmering sea of banners, polished steel, and armored men poised to meet the deadly threat of the larger Atsuhira force. Kanemitsu looked for a response. The braided queue on his uncovered head was an invitation to take it if anyone could.

The archers of both armies had dueled for more than an hour, as was traditional, but now the moment all samurai had awaited was at hand, the formal sword duels. Only in these combats, they felt, was the true spirit of the samurai shown and his mettle proven. The battle that would follow the duels, no matter how fierce, would be only mass butchery, without finesse, offering no true test of skilled swordsmanship.

In a clearing of sandy ground between some smooth boulders to his left lay the bodies of three samurai, two Atsuhira fighters and one Betsuo, already slain on the field of honor.

But the leader of the Atsuhira forces, looking over the backs of his samurai, was dissatisfied with a two-for-one kill ratio, and had sent forward his best swordsman. As he watched and muttered and fidgeted on his camp stool, his retainers brought tea, which Lord Atsuhira refused. With a snort, he opened his fan.

Kanemitsu struck what was considered the classic pose, copied from a temple scroll—chin high, legs firmly apart, *tachi* held low and gleaming. He screamed his defiance again at the green and gold.

The front line of the Betsuo samurai parted, and out stepped a bare-headed samurai wearing the green-and-gold laced laminar armor of the clan. He carried no scabbard that might get in the way, instead resting the back of his bared *tachi* on his shoulder, in a position that reflected readiness for action. His walk was a shuffling gait that puzzled Kanemitsu until he realized his opponent was merely determining the texture of the ground.

"I am Nodai no Kami Tonomori." The samurai stopped some ten paces away. "And I accept your challenge."

Tonomori wore no *mempo*. Unlike Kanemitsu, he needed no mask to advertise his fierceness. Above average in height for a Japanese, but not overly tall, Tonomori was broadchested and thick of limb. At a distance one might think him overweight until he drew closer—but Kanemitsu could see no surplus flesh on his opponent's frame. Fierce black eyes, a twice-broken nose, and a small mouth gave Tonomori the predatory look of a hunting hawk. Though he was only twenty-six, stories of his strength already were being told throughout the Floating Kingdom of Japan.

4

Tonomori's head would be of enormous value and prestige—to any samurai who could take it.

He looks like a hog in armor, Kanemitsu thought. Tonomori brought his sword to guard position, the blade gleaming redly from the hazy late-morning sun at Kanemitsu's back.

Oblivious to everything but his opponent, Kanemitsu brought his *tachi* point out and up in ready position. His straight back and splayed legs were balanced in perfect harmony. *Let the blade push you out of the way*, Kanemitsu's dueling master had taught him. *Be at peace with yourself, and let your courage flow through the blade*.

Still out of sword range, Tonomori twirled his *tachi* in two lazy arcs before returning to guard position, then closed with Kanemitsu.

Feinting first with a side cut, Kanemitsu quickly thrust for the throat, hoping for a fast kill. Tonomori leaned backwards out of range as the tip missed by no more than an inch, then switched positions, holding his *tachi* point behind his body. The blade was low and to the right parallel to the ground for a sweeping leg or belly cut. This checked Kanemitsu's next move, a cut to the right side, and he backed away from the potential counter-blow.

Their world narrowed to a small bright tunnel of whirling death. They were deaf to the sounds from the shifting armor and stamping horses of fourteen thousand men.

Tonomori moved closer, head bobbing slightly from side to side, changing stance again, this time for a suicidal two-handed, over-the-head position. It threw Kanemitsu back into a guard position; he didn't want to double-kill with Tonomori.

Dropping the *tachi* into front guard position again, Tonomori tucked his elbows tightly into the sides of his body armor. He turned his upper torso slightly to the right, taking the blade back with it. Coiling the immense power of his body, Tonomori struck with the speed of a poisonous snake, the *tachi* a blur of shining light. Kanemitsu saw the blow coming into his left side, and stepped into it with a static sword block. He started to move his right foot to position for a counter slash, to be followed automatically by a murderous arc in reverse over his left shoulder, into the unguarded base of Tonomori's thick neck . . .

But the power of Tonomori's blow stunned Kanemitsu, who realized in a frozen instant of time that he should have intercepted the sword with a hard cut of his own. A thin line of white pain, slicing into his left arm, exploded with tremendous force against the lacquered iron scales of his body armor.

Kanemitsu's throat flooded with sick horror when he felt the arm drop onto his left foot. He screamed with rage and pain at the savage figure in front of him, and charged. Tonomori stepped into the attack, then pivoted on the balls of his feet to sidestep into a reversal. He blocked Kanemitsu's blow, using its power to rebound his own blade into position for an overhead cut. With a surging spurt of blood, it took Kanemitsu's head off like a melon.

By the time Kanemitsu's head had stopped rolling on the ground, Tonomori had stepped down from the higher plane where his zen training had taken him, a narrow path of slow motion in which his own senses were as bright and keening as a hawk in full dive. Sound, motion, and color returned to him like a rushing river.

Tonomori picked up the head by its queue, the *mempo* gone, and studied Kanemitsu's face. The duel had lasted less than a minute.

Facing the Atsuhira army, Tonomori raised the severed head. Behind him, *taiko* war drums resounded in his ears, heralds blew conch shells, and the Betsuo samurai gave full cry to their pleasure.

"Tonomor-i-i-i-i! Tonomor-i-i-i-i! Tonomor-i-i-i-i!"

From the Atsuhira lines, nothing except a single arrow, fired by an overzealous archer who was out of range. Tonomori stepped out of its way and flicked a second from the air with the tip of his *tachi*. Then he walked slowly back to his own lines, carrying his grisly trophy by its queue.

On his red lacquered camp stool in the center of his army, Lord Atsuhira resembled a dried barracuda even more than usual. His gash of a mouth hung partly open as, seething, he watched the samurai Tonomori carry off the head of his late champion to the cheering army of the hated Betsuo clan. The kill ratio of samurai was now three to one. Now Kanemitsu's vile spirit was wailing its way into the Great Hereafter, and Lord Atsuhira was in big trouble.

Normally, more duels would have been fought before the armies clashed. But the death of Atsuhira's champion changed all that. Restive at seeing their best fighters falling bloody into the sands, the Atsuhira samurai were boiling for a fight, a chance to take heads and cover themselves with glory or die in the attempt.

And unless they were put into battle order soon and launched into the Betsuo front lines, they would start bolting forward on their own, like old women brooming down a nest of rats. Since these were rats who carried razor-sharp swords and spears, the results would be disastrous. This was no war of manners. Daimyos frequently threw their troops into battle against their peers because of insults, real or imagined. At the spring cherry blossom festival in Kyoto only two months before, Lord Betsuo had compared Atsuhira—within his hearing—to a fish. It was all the excuse Atsuhira needed. This would be no polite battle, no exercise in troop movements to give his samurai a slight taste of blood to keep them combatready. Atsuhira burned with ambition, and he had a plan which could make him military ruler of Japan. He intended to completely destroy the Betsuo clan and take their lands. Now, his first strategic move was in danger because of his champion's failure and the eagerness of his samurai.

Lord Atsuhira's underbite projected menacingly as he signaled with a blue war fan for his generals.

The headquarters staff scattered quickly when the generals hurried toward Atsuhira, bowing low as they arrived. Atsuhira signaled out his commanding general, Takahiro, the *taisho*.

"Keep those fools in formation!" Atsuhira commanded. "Our lines are starting to spread out like a Yoshiwara whore on payday. See if you can draw out some of the Betsuo bandits. I'm not going to show my ass to Lord Betsuo again. Too much is at stake this time. Understood?"

7

Indeed the *taisho* did, having been second in command at last year's battle when the Betsuo forces smashed Lord Atsuhira's samurai and sent him packing with a loss of more than fifteen hundred of his own men. The general who had failed was later ordered to pull a knife across his quivering belly, and Takahiro had no intention of repeating that performance. Takahiro thought Lord Atsuhira looked even more vicious than usual, if that were possible. Takahiro bowed and left.

The officer in charge of the Atsuhira archers was summoned, and Takahiro gave him strict instructions.

"Our master wants some picked archers to crawl close to the Betsuo samurai and start dropping them. The idea is to draw them out of the line and give us a hole we can push through. I want a lot of insults thrown out and I want to see a lot of arrows hitting bodies—and I don't want to hear any excuses later."

The officer in front of him, fully armored and carrying a seven-foot bow, looked unsure. But the deer antlers tied to the front of the *taisho*'s helmet were slipping, and he was in no mood for distractions.

"Do you understand your orders?" Takahiro demanded.

"Oh, yes, General, sir," the officer replied, not sounding sure at all. "It's just . . . that . . ."

"Yes, get on with it."

". . . that you did not say exactly which part of the Betsuo line you wanted attacked."

Takahiro's own mistaken omission did not prevent his roaring in fury: "It's Lord Betsuo's *right* flank, which means you start directly ahead from our *left* flank position! And try to get them to chase you downstream. Far downstream." The officer bowed and fled with Takahiro's screams ringing in his ears. Soon, the Atsuhira archers began creeping into position.

All in the Betsuo camp were exhilarated by Tonomori's victory, a fight which would be discussed and retold for some time to come. Though few blows had actually been struck, the purity of the fight had been beautiful to see. Every move had contained hidden menace and properly countered, except for Kanemitsu's one fatal mistake. These warriors, too, were spoiling for a fight, aching to collect some bloody trophies of their own. Even so, Tonomori noted that their battle formation was tight, ready to deal with any of Lord Atsuhira's treacherous moves.

Old Lord Betsuo sat on his camp stool in the middle of a low platform in front of a lacquered screen covered with a pattern of gold praying mantises, his personal trademark. The clan crest itself was three rabbits running in a circle. He was trying to look stern and pleased at the same time, as Tonomori knelt in the dust before him.

"Well struck, Tonomori-sama," Lord Betsuo said jovially, unable to maintain his usual stony composure. He was fond of Tonomori, and the other retainers noted the favor he was showing his champion by addressing him as "sama," or "great." A champion was the finest duelist serving under a daimyo, and as such received the highest honors.

The severed head of Kanemitsu was propped up against a war fan in front of the platform because the head-viewing stands had not yet been unpacked.

"It was easier than it looked, sire. Kanemitsu-san only knew two basic styles of fencing—both of them bad," Tonomori told him. "At least, Lord Atsuhiro need no longer pay the man."

Lord Betsuo cackled, his heavy jowls shaking. Atsuhira's reputation as a miser was well known. When Atsuhira squeezed a white heron silver piece, the bird broke wind from the pressure—or so the saying went. Betsuo was different. Even if he was too old to take the field in actual combat and could only sit in camp and scratch his rump, Betsuo thought that at least he could properly admire the exploits of his samurai and reward them with an open hand. Tonomori was one of his best young officers, the finest swordsman and archer he had ever seen, and clearly was destined for position and power and renown.

"What now, sire?" Tonomori asked. "The samurai are getting anxious. They, too, wish to take heads. What are your orders?" As Lord Betsuo's aide-de-camp and body-guard, his authority included relaying his master's orders to the generals.

"Tell my generals to hold their positions. We hold

9

better ground than that old woman, Atsuhira, and I don't think the grasping scoundrel can hold his men together much longer. A ragged charge will cost him a lot," Betsuo said.

"And afterwards," Tonomori observed, "Lord Atsuhira will have to go shopping for more samurai again."

Lord Betsuo agreed, and fanned himself. "Tell me, Tonomori-sama, how do you think it will go this time?"

Tonomori stood and gestured toward the front lines. "Lord Atsuhira has more samurai, but ours are better, both in training and in discipline. His men stray from their positions and group where they shouldn't, and it costs him every time. He is ambitious—but he is also too miserly to commit everything he has to total victory. We will win!"

Lord Betsuo agreed cheerfully with this assessment, and issued orders. "Relay my commands to the generals, Tonomori-sama."

His champion bowed and left.

From the sidelines, Lord Betsuo's son, Masanori, watched the scene with disfavor. He, too, hoped to cover himself with glory and now once again he was in Tonomori's shadow. Tonomori. Always Tonomori!

Masanori had cheered silently for Kanemitsu to kill his father's champion, and was disappointed when he didn't, because Tonomori had won an even greater reputation. Masanori did not enjoy other people's successes because his own were few. He rejoiced in the failure of others, and admitted to no fault except lacking opportunity for greatness.

Today, though, would be different. He, Betsuo no Kami Masanori, would show them all that he could take heads in battle even better than that upstart Tonomori.

That the "upstart" had been a champion for five years meant nothing to Masanori. His spirit was forever embedded in a sediment of pettiness, violent jealousy, and greed, with a streak of cruelty thrown in. It did not occur to him that samurai who spent all their time in battle fending off sword strokes were not likely to land any killing blows themselves. Masanori would always blame others for his lack of success.

With his hatred at its peak, Masanori mounted a horse

10

held for him by a retainer, and galloped through the camp to take his position as leader of the center element of the right wing.

A runner soon came through with orders relayed by Tonomori: "Hold your position. Our lord believes the enemy forces will break formation. We'll cut them into small pieces and then chase Lord Atsuhira home."

Masanori glowered at the runner. "I already heard the orders. Get out of my sight." Startled, the runner only bowed and continued down the lines of green and gold. Masanori adjusted his quiver of arrows and dressed the ranks of his mounted samurai. "Hold yourselves ready for action," he said, adding, "by *my* orders."

From his vantage point on the command platform, Tonomori surveyed Lord Betsuo's battle lineup as it firmed into the fluid "Birds-in-Flight" defense. It was a symmetrical formation, with spearmen backed by archers in the vanguard, and with wings of mounted samurai on each side. Three more mounted wings of samurai held the center behind the vanguard. They were flanked by spearmen and more archers. The rear ranks were the same as the front. It was a defense capable of absorbing any wedge of shock troops sent out from the "Crane's Wing" attack formation being loosely formed by Atsuhira. In this, a broad, shallow arrowhead of mounted samurai was ready to charge behind a solid screen of bowmen and spearmen.

With the green foothills to his left, Tonomori knew that the Atsuhira samurai would have to pour across the small bridge, which soon would become a bottleneck, or wade across the river, with its slippery stones, ahead of the plunging horsemen who would ride over any laggards or anyone who tripped.

The Betsuo army waited for the signal. Lord Betsuo waved his war fan, and Tonomori fitted a turnip-head signaling arrow to his powerful bow, sending a screaming insult into the packed Atsuhira lines. Their forces were beginning to pour arrows into the Betsuo right flank, but more than archers would be needed to break those lines, Tonomori thought. All seemed secure.

But those archers were beginning to infuriate Masanori,

who saw three of his samurai topple from their saddles without having had a chance to make a single cut.

Frustrated and still seething, Masanori launched three arrows from his own quiver at the elusive bowmen. The first two shots missed, but the third slightly wounded a careless archer.

The commanding Atsuhira bowman shouted at Masanori, full knowing his foul temper:

"Masanori-san, perhaps you should take lessons from Tonomori-sama. Tonomori-sama would have killed with all three arrows and then beaten the rest of us to death with his bow."

A black rage began to grip Masanori, who reached for another arrow . . .

"Maybe Tonomori-sama will let you retrieve his arrows for him." Mocking laughter followed.

. . . *pulled back carefully, sighting along the shaft* . . .

"And if you are really good, Tonomori-sama will let you carry his slippers."

. . . *releasing the string* . . . The shaft missed widely.

Obscene laughter echoed. "Masanori-san, maybe you should change your name to Tonomori. Then we'd all run from you in terror. Look! It's a Tonomori, only he can't shoot."

Arrows flew along with the barbed insults. Another Betsuo samurai clutched his throat and pitched from the saddle.

Masanori fired another arrow. And missed again.

The Atsuhira archers took up the mocking cry: "Tonomori . . . Tonomori . . . Tonomor-i-i-i-i."

Rage broke over Masanori like a floodtide. Screaming "Betsuoooo," Masanori snapped his men out the right flank and galloped toward the archers, who took to their heels headlong down the riverbank, running for their lives but obeying orders at the same time.

Bound by orders to their commander but also eager to shed blood themselves, Masanori's samurai charged forward—into disaster.

When the last Betsuo samurai was riding full tilt down the riverbank, the Atsuhira *Taisho* Takahiro threw his entire left wing straight as an arrow toward the huge gap Masanori had left in Lord Betsuo's right flank. The shallow river frothed as the spearmen waded furiously toward the Betsuo front lines, followed by a wedge of Atsuhira samurai spurring their horses viciously at the inviting hole.

Betsuo samurai milled into the gap like leaderless ants, but were withered by a storm of arrows. It was too late. The arrows were followed by a wedge of horseflesh and steel that hit the right flank and drove deeply, in an absolutely shattering noise of steel on steel, shrieking men, and screaming horses.

The Atsuhira spearmen, who had parted to let the samurai through, then fanned out to finish off the fallen, and eagerly search for new targets—legs, arms, faces.

From the center of the Betsuo army, Tonomori watched the incredible collapse of the right wing. Instead of dicing the Atsuhira forces like *daikon* radishes, the army was in critical danger of being rolled up. Lord Betsuo was frantically signaling for a ''Half-Moon'' circular defensive regrouping of his men. Sluggishly, the troops began to pull back, except for the bloody right flank locked in a rabid struggle for sheer existence.

On the Atsuhira horsemen came in the hot, thickening dust, their swords darting and flashing like silvery fighting fish in murky waters. The tangle of blood and wreckage widened toward Betsuo's command platform as Takahiro tightened his trap.

Lord Betsuo stood, not believing his ill fortune. He had witnessed Masanori's disobedience of his command and the predictable disaster that resulted. He cursed the day he had ever sired such a worthless son, and could only hope that Masanori would die without further besmirching the family name.

The steady howl of war drew closer, along with the screams of dying horses and men. Arrows hummed their tuneless death song, amidst the braying of the horns and the terrible tocsin of the great *taiko* drums throbbing in Lord Betsuo's ears.

Tonomori relayed orders to shift samurai and bowmen from the left flank for a counterattack. He paused for a glance at Lord Betsuo, who had the look of a drained corpse.

"Tonomori-san, if you think it necessary, send orders for a group . . ." He never finished. A mounted Atsuhira samurai had closed far enough to put an arrow into Lord Betsuo's belly. Another arrow punched into his chest armor.

Tonomori killed the archer with an arrow into the right eye, then covered Betsuo with his own body by standing over him while retainers carried their fallen lord from the platform to safety.

The Atsuhira wedge had driven deeply into the Betsuo flank, but it was turning. Some of the Atsuhira samurai, always a discipline problem at best, were breaking off the attack to engage in personal combat within the Betsuo ranks rather than remaining as a solid point and pushing home the thrust right through Betsuo's headquarters.

The thought of total victory was eclipsed by the prospect of taking heads and gaining personal glory.

Sukehara, an Atsuhira captain leading the head of the wedge, felt the drive faltering. *So close, so close to the goal!* he thought. Sukehara slashed a Betsuo samurai out of the saddle, then turned to rally his forces.

"This way, this way, Atsuhiraaa," he bellowed. The cries fell on deaf ears. Sukehara felt his horse shudder, then drop from beneath him with an arrow in its chest, embedded to the feathers. Sukehara rolled from the beast, its bloody muzzle giving it the look of a horse from hell. Only thirty yards away was Lord Betsuo, his master's ancient enemy. Only thirty yards from victory and a peerless head.

Sukehara pressed ahead on foot, stumbling over bodies and pieces of armor, hacking and hacking and hacking. Suddenly, the way was clear. Only the champion Tonomori stood in their way, his war arrows all spent. He had only a single signaling arrow, with its hollow turnip-like head of steel. It was not a weapon designed for defense or attack, but rather was employed originally to signal the start or end of hostilities.

Sukehara cut down another samurai and turned to take on Tonomori, who fitted the arrow and let it fly from the

14

seven-foot, extremely powerful bow which only he could string.

Sukehara's men stopped in sudden surprise when the impact of the huge, bulbous arrowhead blasted his left leg off just above the knee in a crimson spray. Toppling forward, Sukehara crawled ahead on his right knee, soaking the ground behind him with great spurts of blood.

Casting away his bow, Tonomori charged the weakened Atsuhira wedge, breaking Sukehara's neck with a kick to the head as he began shredding the enemy samurai. His heavy *tachi* rose and fell in bloody arcs, crunching into armored limbs and bodies with a ghastly sound. The ground was covered with blood; the samurai were unable to face such ferocity, and the wedge fell apart as they began tripping over each other to get out of the way of that terrible blade and the might that drove it so deeply into flesh. The Betsuo samurai were now pressing in on the sides of the remnants of the wedge. The charge was turning into a rout.

Then Masanori and his five hundred samurai galloped up from what would later be called the Great Archer Hunt and hit the Atsuhira troops from behind. Trapped on all sides, the Atsuhira samurai began to sell their lives as dearly as possible. Driven into a packed mass, they were unable to swing their weapons, and were butchered by the ferocity of the defenders.

The *Taisho* Takahiro wisely signaled a retreat. Gongs sounded his command to disengage and retreat in order. Atsuhira samurai galloped or waded back across the river with net head bags dripping in the hands of those who had had time to collect trophies.

The Betsuo forces, badly mauled themselves, were in no position to pursue and harass the retreating enemy.

And despite the hard drive into Lord Betsuo's right flank, Lord Atsuhira had lost many men. Atsuhira summoned his *taisho*. He would have preferred a clear-cut victory, to have been able to ride over the corpses of his enemies, but with Lord Betsuo wounded, perhaps even near death, that was almost as good, Atsuhira thought. The son was not the father—witness the son's idiotic behavior in battle—and the next encounter might bring a result even more favorable.

"Regroup my samurai and begin moving them toward my castle. I want immediate word on Lord Betsuo's condition," Lord Atsuhira ordered. "You remain in command, General."

Relieved that he would keep his own head, Takahiro issued orders to assemble his men before marching them back. He knew that if his master were not too cheap to hire capable samurai, he could have won the battle today.

The shadows began to lengthen as the Atsuhira army turned its back on the Betsuo banners, now flecked with drying blood. The west bank was strangely quiet, except for the moans of the dying. Soon, those would stop. Those deemed too far gone for surgical help would be mercifully killed with a stabbing knife. The units began regrouping, the green-and-gold darkly stained, amid heaps of the fallen blue-and-white colors of the Atsuhira samurai.

Masanori rode up to the command platform where his father was being cut out of his armor.

Tonomori was waiting for him.

"Where were you?" Tonomori said coldly, without use of a formal title.

Masanori bit his lower lip. He could see that his father's underkimono had soaked up much blood. The chest wound was not bad but the belly wound was deep, the bowels perforated. Lord Betsuo would die.

"I collected two heads," Masanori said, gesturing to a bag tied to his saddle housing. "I do not have to explain my actions to you."

Tonomori spat. "You collected two heads from some worthless archers—and left the door wide open for Atsuhira to come marching in!"

Masanori did not like the foul taste in his mouth or care for the looks directed his way by many of his father's officers. Here he was, a hero, and they looked at him scornfully. His black mood was deepening.

Tonomori continued relentlessly, "Masanori-san, I understand your five hundred samurai fought among themselves over the archers because they had not enough trophies to go around. Thirty heads to divide among five hundred samurai!''

Masanori drew himself up. ''I am Betsuo no Kami Masanori, and I do not have to answer to anybody,'' he shouted to Tonomori. ''Hold your tongue.''

''I am your father's samurai and not subject to your orders!'' Tonomori countered.

''If you had done your job, my father would not have been wounded,'' Masanori retorted.

''Well, Masanori-san, it was not my head your father heaped curses on for leaving the front door open. It was yours. But if you can think of anything important to say, send me word to my pavilion.'' Tonomori bowed and left. The message was clear: *Send me a challenge and I'll gladly accept*.

But Masanori could not defeat Tonomori on the best day he ever had, and he knew it. Masanori swallowed hard and turned his horse toward where his samurai were waiting. Lord Betsuo had not regained consciousness and was being tied to a litter. Camp would be breaking up quickly for the forced march back to his fortress.

The pale moon was rising, ringed with red, when they reached Lord Betsuo's fortress ten miles to the west of the battlefield. They had changed litterbearers twice for a faster speed, but even before the first step they knew that death was summoning their lord.

Masanori rode at the head of his samurai, far back from the litter, looking somber and preoccupied. Before he had lapsed into unconsciousness, his father's last words had been to curse Masanori to the gods. But in the distance of ten miles, Masanori had managed in his own mind to shift the guilt from his shoulders to those of Tonomori, now riding alongside the litter.

If Tonomori had been that good a bodyguard, those arrows would never have struck my father, Masanori reasoned many times, leaping nimbly over the actual point of his own responsibility, as was his habit. *Still, there are those who will mistakenly blame me*, Masanori thought, *and I must find a way to overcome their faulty reasoning*.

In any event, within a few hours, when his father joined his illustrious ancestors, he, Masanori, would become hereditary feudal lord of the Betsuo clan and master of six thousand samurai, one of whom was the treacherous Tonomori. Time enough then to set matters straight.

On assuming the title, his first act would be to order Tonomori to kill himself to atone for his failure to protect Lord Betsuo. That might set tongues buzzing, but it would set a good example of the type of dedication to duty Masanori, as their lord, would expect in the future. Then his thoughts inevitably turned to his vast inheritance that went with the title—the fortified castle, the samurai, four hundred square miles of rich land, and all the peasants who occupied them.

And he would take proprietorship of the lovely Nobuko, Tonomori's lover. She had been given as concubine to Tonomori by Lord Betsuo, but Masanori lusted after her and would greatly enjoy introducing her to some interesting erotic delights. His own wife was a homely woman— his was strictly a political marriage—but Lord Betsuo would not countenance a concubine for his son. Masanori hoped that Tonomori's last thoughts would be of Nobuko and her new master coupling in bed. It was delightful even to contemplate.

One of the footsoldiers was startled to see Masanori smirking broadly like a small boy telling a forbidden story. Masanori's mottled gums and crooked teeth did not give him a handsome smile, and when he did grin in that way, it usually meant no good for someone. The footsoldier shuddered.

The fortress was situated on eighteen acres of high ground overlooking a small city of ten thousand, mostly merchants and peasants. The city had grown over the centuries, as had the fortress, impressive in the moonlight with its winged roofs and strong towers enclosed by stone walls.

Now, the many trees in and around the city were rustling in the growing winds. All peasants were indoors except for the night soil collectors, and they made themselves scarce at the approach of troops. Few lamps were burning.

At the fortress, all torches were lighted. Couriers had brought word of Lord Betsuo's terrible fate, and preparations were made for his final hours. In the courtyard, bathed in light from the moon, Tonomori dismounted and followed the litterbearers to the Great Hall where the lord's personal retainers and household would gather.

Tonomori knew that he had not much time, that Masanori would be planning some sort of treachery, though he could not conjure the exact form it would take. Tonomori felt his own death approaching with the ebb of his master's life. *Will it be by assassin, or by my own hand?* Tonomori would be patient and wait, but meanwhile he would set his personal affairs in order.

After remaining only a few minutes, Tonomori left the hall, and headed for his quarters in the officers' wing. Sentries saluted and he quickened his pace. Bronze bells began to roll in the depths of the castle, alerting the spirit world to Lord Betsuo's passing. At Tonomori's approach, his retainers slid open the *shoji* panels to his rooms.

As he expected, Nobuko was waiting for him, clad in a golden kimono, kneeling deeply, her unbound hair pooling darkly on the *tatami* mats. He returned the bow, and dismissed the wide-eyed servants who understood that matters were going badly for their master.

Nobuko looked at him through red-rimmed eyes. She had been weeping. "Is it true, Tonomori-san?" In reply, Tonomori took her by the shoulders and raised her from the floor.

"It's true. It has been like walking in a nightmare. Lord Betsuo is dying and what we had between us is also coming to an end." Tonomori looked down at her hands, avoiding her questioning gaze. Like rare Chinese ivory, her soft hands rested among his calloused fingers.

"Listen, Nobuko-chan," Tonomori said, using the intimate diminutive of endearment. "We have very little time. When Masanori takes his father's place, I will not have long to live. And he will take you for his own."

Tonomori paused. Nobuko had the look of a trapped

sparrow. "Then let me die with you. I would gladly share your death," she said, trying not to weep, to disgrace herself before her samurai.

"You cannot," Tonomori said gently but firmly, his spirit crying out in pain. "The old lord gave you to me. That was his right. The new lord can take you back. It will be his right. A wise lord would not, but Masanori is not wise. He is as foolish as he is hateful. He even blames me for his father's wounds, though it was his own folly that let in the arrows."

Tonomori held her chin up from where she had hidden her face against his massive chest.

"You will rust my armor, Nobuko-chan," he teased, forcing a light smile. "How can I face Lord Masanori with rusty plates?"

A small laugh escaped her, despite herself. It would never do for Tonomori to present himself with stained armor; he did not bother to tell her how long a time would be needed for tears to rust his lacquered plates—and time had run out.

He brushed away her tears. She could not help herself. His hands, though thick and strong, were surprisingly gentle. She had touched him deeply. Were it possible to look within Nobuko's aching heart, Tonomori would have been surprised to find love there. Love for him. Loyalty he would have expected, bound inextricably with duty and affection. But love, never. Affection he could understand, but love was a concept alien to him.

As a boy, when he had first heard the word, Tonomori had wondered what it possibly could mean. But he did not take much time to consider the question since his existence was no more than tenuous in this serenely beautiful world that underneath was unbelievably harsh and cruel. Survival was only to the strongest and fittest.

As a samurai, he had two main words in his vocabulary: loyalty and duty. Tonomori was born to the rank of samurai, although it could be achieved by inspired acts of bravery and devotion by those among the footsoldiers. The name *samurai* meant "they who serve." Samurai were the backbone and spirit of the armies fielded by the feudal lords, serving with selfless devotion in peace and war. To preserve his lord's honor, the samurai was expected to give up his life if need be. In the great scheme of things, this was his purpose. Service, duty, loyalty!

Nobuko had shared his bed ever since she was sixteen, when Lord Betsuo gave her to him as a reward for killing the renowned duelist, the giant Tadamitsu. She was as pretty as a butterfly and as fragile. Since she was not of samurai birth, she served only as his concubine.

As it was, she was an excellent choice for Tonomori. The gift bound him closer to his liege lord. Instead of bedding her immediately, as she had expected, Tonomori had done the unexpected (she later learned that Tonomori always did the unexpected), wooing her for two days and nights, allaying her fears, soothing the flutter in her heart with soft words. The night breeze brought the notes of his flute outside her window, welcome as a refreshing rain. He became to her a gentle bear of a man, not someone to fear, and when at last he finally led her to his own bed, Tonomori became her first lover, not just her first man.

Out of loyalty, she stifled her cries of pain—she even yet had not been prepared for the experience—and feigned moans of throbbing passion, full knowing that her serving maids were listening and giggling outside the thin *shoji* panels and eager to spread the story throughout the fortress before morning. She did not even scold them for it, aware that, in their sandals, she would have done the same. Tonomori had already been to bed with most of the maids, and the rest were hopeful. Because of their hero worship, they tended to knock things over or giggle excessively whenever he was around.

So, Tonomori continued to be envied by the other samurai, both for his prowess in the field and abed. He would never be thought handsome. But women found his appearance striking at least, and his formidable reputation was a powerful flame to their moth-like flutters.

Within a few months, Nobuko had learned physical passion from Tonomori, and at the same time had fallen deeply in love with him, although she never told him of this. His deep reserve was something not to be touched.

21

He openly demonstrated his affection and respect for her, so she contented herself with the joy of just being with him. In the four years they had been together, her only regret was that she had never given him a child, a son.

The days had fallen slowly, like cherry blossoms, but now were gone with the last breath of spring. What would happen next, she did not know, but Nobuko already had resolved to never leave his side. She would be there in flesh or in spirit. But rather than die, perhaps he should go on—complete his mission on this earth.

And she would be brave, as brave as a samurai, her samurai. "No long good-byes, Tonomori-chan. Let it end quickly." She paused. "We all have our roads. Yours is the longest, I think the most difficult. Thank you for teaching me so well. My duty is here."

Tonomori started to reply but she touched his lips, the last touch.

"Try to live, Tonomori-chan! Death is easy for a samurai. Do not fear life. You once told me that a little man can chop down the mightiest oak. The strongest dead man can't even lift a little finger to chase away the flies. Don't throw your life away!"

"I must go quickly," Tonomori said. "Farewell, Nobuko-chan. I will always remember you. Always!" In lighter moments, he always called her his Golden Butterfly. That thought came to him now, but he could not speak.

The last she saw of him was his broad back. The final blossom had fallen. Outside, the wind blew, cool and clean, the music silent. Nobuko called her maids to say she was retiring to her rooms to mourn their liege lord and that no one was to disturb her. When she was alone, Nobuko sat upon their sleeping mat, her silk robes gathered around her. She slipped off the outer garment. Her underkimono was white, the color of death. She reflected on their last time together in this room. In the sleeve of her kimono was a small, sharp dagger. She thought it a pity that Tonomori's path should be so difficult while hers would be so very, very easy.

* * *

22

In the hallway, Tonomori was met by one of his closest friends and drinking companions, Obushi, who urged him to return to the Great Hall at once.

"People are noticing your absence and are starting to talk," Obushi said after looking around to see if anyone was listening.

"Masanori is spreading a filthy story that Lord Betsuo's death was all your doing, that you might as well have been in league with the Atsuhira clan. You should get down there and stop those lies," Obushi urged.

He laid a friendly hand on Tonomori's shoulder. "Be warned, Tonomori-sama, Masanori wants your head. Don't give it to him."

Tonomori scowled. "This is no time for jokes, Obushi-san. What am I supposed to say? 'Masanori-sama, all is forgiven'? No, death is my only alternative. I cannot serve Masanori with honor. There is nothing left. What else would you have me do?"

Obushi looked around again and whispered urgently. "You can live! Refuse to serve him. He hasn't taken your oath of allegiance yet. Anger him into casting you out. You are not the only one who wishes vengeance, Tonomori-sama. I and others . . ." He waited, then continued even more quietly.

"You are the strongest man I know, but if you are dead you will be useless to everyone but Masanori, who will rejoice at the sight of your body," Obushi said. "You can find a way to slip the leash. Avenge our master."

To refuse to serve, to become an outcast, a *ronin*? Impossible! The very name samurai implied resolute service. A masterless samurai was a ronin, a disgrace.

"You ask too much," Tonomori rebuked him, drawing away angrily. "I thought you were a friend. Is this what a friend asks?"

"Yes, Tonomori-sama. Don't take the easy way out," Obushi said. Tonomori was shaken. It was the second time within minutes that someone had said that to him. Was it an omen? Must he reconsider his rejection of the very idea of accepting the outcast status of ronin? He began to see the possibility, but would have to give it much more thought in the few moments available for such reflection.

23

Seeing Tonomori start, Obushi pressed what he hoped was an advantage. "Listen, Tonomori-sama! In the days ahead, in the weeks, months, even years ahead, remember our master and give him vengeance. You will need a friend, an ally. I will be that friend, though I may have to denounce you from the rooftops."

"Remember your friend Obushi. You will need someone inside, to give you aid. I and others will help you." Obushi looked around again. "I must go. Remember what I said, Tonomori-sama. You do your duty, and I will do mine even though it means serving Lord Masanori."

Then he was gone, leaving Tonomori in a whirl. Who had the easiest task, Tonomori the outcast, or Obushi the lackey to the despised Lord Masanori, or Nobuko the Butterfly, plaything to Masanori, submitting to his hated touch?

At the head of the steps, Tonomori was met by another samurai. "The lord of the Betsuo clan is dead, sir." He bowed and stood as Tonomori slowly descended the stairs. Tonomori could hear the Shinto priests droning their prayers. Incense filled air already smoky from the torches. Samurai lined both sides of the hall. Most had removed their armor and changed into formal kimonos of somber color. Some of their wives were present but none were weeping. They were samurai. Any tears would come only later, in private.

Tonomori was still in armor. He had taken time only to bathe his face and hands. As for Masanori's hands, they would never be clean, he reflected. Heads turned and the talking stopped when Tonomori swept into the hall, his rolling gait confident and familiar.

His left hand resting on his *tachi*, Tonomori looked only at Masanori, who was standing on a dais. From habit, Tonomori marked everyone's position and measured the distance to Masanori.

The new lord of the Betsuo clan glared, but shrank within the ranks of his samurai who braced themselves for Tonomori's next move.

His face serene despite his inward seething, Tonomori began walking toward the dais, to Masanori, closing the distance and counting the steps.

24

Chapter Two

I am the sum of the past
but a part of the future,
which I can make greater.

The thought of his death poem flashed through Tonomori's mind like a flicker of flame, and was gone. The killing distance between himself and Masanori was closed. Time stopped.

Will the floors be red with their blood or mine? Tonomori thought. His keen senses were tuned to every sound and motion. Every movement had meaning. Fire was crackling in a bronze brazier to the right, and a piece of blackened rice paper used to start the kindling swept upward on the hot air, curling like a dark bat—a lucky sign, but for whom?

Tonomori stood before Masanori and his samurai, as proud as they and as sure of his strength as a hunting bear. He had chosen an overmantle to cover his body armor, a rich brown silk embroidered with the mantis *mon* of the Betsuo clan.

"I, Betsuo no Kami Masanori, claim the hereditary title of lord of the Betsuo clan, and all of its lands and people, as is my right," Masanori said, reading from a sheet of rice paper, hardly knowing whether to keep his eyes on the *kanji* characters of the scroll or on the butcher in armor standing before him.

25

. . . It is as though two archers are standing on the forecourt (Tonomori reflected), *their bows strung, but the arrows still in the quiver . . .*

"Tonomori-san, the day of reckoning has come . . ."

. . . Masanori only has sixteen samurai guarding him, none of them in armor . . .

". . . On the field of battle, you insulted your liege lord . . ."

. . . The arrows are useless once I charge. They'll hit their own men . . .

". . . You have also committed other grievous offenses against the honor of the Betsuo clan . . ."

. . . so when he makes his move, Masanori is a dead man; there are not enough samurai to save him, but enough to make sure I'm dead when I'm through . . .

". . . What is your reply, Tonomori-san?" Masanori said, rolling up the scroll. He waited for Tonomori—would he kill himself or force them to do it for him?"

"Lies! They are all lies!" Tonomori replied quietly, though his voice carried through the stillness of the hall.

"Lies?" Masanori was livid. "How can you stand there and deny them? You insulted me, the lord of the Betsuo clan, on the field of battle."

"I only reminded you of your rash actions, and your father was still lord of the Betsuo. You were his heir, not the head of the clan. The truth is no insult, even if unpleasant. Is that not so, Lord Masanori?" Tonomori's head was down slightly, a dangerous angle, with a sardonic upturn at the left side of his mouth.

Masanori ignored this, having long since made up his mind as to Tonomori's guilt. He had no answer, and while trying to think of a cutting reply, allowed himself to become sidetracked. He saw that Tonomori was wearing his *tachi*, a gross breach of court protocol which demanded that a samurai wear only the short sword in the presence of his master—never the long killing sword, unless permission was given.

"Furthermore, Tonomori-san, you insult me now by wearing your *tachi* in my presence," Masanori sputtered, grasping at anything to shore up the weak framework of lies and distortions of the day's disaster.

"You forget, Masanori-sama, that I was privileged by Lord Betsuo to wear two swords in his presence. As the Betsuo champion, so created by your father, I still have that privilege. Is *that* not so, Masanori-sama?" Tonomori said. The hall was deathly silent and Tonomori could only hear the blood pounding in his own ears. The long path, the short path, whichever—let the gods decide. Tonomori had taken the first step toward death or freedom and he would not stand back. His words were fanning Masanori's hot temper to the kindling point.

"To revoke this privilege, you must accept me into your service as champion, and so be able to take away what was given—or else find someone who can defeat me and take my place. Do you so accept me as your champion, Lord Masanori?" Tonomori put a slight inflection on "lord," which Masanori could infer as an insult, but never prove it.

Masanori wanted to scream with rage and personally hack to pieces the man standing before him. But he, the new lord of the Betsuo clan, had lost the initiative and couldn't think fast enough to retrieve it. Wanting Tonomori dead and out of the way, Masanori had not thought out the legalities in drumming up distortions to achieve his end, nor had he bothered to consult anyone.

Because Tonomori had only sworn allegiance to his father, Masanori could not, under law, issue a command to Tonomori to kill himself as punishment. Masanori angrily realized that to be able to do this now, he would first have to accept Tonomori into his service—but since it seemed unlikely that Tonomori would enter it, Masanori would be about to lose face before the clan.

The other obvious course open to Masanori would be to have a swordsman issue a deadly insult to Tonomori, provoke a duel, and kill him. But the champion stood before him, unbeatable—and as unyielding as the onslaught of a summer storm. Masanori was wavering before his samurai, and he knew he must act quickly or Tonomori would beat him again.

27

"Well, Lord Masanori? As your champion?" Tonomori was baiting him now.

"No!" Masanori said in a harsh whisper. Several of the elder court nobles looked aghast. Had Masanori asked them, they would have advised dispensing with any legalities, overpowering Tonomori with heavily armed samurai—enough to be sure of killing him—and later bribing or intimidating the witnesses for the imperial court inquiry.

"My decision is to cast you out, Tonomori-san. From this day on, you are without a master—a ronin." Masanori looked around, pleased with himself. At least, Tonomori would be disgraced. He would pay.

To Masanori, it seemed unthinkable that Tonomori would prefer to be an outcast ronin rather than to accept an honorable death, but Masanori now could not keep track of his own illogical arguments. And to Tonomori, almost anything, including the outcast status, presumably would be preferable to the dishonorable service Masanori represented.

But Tonomori was not through. He would need resources and he did not intend to walk out of the castle barehanded.

"Lord Masanori, while dispensing with my services, do you intend also to confiscate my property, the gifts which your father freely gave me?" he demanded.

Masanori was livid. He was losing his confidence again. He had not uttered a single one of all the things which he had rehearsed in his mind. Tonomori should have been cowering before him, or at least currying favor as everyone else did.

"N-no. You may take your property, all of it . . . except," Masanori recovered long enough to get in one blow, ". . . except the concubine Nobuko. She remains. You are ordered to leave the castle, with your property, by dawn." Masanori paused, then remembered one other thing to say.

"Any other of my retainers who wish to join this ronin may do so. Be gone from my castle with him!" He turned away together with his samurai, with dread clinging to his heels as if someone were walking across his grave. Moving swiftly to one end of the hall, Masanori paused by a painted wall-hanging which depicted Lord Betsuo's trademark, the praying mantis. "Take it down and burn it," he ordered brusquely. Masanori's conscience was throbbing, and he wanted no reminders. "Have every one of those removed from the castle. Every one! My mark will be the eagle," he shrieked, and swept on. Tonomori's crest was three ravens within intertwined circles, and Masanori was determined to make a point of choosing the more exalted eagle.

Masanori's samurai edged away from Tonomori, not caring to share his disgrace. His friends would not look him in the eye, except for Obushi, who said, "So you escape unharmed once more, Tonomori-san. It is always too easy for you. Lord Masanori should have killed you."

I will be that friend, though I may have to denounce you from the rooftops.

Tonomori said nothing. His piercing gaze burned them all. Even Obushi moved back. Tonomori walked away calmly to collect his property.

"What insolence," he heard behind his back. Tonomori ignored a babble of suddenly raised voices. At the foot of the steps, he was stopped by four samurai.

"Tonomori-san, please excuse us," one guard said. "But Lord Masanori has just issued orders that you are not to be allowed beyond these stairs. Your concubine has been instructed to give us your possessions, and we will bring them to you in the courtyard. If you bring us your horses, sir, we will assist you in loading them. We are very sorry."

"Meet me in the stables then," Tonomori said, returning the guard's bow. He headed quickly for the stables, wondering if Masanori would realize the stupidity of his actions, and send an armed party of samurai to kill him. Perhaps, but not immediately and not within the castle walls. Tonomori decided that Masanori could not make him an outcast in one breath and then order him killed with the next. If there were a few hours remaining until

Masanori's treachery surfaced, Tonomori would make the most of them.

Though Tonomori was in disgrace, the sentries saluted as he walked to the stables. The champion was quite capable of plastering the walls with their bodies, and Lord Masanori or no, they did not want to offer any possible insult.

The master of horse, Sadamitsu, was waiting for Tonomori at the stalls, his *eboshi*, a curved felt hat, tugged over his gray hair and a well-worn leather apron covering the front of his kimono. The master was glad for one last chance to see him, despite the circumstances. His was the first friendly face Tonomori had seen since his private talk with Obushi.

"So sorry, Tonomori-san. I am ordered to assist in your quick departure," the master said. Small and lean, leather-tough, he was as bad-tempered as the mounts he had in charge. For some reason he had always liked Tonomori, unusual in itself, because the horse master didn't like anybody.

Perhaps it stemmed from the day that he met the champion. Lord Betsuo's favorite war-horse, Denji, a vicious brute, had bitten Tonomori, who immediately responded by knocking it to the ground with a punch between the eyes. The horse had staggered back to its feet, but it never put a tooth to anyone again. The stallion had bitten the master and others many times before, but no one ever had the temerity to strike Lord Betsuo's favorite mount.

When Lord Betsuo remonstrated with Tonomori for striking a valuable horse, his new champion had replied, "Sire, I am not obliged to suffer insults from samurai, let alone a horse, even of the best antecedents."

The bite was still throbbing, but Tonomori had added cheerfully, "If he bites me again, I'll break his neck. However, if you wish to adopt him and lend Denji the protection of your name, I might change my mind." Old Betsuo had roared with laughter at the thought, and agreed that his champion should uphold his dignity and defend himself on all occasions. When he jovially offered to name Tonomori as *Unawara*, official horse breaker, Tonomori respectfully declined while rubbing his sore shoulder.

The master already had saddled Tonomori's favorite horse, Kaminari, whose name meant thunder. He also slipped elaborate bridle-muzzles over Kaminari and two other of Tonomori's war-horses for use as pack ponies. Japanese war-horses, mostly stallions, were notorious for their bad tempers, much like their owners, and frequently were muzzled since they tended to sink their teeth into friend and foe alike.

The other two horses did not like their role as pack ponies, but mellowed at the approach of Tonomori, whom they recognized as the Giver of Sweet Fruit and Hard Kicks. All the horses would take turns acting as Tonomori's mount, giving them each a breather, since the packs were lighter than their master.

Retainers arrived, carrying the rest of Tonomori's gear, which he checked thoroughly before they lashed it to the pack saddles and covered them with rainproofed oilcloth. Tonomori could tell from the weight of one traveling case that it still contained the gold and silver given generously to him by Lord Betsuo. Theft, ordinarily of little problem because it was punishable by death, was the least of Tonomori's worries. The great lords of Japan were in the business of stealing each other's lands. Purses were for petty thieves.

The guard who had stopped Tonomori at the stairs brushed into him, and apologized while slipping a small piece of paper into his hand.

"Obushi-san sent this," he whispered, then said more loudly, for the benefit of the other guards, "It was my clumsiness, Tonomori-san, please excuse."

"It was nothing," Tonomori said as he slid the paper into his white sash.

The guards were anxious to finish their work and return to their posts. They, too, did not know what Lord Masanori might do next, and did not want to become involved if it meant an attack on Tonomori, whom they had seen in action. If they were going to commit suicide, they would like it to be their own idea.

They bowed and left without speaking. The horse master waved a farewell and went with them. Tonomori was alone.

Outside, he could see the moon begin to dip. Dawn was still hours away, his first day as a ronin. To be outcast was in some ways worse than death. To have existence was to have purpose in life. To be a samurai was to serve a lord. A masterless samurai was a useless samurai. Many became outlaws. Their life had no meaning, they wandered without purpose as ronin.

Tonomori, though, had purpose, ronin or not.

He still had a few moments, and took the folded paper from his sash. He smoothed out the paper on a feed bin under the only lantern. The message was very simple, a few brush strokes to make the wings and a touch of the tip for the delicate antennae of a butterfly. And the *kanji* ideograph for "Sayonara." Below that was the tiny mark from a fallen tear. Tonomori paused. He had said his good-byes. Before dawn he must be gone.

The courtyard was deserted, except for the guards on duty, and they had orders not to speak to the outcast, although they wanted to. Tonomori was a stickler for etiquette and military discipline but he was fair in dealing with subordinates and the guards appreciated that.

Tonomori's sadness was overflowing. The fortress had been his home for six years, the happiest he had ever known, especially the last four with Nobuko. He was leaving behind his friends, men with whom he enjoyed brawling, womanizing, and drinking to excess. He had put a harmless snake in the bed of one friend as a joke, brushed fresh paint in a place where another was sure to sit on it, and doused others with buckets of cold water when they least expected it. In turn, he suffered the cheerful insults of his companions. Everything was gone in the capricious action of cruel fate, the *karma* which controlled all their destinies. There was no going back. If Lord Betsuo had lived, Tonomori would have asked him for permission to take Nobuko as wife, since she pleased him so. Kaminari jerked Tonomori out of his reverie. The other two horses did not like being led, and one had tried to nip

Kaminari. Tonomori pulled back, lashed out a foot, and restored order.

Once across the bridge spanning the moat, Tonomori turned in the saddle on impulse. "Sayonara, Nobuko-chan," he called softly, then spurred Kaminari onward. He did not look back again.

"I will return, and I will have all their blood," Tonomori said to the silent skies. The horses whickered. Tonomori did not expect an answer to his promise of vengeance against Masanori and Lord Atsuhira. Not immediately. It would come in time if he was fated to spill their blood.

The streets of the city were quiet. The few people he did encounter bowed and then scuttled away. When a samurai was on the move, a wise peasant got out of the way. Tonomori smiled grimly; how unfair. In his occasional dealings with the long-suffering peasants, who had few rights, Tonomori was honest, with a sense of justice and fair play. He would not allow a samurai to bully or mis-treat a peasant or merchant unless they proved to be dishonest.

The road east lay ahead stretching out along the countryside. The wind was rising from the east and dark clouds streaked the moon. The air smelled of approaching rain. The air was crisp, so Kaminari was full of frisk, as were the other horses. To them every morning was the same, and Tonomori thought how lucky it would be to be reborn a horse with nothing to worry about except when it was time to eat and when to rest.

Who had the easiest road? Tonomori was eager to put some miles between himself and the Betsuo fortress. He did not want an armed clash with Masanori yet. Tonomori had no plan and only limited resources.

Yes, but unlimited time, Tonomori told himself. *You have been schooled by many masters. One of them must have taught you something.*

He thought hard. *Even the strongest ox is easily led. The weaker fox is hard to catch.* Tonomori had heard those tired sayings many times and he was sick of them. Much better was some really practical advice he once got from an old samurai: *A well-turned insult is nice, but a kick in*

33

the groin will gain your opponent's attention and keep his hands busy at the same time. And, *Never gamble in a whorehouse. You're already taking a chance by walking in there.*

Tonomori knew he would need more than philosophic aphorisms. He also knew enough to come in out of the rain. A light drizzle was starting to fall, with the promise of more to come. He stopped to dig some rain gear out of his pack, and a lacquered waterproofed conical hat. Then, after checking the coverings on his personal effects, he proceeded on his way.

In a hour, rain was falling steadily, a soaking downpour. The neat, checkered fields of rice and vegetables were disappearing under it. Occasionally, Tonomori could see some thatched roofs clustered together and the bamboo pipes extending from the irrigation ditches.

With the road worsening and visibility becoming even poorer, Tonomori gave up and began pitching camp. He made quick work of it, despite the lack of retainers to perform such a menial task for him. Tonomori was glad for something to keep his mind occupied. Once he had trenched the tent and had thrown his armor into it, Tonomori thought of food, and was astonished to realize how hungry he was.

Since the traditional ''lucky'' meal before yesterday's fighting, he had not eaten. That meal had consisted of some dried abalone (which he despised), chestnuts (which he liked), and dried seaweed, something he deemed palatable only when wrapped around some pickled rice and bits of ginger, which had not been available. He hated to think what fortune an *unlucky* meal would have brought yesterday.

Digging into his pack, he brought out some rice balls, pickled vegetables, and some smoked fish—simple fare but good. He was ravenous and ate without pausing, washing it all down with plain water, while silently thanking whoever thought to pack some food for his exile. Being tired—Tonomori had not slept since the night before—the dampness chilled him even more deeply than normally it would have. Tonomori lighted some coals in a small hiba-

34

chi and set on a pot of water to brew some tea, really good *o-cha*.

While waiting for the water to boil, Tonomori also warmed his hands. Tea would not have been as popular with the nobility in Japan if the shoguns and emperors did not think it helped soothe their hangovers. Tonomori also thought tea to be efficacious after having dipped his nose in a sake bowl all night. But it was expensive. His own jar of green *o-cha* from China had been one of the lavish presents from his late lord.

The tea brewed, Tonomori sipped slowly, having been taught to appreciate the jade color and the smell as well as the taste. Tea was already gaining a mystique of its own in Japan and complex rituals had been formed for its serving. Though Tonomori hated rituals, he had found no way to avoid them.

So many masters, so much learning. *Why?* It was a thought which had puzzled Tonomori for the past few years. Tutored by the finest masters affordable only by the richest lords, he knew that his own origins were obscure. His foster father, a Satsuma baron named Shijame, had told Tonomori only that he was samurai and of high rank. The childless Shijame, though a backwoods baron, was well educated himself. His wealth and manners made him a favorite at the imperial court in Kyoto, so Tonomori did not see much of him.

Still, Tonomori, with the curiosity of all children, had kept badgering when his foster father paid the occasional visit home in order to keep affairs running smoothly. This finally angered Shijame, a widower not overly fond of bothersome boys.

"Your father is a great man but he committed an indiscretion. Enough now!" Shijame said to the small but obstinate Tonomori.

"What about my mother? Is she a great woman?"

Shijame took on a bemused look.

"Your mother was hideous. You were taken away from her at birth so her glance wouldn't turn you into stone," Shijame said. At that point, servants swooped down on young Tonomori and carried him away before he angered

Shijame any further. Tonomori's shrill protests could be heard far down the hallway.

Tonomori had not believed the story. If his mother's glance would turn him to stone, then how had his father managed to get into bed with her? Tonomori did not have long to consider that problem; soon, he was in a struggle for his very existence.

First, he was assigned harsh physical tasks, for which he was beaten severely if they were not accomplished quickly and correctly. His taskmasters were not kindly men, so every minor infraction brought Tonomori a sound thumping. Since he was samurai, he was not allowed to cry out. The undeserved beatings had a reason behind them: Learn to accept discipline; never question it; a complaint will only bring more thumpings; to strike a superior would bring death. A servant or underling must never strike a superior, no matter under what provocation.

Once, when he was eight years old, he was given the almost impossible task of building a long, stone wall at the edge of Shijame's lands near the coast. All spring and summer he toiled, carrying rocks and hauling or levering huge boulders into place. He already was a strong child, but to toughen him, he was given little food. He caught fish trapped in tidal pools and ate them raw, flavored with a fermented bean curd sauce brought by a sympathetic servant along with his meager meals. Tonomori even caught a hare and roasted it in pieces over a small fire; it was a feast. He caught other game when he could, ignoring the Buddhist strictures against eating meat, because he was really a Shintoist anyway. The Shinto spirits who inhabited this desolate stretch of coastland, he thought, must be few and far between, commanding very little power and influence and even less of Tonomori's respect. So, he concentrated on survival. And the wall grew. With it grew his strength.

In the fall, Lord Shijame surveyed the wall, grunting once—whether in approval or not Tonomori never knew. Then Shijame ordered the wall dismantled, the rocks put back in their original resting places. By this time, Tonomori knew better than to ask questions, and did as he was ordered. When the first winter winds churned the seas into the gray of an old sword blade, he was brought back to the baron's mansion, given clean clothing, and turned over to tutors. Their daily instruction was in writing, in brush painting, in speaking Chinese, and appreciation of fine porcelain, ivory, lacquer work, and the forging of sword blades. He learned the management of horses, the handling of a bow, and finally, but most important, the use of a sword.

Tonomori had received his first sword at the age of five, and wore it on the few formal occasions he was allowed to attend. Before he could join the adult world, he first had to learn how to function in it. Twice a week, he had instruction on the etiquette and elaborate protocol of the imperial court. For the uninitiated, this was an endless maze of rigid rules, customs, and ritual.

The coals under the teapot were burning out, so Tonomori stirred them with a stick and added more charcoal. He wanted some sake now, and though it should have been heated, Tonomori drank two flasks cold while waiting for a third to warm.

The end to his riddle still eluded him. Perhaps in seeking the answer to who he was, Tonomori thought, he might find a way to bring down the clans of Betsuo and Atsuhira. Vengeance would put Lord Betsuo's spirit at rest and perhaps give Tonomori some peace, though the long road would not end there.

The rain was still falling but the pavilion was dry. Tonomori had trenched it well. He had fought in enough rain-drenched campaigns to cause him to be repelled by the idea of sleeping in wet clothes, so he had tried to make camp as thoroughly as any of his retainers might have.

The drops falling from the pavilion canopy reminded him of sweat and his fencing school. The smells, the sheen of the polished wooden floors, the racks of bamboo weapons, and the weight of padded armor came back to him as if he had seen them and smelled them and handled them yesterday.

The fencing master was a disciplinarian, and because

Tonomori was his special charge, he let nothing escape his notice. His first tactic of pitting Tonomori against taller, older boys would have had other young students almost in tears. But Tonomori's sheer strength and natural ferocity wreaked havoc among the senior ranks, and the master had to change his tactics. He engaged Tonomori himself and thoroughly thrashed him in mock combats.

"Examine the whole and study the parts," the master said obliquely to Tonomori one afternoon after the other students had put away their equipment and left. Kneeling on the floor, Tonomori was still wearing his padded practice armor. His *bo-ken,* a stout hardwood sword balanced to match the real thing, lay in front of him.

"You win matches, Tonomori-san, but you do not know why you win," the master said, running thin but strong fingers through his hair. "A sword in the hands is not enough. You must learn to use your feet also. Your wits must be nimble—faster than the blade—or you will lose them when someone smarter cuts off your head!"

By then, Tonomori had learned the lesson of the stone wall, so he listened carefully to the ugly little fencing master whose catlike movements were so beautiful.

And each time his fencing master spoke, Tonomori paid attention to every word. The master preached patience, but did not practice it with his high-ranking charges. Each lesson must be quickly learned at once—or painfully learned twice. The third time was something Tonomori did not like to even think about. He assimilated the basic moves with ease, and advanced with confidence toward the dueling ground of the master swordsmen.

Satsuma samurai were a quarrelsome lot, so their skills with a sword needed to be excellent in order to ensure their very survival. Tonomori's Satsuma instructor was among the best, and one of the most satisfying moments in Tonomori's life occurred when, at the age of twelve, during a practice match, he broke through the master's defenses and knocked him unconscious with a wooden *bo-ken.* Older boys' respect for Tonomori grew steadily after that. Even the oldest boys, those almost ready to enter into service as samurai, stopped antagonizing him.

Baron Shijame took to visiting the school occasionally, unannounced, to view his progress. He made no comment, but other instructors began to appear at the school to engage Tonomori in mock combat.

Finally, the baron summoned Tonomori before him in his formal gardens and offered a rare explanation. "Your fencing instructors are pleased with your progress, as am I in discharging my obligation to your father. However, the masters have taught you only how to fight them and the other students. In order to perfect the duel, you must learn the techniques of many others. Otherwise, a samurai of lesser skill might defeat you because you had never encountered his style of fighting. Learn all styles so that you will know how to counter and overcome them."

Tonomori was not invited to speak, and so he did not ask any questions, but bowed unemotionally upon his dismissal. He had learned well.

His only other ally—if the Satsuma fencing master could be called one—was his archery instructor, Nakamura, a Zen Buddhist priest who was encouraging and kind and gave Tonomori his only holidays. These were extended hunting expeditions into the green hills in the northeast of Lord Shijame's lands.

The priest did not kill game, but Tonomori was allowed to shoot deer—though always under the most difficult of circumstances when they were on the run. The meat was given to Shijame's peasants, the hide tanned into leather, and the horns made into sword stands. The holidays were always too brief, but they helped improve Tonomori's skills as a marksman.

On his fifteenth birthday, Lord Shijame himself presented Tonomori with his two swords, the long slashing *tachi* and the shorter stabbing blade; under strict law only samurai could carry both. Those of lesser rank, merchants and craftsmen, could carry only the short sword, under penalty of death.

Late that afternoon, Shijame met Tonomori at the fencing school. No one, not even the master, was on hand. Over his medium frame, Shijame wore a faded kimono with the sleeves tied back and well-worn *hakama*, the loose, baggy trousers worn by samurai and often by other warriors.

"Let me see what you have learned, Tonomori-san," the baron said, drawing his long sword.

Tonomori was unprepared for this, but obeyed promptly, sensing that Lord Shijame was hardly acting on a whim. His face might be heavily lined and his hair iron gray, but this Satsuma baron carried himself like a professional soldier. Tonomori moved with caution.

Shijame threw a blow. Tonomori blocked. Shijame threw another blow. Tonomori blocked. The baron threw a third blow, this time with deceptive speed, and Tonomori blocked the countercut. Shijame began pressing him with combinations of blows, working both his right and left sides, but steadily pressing Tonomori backward across the *dojo* floor.

Tonomori began changing his own positions, switched to the stance of a left-hander, and began forcing Shijame back. The fighting was relentless, the blades silvery blurs; this was no game of wooden swords.

Tonomori cut through Shijame's kimono at the shoulder, and moved in for a downward block. Without warning, Shijame stepped backward and out of range in one fluid motion, then bowed to Tonomori.

"You have done well! I am pleased. You do your father credit," Shijame said, hardly showing a sign of physical exertion.

Tonomori could hardly believe the ease with which the baron had fought. He had not credited the baron with any skills at all, except a flair for poetry and for court intrigue. Tonomori would never take anybody for granted again.

"You will go far, I predict," Shijame said. "You are dismissed."

The following day, Tonomori was sent to begin service as a samurai with Shijame's cousin Lord Munetaka, whose holding was far to the northwest of Satsuma.

It was an excellent training ground. Lord Munetaka was involved in continual border warfare with feudal lords whose land he coveted. Assigned as a mounted archer, Tonomori showed impressive skill that soon placed him in Munetaka's vanguard. He rose quickly within the ranks, and by the age of twenty was Munetaka's bodyguard and champion. His renown was spreading. Other samurai on meeting him seemed surprised that he was not the giant they had supposed. Those who doubted his abilities challenged him only once. Their friends disposed of the remains.

Tonomori accompanied his master to Kyoto for the viewing of the cherry blossoms at the imperial court. The other great daimyos also attended. To refuse was an insult. Tonomori came to the attention of Lord Betsuo in winning the archery competition. The prize was a carved steel arrowhead by a great artist who had put all his genius into forming a mountainscape in the narrow triangular field of the arrowhead; it was beauty in miniature.

When Tonomori killed three samurai who had ambushed him in a Kyoto street in retaliation for his slaying of a kinsman of theirs, Betsuo approached Munetaka with a business proposition: Lord Betsuo's champion, having grown old, was retiring to the priesthood. Betsuo needed a new champion and would like to sign on Tonomori; of course, he would reimburse Lord Munetaka for his great loss. They bargained and drank all afternoon, but Betsuo knew that Lord Munetaka needed funds to continue his predatory attacks against his equally rapacious neighbors.

In the morning, Tonomori said farewell to his friends and rode eastward with Betsuo, after the lord took leave of the emperor. It proved to be a bad bargain for Lord Munetaka. Not long afterward, he could have used his best archer while storming a position across his disputed borders. He was slain by an enemy bowman.

Lord Betsuo, on the other hand, was pleased with his champion who, each year, won the coveted archery prize at the Golden Pavilion in Kyoto. Other samurai seeking to build reputations as swordsmen occasionally appeared at Betsuo's fortress to challenge his champion.

By organizing the duel on a grand scale, Lord Betsuo gained much favor among the nobility, inviting them to watch the fighting in comfortable surroundings while enjoying the rarest delicacies and the finest sake.

Once, Baron Shijame had been in attendance. It was a highly touted match between Tonomori and a large swordsman from the north, named Amanari. The betting was heavy; the fighting long and vicious. Halfway through, Tonomori began making a patterned attack, using a series of sequential moves to measure his opponent's reactions— cut to the left leg, then the right shoulder, then the left shoulder, and a chop to the head. Again, left leg, right shoulder, left shoulder, chop to the head.

When Amanari's response was measurable, Tonomori began the final deadly sequence, pressing the attack harder: Left leg, right shoulder, feint the move for the left shoulder, shift body weight to the right, and bring the *tachi* straight down instead. Amanari fell silently, blood welling from the deep cut through his forehead. The feint had been so subtle, the blow so swift that the barons were caught by surprise.

Afterward, the talk was of nothing but the fight. Many nobles were eager to pit their champions against Tonomori or to take him into their service. Betsuo, basking in Tonomori's victory, respectfully declined both offers. Too many duels would defeat his purpose of providing a unique entertainment. He preferred to ensure the future attendance of the nobles, and so remain in the mainstream of their politics and intrigues.

The barons sent Tonomori expensive presents of swords and equipment, and one even presented a handsome saddle and matching stirrups inlaid with mother of pearl. Lord Betsuo presented Tonomori with a *tachi*, the blade almost three hundred years old and the mountings done completely in leather marked with the solid-gold crest of the powerful Hosokawa family, allies of shogun and emperor alike.

Baron Shijame appeared last of all, delivering a simple but exquisite gift wrapped in gold silk. It was a sword guard which had belonged to Tonomori's father. The *sukashi tsuba* was a round iron guard made by a master whose pierced work depicted geese flying in the rain. The guard was delicate, yet had great strength. Near the opening in the center for the passage of the blade was an engraving of a sixteen-petal chrysanthemum, the imperial *mon*. It indicated either its ownership, or a favor conferred upon its maker by an emperor. But which?

"I regret that I cannot answer any questions in connection with your father," Lord Shijame replied to Tonomori's expression of gratitude and curiosity. "Your father did not wish to make himself known to you, although I am at liberty to say that you please him greatly and that there was no disgrace in your birth. You are of the highest daimyo rank, though unfortunately you have no lands. I cannot say more. I also am pleased. You have brought much honor to your foster father."

"Thank you very much, Shijame-sama. Would you enjoy some *o-cha*?"

Shijame declined politely. "There are pressing matters in the north, and I must return quickly. Thank you for the fight, Tonomori-san. It was very enjoyable, just like the old days. Perhaps one day you should go on a quest. Then you would be enshrined in Japanese legend forever." Shijame made ready to leave.

Tonomori was eager to detain him for another moment. "Is it permitted to convey respect to my father, to wish him good health?"

"Consider it done, Tonomori-san," said Shijame. He bowed and left Tonomori puzzling.

Those times were gone now. As a ronin, Tonomori would not command the respect of the barons. But at least I found out that my father is still alive, Tonomori thought as he reached for another flask of sake. But why does he not recognize me? What did he do that I had to be sent away? If my birth was no disgrace, then why was I raised by Lord Shijame?

Riddles, riddles. Earlier in the year, at a request from Tonomori, Lord Betsuo said he would make discreet inquiries into his champion's origins. At great expense, Betsuo maintained connections among men in high places. Because he also owned one of the strongest fortresses in the strategic Yamato plain, those men would have been glad to oblige him for past services rendered and for future support. Betsuo's death changed all that.

First, Tonomori had the business of Masanori and Lord Atsuhira, and only then, the quest for his own beginnings. As a ronin, Tonomori could not go back to Lord Shijame, nor did he want to. Nor could he go to the imperial court, where he had influential friends. They would not open their doors to a ronin. Tonomori drank deeply from the flask, then suddenly reached for the *tachi* beside him.

His horses were looking into the darkness, their ears pricked up. It could mean nothing; it could mean everything. Tonomori unsheathed the *tachi* and moved into the darkness away from the pavilion, keeping low.

Trying to clear his swimming head, Tonomori welcomed the steady dripping from the branches overhead. Being so close to Masanori, he should never have drunk so much sake. It was a stupid mistake that now might cost him dearly.

Men were somewhere in the darkness, moving lightly. But with the wind rustling in the trees, he could not distinguish how many men. Heavy cloud cover still obscured most of the light from the moon. The rain had stopped. Tonomori thought he saw a blink of bare steel.

The horses were muttering now, swinging around to meet whatever was coming toward them from the cover of night. This pinpointed the source of attack, and Tonomori moved from the cover of a tree to meet it.

The clouds suddenly unveiled the falling moon, bathing everything in a yellow light. A demon shape screamed with an unearthly howl and scurried from a bush just three feet away. Completely rattled, Tonomori turned and slipped on the wet grass, dropping the *tachi* as the dark shapes rushed forward.

Tonomori reached frantically for the sword, fumbling in the wet grass as those terrible screams shattered the night air.

A wicked spear blade gleamed toward his throat.

"It's him, it's Tonomori."

How stupid, Tonomori thought. *I will never have the answer to my riddle.* He braced himself for the death cut.

Chapter Three

"Tonomori-san is wounded," said the voice behind the unwavering *naginata* angled at Tonomori's throat. The moonlight gleamed like pale death on the undulating temper line of the spear.

"No, you idiot," another voice hissed. "Can't you see that our master has fallen afoul of demon forces?"

His blood still singing in his ears, Tonomori saw hands reaching toward him, helping him stand. He recognized those voices. They were not those of assassins, but of two lowly footsoldiers, *ashigaru*, who until yesterday were in his service.

The spearman he recognized as Yamahito, the man-mountain who was even taller than he. The other, Oshabiri the chatterbox, gathered up a small monkey that had scrambled to him from out of the darkness. So *that* was the demon from hell that had shivered his soul with screams!

Swaying unsteadily, Tonomori laughed until tears streamed from his eyes. "I thought you were demons," he told them, brushing the tears from his face.

The *ashigaru* stared, their suspicions of demons confirmed, but they hoped that Tonomori had not lost his reason from grappling with such dark powers on a howling night like this. Yamahito picked up Tonomori's sword and, hesitantly, offered it to him.

"You have come a long way," Tonomori said. With his kimono sleeve, he wiped the moisture from the sword blade. He could not afford to have rust mar its fine polish.

"The castle seemed empty without you, Tonomori-san, so we left to join you," Oshabiri said. He was awed. Oshabiri had never heard of anyone before who had been successful in wrestling with devils. He wondered if the devils had been summoned by Lord Masanori, whom he considered capable of anything.

Yamahito interrupted. "Yes, Tonomori-san. Lord Masanori decreed that anyone who wished might go with you." Out of politeness, Yamahito left out the words, *in disgrace*.

"Oshabiri-san and I discussed it. We thought it would be exciting to be wherever you might go, and we also decided that you might need some help. I have some skill with the spear, and Oshabiri-san is a very fine bowman, whatever else are his many failings." Oshabiri shot him an indignant look.

Tonomori was instantly touched by the loyalty displayed by the two *ashigaru* who looked at him so expectantly. But he knew the road ahead might be dangerous indeed, and short. He felt he must advise them frankly to seek employment "with a lord who is in a better position than I to reward your services."

"Please, Tonomori-san, we would rather stay with you without any money. Besides, we cannot go back now," Oshabiri said. As Tonomori staggered slightly, Oshabiri became very excited; he would have given much to see that struggle with the demons. Obviously Tonomori had won. But how did he win? How big were the devils? Oshabiri was determined that he would worm the story out of him. But Tonomori was no boaster—others spread his fame before him. Oshabiri would have to do some careful coaxing.

"See, we can start by cleaning up your camp and packing it away. What a mess," Yamahito declared. Tonomori looked at the pavilion now leaning at drunken angles. Equipment was scattered carelessly. His camp-making skills obviously were out of practice. Tonomori was shocked. He would have strongly reprimanded a subordinate for leaving a camp in such condition.

"Er, yes, it has been a long day," Tonomori agreed. He made up his mind. "After thinking it over, I've decided that you may stay." Amid their bows and profuse thanks, he wandered over to his camp stool and sat before he might fall down.

"Excuse me, sir," Yamahito said, bowing once more. "But we have to pack all this immediately."

"Pack? Why?"

"Because when we left, Lord Masanori was very angry. I am sorry that I must tell you this, but Nobuko-san has killed herself. Lord Masanori found her when he went to claim her for his own," Yamahito explained. "She had cut her throat. I heard Lord Masanori screaming. Afterward, many samurai were arming themselves. I think Masanori-sama blames you. We ran very fast, but I think they will be here soon."

"Why didn't you tell me this before?" Tonomori asked angrily.

"Because you might have left without us, Tonomori-san."

Tonomori had no reply to this and turned away. The drops from his pavilion were falling like tears, but he had none to shed. Nobuko had found life unbearable and had left it. Tonomori understood. Life was so delicate in the balance, a butterfly skipping on a warm breeze through a summer garden, and gone before the first fallen leaf of autumn. He would honor her sacrifice.

"Break camp. We're leaving!" he ordered suddenly. Tonomori began lashing the pack saddles to the horses as soon as the *ashigaru* had finished loading them. The camp was struck within fifteen minutes, and Tonomori was back in his armor.

The rain was starting up again, and he hoped it would come down hard enough to cover their tracks. He planned to cut across his own trail, give the Betsuo fortress a wide circle, and head for the eastern sea, where he might find a better answer to the riddle of how to flee Masanori successfully.

Despite protests by the *ashigaru* that they would rather

run, Tonomori mounted Oshabiri behind him on Kaminari and put Yamahito on one of the pack ponies. The other pony did not like carrying the extra baggage but would have to become used to the idea. Tonomori had no intention of leaving his possessions for Masanori's samurai to divide among themselves.

Tonomori wrapped the lead line of the pack pony around his left hand and spurred Kaminari. Yamahito's horse followed in eager pursuit. Rain was falling heavily now, and that suited Tonomori; it would be more difficult to track them. He drew his waterproof cloak around him tightly. Oshabiri burrowed his face into Tonomori's back and gripped the saddle tightly. The monkey's chittering of complaint from inside Oshabiri's cloak echoed the *ashigaru*'s own feelings.

Behind them, Yamahito hung on in grim determination, catching all the mud flying from the horse's hooves. Each black lump which he blew away from his lips had Masanori's name on it.

Luckily, Tonomori had hunted this area before. In doubling back, he would remain in the foothills away from the plain. If any helpful spirits were smiling on him tonight, the samurai hunting Tonomori would not find the camp until dawn, and by that time they would be far away. With the wind and driving rain at his back, Tonomori plunged deeper into the night on the path to the eastern sea.

At dawn, the Betsuo samurai ran across his camp. Before their horses churned the entire area into muddy soup, the commander dispatched outriders to find Tonomori's trail.

The commander, Kanegama, did not have much hope of finding the ronin, and dreaded the prospect of returning to face Masanori's wrath. The camp appeared to have been briefly occupied. The wood fire had been extinguished by rain during the night. Kanegama wiped the water from his face. His armor lacings were soaked and his weapons probably already rusting. That did not matter. That Tonomori had been a friend did not matter—only duty mattered.

Kanegama was afraid of failure. They were all afraid of failure.

A samurai came pounding into the camp. "He has doubled back, sir! I think he must be heading for the coast."

"You are sure?" Kanegama was wary of chasing false leads. They couldn't afford to waste time, and Tonomori was a fox.

"I am sure, sir. The trail is hours old but there are freshly broken branches. He has companions, and they were in a hurry." The samurai's helmet cord had loosened and he paused to retie it.

"Call in the others. We head for the sea!" Kanegama retied his own helmet cord. They had a hard ride ahead of them. He left one rider in camp with instructions to follow when the other outriders regrouped. Kanegama had no time to wait for everyone. A signaling horn blew and the main group disappeared into the low gray clouds covering the foothills. The hunt was in full cry.

Chapter Four

The novice meditated in the lotus position, his right hand extended and open upon his thigh. He looked with pleasure upon the two combatants before him, fencing in the garden with practice spears. The pop and clack of the *naginatas'* bamboo shafts brought back pleasant memories of his youth, when he had trained to be a samurai.

Bitter was the young man's lot when he could not meet

the physical standards for a samurai. But God, in His own wisdom, had called instead.

The black rosary hanging from his neck over his thin chest was as comforting as his own Buddhist beads once had been. It still seemed odd how much the gentle teachings of Buddha blended in so easily with those of the Christ. Atsue, the novice, hoped that Buddha would understand his conversion. He felt that it was possible to follow the teachings of both, although he would never say this to the priest. Father Ochoa would rant and rave as usual, and he would have resolved nothing.

The slap of the bamboo poles stopped. The novice gazed fondly as the combatant on his left removed her headgear and brushed a few loose strands of dark hair away from her face.

The Lady Toriko was an excellent instructor, a true samurai and so graceful, he thought. The other, who shook her hair out in a gold cloud, asked with a broad smile, "How did I do, Atsue-san?" She spoke in Japanese.

"Very well, although I must confess I am but a poor judge of fighting ability," Atsue replied.

Toriko was a samurai of a rank slightly higher than his and to criticize her ability would be a gross act of impertinence, one which would entitle her to remove his head. Toriko had been born a samurai. Otherwise, it would have been difficult for her as a woman to achieve that rank.

But the blond woman, Lady Diana, was quite another matter. She had no rank at all in Japan, though she was said to be of a noble house in her own country. Only eighteen years old, she was under the protection of their ruling daimyo, Lord Hoju, so she was called Diana-san, the -san being interchangeable as *Miss, Mr.,* or *Mrs.* Only lords of very high rank were addressed as -sama.

Foreigners were barely tolerated, so Diana usually kept her extravagant blond mane piled under a black lacquered wig so as to better blend into her surroundings, and plucked her eyebrows in the arched Japanese style. But nothing could disguise those deep blue eyes with their quite unintentionally intimate gaze.

Atsue, as always, found her face and figure temptingly beautiful, and his loins stirred at the vision of her sensuously rounded body entering her bath. To even contemplate fornication was a mortal sin—Father Ochoa had reminded him often enough—and Atsue would say several *Aves* and *Pater Nosters* tonight for the benefit of his soul. In his heart, he knew that even these would not be proof against the allure of the mission cook's pretty daughter; Atsue had been pillowing her for weeks. *Pillowing* was a fine, soft word, much better than the harsh term of fornication, Atsue reflected. The cook's daughter had proven so adept at sin, especially in the stirring "Shouting Monkey" position, that Atsue realized he would have to renounce his novitiate vows and remain simply a convert. He hoped the Christ would understand even if Father Ochoa didn't.

Diana smiled again at the small novice in his overlarge white robes, then dismissed him from her thoughts. Her efforts in the *naginata* practice had been good, Diana knew. Then why was not Lady Toriko smiling in approval? Why was she so quiet?

"You do well, Diana-san. You show much promise," Toriko finally said. She rested the practice *naginata* in the curve of her arm and untied the *hachimaki*, a headband used to keep sweat out of the eyes.

Twice, Diana had slashed the edge of her *naginata* against the side of Toriko's *do*, the lacquered leather chest protector used in fencing practice. Usually, Toriko would have had great praise for her student. Today, she seemed moody.

"Is something wrong?" Diana asked. She moved to retrieve her head protector from the ground, but Toriko stopped her.

"We will have no more practice today. The servants will put away the equipment. We have time to bathe before the midday meal. Shall we go?"

The bathhouse was at the lower end of the mission grounds. Originally located behind the low winged-roof building used for the chapel, it had been moved two years ago, after the arrival of Father Ochoa. He considered frequent bathing an invitation to sin. When he found that men and women bathed together in complete nakedness, his fury knew no bounds. His converts had listened politely to the rambling sermons translated for them by Atsue, and then had moved the bathhouse to another place, where they bathed as before.

Diana, who had accompanied Father Ochoa to Japan, had become used to the public baths. She found the scalding water refreshing after an energetic practice session with Toriko. Once the novelty wore off, along with her modesty, she did not notice the nude bodies at all, though she never soaked in the bathhouse unless Father Ochoa was at private prayers. These days he had been spending more and more time in mystical contemplation.

"Leave us," Toriko commanded the servants after they had carefully arranged fresh kimonos and towels on a low table. To discourage eavesdroppers, Toriko had propped open the slatted sides to the bathhouse. It was unlikely that anyone else in the village could speak or understand Portuguese or Dutch, but Toriko did not want, in any case, to be overheard.

Diana already was in the water. Now Toriko settled in and splashed her face.

"Ah, that is much better." She reached for a sponge and began washing. Diana noticed that Toriko's dagger, a *tanto* in exquisite *aikuchi* mounts, was lying beside her at the edge of the sunken pool. What now?

"Trouble is gathering!"

"What kind of trouble?" Diana asked.

Toriko had resolved to be blunt. "Your presence here and that of the mission has become intolerable to some of Lord Hoju's neighbors. They wish that you leave."

Diana, who had never met Lord Hoju, looked perplexed. "We have an agreement with Lord Hoju. How can he break it?"

"Believe me, if Lord Hoju considers you to be more trouble than you are worth, he will find a pretext to break it—or do so without one. Great pressures are being brought to bear on him. The other daimyos do not like the converts to this new religion, and they have never liked foreigners."

Toriko did not have to add that only Lord Hoju's notorious streak of stubbornness had kept him from caving in to the pressure immediately. Lord Hoju did not like to be pressured. As someone had once said, try to force Hoju to become a profligate, and he would have become a celibate out of spite.

Diana ducked her head beneath the water and came up sputtering. Her hair needed washing. While she closed her eyes to the suds, Toriko kept constant guard, her hand never far from the dagger.

"Do you think the samurai will do anything?" Diana said. She rinsed her hair carefully, then twisted it to squeeze out the excess water.

"Yes, I am sure that will happen, but I don't know when—soon, I think." Toriko was out of the water, drying herself carefully. The dagger was on the low table near her. Diana understood the knife would not be used only to repel attackers. Toriko would cut her own throat with it before allowing herself to be captured.

"Lord Hoju sent a message last night," Toriko explained now. "He has contacted the captain of the *Schoen*. If the ship arrives in time, you will be safe. Lord Hoju said he sent for the captain weeks ago, and expects him at any hour."

Diana had arrived in Japan on the *Schoen*, a refugee from Spanish assassins who had murdered most of her family in the Netherlands. Her father, Count de Edgemont, had used his influence and connections with Dutch traders to hide his remaining child on the other side of the world.

The *Schoen*'s captain, Peter de Wynte, a trusted family friend, had made the arrangements with Lord Hoju before bringing her from India, the first haven in her flight. De Wynte, searching for a solution to the problem of finding a place where she could be safe, had thought of Father Ochoa, who was in India establishing missions. For many years, de Wynte had known Father Ochoa, and he trusted this Portuguese friar, a born evangelist with a drive to see the world. In return for obtaining the land for a mission in the heathen land of Japan, and permission to build a church, albeit a small one, Father Ochoa readily agreed to hide the girl there. As part of his complex arrangement, de

Wynte gave Lord Hoju two hundred muskets and four cannon, plus powder and shot. Guns were priceless to Japanese warlords, who were quick to learn their value in battle.

De Wynte felt secure in his bargain. And Lady Diana would be additionally safe because Father Ochoa despised the Spanish—even though that earlier missionary to the Orient, the Jesuits' co-founder, had come from Pamplona.

But now, Lord Hoju seemed to feel that the bargain counted for nothing. Diana's stomach felt like lead. Where would she go now? To the New World? No, the Spanish ruled there, also. Their influence spread like a hideous disease, strangling and corrupting everything in their greed and consuming lust for power and gold.

And would Captain de Wynte arrive in time with the *Schoen*? In some ways, Diana did not care—she had nowhere to go. But she thought carefully. So, Lord Hoju must know where the *Schoen* was ported, and he even had a way to send messages across the sea. His spy network must be very good, indeed. Now, it seemed, she must go from one peril to the next.

Toriko studied Diana's troubled face. "I think the captain will be in time." She smiled.

Diana returned the gesture and was pleased to discover that her conversation in Japanese was almost effortless.

"Your Japanese is becoming very good," Toriko remarked approvingly. "It is regrettable that your study of our language will be suspended now. But I wish even more that we had time to continue your other studies."

"So do I," Diana said. That Toriko was teaching Diana the subtle art of spying and assassination as well as the Japanese language would have been a startling revelation to Father Ochoa and to many others.

Lady Toriko's presence at the mission was, in fact, a mystery to the priest. Lord Hoju had insisted upon it as part of the bargain, and so de Wynte had agreed; he had no choice. It soon became apparent to everyone in the mission, except to Father Ochoa, that Lady Toriko acted as Hoju's eyes and ears there, as well as Diana's guard.

In some ways, it was a humiliating assignment for Toriko. A male samurai would have been more appropriate, but Lord Hoju feared that might seem to lend an air of approval to the mission, and this he wished to avoid. None of the samurai would take a woman seriously, even if she was of their own rank, though in theory they were supposed to.

Toriko was aware that her rank merited a more important assignment, and that her orders to observe the mission must be somehow a punishment. Or perhaps a safeguard? She smiled inwardly. Lord Hoju had respect for Toriko, knowing that she was a *ninja* assassin. From early girlhood, the Hoju family had paid for her training and she had repaid them well. Even the grasping Lord Hoju would admit as much. But a *ninja* could be a two-edged *ken*, an ancient blade which cut both ways. A *ninja* conceivably was susceptible to being corrupted and turned against her employer. This could explain Hoju's nervousness when Toriko lived within his fortress.

Lord Hoju, however, remained her master and, within reason, could assign her to any duties he wished. Then, too, few Japanese within Hoju's domains could speak a European language, and this was a further reason for her assignment to the mission. Her second language was Portuguese, for she had lived in Tanegashima, a small island where seamen from Portugal had been the first visitors. There, too, they had introduced guns to the Japanese.

Toriko had at first resented the assignment, but she did not object to leaving the fortress. She considered Hoju's men to be little more than a collection of backwoods boors calling themselves samurai. To a man, they resented her, both for her influence with their master, and for her aloofness. She spurned their advances, few of these subtle, for sexual liaisons. Toriko remained an enigma to them. They did not understand her, nor would they even try.

She found the mission dull. Father Ochoa, while pious and sincere, hardly could be called an intellectual. And he seldom bathed. Toriko wrinkled her nose at the thought. But with him had come Diana, pretty as a flower. Her eyes sparkled with intelligence. In Diana, Toriko recognized a soaring spirit so much like her own, but one whose wings would be kept clipped—like her own—by men in a world created for men.

Within a month, Diana was conversing painstakingly in Japanese with Toriko, who in turn responded haltingly in the complexities of the Dutch tongue. During one of these lessons, Diana saw the *naginata* hanging on the wall in Toriko's room, and had been intrigued.

"It is a spear," Toriko explained.

"Do all samurai women know how to use one?"

"No, not all—but many do. It is an approved weapon for women, like the dagger. Very few samurai women use the sword. It is not encouraged. Three hundred years ago or so, the women would sometimes fight alongside the men, but no more. It is almost unheard of. Women are expected to support their samurai husbands by defending the home and children. That is enough. I am one of a dozen women in all of Japan who still use the sword."

In Toriko's room also, Diana had seen Toriko's dagger for the first time, a thing of beauty with finely carved silver mountings depicting the waves of the sea inlaid with fish of gold. The scabbard's green lacquer was mixed with crushed mother of pearl. The mountings were new, but the blade, Diana learned, was more than three hundred years old, and sharp enough to shave a peach.

Diana found that the Japanese had little use for gems or jewelry of any kind. Their riches were in poetry, fine silks, carvings of ivory, and their weapons the finest blades in the world. Toriko kept her dagger tucked into her kimono sleeve.

She had not intended to introduce Diana into the darker side of the Japanese martial arts. But it had happened suddenly. Eager to please her teacher with some freshly cut flowers, another Japanese favorite, Diana padded into Toriko's room late one evening to find her clinging to a wall by an open window. Diana, frightened, held her ground. Toriko leaped from the wall to the floor with fluid grace. She was a menacing form, wrapped completely in black cotton. Steel hooks gleamed from the tips of her dark gloves.

"Well, well, Diana-san, you move very quickly, like a cat. Perhaps you should be called one. Should I call you Nekko-san?" The figure moved closer. Diana did not move.

"I apologize," Diana said. "I should have knocked. How—how did you do that?" Diana studied Toriko's guise more closely. "I want to know how to do that."

"Curious cats can get their whiskers singed," Toriko admonished, furious that Diana had discovered her secret. Diana was but a hair's breadth away from being killed.

But Toriko made a spontaneous decision, and the danger passed. "In the future, Nekko-san, knock and receive permission before you enter a room." Toriko began unwrapping the cloth which muffled her face. "To do otherwise might get you a broken neck or something . . . equally unpleasant."

Having refrained from killing Diana, Toriko now had to decide what to do with her. She examined the young woman closely.

"I want to learn," Diana said. "I will do anything you tell me. *Anything*. You—you are not what you appear to be, I think. Neither am I!"

"You may not like what you become." Toriko was testing her.

"I do not like being helpless. Women are so—so helpless."

Toriko acknowledged the statement. "That is true up to a point. But in some things we can be more deadly than the samurai. They are like the waves that smash upon the rocks in the storm. We are like the reeds that bend before the mighty winds, while within those reeds lies a small poisonous snake waiting to strike. If you choose to learn, there will be no turning back."

"I would never turn back. Never!"

"I choose to believe you. Very well; then first you must be prepared to learn what is reality and what isn't. The world of the *ninja* is far different than that of the samurai."

"A *ninja*—what is a *ninja*?"

This time Toriko did not smile. "The shadow people. What you are, I once was. What I am, you will be. There

57

is truth in death, and in little else. We have much to talk about before you can begin your work.''

It was the first careful step. Toriko, a recent convert to the church, had yet to reconcile her new faith to that of her profession. Diana, she warned, must face the same dilemma.

Diana's answer put some of Toriko's doubts to rest. ''Is it 'just' to allow a murderer to live, to continue to slaughter? I think not! Most of my family was murdered by one man, a man who not only lives above the law, he *is* the law. If my father had not sent me into hiding, I would have been killed with the rest. Look, the kings and knights of Europe are professed to be very devout Christians. That hasn't stopped them even one bit from pursuing their cruel and evil ways. I have seen death hide behind many smiles. If I am to survive, to ever return to my home, I must learn to smile back.''

Toriko looked into Diana's eyes. *Men will be enchanted by those eyes, lost in them. They will never know what killed them,* Toriko thought.

Diana would need every advantage she could get. Her homeland, the Netherlands, was ruled by the King of Spain and occupied by Spanish troops who in theory were there to protect the Hollanders, but who in fact were there to keep them in line.

Commanding general of this occupation force was the Duke of Alvino, the implacable enemy of Diana's family and any other noble house hinting rebellion to the Hapsburg dynasty that ruled Spain. When the Hapsburgs needed money, as they always did for their grand plans of dominating Europe, they squeezed it from their subjects, loyal or not.

The Duke of Alvino was an expert at turning the screws, a judicious murder here, a hostage taken there, the burning of heretics in an *auto-da-fe* on behalf of the feared Inquisition.

But the Count of Edgemont suspected Alvino of ambitions of his own, of dominating the king and beginning his own dynasty with money looted from the estates of families he had slaughtered. Fearing this, Edgemont had sent his daughter, his only weakness, beyond what he hoped was the reach of the Spanish empire until the Netherlands were safe once more.

At times the count was overprotective, and it was well that he did not know of his daughter's studies with the Lady Toriko. With each passing day, Diana grew in skills and a grace that was at times feral and chilling to see.

Months passed before Toriko would allow Diana to take a step outside the mission. First, she had to learn how to walk properly, to understand the difference in walking in the city, in the country, along the beach, in the mountains.

"Peasant women walk differently than samurai ladies; they take larger strides. Courtesans are another world altogether. Learn the differences. Watch everyone," Toriko instructed her. "When you return to your own world, study everyone, peasant and nobles alike.

"Look for patterns in behavior. Does your enemy walk or ride? When? Where? How often? What hour? What is his favorite food? When does he sleep, and where? Is he right- or left-handed? These are important things. Remember them well."

She guided Diana in learning how to remain completely still for hours, how to move from shadow to shadow, and how to step but make no sound. Toriko began to teach her the rudiments of the *naginata,* presumably for something to do, as the servants were told. It was the only exercise Diana was allowed to perform openly. But she was learning to climb sheer walls, to breathe underwater, even to walk across water.

When Toriko thought Diana was physically toughened enough, she was taken for brief forays at night into the country. And as Diana grew more sure of herself and more skilled, the expeditions became longer. One moonlit night, Diana shivered in delicious excitement as she watched Toriko elude the samurai guards at Lord Hoju's castle and scale its walls. Three times, Toriko penetrated the castle's defenses. The fourth time was Diana's turn. The guards never saw her, though one thought he might have noticed a cat in the shadows. She was mastering the black art of blending invisibly into one's surroundings.

But Diana still did not know how to kill. When Toriko

thought she was ready, she gave Diana a small strangling chain and a bundle of *shuriken*, the legendary throwing knives of the *ninja*. Handforged and razor sharp, most were star-shaped but some were double-bladed, hammered from a single piece of steel.

"Sometimes they are poisoned," Toriko told Diana. "These are not. They are to practice with. When you can hit a small target seven times out of seven, you will be ready."

"Ready for what, Toriko-san?"

"Ready to begin your practice in earnest, Diana-san."

Diana groaned later while soaking her aching muscles in the hot tub, but she was learning. Toriko had the muscles for it, a flat, lithe figure with small breasts and boyish hips. Toriko was lovely and demure in appearance, which is exactly what she strove for; people were put off guard. Diana bemoaned her own full breasts. They ruined the smooth flowing lines of a kimono, and had not been fashionable in Europe either. She flattened her breasts by binding them, which was not only desirable when she was in European dress, but also for protection when she was in *ninja* gear.

As Diana's skill improved, so did her eagerness, and the aching muscles were forgotten. She began to look forward to sundown and to the quiet late hours when the crickets called. She could slip undetected from the mission like a wild night creature, free to roam at will.

And so it went. During the day, under Father Ochoa's eye, she remained the Lady Edgemont. Diana had no work to perform, so she embroidered vestments and altar cloths for the chapel. "You must be fatigued with boredom," Father Ochoa happened to remark sympathetically. Having just learned from Toriko of Lord Hoju's breach of faith, Diana merely looked at him, barely managing to stifle a yawn. She would have to tell him soon, or perhaps Toriko should do it.

"It is a pity you must be tucked away here so far from home," the priest said. "I wish there was something for you to do."

"So do I, but there isn't," she responded. "Lately, I

have started taking long naps in the afternoon. I do enjoy the evenings more—they are so cool. I can see some of the lights in the town, and occasionally a basket of fire is visible when one of the fishermen is working at night offshore. I can only imagine what things must be like in the cities. It must be like another world. I do wish Lord Hoju would allow us freedom to go beyond the mission boundaries.''

"God moves in mysterious ways, my child. You are beginning to learn patience, something very valuable in the young," Father Ochoa said. He did not understand women at all, or care to. His only interest was in the church. He did, however, think it a shame that a nice young lady like Diana had to be shut up in a mission with no friends, and with almost nothing to do but worry about those at home remaining in the shadow of Spain. The priest was understanding about this; he did not care for the Spanish who had annexed his small homeland of Portugal. From what he had been able to observe, Father Ochoa found the Japanese princes little different from what he knew of their European counterparts. They were all treacherous and greedy. He pondered as he looked at Diana who was setting some small stitches on a silk surplice—were the Spanish hunting her father even now? Were they still looking for her? Poor Diana, alone and so defenseless!

As she yawned and stretched now, she seemed much like a cat, Father Ochoa thought, very much like a cat. He would pray for her safety again this evening.

Chapter Five

They ran along a narrow foot trail paralleling the main road, leading the tired horses. Tonomori knew that Masanori's samurai were not far behind—maybe two hours, at best. His lead was dwindling but Tonomori thought it would hold long enough. They had to go on. With enough men, Tonomori would simply have ambushed his pursuers, and be done with it. But the pursuers were just too many. Tonomori and his two men would be overwhelmed and their heads taken.

A burning rage drove him relentlessly. He would give Masanori no satisfaction. If need be, he would drown himself in the depths of the sea before he would allow Masanori's samurai to take him.

"We stop to rest," Tonomori ordered. His *ashigaru* dropped where they stood. Even the horses' flanks were heaving. Tonomori left Kaminari tied to a tree, and scrambled up a hill to scout the terrain. At the top he looked back but saw no sign of pursuit along the muddy road. But he knew the samurai were closing the distance; they would kill their horses, if necessary, to get him. He would, too, were the situation reversed.

Ten miles away, through the winding cleft in the coastal range, was the sea. Five miles farther, along the seacoast, was the city of Murashima, seat of Lord Hoju, with whom Tonomori was slightly acquainted. He had been at one of Betsuo's dueling entertainments. Tonomori thought he could run another five miles and then ride the rest of the way. If they did not find a boat, Tonomori would attempt to buy fresh horses from Lord Hoju.

Such a course would be risky. Hoju was a well-known eccentric. He might sell them the horses, but then again he might hold Tonomori and his *ashigaru* and for a price turn them over to Masanori's samurai. Tonomori hoped he could find a boat; there he could sleep. He was very tired. Tonomori had not slept since long before the battle. He really did not even want to contemplate riding beyond Murashima any more than he wished to chance Lord Hoju's whim.

The *ashigaru* barely looked up when Tonomori returned.

"A few more miles, and then we can ride," Tonomori told them. He sat down and leaned back against a rotted log. He would close his eyes for a few minutes, no more.

Oshabiri and Yamahito said nothing. Their broken blisters burned with each movement. Their feet were in torment. But they would run without complaint. They would not shame themselves before a samurai.

Little Saru grumbled noisily. Oshabiri fed him part of a rice ball that Tonomori had carried away from the castle.

"I wondered how big the demon was," Oshabiri whispered to Yamahito.

"What demon?"

"The demon that Tonomori-san was wrestling with all afternoon yesterday," Oshabiri said indignantly.

"I didn't see any demon."

"Of course not. Tonomori-san defeated it."

Yamahito looked at Oshabiri in great weariness. If his young friend was certain that a demon had been present, Yamahito knew from experience that nothing he might say would persuade him otherwise. His practiced nose told Yamahito that Tonomori's breath last night would have intoxicated three normal samurai, but he said nothing. If a devil had been there, it would have been washed away in the sake bowl. In the meanwhile, he would rest and watch and await his master's orders.

In turn, Tonomori regarded his men, through eyes opened in their slits, with some amusement. Oshabiri strongly resembled his pet, Saru. He was young and slender, though with a tough wiriness that sent his arrows far and true. But Oshabiri had missed his true calling. He was an even finer mimic and was renowned among the lower ranks for his uncanny ability, with both voice and body movements, to ape the personalities and affectations of his betters, a talent he was careful to conceal from them, but which nonetheless was known to Tonomori. He wondered what Oshabiri's imitation of him was like.

Yamahito, on the other hand, was a quiet tower of strength, who looked as if carved from stone. His long spear had killed many men, and he had a reputation of wading into the hottest battle with a cool head. Even more fearsome was his prodigious appetite. Yamahito had won many bets with unsuspecting *ashigaru* who had not heard of his feats with chopsticks.

As Tonomori stirred, Oshabiri offered some smoked fish and a rice ball, along with some cold sake.

"How much do we have left, Oshabiri-san?" Tonomori said between swallows.

"Very little, sir."

"Too bad. Well, we can always eat the monkey."

"Yes, . . . sir?" Oshabiri's eyes grew wide.

"A joke, Oshabiri-san."

"Thank you, sir." Oshabiri looked relieved. He offered more sake. "Would you like some more food to replenish your strength? The struggle must have been terrible—you must be very tired."

Tonomori raised an eyebrow. "No, I don't want anything more to eat but as I am very tired, don't wear me out any further with questions." Tonomori lay back with his eyes closed. But he thought for a moment, and curiosity won out. "What struggle?"

"Yesterday afternoon—with the fiend. The evil one. The bad *kami* that put your camp on end. Was it sent by Lord Masanori?"

Tonomori scowled at the mention of Masanori's name. "I didn't ask," he replied dryly.

"What color was it, Tonomori-san?"

Tonomori was about to reply angrily that he did not

want to be bothered, but then said with enthusiasm, "It was blue with white veins all over its body. It had tusks like a boar and claws like *naginata* blades."

Oshabiri's eyes grew even wider. Tonomori heard a noise.

"Is something wrong, Yamahito-san?"

"No, sir, I must have swallowed wrong. It must be the damp air."

Tonomori decided to humor Oshabiri. "It had a great voice like thunder in the mountains. It said it was hungry and wanted to eat one of my horses since it could not find any young *ashigaru* in the vicinity. They are the demon's favorite meal and it wears their leg bones around its neck. A most fearsome sight."

Oshabiri peered into the trees.

"Naturally, I refused, and it attacked. I think we fought for a long time. Just when I was about to strangle it, the demon transformed itself into a bottle of sake."

Oshabiri nearly dropped the one he was holding.

"There was only one thing I could do . . ."

"Yes? . . ."

"I quickly drank the sake. The demon tried to get out but I washed it back down with another flask and another." Tonomori's voice rose to an urgent pitch. "Quick, Oshabiri-san, more sake, I think it's trying to get out again!"

Oshabiri fell back against the ground in fright. He waited for the apparition to spring forth. But a glance at Yamahito's silently heaving shoulders and then at Tonomori's bemused expression told him that once more his imagination had gotten the better of him.

Abashed, Oshabiri sat up. "What will you do now, Tonomori-san?"

"Lose Masanori's samurai at the first opportunity," Tonomori said. "As to that demon—instead of its sending me into the Great Void, I voided it this morning instead. On a rock. Any more questions, Oshabiri-san? Good!"

Tonomori did not want any more interruptions. He had an impossible task ahead of him—to achieve the destruction of both Masanori and Lord Atsuhira. Both had vast holdings and armies of samurai to protect them. His cause

65

seemed a hopeless one. But hopeless causes and samurai who pursued them, always had been the stuff of legends in Japan. On those many causes, countless samurai had expended their lives.

Think of Yoshitsune. For destroying the rival Tiara clan in the famed Gempei war four hundred years earlier, his reward was to be hounded all over Japan by his jealous brother, the Minamoto Shogun Yoritomo. The harassed Yoshitsune finally killed himself, and passed into national legend.

Tonomori wondered if he had made a mistake. It would be so easy—a quick cut, and his spirit would be free to be reborn again in someone else, surely a better life than the one he was leading.

Shaking his head, Tonomori knew he could not. Already, he was on the road he was fated to take. Time enough later to atone for any defeat, any failure.

Tonomori knew the strengths of Masanori and Atsuhira, but what of their weaknesses? *Examine the whole and study the parts,* as his fencing master had said.

Masanori has great wealth and many samurai—but he is also vain and impulsive, easily manipulated. Atsuhira is ambitious but too cautious, and cheap in the bargain. His ambition is a flame that could be fanned into a funeral pyre, Tonomori thought.

Both lords must die, he told himself, or he would have failed in his duty to Lord Betsuo.

> *Death is a samurai*
> *both blind and deaf,*
> *and groping with swords.*

As Tonomori wrote the poem in his mind, the specter formed of a ghastly warrior, reaching out into the silent darkness ahead, with sharp blades to feel his sightless way, oblivious to the pain and suffering he inflicted in passing through the world.

There had to be a way for revenge. And, as in a duel, Tonomori knew he must wait for an opening. Or, perhaps, force one.

He looked up. It was time to move. The road behind them was still quiet, but would not remain so forever. He nodded to his *ashigaru* and plunged down the path, with Kaminari following. The *ashigaru* struggled to their feet and trotted on behind him, leading the horses. They thought themselves fortunate in one aspect—they were, at least, now running downhill.

Chapter Six

To the Honorable Captain de Wynte,

It is my duty to inform you that permission to allow the Lady Diana de Edgemont to remain at the mission in Murashima is hereby revoked. Recent portents interpreted by the priests at Kuwara shrine indicate possible calamitous upheavals if she remains in Murashima any longer. Lord Hoju regrets that he can no longer ensure her safety nor that of anyone within the mission. You are to remove them at once. Lord Hoju will retain the guns under the agreement since he has maintained the lady's safety in good faith. As a further sign of good will, Lord Hoju has enrolled the Lady Diana on his family records as a samurai, under the name Mitsuko. May the gods prosper her and may she bear many sons. Please retain this letter as your safe conduct pass.

Sukeyoshi
Scribe to Hoju no Kami Tadawara
Written February, second year
of Ko-ji

Captain Peter de Wynte looked beyond the faces of his two crewmen straining at the oars and saw the waves crashing on the beach below the mission at Murashima. The captain swore inwardly at the perfidy of the Japanese, especially Lord Hoju. It had been difficult enough to bribe the old scoundrel, what with the immense amount of protocol, endless tea ceremonies, and interminable waiting for the head of an arrogant and powerful clan who sometimes forgot to show up. De Wynte believed in the sanctity of written agreements, and it now appeared that Lord Hoju did not.

Nor would Lord Hoju return the guns which were worth their weight in silver to the Japanese. A few swordsmiths had been persuaded to make copies of the Portuguese matchlocks, the first ever seen in Japan. But these first guns were sorry affairs, more likely to blow up or pop off the stock after only a few shots. Japanese guns of recent manufacture had been better but the European guns were highly prized. And now Lord Hoju still had the guns. And the cannon. And the precious powder. A plague on all Japanese nobles, de Wynte thought.

It had been a black week when de Wynte received Lord Hoju's letter in Tanegashima, where the *Schoen* was unloading a cargo of Chinese silk and steel from India in exchange for lacquerware, porcelains, and silver. Only a few days before, de Wynte had learned, by dispatch from another Dutch trader, that the Count de Edgemont was dead, "struck down by highwaymen" while in Spain to petition the king for redress against Spanish misrule in the Low Countries. *Murder by ducal assassins was more like it*, the captain thought. The duke of Alvino had a long arm, reaching all the way from his unassailable position as military governor of the Low Countries to the court of the Spanish king. De Wynte wondered if the duke was groping around the world for Lady Diana—correction, *Countess* Diana. She was the last of a noble house. And he would have to be the one to tell her.

De Wynte shifted his position in the longboat for better balance. They were almost to the edge where the swells were breaking.

"Hans? Volmer? Look lively, now. Pullllll!" The crewmen pulled expertly at the oars, and the longboat bucked gracefully through the combers. At the water's edge, Hans and Volmer jumped out and tugged the boat far onto the dry sand. At the rise of a dune, two children stared pop-eyed at de Wynte's cape, hose, and doublet and the milky skin of his face, and then ran for their village as if demons were snapping at their bare feet.

The captain licked the drying salt spray from a sore at the corner of his mouth. His light brown hair, peppered with gray, needed washing. De Wynte's experience as a ship's captain made him seem older than his thirty-seven years, but his back was straight and his carriage youthful.

"See to your weapons," De Wynte ordered. He scratched at the salt in his beard and hoped they would find no trouble. Hans and Volmer jammed swords into their waist sashes and reached into the longboat for their matchlocks. The captain himself carried a sword and two wheel-lock pistols crafted out of solid steel. Weighted in the butt for use as maces after the balls were discharged, the pistols fired when sparks were struck from a flint by a revolving wheel. Beneath his doublet, de Wynte wore a tight-fitting steel breastplate. He had heard legends of the samurai's fighting prowess and was not eager to experience it firsthand.

Under other circumstances, de Wynte would have been able to enjoy his visit to Murashima. Japan was the most beautiful country he had ever seen. And it was always shipshape, with a place for everything and everything in its place, including its people. De Wynte, knowing how some of the Japanese worshiped nature, was hardly surprised by this. Their homes and villages fitted perfectly into their surroundings.

The captain surveyed the area. To the south, a short distance from the city proper, was the fishing village. But it appeared to be deserted. Most of the boats were out to sea. The few fishermen remaining would be drying their catch, repairing their nets, or replacing the hollow glass balls they used as floats instead of the European's cork. It all looked peaceful and idyllic, but de Wynte knew appearances were deceiving.

Lord Hoju's advisers had hoped that, by keeping the mission at a distance, it would not disrupt the peace of the province. They were wrong. The villagers and townspeople would tolerate it because Hoju ordered them to. Hoju's neighboring peers, masters of their own lands, were outraged at the presence of foreigners so close to their domains. Never mind that other missions had been allowed elsewhere in Japan—this was too close to home.

The crewmen lighted the matches for their guns from a box of coals they brought from the galley for that purpose. Each matchlock carried about twelve feet of fuse wrapped tightly around the stock. The rate varied slightly, but the fuses would burn slowly, at about a foot each hour. The fuse, held in an arm curving over the breech, could be lowered so as to ignite the charge with its glowing tip.

"Look sharp, men," de Wynte warned. "Things should be peaceable, but it doesn't hurt to show them we are ready to deal with troublemakers."

Hans and Volmer gripped their guns tightly; they, too, had heard of the legendary samurai, but dismissed the stories as fairytales. They did not believe that such small men could do them any damage. A few shots from the guns would send them packing. Nevertheless, they kept an eye on the slow-burning fuses. They had twelve hours, no more. But de Wynte expected to collect the Lady Diana and the priest from the mission and be back aboard the *Schoen* in less than four hours, perhaps five at the maximum; plenty of margin.

De Wynte gave a backward glance at the *Schoen* lying peacefully at anchor. He felt a swell of pride. He had taken that ship around the world to lands that, as a boy, he had not even dreamed of, and he would take her back again as a rich man. His many months of sailing from port to port in these strange lands, trading as they went, had filled the coffers to overflowing, as well as the hold. Those who had invested in the cargo would also be wealthy. De Wynte would never have to sail again, but in his heart he knew he would return. To sail where no European had ever been seen before—the lure was too great! But now it was indeed time to head for a home port. Diana would be the last cargo to be taken on.

The *Schoen* disappeared from their sight as the men trudged up the path. Other than a few birds, they saw no living thing. Within minutes, they were at the mission gates.

"*Konnichi-wa,*" the gate attendant said, bowing deeply. De Wynte noted that the attendant displayed no surprise upon their arrival, and assumed they must have been expected.

"*Konnichi-wa,*" de Wynte responded, and returned the bow. "*Anata no shimpun-san wa kyokai naka ni imaska?*" Is the priest within the church? It was one of several useful phrases de Wynte had committed to memory by rote.

"*Hai,*" the attendant greeted them. He extended a hand. "Papers, please," The smile was polite but firm. De Wynte handed over the safe-conduct pass.

The attendant studied the paper carefully, bowed again, and scuttled through a small trapdoor within the gate itself. The use of such a door was a common practice in any time of danger. In times of peace, the main gates could be left open to daily traffic. Now they could be secured, but people could come and go, one at a time, through the smaller door, which could be more easily defended in case of a surprise attack.

Father Ochoa was shortly puffing through the gate, full of warmth and greetings, but his eyes were darting questions.

"Good day, good day; we were not expecting the pleasure of a visit for months," he said, clasping de Wynte's hand in his own.

"For months," he repeated. "But . . . well, we certainly can use some fresh news of home. And how goes it with the Chinese missions? Does the church prosper there?" Searching de Wynte's impassive face and seeing nothing, his alarm grew.

"Please excuse my bad manners. You certainly must be weary after your journey. You will be wanting some refreshment," the priest said hurriedly. "We have some *cha,* some hot tea, and lunch will be served in an hour or so. If we only had some warning, I could have served you

71

something more substantial but it will have to suffice.'' Father Ochoa babbled on, fearful of hearing bad news.

The captain's words hit him like a body blow. ''I am afraid that the mission will have to be closed, Father Ochoa,'' de Wynte said in Portuguese. ''We have received a letter from Lord Hoju's scribe. You and the Countess Diana must be removed at once. The situation here is described as potentially explosive, and Lord Hoju can no longer offer you his protection.''

Father Ochoa twisted his rosary beads. ''But things have been going so well here. I am sure this is all a great misunderstanding that can be cleared up with time. I have heard of trouble beyond Lord Hoju's borders, but we are under his protection. I have met with his representatives. One of them lives on the grounds. Lord Hoju even sent rice and wine to us from his own storehouse.''

''Nevertheless, Lord Hoju has removed his protection and you all are in great danger. You must be ready to leave as soon as possible,'' de Wynte said. He looked around. The converts within the mission were trying not to show bad manners by staring at him and the two crewmen. They had seen few foreigners. The garments and weapons were completely alien. When they saw de Wynte look at them, they bowed politely and began to leave in ones and twos.

Father Ochoa looked desperate, then defiant. ''I will not leave. I will not abandon the work which God has appointed me to do. . . .''

De Wynte was beginning to feel exasperation. The man simply did not understand. He was being thrown out. There could be no question of his staying.

''You cannot defy Lord Hoju's edict. You will be killed if you do.''

''No man who has put his hand to the plow and turns back is fit for the kingdom of God,'' Ochoa said. His chin was up.

''Lord Hoju is revoking your farming permit, father,'' de Wynte said dryly. ''You have no other choice. God will later revoke Lord Hoju, and at least there will be some justice in that. I am sure you can find your proper place somewhere else.''

Father Ochoa was despairing. He had tried with such tireless sincerity to carry on the great works of a predecessor in Japan, the revered Francis Xavier, and now it would be sacrificed. ''But we have come so close to making great progress. Two of Lord Hoju's samurai are nearly converts. They come here daily. . . .''

''Spies!'' a voice said.

De Wynte turned. Lady Diana and a beautiful Japanese woman he had never seen had approached, seemingly out of nowhere.

Diana had matured much since that windy day in Antwerp when de Wynte had hidden her aboard his ship. Her figure had rounded seductively. The downturned mouth seemed wider; it was slightly parted as if ready to frame a question. The cheekbones were more taut, making them appear higher. It was the almost triangular face of her father, softened by femininity and glowing with vitality. She was now a lovely young woman, who would unfold her true beauty with greater maturity, like a precious flower.

The other . . . Dark in contrast to Diana's fairness, and though of almost the same height, slimmer, more lithely compact. An oval face lustrous and golden, and crowned with hair of silk jet, swept back and tied at the nape, from where it fell flowingly to brush her pinched waist. The full lips were rounded; de Wynte saw a suggestive gleam of even, white teeth. He was put in mind of an exquisite porcelain, yet . . . Something about the dark almond eyes seemed to sparkle, to enchant, to question sharply with a mere look. Or turn one to stone, killing a foe with a glance like that of the mythical basilisk, that lethal reptile.

Diana spoke, and the captain shook himself out of his speculation.

''They are spies,'' Diana repeated. ''They come here every day to spy on us, Father Ochoa. I am very sorry.'' She turned to the captain. ''It is good to see you again although I wish it were under better circumstances. What now?''

De Wynte looked at the sweet face of the daughter of

73

his old friend and patron. "I, too, wish circumstances were better. I wish I were not the bearer of bad tidings. Your father, I am forced to inform you, is dead. You are now the Countess de Edgemont."

Prepared to see tears, he was surprised. It was as if she had been expecting the news.

"How and when, if you please, Captain, did my father die?" Diana looked and sounded grim.

"It was more than a year ago; the news takes so long to get here. He was struck down while petitioning the king in Spain . . ." De Wynte tried to let her down as gently as possible.

"You mean *murdered* in Spain. . . ."

"We have no proof, Countess," de Wynte said. "Highwaymen were blamed. He was stabbed to death. The message hints that it was ordered by the Duke of Alvino from the Netherlands. I can only offer you my most profound sympathy, and that of all your father's friends."

"I need neither proof nor sympathy! The Spanish will do well to remember my father," she responded in a clipped tone. De Wynte received the impression that she left unsaid the expectation that the Spanish would have cause to remember her also.

"When do we leave?" Diana's voice had taken on a cold and distant ring, and de Wynte shuddered at the sound from one so young and presumptively innocent.

"We will leave when you have packed, Countess," he told her gently. "And that should be as quickly as you can arrange it."

"I, too, shall be leaving, Diana-san," said a voice over de Wynte's shoulder. It was Toriko.

"I am Lord Hoju's representative. When you leave, I must return to the castle. I am very sorry, but this leaves me no alternative."

Diana wanted to reach out, to touch her in farewell, but did not. To touch a Japanese was an infringement on the person. Samurai kept their distance. Diana simply bowed.

"I understand," she said, "but I will miss you greatly, Toriko-san. I wish we could remain together."

74

"So do I, Diana-san, but it is not to be," Toriko said, returning the bow formally. Their relationship was finished and to display emotion would mar the beauty of that friendship. Not that they would ever forget. The dew on a rose, the path of raindrops on a windowpane, such things would one day remind them of the tears that were not shed, could never be shed. Toriko was samurai, and with her duty completed, as she saw it, she must return to Lord Hoju to await his pleasure.

Diana's eyes were brimming but she, too, displayed no outward sign of emotion. Toriko smiled. She understood.

De Wynte did not understand at all the exchange between the two women, but it did not matter. "Then it's settled? Good!"

Father Ochoa's stubborn streak again emerged. "I refuse to go. I am a servant of God and my mission is here."

Toriko sighed. She disliked scenes and the priest was exhibiting bad manners and even worse judgment. She spoke to him in Portuguese in a tone one might use with a child.

"Do not be foolish, priest of Christ," she said. "When the samurai come here—and be certain, they will come—you will be slaughtered. Your church needs men, not martyrs. Sow your seeds elsewhere, on more fertile ground. Do not leave your blood here."

Father Ochoa wavered. He looked tired. So much work, and now all for nothing. "I . . . don't know." His dark eyes searched the sky for a sign—something, anything. He found nothing but the wind. A sigh escaped him, and his head slumped in what could have been a nod of acceptance.

De Wynte was brisk. "If you will get packed, then, I will have your belongings carried to the longboat. I think we should hurry, under the circumstances." His men stood at ease, gawking at their surroundings and making rude remarks about the Japanese. De Wynte noticed this and walked over to them.

"Watch your manners," he hissed in an undertone. "These people are very touchy. We already have enough trouble and I don't want any more. They may not be able

75

to understand what you say, but they might figure out that you are insulting them.''

''Aye, aye, sir,'' came the simultaneous echo.

They watched as Toriko issued orders and the servants scrambled to obey. Father Ochoa went to the chapel to supervise the packing of the vestments, the censer, and the few precious books he possessed, along with his priestly robes and two saints' relics. Father Ochoa owned little else, having taken a oath of poverty as a young novice.

Within a half hour, all the baggage was packed and piled neatly in front of the living quarters to the right of the chapel. The packed earth was hard and damp, but the chests had been wrapped in canvas for protection. The adjoining garden was strikingly lovely, the captain thought as he waited. Its moss-covered rocks and flowing trees seemed to draw the eye. The captain blinked. *It must have been designed that way,* he realized. *How clever!*

The servants, ready to return to the castle, lined up to receive a parting benediction. The porters who were to carry the baggage to the beach squatted nearby, naked except for breechclouts, though they did not seem to mind the cold. Father Ochoa's thoughts were as dark as the clouds scudding along overhead, but he raised his arms and intoned the benediction in a mumbling monotone. Although the servants did not understand, the foreign words seemed to give them comfort. The priest droned along just as the Buddhist monks had done for them, and they found it to their liking.

De Wynte, pacing nervously, did not know if they could withstand an attack by determined samurai. He did not want to be forced by circumstances to tempt the fates. Rain would soon be falling again, his experienced weather eye judged, and it would render the matchlocks useless except as clubs. His own wheel-lock pistols might withstand the rain for a few shots, but in the end it would be the same. And the guns were the only edge they could expect to have against samurai.

The captain was dumbfounded by what he saw next. Father Ochoa, having put on his vestments, picked up a heavy silver crucifix. The bewildered converts crossed themselves and began to follow the priest as he walked to the chapel. The ways of foreigners were odd, but they were not expected to ask questions.

"What in God's name? . . ." De Wynte was totally exasperated now. Didn't the priest understand? They had to leave. Now!

He ran into the chapel, holding the sword to keep the scabbard from slapping against his leg. By now, Father Ochoa was lying face down in front of the stripped altar in a posture of absolute submission, arms outstretched, a humble figure of transfixion.

"Father Ochoa! . . ." De Wynte began shouting, but the priest appeared to have not heard him. Minutes dragged. Despite the chill, the captain found himself sweating slightly. When Ochoa finally did stand, he turned to face the handful of converts. They looked puzzled, their peasant faces eager, but Lady Toriko was not there to translate for them. Father Ochoa's plainsong Latin was incomprehensible, but they recognized the emotion in his voice. When they heard the pattern of the blessing, they understood that he was saying farewell, and they bowed as one. Father Ochoa turned to face the altar once more, the converts crossed themselves, and then quietly filed out through the entrance. In the distance, de Wynte could hear the attendant bolt the trapdoor as the last of them left. Atsue waved good-bye and ducked through the door.

"I am ready now, Captain." De Wynte turned; the priest sounded emotionally weary to the point of exhaustion.

"There really isn't any time left, Father. We must leave at once." De Wynte spoke quietly, gently. He felt sorry for the priest but no one could change the situation. The sun had disappeared behind the buildup of clouds and a shadow passed over the compound. De Wynte could smell the tension.

Outside, Volmer and Hans had amused themselves by ogling Toriko and laughed among themselves when she glared at them. Toriko said something to the countess, who translated for them.

"This is Japan," Diana said levelly in her native Dutch language. "She is samurai, of a lineage more ancient than

77

any European king. You are lowborn. She cares for neither your stares nor your rude jests. Those are *her* words. *My* advice to you is to mind your own business and your manners. If you persist, she will kill you."

Volmer regarded the blond woman with amusement. "That little monkey? These heathen are all the same. What she needs is . . ."

"If you are about to refer to your unwashed manhood, the Lady Toriko will probably slice it off and feed it to you," Diana interjected. "And if she doesn't, I will!" Her blue eyes were level and unblinking. Volmer stepped back.

"We were only jokin', Hans and me." Volmer's grin revealed brown teeth. Diana wanted to shrink from the reek of a man who probably had not bathed in a year, if ever, but she held her ground.

"The joke is on you, seaman," she said. "There is more to these people than meets the eye. If I were you, I would watch what I say. By the way"—Diana tapped his chest for emphasis—"the lady understands your language very well. But you disgust her and she does not wish to speak with you."

Volmer gritted his teeth and said nothing. It was not for him to bandy words with a countess who could have him flogged or possibly worse, but he did not like the idea of being told what to do by a woman. The fact that Hans was openly enjoying his discomfiture was equally galling.

"That's a cold one," Hans snickered after Diana had walked away. "Have you chokin' on yer cod, will she?"

"Shut yer face, Hans, or you'll be chokin' on somethin' else."

"Some lady!" Hans was not to be stopped so easily.

"They all talk the same, highborn and low," was Volmer's reply.

In his assertion was a lot of truth. If it was an age of enlightenment, progress, and discovery, it was also one—on every level—of ribaldry, debauchery, and profane speech, which Diana could hardly have escaped in her youth even if she had wished. And many of the clergy committed the very sins they openly protested against in the pulpit. It was no time for a prude.

De Wynte and the priest were approaching, so the two crewmen attempted to look alert. They had hoped to meet some village girls who would be more biddable, and thankful to earn a few coppers from a pair of lusty sailors. It appeared now they would hustle right back to the ship with no time for amorous dalliance.

"Now if that ain't fuckin' wonderful," Volmer said sourly.

"Too bad it ain't vice versa," Hans added thoughtfully.

"Shut up!" Volmer retorted.

"Shut up, yerself, here they come."

De Wynte nodded to his men. "We are leaving. Now! Take the point and keep a sharp lookout. Look to your powder."

Volmer and Hans looked at each other. What did the captain know that they didn't? "Aye, sir," they said.

The captain bowed to Diana. "Countess, if you will be so good as to accompany me, we will be back aboard ship. . . ."

Suddenly, a pounding at the gate was heard, mixed with the sound of angry voices.

"What the? . . ." de Wynte began.

"Ron-i-i-i-in!" the gatekeeper screamed, and took to his heels across the compound. De Wynte looked wonderingly at him, then turned in time to see the first grappling hook fly over and grip the top of the wall.

Lord Hoju's neighbors had decided not to wait.

"Who the hell are ronin?" de Wynte shouted to Diana.

"They are samurai—masterless samurai—and it appears that they are about to come over these walls!" Diana yelled over her shoulder as she ran for her *naginata*. Toriko had already disappeared into her quarters, emerging with armor, two *naginatas,* and a bow.

"This isn't the best armor, Diana-san, but it will have to do," she said hastily. "The breastplate won't stop a sword, but it will take the shock of an arrow."

Diana did not take time to reply. Fortunately, the armor was light and consisted only of a breastplate with attached tassets to protect the thighs. Diana was not strong enough yet to wear full armor for very long. No helmets were on hand, but Toriko offered her a mailed *hachimaki* for use as a sweatband and to guard against stray cuts. Diana pulled the sheath from the *naginata* and held the blade ready at guard position. Toriko's training must stand her in good stead now—or never!

The first ronin topped the wall and fell back with a bullet reddening his chest. A second made it over, followed by another ronin, and then another. They raced across the compound with swords raised for the kill, screaming as they ran. Their disreputable appearance, distinguishing them easily from proud samurai, matched the wildness of their bloodcurdling cries. Volmer's gun fired but missed. One ronin went down with an arrow in his throat. De Wynte braced himself and leveled the pistols. He could shoot only at close range, and hoped to God the guns didn't misfire.

"Nambanj-i-i-i-n!" One of the ronin in surprise howled out the name for foreigners. De Wynte fired and the man's head snapped back with a bright red wound flowering across his face. The third ronin tore into the line of defenders, concentrating on the crewmen trying to reload their guns. As Hans blocked a vicious slash, the sword tore a chunk out of the stock of his gun. All that Volmer could see were teeth and gums and a flash of silvery steel as the ronin turned on him. Then the invader sagged, his chest impaled on Diana's spear point. She lashed out and kicked him off the end of it. Toriko nodded in silent approval. Diana had met the test. She had skillfully killed for the first time in her life, a life that was meant to be protectively shielded—and she had not shrunk from the need at the crucial moment.

More grappling hooks were sailing over the walls like gray spiders.

"Retreat to the chapel," de Wynte ordered. Black smoke was beginning to billow up behind the gate. *Christ,* de Wynte thought, *they're firing it!*

Five ronin dropped over the wall and hit the ground running. Volmer fired, and this time didn't miss. A ronin with a black headband and a livid scar across his cheek fell limply; Volmer bent over his gun to reload. Hans wounded one attacker, who kept on coming. Toriko wounded a third as they boiled into the line, swords slashing.

Toriko, dropping her bow, stabbed a man in the armpit with a spear just as he lunged at Diana. De Wynte blasted one raging ronin into eternity with a bullet in the chest and wounded another with a second shot. Diana finished him off with a stab in the throat. Toriko took another ronin in the belly and pinned him to the ground as he writhed. The last of the attackers was hacked to death by Hans and Volmer after they knocked the sword from his hands. They wiped their own weapons and sheathed them, then began the laborious process of reloading the matchlocks. Three minutes had gone by. An eternity.

In a new suicidal charge over the wall, two ronin sacrificed themselves. Then, while the defenders were occupied with those invaders, archers sent fire arrows into the compound.

The dreaded rain had begun.

"As if we needed anything more," Volmer commented. "How many of them are there?"

"Why don't you stick your head over the wall and ask 'em, Volmer boy," Hans said.

"Save your breath," de Wynte snapped.

"What do we do now, Captain?" Diana asked. She wiped her perspiring face with a kimono sleeve—no time for niceties now—and leaned on her *naginata*.

The back of the chapel was already in flames, and it would all be utterly consumed despite the steady rain. And its overhang, where they all crouched, was the only thing that kept the matchlock fuses dry. Without the guns, they were going to lose. If the gatekeeper had not had the presence of mind to remain inside the wall and watch through a spyhole, the compound would have been overrun by now. They were at least relatively fortunate in this.

"The bathhouse!" Toriko interjected now. "The walls are made of stone and there is an ample supply of water."

"The bathhouse it is, then," de Wynte commanded. "Hans, Volmer, cover the fuses with your hands. Keep them dry at all costs. We are going to run for it. Father Ochoa, if you will be . . ."

The priest had fallen quietly on his side, his black cassock glistening with blood. The boards beneath him were dark. One of the ronin had found his mark.

De Wynte retrieved the crucifix Father Ochoa had cradled. "We can do nothing for him. Leave him. Here!" He quickly dragged the priest's body into the chapel. "It was his life. Let it be his funeral pyre!"

They all crossed themselves, but there was no time for a prayer. The heat drove de Wynte from the chapel. The main gate, smoking and spitting because of the rain, was nevertheless burning furiously. The ronin would be through soon, in a body, and then . . .

"Run for it. Now!" de Wynte commanded.

Afterwards, Diana thought it had been like running in a nightmare, moving with such unearthly slowness, as in loose sand. They reached the bathhouse, chests heaving. They were safe, for a time.

But another pounding came at the gate. They could hear the weakened timbers giving way before a battering ram. The ronin would be inside the compound soon, waves of them. De Wynte heard them yelling.

"What are they saying?" he asked Diana.

"They are shouting themselves into a frenzy," Diana said.

"Judging from the sound, I would estimate at least twelve of them are left, perhaps fifteen," Toriko offered.

"More than enough," de Wynte observed.

"Perhaps not," Toriko said. A questioning look from the captain prompted her to elaborate. "I think Lord Hoju's neighbors were reluctant to use their own samurai, so they hired ronin to do their work for them. These men are masterless for a reason. They are not very good. True samurai would have come over those walls in a rush and slaughtered all of us."

It was yet another shock for de Wynte. If these men were not true samurai, what were *real* samurai like?

"They will be at us in a few minutes, Captain," Diana said.

Outside the gate, Tadetomo, leader of the ronin, seethed as his men battered at the burning timbers. The Aizuni and Noyabe clans had told him that only a few *nambanjin*—hated southern barbarians—were present at the mission and that killing them would be easy and a service to Japan. They had given him this scabby collection of ronin and expected them to act like samurai. Samurai, ha! Tadetomo snorted. *Basket hangers was more like it,* he thought. Tadetomo had already been forced to kill one of his own men for disobedience, and then the rest had more or less fallen into line—for the moment. They still were a disorganized lot, prone to shouting and hysteria. If Lord Hoju chose to send samurai at this moment, all the heads of this sorry group soon would be on the ground like melons.

As it was, Tadetomo had lost eight men to the *nambanjin* and their stinking guns.

"Hit it one more time, then stand back!" he bellowed.

The ronin lifted the log and battered the gate, which groaned from its hinges and fell inward. The flames shot backward, catching one ronin by surprise. His kimono and *hakama* caught fire, and he rolled on the ground in agony.

"Serves him right for not listening," Tadetomo muttered. He issued orders to smother the flames on the gate with sand, and then regrouped his men. A few had bits and pieces of armor, but most had only their own garments and their swords. *I'll bet their swords are third-rate, too,* Tadetomo thought.

"When we go in, hit them solidly—and don't bunch up," Tadetomo said. He berated them for being an ungrateful lot and being in danger of failing in their duty to their new masters.

The ronin showed little unity except a common feeling that their hatchet-faced leader was guilty of gross incompetence for sending in two small groups of men when he should have sent them all. They could have been safely out of there by now but for Tadetomo's inept leadership. In fact, two of the ronin who had lost friends during the first ill-conceived assault had already privately agreed that Tadetomo would not be rejoining them at the staging area when the *nambanjin* were dead. Better he rejoin his leprous ancestors as soon as they could possibly arrange it.

When the last of the sand had been scooped into place, Tadetomo drew his sword.

"Leave none of them alive," he shouted, then turned and led them, roaring, into the compound.

The defenders heard them coming before they could see them.

"Here they come," de Wynte said levelly. "Fire when they are in range. Careful now!"

"Captain," Volmer said while sighting down his musket barrel, "we only have a few bullets left."

"At this point," de Wynte replied somberly as the line of ronin raced toward them, "I don't think it is going to make much difference."

Chapter Seven

The horses were tired and starting to stumble. Tonomori knew that he and his men would not last much longer without some rest. Theirs had been a bone-numbing pace, riding through wind and rain, when they were not running on foot in order to give the horses a breather.

They had reached the ocean but kept to the coastal foothills to avoid being seen by Masanori's samurai. It would have been easier going along the narrow strip of flatlands between the foothills and the rolling waves, but Tonomori preferred the covering trees and scrub. In less than an hour now, they would be in Murashima, then they could rest. Masanori's samurai would not dare pursue them into a Hoju stronghold.

"How much farther, Tonomori-san?" Oshabiri did not usually complain but he was ready to drop.

Although accustomed to setting a relentless pace, Tonomori knew they had passed beyond the limits of their endurance and he felt concern.

"Within an hour. Hold on for that much longer, and then we rest," Tonomori said.

Rest! Oshabiri and Yamahito at that point were ready to embrace the eternal rest of the grave. Their bodies ached for sleep. The torment of their raw blisters had become a part of their existence.

Tonomori pulled up on Kaminari's reins. The horse was inclined to be bad-tempered but too weary to do much about it now but snort. Also, he smelled fire, which he did not like.

Tonomori, too, smelled it. "Wait here and eat," he told his companions. "I'm going on ahead and look around. Something is wrong."

Tonomori crammed his mouth with the last of some dried fish he had been hoarding, and spurred Kaminari ahead. About three hundred yards along the winding path, the scrub trees thinned and Tonomori could see all the way to the beach, despite the rain. Flames were shooting up from an enclosed compound and Tonomori could make out an armed party of men pounding away at the burning gate with a log.

Tonomori had only one thought. *Masanori! His samurai have followed the wrong trail and they think that I have gone to ground in there.*

He felt the weariness falling away from him like the rain. Tonomori had enough strength left for one good fight. He wheeled Kaminari around and returned to his men.

The *ashigaru* looked up when Tonomori returned more suddenly than they had expected.

"Samurai ahead!" Tonomori snapped. "Somehow they got past us. They are attacking some dwellings, so they must think we are in there. I do not intend to disappoint

85

them. I will run no farther. I will die like a samurai. You," he continued, with a wave of his great bow, "are free to leave. You are under no such obligation and need not share my fate."

He smiled. "In fact, I think that if you are smart, you will go."

Yamahito responded with a wry grin. "Then I am very stupid, sir. But in fact I am too tired to run anymore."

"I also, sir," Oshabiri said. "But not too tired to fight."

Tonomori bowed, touched by the show of loyalty. He only thought it a pity there would be no one to record this final act of devotion by two footsoldiers who were not even expected to live up to the high ideals of Bushido, the code of the warrior.

Tonomori dismounted and from the saddlebags extracted some carefully padded bottles in one of the panniers. It was the last of their sake.

"Take two swallows each and pour the rest into the horses," he instructed. After they drank, and felt warmth flooding back into them, Tonomori and his men forced open the jaws of the horses and emptied the bottles.

Tonomori remounted. "I am going straight in. I don't think they can be prepared for a rear attack, but be prepared for anything. When you are through the gate, dismount and fight on foot. You have no experience on horseback, so you would be at a disadvantage."

"Once I am off this beast, Tonomori-san, I will die happy," Yamahito said fervently, and Oshabiri echoed his feelings.

"It is an excellent afternoon for a walk in the rain, Yamahito-san. It would make a fine poem," Tonomori told him with a short laugh. "But for now, let us go and inform Masanori's samurai that they are knocking on the wrong door."

The *ashigaru* followed as Tonomori spurred Kaminari at a gallop toward the mission compound.

Inside, the defenders braced for the impact of the ronin onslaught.

"Fire a volley, and then draw your swords," de Wynte

ordered. The guns jerked from the recoil of the muzzle blasts and nearly deafened them inside their bathhouse retreat. The rapidly advancing line of ronin showed a few more gaps, but did not waver, like raptors after their prey.

"Steady on," de Wynte said, guiding his men. He wondered if their courage would hold, and hoped his own would not fail him. The fuses sputtered out because of the pervading dampness, and they had no way to relight them. Without the fuses, the guns were useless. Without the guns, they could not possibly withstand the charge of a dozen determined swordsmen—but they could sell their lives as dearly as possible.

"Thrust with the tip only," de Wynte called. "There's no room for slashing. Go for their faces and their bellies."

"Jesus; we're in for it this time," Hans said.

Toriko readied her *naginata*. Her bow was behind her on the floor, useless; the string was cut during the last assault on the chapel. She and Diana exchanged glances.

"Today shalt thou be with me in paradise," Toriko said, repeating the words of Jesus to the thief on the cross at Golgotha.

"Sayonara, Toriko-san," Diana said, lowering her head to brace for the clash just seconds away.

Then . . . out of the smoke from the burning chapel and the misting rain, a dark horse and rider swept into view, like Shinto demons out of hell. The crest of his black helmet swept back from the brim in a golden "V," flaring at the tips. No mercy could be seen in that face. *This* was a samurai, and de Wynte's heart fell, until the first pale shaft from the rider's great bow sent a ronin pitching forward on the freshly raked gravel around the bathhouse. Another swordsman fell, impaled, before the rest sensed the peril thudding behind them and turned to meet it.

When Tadetomo fell, blood gushing from his mouth with an arrow in his chest, the rest scattered for cover. The ronin archers attempted to hit Tonomori, but their target had galloped between the buildings. When he did reappear, it was only for an instant, to shoot once more with lethal effect, then disappear behind another building. Three of the ronin tried to flee but ran into Yamahito, who cut one down with his *naginata*, and Oshabiri, who killed the other two with arrows.

Cut off from retreat and flanked on all sides, their leader dead, the remaining ronin rushed the bathhouse in desperation, hoping to overwhelm the defenders and find refuge there. They never made it.

With his arrows gone, Tonomori crashed into them with Kaminari. His sword was out and flashing. A ronin was down with his skull split to the chin. Another swordsman in a poorly laced half armor charged Tonomori from the left. But in his eagerness to kill the samurai, he failed to notice the small triangular spear points, *yumi yari,* socketed to the tips of Tonomori's bow.

Tonomori whipped the point into the ronin's forehead and he fell without a sound beneath Kaminari's hooves. The horse shied, but before Tonomori brought him under control, Yamahito and Oshabiri had joined the fray, and suddenly it was over. Dismounting, Tonomori carefully examined the bodies. *They were not Masanori's samurai!*

They were not even well equipped. Their armor was poorly made, what there was of it, with large patches of rust where the cheap lacquer had chipped and cracked. Their kimonos and *hakama* were shabby and patched. Most likely, they were ronin. *Like myself,* Tonomori thought bitterly.

Tonomori was puzzled. If Lord Hoju was incapable of keeping the peace within his domains so near to his fortress, then it was not likely that he would be challenging Masanori's samurai, either. Tonomori wanted some answers. Fast.

"You. In the bathhouse. Come out at once," Tonomori ordered. De Wynte emerged slowly, followed by Hans and Volmer and the two women. They, too, were confused— was this the reinforcement Lord Hoju had sent? One samurai and two footsoldiers?

Tonomori approached them. The defenders held their weapons warily, he noticed.

"Drop your weapons. At once," he commanded. He had sheathed his sword after the last man had been killed, but still held his bow in his left hand, poised on his shoulder. When they showed no intention of complying, he slashed it across Toriko's shoulder and neck, knocking her to the earth. Diana lunged forward but Tonomori sidestepped the thrust with ease, grabbed the haft, and kicked her backward.

"Drop your weapons," he repeated. "I will not say it again." He looked to de Wynte, who from his bearing and clothing obviously was in command, but received no response. It was apparent to Tonomori that the commander did not understand Japanese.

De Wynte and his men tensed their muscles to fight, but Diana's voice stopped him. "Drop your weapons, Captain, or he will kill us all." She looked to Toriko, who had been stunned by the blow.

"I am not hurt, Diana-san," Toriko said. She managed to gain her feet unaided, but made no attempt to retrieve her weapon. She had met many samurai, but this was the best she had ever encountered. She might be able to kill him with *ninja* cunning, at night, but never in regular combat.

Diana was standing again, head high. If this man, who quite evidently was samurai, intended to kill them, she, for her part, intended to meet death unflinchingly.

"What are you doing here? Why were these men attacking you?" Tonomori demanded, addressing Diana. Normally, he would have spoken to de Wynte, a man, obviously the leader because of his better clothing and superior weapons. Since this leader of the barbarians said nothing, Tonomori assumed he did not speak Japanese.

Tonomori's curiosity was intense. He had never seen *nambanjin* before. *These southern barbarians are big*, he thought, using the descriptive term for Europeans. But it was Diana who interested him the most. Her lustrous hair was the color of the sun, her fragile skin pale, and her eyes like a clear sky. All Japanese had dark eyes and black hair, unless it grayed with age.

The eyes do not slant, either, Tonomori noted. Briefly, he wondered if they could see colors, as the Japanese did.

Diana's reply was in Japanese. "This is a mission of the

89

Catholic Church. Its existence was permitted by Lord Hoju under an agreement reached with Captain de Wynte here. My presence is part of that agreement.''

''You speak Japanese,'' Tonomori noted. ''That is very interesting. But your accent is terrible. Who taught you?''

''The Lady Toriko—here,'' Diana told him.

''She is not a very good teacher.''

''Yours is a difficult language. I am not a very good student,'' Diana retorted, instinctively coming to Toriko's defense. ''And who are you?''

He ignored her question. ''You are getting away from your story. I want answers.''

''It was *you* who interrupted me when I was attempting to give you the answers,'' Diana said in exasperation.

''So I did. That is my privilege. Do not argue with me again,'' he warned. ''Continue with your story.''

Diana choked back her rising temper. The sheer arrogance of the man galled her. But the situation was hopeless.

''The other daimyos have been angered by the presence of foreigners, and they demanded that Lord Hoju send us away. He resisted them for a time, but has finally ordered us to depart. We were preparing to leave in Captain de Wynte's ship when we were attacked.''

''Where are the rest of the people who must have been here?'' Tonomori now wanted to know.

''They fled.''

''What about the priest? Did he run also?''

''The priest was killed in the fighting,'' Diana said. ''He was a good man.''

''He is dead now, like the rest of you will be if you don't leave at once.''

Diana decided to risk angering the samurai by asking him to explain.

''Many samurai are on their way here. They are hunting for me,'' Tonomori said. ''If they find you here with me they will kill you also.''

De Wynte could not understand much of what was being said, and was impatient. ''Ask him if we can leave,'' the captain told Diana.

She turned on him. ''He says we are free to go. In fact,

he urges us to leave quickly. He says many samurai are looking for him to kill him.''

De Wynte responded reflexively to the warrior's dilemma. ''Thank him for me, and tell him he is welcome to leave with us on the *Schoen*, if he so desires.''

Diana was certain that getting on a foreign ship was the last thing a samurai would want, but she was surprised. It appeared that an instinctive relationship had sprung up between the two men, who saw themselves as equals. ''Is the ship large enough for my men also?'' Tonomori asked.

''Yes, more than enough, if they wish to go,'' Diana assured him.

''Where I go, they will go. And I suggest, in any event, that we leave immediately. I do not know how far the samurai are behind me.''

Diana and Toriko were already in traveling clothes—heavy kimono and *hakama*—they had put on just before the fighting began. They carried only bundles of their most personal possessions—plus their weapons. The crewmen picked up one of Diana's chests to carry between them. Neither Tonomori nor his men offered to help.

Diana looked wistfully at the pile of luggage that would have to be left behind—a pity. But at least she had her silks, and she could always have new clothes made when she finally arrived back in the Netherlands.

The flames and smoke were becoming worse, making them all cough vigorously and their eyes water. As de Wynte led the way out of the compound, Diana noticed that the small bowman with the monkey was collecting arrows. The bodies looked like fallen bundles of clothing. The rain had washed away most of the blood. The head wound in the man that Tonomori's sword had killed gaped horribly. Diana, forcing herself to look straight ahead, tried to remember the mission as it had been. Tonomori had remounted and brought up the rear with his men. He and the archer kept their bows at the ready, arrows nocked for instant firing if necessary.

Soaked to the skin, Diana tried to keep her teeth from chattering. A slight wind seemed to make the chill even more pronounced. By the time they reached the beach and the *Schoen* loomed into view, her fingers were becoming stiff.

The crewmen loaded Diana's traveling chest into the longboat, then she and Toriko packed their meager belongings alongside it. When Tonomori threw his packs and saddlebags into the boat also, Diana was highly incensed. She had left many treasured belongings behind.

"You said we had to move quickly," Diana objected hotly. "I had to leave most of my things."

"So I did," Tonomori agreed.

"But you brought everything you had!"

"You are very observant," he said genially, with a slight smile that Diana found highly annoying.

"You *could* have helped us carry our things," Diana pointed out sharply.

"That is true." Tonomori was removing the saddles from the horses. If anyone wanted a horse, they would have to catch him first. With the bridles off, the horses bolted for the hills.

"*Would* you have helped us carry the baggage if we had asked?" Diana asked narrowly.

"No, I would not."

"Oooooo! I could kick him," Diana said in Portuguese to Toriko.

"I would advise against that, Diana-san," Toriko replied quickly. "This is Japan, and he is samurai. He would kick you back, or worse, for such an insult." She paused. "I don't think I would be able to stop him."

Diana bit her lip. She would question Toriko later on the subject of samurai and why a *ninja* would fear and respect one. She *had* detected a note of respect in Toriko's voice.

"Into the boat quickly," de Wynte shouted. "I see horsemen coming!"

Mounted samurai, sweeping down the beach from the north, were several hundred yards away and closing rapidly. Tonomori estimated the range, and as he helped the crewmen launch the longboat into the surf thought that time would just about permit their departure before the samurai could arrive.

Saru panicked and decided to abandon ship, but Tonomori

scooped him up and tossed him lightly back to Oshabiri, who appeared as frightened as his pet.

"Must we go in this boat out there, Tonomori-san?" Oshabiri chattered.

"Not if you'd rather swim," Tonomori answered shortly.

"I would rather stay and die," Oshabiri complained miserably.

"You have no choice. You are ordered to stay put!" The nose of the longboat pitched upward from a wave, and then dropped, sickeningly. A loud report, a puff of white smoke—and a heavy-caliber bullet sprayed them with sea water.

"Pull, for Christ's sake! They have guns!" de Wynte shouted to the straining crewmen. A samurai gunner crouched low in the saddle to avoid being hit by an arrow from Tonomori's bow. Oshabiri moved to fire also, but Tonomori stopped him.

"You could not hit him from here. Your bow is not strong enough. Also, this is like shooting from a moving horse, and you are not used to it. Save your arrows."

The samurai gunner had reloaded. He rode his horse into the surf chest-high, and fired again. The bullet whizzed over the boat harmlessly.

"How in hell can he shoot in this rain, Captain, and we can't?" Volmer spat.

"I don't know. Pull!"

Masanori's samurai now caught up with the gunner and were milling on the beach.

Diana directed a question to Tonomori. "Why is his gun not damp as ours are?"

Two of Tonomori's hawk-feathered arrows bristled from the samurai gunner's chest.

"His armor is very good. What a pity," Tonomori said, nocking another arrow. He replied to Diana without turning his head. "There is a lacquered box fitting which goes over the lock in rainy weather. I am surprised your gunners do not have them."

Diana said nothing. The gunner was taking aim again and Diana was trying to make herself as small as possible. She heard the gun fire, and ducked.

"Ha, a noodle gun," Tonomori laughed. The samurai gunner was yelling. The barrel had slipped off the stock and curled. The gunner flung it into the sea. Tonomori's arrow caught his horse in the neck and it went over sideways, hooves lashing the foam. The gunner disappeared beneath the waves and did not resurface.

"What is a noodle gun?" Diana asked. The rest of the samurai were pounding farther down the beach.

"It is a gun that curls up like a noodle after a couple of shots," Tonomori said, keeping an eye on the samurai. "Some of the early guns were poorly made. The son of my late master had a few of them. My master himself did not think much of guns." It was apparent to Diana from his tone that the samurai did not think much of the son.

Tonomori pointed suddenly with his bow. "Look! They are trying to cut us off." Masanori's men flogged their horses along the promontory where the deserted fishing village lay. They dismounted and began piling into the two fishing boats left on the beach.

"We can't make it," de Wynte muttered. "They'll intercept us before we reach the ship." The promontory jutted sharply toward the *Schoen*, giving Masanori's samurai a good position to head them off. A dozen were crowded into each vessel and were pulling hard for the longboat.

"If only we had a sail, we could tack away from them, and then cut back," Diana remarked to Toriko. It looked hopeless. The two fishing vessels bristled with shining spears.

"Yes, and if we had wings, we could fly across the water," Tonomori said before Toriko could reply.

Diana ignored him. "Captain de Wynte, can the *Schoen*'s crew do anything to help out?"

"Not unless the ship is directly attacked," de Wynte said with some regret. "Any landing party must take its chances. Those are standing orders, and can't be broken. The other daimyos would hear of it if the ship fired on samurai, and they would slaughter every last Dutchman in Japan. No, the crew won't interfere. I wouldn't, if I were in their place.

94

"And if we go down, the ship's pilot will take her out of here as quickly as possible—without looking back. He could do nothing else."

If we go down? de Wynte thought desperately. *When* was the more likely prospect. The samurai were rowing furiously and the distance between them was closing rapidly. It was only a matter of time. De Wynte noticed that their newest ally was looking as impassive as a statue. The captain thought wildly of pushing him over the side, but knew he could not abandon a man who had saved their lives. The samurai probably would kill them anyway.

Tonomori untied the heavy cords securing his helmet and removed it. Diana saw that his head was not shaved in the fashion of the other samurai she had seen. His hair was brushed back tightly in a thick braid which was pulled forward and pinned. His *hachimaki* was white against his glistening forehead and was marked with Japanese writing which Diana could not read. Who was this masterful samurai, so accustomed to command, with skills to equal his authority?

"Oshabiri-san, that store of arrows you have been hoarding . . ." Tonomori said almost casually.

"Yes, Tonomori-san?" Oshabiri sounded eager.

"Please deliver them now to Masanori's samurai with my compliments. Aim primarily at the rowers."

"A pleasure, sir," Oshabiri replied with alacrity. Yamahito said nothing, but thought it fortunate no bowmen could be seen in the other boats.

Oshabiri's arrows began to take immediate effect. One rower slumped with an arrow in his neck and the boat began to pitch between the wave troughs, broadside to the longboat.

"Now, Oshabiri-san, engage the other boat. Quickly!" Tonomori urged. While Oshabiri swiveled to send arrows into the other crowded vessel, Tonomori fitted a shaft to his bow. The highly polished tip was blunt and weighed almost two pounds. Toriko recognized it to be a stun arrow, ordinarily used to take high-ranking daimyos alive. Tonomori watched carefully as the first boat bobbed between the waves and waited for the rowers to gain control

95

and bring it around. When its prow lifted above a swell, Tonomori released the arrow. The heavy tip punched a hole below its waterline. The prow came down and cold sea water gushed over the feet of the samurai. Too late, they realized their peril. Overcrowded as it was, the boat settled heavily in the waves until a swell crested greenly over the side, swamping it.

The screams of the samurai were choked off swiftly as their ponderous armor dragged them beneath the swells.

By then, Tonomori had turned his attention to the remaining boat. Oshabiri peppered them with arrows, and Tonomori carefully timed the lifting of the prow. Only one stun arrow was left, and he had to aim it to hit perfectly.

The arrowhead crunched into the side of the craft. Samurai moved swiftly to plug the gap with strings of cloth torn hastily from their leggings. Too many of them moved to the side and the boat overturned. The samurai sank quickly. Two of them clung desperately to the overturned craft, but Tonomori and Oshabiri picked them off with arrows. Soon, the boat settled and slipped beneath the waves.

In the distance, Tonomori could hear the cry of gulls like the spirits of the dead samurai shrieking forward into eternity.

Diana broke the tense silence. ''That was the most incredible thing I have ever seen,'' she said to Tonomori.

Tonomori only grunted. It had been a terrible death for the samurai, but Tonomori could feel no regret. They had once served the same master as he, true, but they had sought their own fatal *karma,* the fate that had carried them to destruction in the pride of their strength.

His mates in the longboat said nothing more, awed into silence by the total devastation wreaked by Tonomori's bow. If ever there was a perfect subject for a *Noh* drama, it would be the Battle of the Rowboats, Toriko thought. The timing and execution had been as perfect as the brush strokes of a haiku poem. She would not speak now, to intrude upon the beauty of the death, and the serenity his soul must now feel. She was proud to be a samurai.

Toriko would write a haiku and perhaps give it to Tonomori some day in memory of this moment.

Green was their armor,
green like old grave stones,
beneath the shining sea.

She thought of a similar fight, some four hundred years before, across the face of Japan to the east, when two mighty clans had clashed on the inland sea in the battle of Dan-no-Ura. The proud *Taira,* masters of the shogun, regents for the infant emperor, bounded forward on the tide to crush the challenge of the rebellious Minamoto. Before the day was done, the *Taira* were no more, their banners rippling on the waves in the ebb tide. Rather than face defeat when the battle had turned against them, every last one of the *Taira* samurai had leaped into the sea to drown, taking the emperor with them.

Perhaps Masanori's samurai would take on the form of crabs, as legend had it the *Taira* had done, doomed to wander forever beneath the waves. Tonomori turned at the sound of fighting on shore, and saw samurai on foot swarming through the fishing village. The remainder of Masanori's men wheeled to meet them but were quickly overrun. Tonomori could see the rise and fall of their blades. Lord Hoju had finally decided to rid his realm of ronin.

Tonomori returned his gaze to the ship as they approached it, the crewmen strained at the oars. He was very weary, and all he wanted to do was sleep. His bones seemed to creak like the oarlocks. He could not remember ever having been so tired. The day was becoming a bright blur. But soon the longboat was bobbing alongside the *Schoen.*

Diana and Toriko had little trouble scrambling up the ship's ladder, while de Wynte and the crewmen secured the longboat so it could be hauled aboard and lashed down. At one point, when the ship rolled outward on the worsening sea, Tonomori thought he would lose his grip and drop into the dark green waters. He had exhausted all his reserves; no more strength was left in him. Somehow, he managed to hang on. Once on board, he leaned against the railing for support while the longboat was hauled up by pulleys. He ignored the stares of the crew members.

"Tell the samurai," de Wynte told Diana, who translated, "that he and his men can sleep in the chartroom until we can make other arrangements. His baggage can be stored there, and I'll have pallets laid out for him and his men on the floor."

Tonomori nodded while staring at the huge ship numbly. He had many questions to ask but was too tired to speak. Later, he did not even remember Yamahito and Oshabiri helping him out of his armor. Warm in a dry komono and wrapped in a thick blanket, he let sleep take him in a dark grip.

On deck, the captain gave instructions to the helmsman and crew. "Set the course for Nagasaki, and shorten the sail. From the looks of the storm, we can run before it. Keep a sharp lookout for gusts. We don't want to lose a mast."

That taken care of, de Wynte saw to his crewmen, Hans and Volmer, who had sustained cuts and bruises during the fighting on shore.

"It was a close thing, Captain," Volmer mentioned.

"Any closer and we'd have been cold meat," Hans added.

"Aye, it was close," de Wynte agreed. He handed each of the men a cup of wine. "Drink this and rest. Your actions today will be noted in the ship's log, and I'll be recommending you both for a bonus when we return home."

Hans and Volmer accepted gratefully. Home!—so very long since they had seen it. When de Wynte left, Volmer had a quick talk with Hans.

"If they all fight like that big heathen, it is going to be a long voyage home. If we ever get there, that is!"

"Amen to that, mate," Hans said.

"And I'll tell you another thing: I'll never call them Japs monkeys again, long as I live," Volmer vowed, gulping his wine.

"At least not when they can hear us, eh?" Hans grinned. " 'Cause if they do hear, I have a feeling the living won't be long."

The women had changed into dry clothes and Diana was combing the tangles out of her damp hair when de Wynte knocked on their door. They had been given the small cabin shared by the first and second mates, who went to sling their hammocks with the crew forward beyond the hold.

"Are you comfortable?" de Wynte asked solicitously. He still had many pressing duties in command of the *Schoen*, but a few items of business claimed priority.

"Yes, very comfortable, Captain," Diana assured him, pleased to be able to speak Dutch again so freely to a countryman. "Thank you for your concern. But you needn't bother about us."

"It is no bother at all. But I do have some matters which we *will* have to discuss and which you must know about." Diana gave the captain a questioning look, and so he continued.

"First, the *Schoen* and her cargo are yours. I was not sure if you knew of your father's business arrangements. He was a generous man and I have a share in the profits under contract. Under law, though, you are now the legal owner, and I still retain command. I hope that the trust your father placed in me will continue."

"Of course, Captain, you have proven yourself to be a faithful steward for many years. I have no desire to make any changes. I hardly would wish to be an ingrate," Diana told him.

"Secondly, then," de Wynte said, "I am responsible for your safety. And that of the lady here. Men being what they are, it is risky business having women aboard ship. It can cause trouble."

Diana interrupted. "We can take care of ourselves, Captain, as you may have noticed."

"To be sure you can, to some degree," de Wynte agreed smoothly. "But the closer we get to Europe, the more my concern will grow."

"The Duke of Alvino, you mean?"

"Precisely. The man is determined to exterminate the de Edgemont family, and has nearly succeeded. You need

99

protection, and I simply can't be everywhere at once. The ship must come first. I hope you understand.''

Diana looked thoughtful. ''I understand completely, of course. My father's ships are responsible for a good deal of the family's wealth. The Lady Toriko, if she could only stay, would be the perfect companion, but I am afraid that when we reach Tanegashima, she will be leaving . . .''

Toriko interrupted. ''If you consent, I will go with you beyond the edge of the world, if necessary. My Lord Hoju did not live up to my agreement with him. For whatever reason, he allowed ronin to attack the mission. At that moment, my service with him ended. In fact, I am now a ronin myself, and this, I am obliged to point out, is a most shameful state. If you would be so kind to accept me as your traveling companion, and perhaps continue in your *studies*''—Toriko emphasized the word to avoid unnecessary explanations to the captain—''then I would be happy to serve. I would require no salary, only my meals and a place to sleep.''

Diana clapped her hands in delight. ''Perfect! Of course I would accept you. And there won't be any argument about your pay, either.''

Toriko looked inclined to argue the point.

But Diana reminded her cheerfully, ''Remember, in my own land, I am a daimyo of rank.''

Toriko smiled.

De Wynte cleared his throat. 'This is all well and good, but it still leaves unresolved the matter of your personal protection. . . .''

''But I now have Toriko-san . . .'' Diana was starting to dig in her heels.

''Excuse me, please, but I feel it my duty to suggest that the captain is right and wise,'' Toriko said. Diana gave her a quizzical look, but de Wynte appeared to be relieved at acquiring an unexpected ally. The de Edgemonts were notoriously stubborn in some matters.

''You have a suggestion then?'' Diana inquired.

''Yes, if he would agree, hire the samurai who has already saved our lives on land and on the sea,'' Toriko suggested, bowing.

"Him?" Diana's vehemence surprised de Wynte. "I would rather die first! He is the most arrogant, maddening man I have ever encountered, as proud as Lucifer, whom I suspect he probably greatly resembles . . ."

"Please excuse me again, Diana-san, but I think you are making a mistake. He is a samurai of great renown. His name is Tonomori . . ."

"At least I now can know his name. How nice!" Diana spit out bitingly. *"All* my good kimonos are lying there back at the mission because this great samurai wouldn't *think* of carrying a package . . ."

De Wynte rolled his eyes. "Let me interrupt, please. I have pressing duties and I must leave. Diana, do please listen to what the lady has to say. She is talking good sense. If you will take the time to think about it, you will find she is right. The man is an excellent fighter. I have certainly seen nothing like him before. Discuss it now between you, and then we can all talk when we dine together this evening. I must leave you now." Once outside the door, de Wynte ran his hand over his hair in exasperation. He hoped the Countess Diana would listen to reason. He could hear the debate continuing, now in rapid Portuguese, as he departed.

Inside the cabin, Diana sat on her small bed, and ticked off on her fingers all of Tonomori's shortcomings, ending on a defiant note ". . . and his arrogance is exceeded only by his impertinence, and, and . . . I've run out of fingers, so there!"

"Of course you are right, Diana-san, but these very qualities . . ."

"Qualities?"

"Yes, qualities, and they make him an excellent choice as your bodyguard. If he had acted any differently, he would not be samurai, and would be useless to you," Toriko pointed out sharply.

"He is useless to me now."

"If the captain thinks you are in danger, then you probably are. From what you have told me about Europe, we cannot go around carrying our *naginatas* without prompting some odd looks."

Diana laughed. Toriko had a point.

"See, already you are starting to agree," Toriko quickly continued, because Diana was opening her lips to begin debate anew.

"That man was born to protect with the utmost devotion and loyalty, anyone he serves. Whoever tried to harm you would have to do so over that samurai's dead body. All that I have heard of this Tonomori, and have seen with my own eyes, assures me that is not at all likely to happen."

Diana bit her lip in thought. "All right, for the sake of argument, supppose that you are right. Suppose this Tonomori *is* the perfect bodyguard. Won't he refuse to serve *me*, a woman, because of his precious pride?"

"He might, but I don't think so," Toriko said, explaining that she heard his men talking and asked some questions of her own. She learned, Toriko now told Diana, that Tonomori had served a great diamyo, Lord Betsuo, until a few days before. "In a battle, Betsuo's son, Masanori, made a foolish error in judgment and got his father killed. To cover up his own mistakes—once he had assumed the title—Masanori exiled Tonomori as a ronin. Later, he sent his own samurai to hunt Tonomori down.

"And if I am not mistaken, Tonomori does not like being a ronin any more than I did. It is very shameful to a samurai. He could serve you with honor, and I am sure that is all that he cares about."

Diana still looked dubious, but in the end, Toriko won. Diana would ask Tonomori to serve as her bodyguard, along with his men. Toriko listened carefully as Diana explained the course the *Schoen* would take in returning to Europe, a voyage that would take a year and a half or more.

"Samurai can be very difficult to manage unless you know how. I will be there to assist you, Diana-san," Toriko assured her.

"To make sure I don't wound his pride?" Diana asked glumly.

"If I did so, that would be of benefit to all concerned," Toriko replied as she inwardly chuckled. *Oh Diana-san,*

*when it comes to pride, you could show Tonomori a thing
or two. You are truly a samurai in spirit.*

That evening, in pouring the wine before dinner, which
was served on a plank table in the chartroom, de Wynte
was relieved to discover Diana had finally listened to
reason. Instead of saying so, he proposed a toast, "May
you find peace and happiness in returning to your home."

Diana raised her tumbler of finely blown Venetian glass.
She was mulling over the occurrences of the day, and it
was slowly dawning on her that Lady Toriko could be as
stubborn as she was. It appeared that life certainly was
going to continue to be interesting.

"Then you will offer employment to this samurai,
Tonomori?" de Wynte inquired.

"Yes, as soon as he awakens. Toriko-san told me that
he had gone a day and a half without sleep while the other
samurai were hunting him," Diana explained.

The candle flames bent, and Tonomori was suddenly in
the doorway, filling it. He wore dark *hakama*, with a
short sword tucked into his sash, but from the waist up
he was naked. His left hand held the two-handed *tachi*,
while his right gripped the crossed wrappings of the
handle. Even in the dim light, they could see that he was
powerfully built, with thick veins cording his massive
forearms.

"Where are we bound?" Tonomori directed his question at de Wynte, but it was Toriko who stood and
bowed.

"Ah, Tonomori-san, we hope you have slept well.
We will be staying at Nagasaki for a few days to
gather provisions. Then we sail for India and beyond,
to Europe, to Diana-san's homeland. We wish to thank
you for saving our lives today at the mission, and again
in the boat. . . ."

"You are welcome. And I see that you know of
Tonomori." His voice held no emotion.

"In return, Diana-san, who is a daimyo in her own
land, wishes to engage your services as head of her
bodyguard. She would deem it a great honor if you would
accept."

De Wynte did not fully understand what was being said, but he could see that something was going terribly wrong when Diana's eyes narrowed. Her temper visibly boiled to the surface as she heard Tonomori say, almost contemptuously, "I refuse."

Chapter Eight

Tonomori had surfaced suddenly from a deep sleep, clear of mind and completely alert. He heard the whining of the wind and felt the rhythmic lift of the ship as she plied through the heavy sea, but these were not the sounds which had wrenched him awake.

Then groans came from his men in the corner, as if they were in great pain. Tonomori unsheathed his short sword and went to them.

"Tonomori-san, I die," Oshabiri said, sweating. Tonomori heard the light chittering of the monkey, so he knew there had been no sudden attack of treachery. The little fiend would have awakened him with his shrill screams, and that was not what Tonomori had heard.

"I also am very ill, sir," Yamahito said weakly. "Ever since we came aboard this accursed foreign ship, it has become worse."

Tonomori laughed in relief. "What you are, my friends, is seasick," he said. "I have heard of this. You will live."

More groans greeted this unwelcome news.

"I had hoped to die quickly, Tonomori-san," Oshabiri said.

"Not yet, Oshabiri-san," Tonomori said in a soothing tone. "The sickness affects the belly and lightens the head. You will be well in a day or so. Try to drink some water or some wine but eat no heavy food."

The mention of food brought fresh moans. "I never want to eat again," Yamahito exclaimed weakly, but with feeling.

"I will return shortly," Tonomori promised, and left the cabin to find the women. He needed to find out where they were heading.

Now, standing before them and the captain of the vessel, Tonomori was acutely aware that he had angered the golden one, the young woman called Diana, but that could not be helped. He had sworn to avenge Betsuo on Masanori and Lord Atsuhira, and he could not waste his time doing anything else.

"Would you mind explaining why?" Diana demanded. Her eyes were smoldering, but she kept her temper in check—barely.

"I have sworn an oath of vengeance," Tonomori said shortly. Then he troubled himself to add, "Also, you are not samurai."

The captain's knowledge of Japanese was only rudimentary, but he understood the gist of the last sentence and interrupted.

"Did he say she is not samurai?"

"Yes, he did."

"But that is not the case. The Countess Diana is indeed samurai. I have it in writing."

It was Toriko's turn to be stunned. Diana looked puzzled. Tonomori waited impatiently.

De Wynte produced the letter from Lord Hoju's scribe. "I had it translated when I received it, but this is the original," he told them. "In it, Lord Hoju grants her samurai status."

Toriko read carefully. "There is no mistake. Here is Lord Hoju's seal. Diana-san, you are samurai. This is a tremendous boon." Toriko relayed the information for Tonomori.

Diverted, Diana turned to Toriko. "But why should he

do such a thing? I made no such request. In fact, the thought never crossed my mind."

"I have heard of Lord Hoju," Tonomori interjected. "He probably did it to annoy his neighbors, the other daimyos who sent the ronin to attack the mission. This would really stick their noses in it."

Toriko smiled. "Yes, it would be just like him. Well, Tonomori-san, does this change anything? Will you serve?"

Tonomori looked uncomfortable. As a foreigner, Diana could be refused easily enough. As a samurai, she now actually had an edge on him. Tonomori was still a ronin.

"It does, but I still have my oath of vengeance against those responsible for the death of my master. You must understand. It takes precedence over everything."

"Yes, I also am samurai and understand duty. It is too bad, because I think you would have found service with the lady very interesting. She faces grave dangers for one so young," Toriko told him. To the captain, she explained Tonomori's dilemma.

"If you would please translate for me, perhaps my words would have some effect," the captain said, and then addressed Tonomori.

"Knowledge is the most dangerous weapon of all," he said to the ronin. "You could learn much in Europe. We are not the barbarians you think we are. Consider this: Until fifteen years ago, the Japanese had never seen a gun. Has a Japanese ever been able to build a ship like this one and sail it around the world?

"Also, to take revenge against someone requires resources, and I take it yours are limited. I mean no insult in this. We are returning to Europe. Any spices or silks you might purchase here or in India would return you a hundredfold, two hundredfold of their price. Buy guns and powder in Europe and return to your home. With these resources, you could blast your enemies to pieces."

Toriko translated rapidly, and Tonomori seemed to ponder the remarks.

"Then I must describe another matter, perhaps an even greater danger to all of Japan. I am Dutch." De Wynte struck his chest for emphasis and leaned forward.

"My country now is a possession of Spain, a country that has been embarking on a successful mission of conquest. We pay taxes to Spain, and Spanish soldiers march on our soil at our expense. Japan is tiny compared to the nations of Europe, but Europe is small when measured against the vast new lands that Spain has claimed and conquered. I urge you to consider this: Every day, Spanish warships are closer to Japan. Spain has thrown down mighty nations and enslaved their people, stolen their wealth.

"My country is trying to get out from under the weight of the Spanish throne. You could be a part of our success. Spanish troops are everywhere, and they grow more numerous with time. It would be a long road, but not only would you have honorable service as a samurai, you would be doing the world and your emperor an even greater service. Please consider this before you reply."

But Tonomori's thoughts had wandered off before Toriko completed the translation from the Dutch into Japanese. *The long road.* This was the third time Tonomori had been urged to take it, and he accepted it as an omen. Very well—he would set aside his oath, he would go to the ends of the earth, he would learn the secrets of the *nambanjin,* the southern barbarians. But he would return. The day might be distant, but he would return and his revenge would be nothing less than total destruction of Masanori and Lord Atsuhira.

"I accept!" Tonomori said suddenly. Diana looked to Toriko, to the captain; it was now up to her. She did need protection and Tonomori could be a powerful ally. Her hostility vanished.

"Very well, Tonomori-san, I welcome you into my service," she said, bowing. Tonomori returned the gesture stiffly, bending his own pride. It was an awkward moment, but he broke the silence.

"What are your first orders?"

"You are welcome to dine with us if you like, but after that you should rest until you completely recover your strength. You have only had a few hours of sleep and it seems to me that you must need more. When you and your men have rested, we will begin your studies," Diana said.

"Studies?" Tonomori was dubious.

"Yes, if you are to be able to function in my world, you will need to know how to speak Portuguese and Dutch, and the customs and etiquette of my country as well as those of other lands." Diana smiled brightly in encouragement. "I will teach you. In return, you can teach me more about Japan. I liked your country very much and I would like to return some day. Many months are ahead of us on this voyage, so we will have plenty of time to learn."

"Very well," Tonomori agreed with an enthusiasm he did not feel. Already regretting his action, he did not relish the idea of being taught by a woman. "If you do not object, I will take my leave." He bowed and returned to his men.

When the latch had closed, de Wynte breathed easier. "This resolves many difficulties; more than you know," he told Diana.

"How is that?"

"This is a trading vessel, not a ship of war, although we have sixteen cannon for our defenses. It is a policy of your father's that, except in times of danger, neither crew nor passengers go armed. All arms are kept under lock and key, in my control. On long voyages, tempers can wear thin, and I want no bloodletting. It would have been difficult to take the weapons from the samurai—impossible, one might say, having seen him in action—and I rather doubt he would have given them up freely."

"True," Toriko said, "a samurai is never without his weapons. Never."

"As the Countess Diana's guard, however, it becomes necessary, even mandatory, for Tonomori to remain armed at all times," the captain pointed out.

"I see," said Diana, who was beginning to look pale. She had picked at her dinner earlier. The chartroom was stifling.

"Are you well, Countess?" de Wynte asked.

"No, no, I think the motion of the ship . . . I think I-am-going-to-be-sick," she wailed thinly.

"Take her on deck for some air, but be careful," de Wynte instructed Toriko. "The sea is running a little heavy and it doesn't pay to take chances. When she feels better, she would do well with some rest; do you agree?''

On deck, the wind was sharp and piercing, but it did not bother Diana. The cold, in fact, felt good, and if only her stomach would stop churning, she could be content. Finally, it was the odor of grease, wafted from the galley, that did her in. Diana leaned over the railing and retched. Toriko afterward led her below deck, made her drink a small cup of cold tea, which actually proved to be soothing, and put her to bed.

When Diana slept at last, Toriko changed into a plain brown kimono and slipped silently out of the cabin on bare feet. When she was satisfied, hours later, she had committed every inch of the ship to memory. Toriko knew precisely the width of the passageways, which hatches creaked on opening, and which of the decking planks squeaked when stepped on. She could have found her way around the *Schoen* blindfolded. No one saw her, except Tonomori, who was doing precisely the same thing.

Very interesting, Tonomori thought. He had seen her slip sideways through the shadows of a passageway, nimbly avoid a spear of light thrown by the opening of the galley door, and shoot up the ladder to disappear on deck. If the lady Toriko was what he suspected her to be, Tonomori would have to watch her very closely. His honor as a samurai, and his loyalty to his mistress, foreigner or not, demanded it if the countess was in danger from a *ninja*.

Before he returned to his pallet, Tonomori carefully spread some sand behind the door to the chartroom where he and his *ashigaru* unrolled their sleeping mats. The crunching of the sand would alert him to the presence of anyone who put a foot on it. He took a small handful of sand from each of the ship's fire buckets so it wouldn't be missed, and stashed a sackful in his belongings. Then he slept securely with the thought of later carefully wetting the decking outside his door. When the boards swelled slightly from the moisture, they would shriek an alarm when stepped on, exactly like the ''nightingale'' floors designed to signal the presence of intruders in Japanese castles.

They reached Nagasaki the following evening and spent the night aboard ship. The skies were leaden in the morning but the rain appeared to have passed. De Wynte returned to the ship in late morning after obtaining passes for Tonomori and the women.

"I experienced some difficulty at first," he explained, "but when I showed them Lord Hoju's letter and mentioned Tonomori's name, they showed great respect." Many samurai patroling the harbor could understand Portuguese, so de Wynte had less trouble trading there.

Tonomori was inclined to be belligerent, even more so than usual, on the subject of his new employer. But on leaving the ship in attendance on Diana, with Lady Toriko following closely, he encountered no difficulty.

"I am very pleased to meet you, Tonomori-san. Please excuse any delay," said the captain of the harbor guards. "Your papers are now completely in order. Please enjoy your stay in Nagasaki."

So his fame had gone before him. Tonomori gave a mental shrug. Perhaps city-bred samurai had better manners. He knew the samurai of the backwoods regions would have twitted him for serving a woman, samurai or no. He was not to know, as the captain of the guard glared murderously at his back as they shouldered through the market throng, that the harbor samurai ordinarily would have done the same thing. None of them, however, had a death wish that day.

Diana was wearing her lacquered wig, and she kept her eyes cast down so the Japanese would not be startled by their color. Her face was powdered white and she walked in the correct fashion of a city woman, as Toriko had taught her. Tonomori's menacing presence discouraged any comment from those who noticed anything odd about her appearance.

"The fabrics are exquisite, don't you agree, Toriko-san? I have never seen anything so lovely," Diana exclaimed inside a silk merchant's shop. Tonomori cooled his heels and gritted his teeth. The women carefully examined every bolt, each inch of trim and discoursed upon them interminably, he thought. At last, he gave up his private grumbling and strove to cultivate patience. It only seemed as if they had been there for hours.

When at last it appeared that Diana and Toriko were through examining every fiber of silk in the place, the merchant's assistants brought out tea and refreshments, and they fell to haggling over price. Tonomori felt like running outside and picking a fight with the first unlucky samurai who crossed his path. To abandon his post, however, would mean tremendous loss of face, not to mention the dereliction of his duty as a samurai.

To exercise self-control, he passed the time by scrutinizing the portly merchant and his fawning manners, and contemplating his early demise. The belly of a mongrel cur would be an appropriate tomb, Tonomori thought. That way, he would be reborn in the next life as a dog turd.

"See, Tonomori-san, that did not take long at all," Diana called cheerfully, drawing fiendish satisfaction in knowing that Tonomori was chafing at the delay. "It was a pity that we lost all our things at the mission, but it is so pleasant to be able to go shopping again."

"Diana-san, perhaps now would be a good time to stop for the midday meal," Toriko suggested. "I am sure that Tonomori-san would enjoy some refreshment." Seeing that Tonomori was restless, she hoped ardently that Diana would not push him too far by antagonizing him. Samurai were short-tempered and this one looked as if he might explode.

The excellent meal they enjoyed of grilled shrimp, boiled rice, and freshly pickled vegetables at a small eating establishment eventually helped to restore Tonomori's spirits. Being on duty, he declined the offer of sake, but accepted a second bowl of *o-cha*, the bright green tea the Japanese preferred over the darker Chinese tea, *ko-cha*.

The women finally finished poking through the other shops and selecting tortoise shell combs and pins, plus mirrors, fans, and umbrellas, not to mention several silk kimonos to replace those abandoned at the mission. By this time, Tonomori was resigned to his fate, the evil *karma* that was out to teach him patience.

Diana surprised Tonomori by stopping at the stall of a maker of sword furnishings, then presenting him with a matched pair of sword guards, crickets carved in iron. The few gold highlights on the blades of grass had been added after the iron had been pickled and then baked in a small oven for two weeks, giving a dark lustre to the iron. One had to touch the crickets to be assured they were not real. Tonomori received the present with appropriate gratitude, and Toriko heaved a sigh of relief. She was already in a good mood from the expensive present of richly patterned silk she had received from Diana, and she had hoped Tonomori would do nothing to spoil the feeling of good humor that now prevailed.

Nagasaki was like a city out of a fable, Diana thought; she had never seen anything so lovely. Nothing in Europe could compare to its jumble of buildings and the bright colors. The streets were clean and neat, even if one was not used to men blithely hiking their *hakama* in order to urinate against the side of a building. Everything was as tidy as a pin box. The people looked happy and prosperous. Diana thought their manners were impeccable. Even the children scrambling in the narrow back streets seemed well scrubbed and well behaved.

When she remarked on the difference between the towering houses in Antwerp and dwellings in Japan, Toriko explained. "Our architecture is subject to earthquakes, Diana-san. If we built them any higher, they would fall down when the ground shakes. Some of them do anyway. The earthquakes can be very terrible."

The shadows were growing long, and Captain de Wynte was relieved when they returned aboard ship. So far, the Japanese had been quite tolerant about foreigners in Nagasaki, but one never knew when their attitudes might change; consider Lord Hoju.

Diana dismissed his concerns. Her packages and carefully wrapped bolts and bales of silk had arrived from the merchants, and she was busily supervising their storage below decks.

His duty finished for the time being, Tonomori went to find his men. He found them carefully cleaning his armor.

"See, Tonomori-san, the lacings are almost dry," Yamahito said. He and Oshabiri had been carefully patting the *odoshi* lacings dry with squares of soft paper used by the Japanese to wipe their noses. Care had to be exercised with wet armor or the lacings bred lice and foul odors, Tonomori knew from experience on long campaigns, and he was glad that his men were already seeing to it. When they were through, they would store each piece of armor in its own silk bag and then pack them in a stout, ironbound chest.

Tonomori turned to a bundle of swords Yamahito had looted from the bodies of the ronin at the mission. He examined them with the same thoroughness of the women in the silk merchant's shop, although if anyone had been rash enough to point this out, Tonomori would have bitten his head off.

"Only three of these swords are any good," Tonomori said. "The rest are mediocre quality, and two of them are real trash."

"Yes, but that *tanto* over there is of a very high quality and should fetch an excellent price when in full polish and in better mountings," Yamahito told him, pointing to a heavy dagger which Tonomori had overlooked.

"Yes, you are correct, Yamahito-san," Tonomori agreed, after popping out the *mekugi-ana* pin, removing the handle, and examining the signature on the *tang*. "It is signed, Miyatsu Nyudo Munetade. Yamato school, I believe."

"Yes, Yamato work. Notice the temper turnback at the point, sir, and the V-shaped file marks on the *tang*. Always a sign of the Yamato smiths," Yamahito pointed out. He pressed the lacings with a dry piece of the fine tissue, and was satisfied that no more moisture was left to draw from the lacings.

Tonomori raised an inquisitive eyebrow. Common footsoldiers were not noted as connoisseurs of fine swords, and Tonomori wondered where Yamahito had obtained his knowledge. The Munetade blade was indeed as fine as Yamahito had said it was.

"My father was a swordsmith," Yamahito explained. "My older brothers joined him at the forge. My interest was always in using weapons, not making them, so I became a soldier. If we can obtain the proper stones, I will polish that dagger for you."

"Very well, Yamahito-san. Thank you very much," Tonomori said. Oshabiri began packing pieces of Tonomori's armor into its storage chest. The monkey Saru was not present, and Tonomori hoped it was not causing difficulties aboard ship. In fact, the monkey was in the galley, shamelessly ingratiating himself with the ship's cook by performing somersaults and other tricks it had been taught. The cook would have been less amused if he knew that every time his back turned, Saru was stealing him blind. Saru seldom missed one of his five meals a day.

The smells from the galley drifted to the deck, but Tonomori was not hungry. He had left his men to come topside. On the tide, they would weigh anchor, and Tonomori intended to fill his being with the mountains and the greenness, the oneness that was Japan. If his long road was taking him from the land of the gods, then so be it. He would be patient. And he would return, of that he had no doubt. But when? That was another matter. He wanted to fix those towering mountains in his mind so that if the days should darken ahead, he could draw his strength from them, to return to the land of the gods as the hawk does to nest despite the lure of the open skies and the teeming meadows.

And Tonomori recognized one more pilgrimage which he should not neglect, perhaps a place even more important to him than the great *torii* gate of the famed shrine at Ise. And he would so inform his men. A good commander would always see to all their needs.

At dinner that evening, de Wynte remarked on the absence of Diana's bodyguard, but was reassured.

"Tonomori told me that as we are leaving Japan on the morrow," Diana said, "it would be most appropriate for a samurai to take his leave in the proper fashion, and that he was taking his men for their own good. I had no idea that the samurai were so devout, Captain."

"Nor I, but I must voice concern that you dismiss your bodyguard so lightly. I urge you to consider your safety at all times."

"And so I will. But here aboard ship, surrounded by all your men, and with the samurai on guard here in the harbor, I have never felt so safe before," Diana assured him. "Besides, I think it is important for a man to be able to pray, although it is a pity he worships false gods. Perhaps in time, he will find the right path to paradise."

"I certainly hope so, Countess," de Wynte acknowledged.

At the first light of dawn, Tonomori stood on deck, muffled in a thick cloak, watching the wrinkled outline of the mountains shrink into the gray sea. But his spirit was at peace. It was fortunate that he had returned ashore for one last time.

"Now there is a true samurai," Oshabiri whispered to Yamahito. The two men squatted on deck, keeping a somewhat silent vigilance with Tonomori.

"Did you see those two courtesans Tonomori went up the stairs with, Yamahito-san? I nearly wet my *hakama*, they were so beautiful," Oshabiri said. He was still in a delirium from the events of the night before, having never been in so prestigious a brothel.

"Yes, our master certainly is capable of taking care of himself, while at the same time looking after us," Yamahito said.

"And the girl I was with, what's-her-name, I will never forget her. Ever."

"I'm sure," Yamahito said dryly.

"Thighs as white and strong as the Sacred Ropes at a *Sumo* match . . ."

"I'm sure she would enjoy the comparison," Yamahito amended. He considered Oshabiri's companion of the evening slightly on the porcine side, but she certainly had seemed eager enough.

". . . even her crotch was perfumed, I tell you. . . ."

"Quiet, you idiot," Yamahito interrupted. "I do not think our master wishes to be distracted with your ravings."

115

Besides, Yamahito wished to reflect on the joys he had sampled himself.

"Listen, I heard some of the girls say the two women Tonomori was with would be walking with difficulty for a week. How about that!" Oshabiri whispered triumphantly.

"Enough! Give me some peace," Yamahito groaned.

Oshabiri lapsed into silence. He could not understand his friend's reticence. The kind of whores Yamahito consorted with usually smelled like a couple of tuna *sushi* left in the sun. Now, after a few hours of thrashing on the *tatamis* with a goddess, Yamahito had the conversation of a clam. Oshabiri was incensed. But maybe they could compare experiences later.

But Oshabiri's sense of outrage was nothing compared with the chagrin of Diana when Toriko mentioned Tonomori's destination of the night before.

"You mean to tell me that Tonomori spent the night in a whorehouse?" Diana exclaimed, in some surprise. "I thought he had gone for prayers."

"Of course," Toriko said, unprepared for the emotion in Diana's voice. "We are leaving on a long voyage. What did you expect, mistress? He is a man."

"I'm such an innocent. I should have known," Diana said, crestfallen.

"It is all for the best. He is not Christian and we have no such restrictions here. And when I saw Tonomori this morning, he was almost civil," Toriko mentioned.

In spite of herself, Diana laughed, "I suppose that his prayers were answered."

Even the crew ultimately became accustomed to Tonomori and his ways. He tended to startle them at first, popping up when least expected and regarding everyone with suspicion when in attendance on his mistress. The women were a mystery, but then all women were a mystery to the crew, except the sort they consorted with off the ship, and those, too, were frequently a puzzle.

That little trouble turned up between the crew and the "slant-eyed foreigners" aboard ship was partly due to Captain de Wynte's orders to extend courtesy to the passengers. That the crew was not only civil but almost respectful was partly to be credited to Hans and Volmer, who described in vivid detail to a slack-jawed crew what had actually happened at Murashima.

"And just when they was about to carve us up and serve us in chafing dishes, out roars this whacking great samurai, Tonomori, riding a horse that looked like it was breathing fire and brimstone, and starts hacking them savages like they was chickens, just as cool as you please," Volmer told them.

"Don't forget the women," Hans interrupted.

"I was getting to that. And before that, the women gutted a couple of them savages with long spears like they was fixing Sunday dinner," Volmer went on. "So if I was any of you, I would think twice before I stirred 'em up, or your tripes will be all over the deck before you know what happened. Especially that samurai. From what I've heard and seen, them samurai can be as touchy as a scalded boil. Worse, maybe."

"How do you know when you've done something wrong?" asked one of the crewmen uncertainly.

"That's just it; you don't know until he hands you your head by way of explanation. Just stay out of their way."

The crewmen gave Tonomori and his men a wide berth, but that did not stop the grumbling. As the days passed, the return of sunny weather failed to improve their mood. The men quarreled over minor matters and not until de Wynte had one man flogged did it stop, and then only temporarily.

"I hear men saying that this is a ghost ship," Tonomori overheard de Wynte telling the first mate. "I don't know how these things get started, but this is one I am going to put down—hard."

Tonomori's hated daily language lessons in Portuguese and Dutch had finally begun paying off. Now he knew exactly what the problem was, and how to stop it. Almost every night, Diana and Toriko had been slipping out of their cabin for a few hours and roaming the ship like cats on a ratting expedition. It was becoming a dangerous game, and Tonomori thought the time had come to bring it to a conclusion.

But Diana did not want to quit. Nothing could compare to the delicious sensation of freedom. All her life, she had been hemmed in by her sex and her skirts, forced to be accompanied by a chaperone, told what to do and when, given instruction for her own good, never allowed to be her own self—only what others expected of a woman of Diana's rank. Now, on this moonless night, Toriko had led her along the shrouds, with the deck pitching dizzily below and the masts swaying like tall trees. This freedom was seducing her as a lover might, leaving her weak and sleepy after every embrace with the night, and wanting more.

The helmsman and the watch were attuned only to the sea, trained to detect any contradictions between wind and wave and the roll of the ship. They did not see the wisps of shadow slip beyond them.

Once back inside their cabin, Diana lifted the shade from the candle which might have betrayed their coming and going with a splash of light when they opened the door. She loosened the wrappings which muffled her face and . . . her heart stopped.

"*Konban-wa*, Diana-san." Though his "good evening" was polite, Tonomori loomed in the corner, a menacing figure. Toriko spun instinctively to meet the unexpected challenge, but steel flashed at her throat.

"Enough!" Tonomori said. The blade of his *wakizashi* was heavy and brutal. And unwavering. He was aware of Diana, her face white and breasts heaving in the flickering light, but Tonomori never took his eyes off Toriko for even a split second.

"Wait! Do not quarrel," Diana interposed. Toriko gradually relaxed her tense body which had been ready to spring, and the *wakizashi* then disappeared into the sheath tucked into Tonomori's sash.

"Diana-san, if I am to guard you well, to serve you as I must, then you must be straightforward with me," Tonomori said. His eyes never left Toriko. "She," he said, pointing, "is a *ninja,* an enemy to samurai." The *ninja* killed by

118

stealth. The samurai thought they used cowardly methods, but they nonetheless feared the *ninja* assassins.

"Yes, but she is my servant and my friend and she serves me well. She is also samurai, Tonomori-san," Diana said.

Tonomori spoke sharply to Toriko. "If you move that leg one more inch I will kill you." Toriko had casually been moving into position to balance her weight on her right leg so she could lash out with her left if the opportunity arose. Tonomori blocked that avenue, but Toriko was already furious at being caught off guard. Her face remained passive but alert.

"Stop it, please, both of you!" Diana pleaded. "Do not fight on my account. Tonomori-san, listen to me and then decide. Only a little while ago, you refused to serve me because you said you wanted to make your enemies pay. When you told me that, I understood, because I want revenge myself."

Tonomori indicated his understanding, but kept his full attention on Toriko.

"My father, whom I loved more than anything in this world, was murdered," Diana continued. "Because I am a woman, our customs say that I may not avenge my father. I know who the murderer is. He is a man who is very powerful—almost like a king. It would be very difficult to have him assassinated." Diana chose her next words carefully. "But now I myself have killed men. I have not found it difficult. Toriko-san has showed me the way. And when I have learned more, when I am ready—when Toriko-san thinks I am ready—I will kill this man! I want to do it myself. I *will* do it myself. But I need Toriko-san to teach me further. Do you not understand?"

"I do. Perhaps better than you might think," Tonomori said. "What do you propose doing now?"

"Be with us. I need you *both*," Diana answered quickly. "As allies, we could accomplish almost anything. You, Tonomori-san, will be the key."

"How so?"

"Consider this: You are a samurai of renown. There will be times when your skills and strength will carry the day, when just your presence will keep danger from us. But there will come a time for stealth and cunning, when nothing else will do. When we return to my country, my enemies will have me carefully watched. I think it will be you that they will guard against. And when a man has his eye on the tiger, perhaps the foxes can run riot.''

Diana tilted her head and waited for Tonomori's reply. She was surprised to see him smile.

''Your eloquence is surprising, Diana-san,'' he observed.

Diana exhaled slowly, in relief. ''Then, would you agree to work with Toriko-san, with me, against my enemies? It will be very dangerous.''

Tonomori bowed. ''Yes, I agree. I give you my word as a samurai. The danger is not a consideration.''

''And I,'' Toriko echoed, also bowing. Tonomori relaxed his vigilance.

''Perfect!'' Diana exclaimed. ''Tomorrow we will begin. I still have much to learn from you. And you need to learn more from me, especially about my enemies, and together we must decide how they are to be defeated. A vast struggle for power is going on in Europe. It is even possible, I think, to affect its outcome as I take my own personal vengeance.''

She felt drained by her efforts, both the exertions of the night exercise and the persuasion of Tonomori. After he had left and Toriko had snuffed the candle, Diana burrowed gratefully under the covers and let herself be carried by the gentle swaying of the ship, matching her rhythms to its own. It was a good start. Toriko and Tonomori may never become friends, she thought, but they will work together. The three of us would be a force to be reckoned with . . . She drifted into sleep.

In the morning, Diana awoke to discover an unsuspected ally: Tonomori's pride. After a light breakfast, it was he who suggested an early start. Diana soon discovered the reason. It became apparent that Tonomori would rather run barefooted through red-hot coals than be bested by a woman at anything.

He realized that Toriko was far ahead of him in her comprehension of Portuguese and Dutch, but he intended to whittle her lead as soon as possible. Diana now decided this was so promising an opportunity that she must exploit it, and soon she had Toriko and Tonomori deeply engaged in a healthy competition. Toriko was not willing to let herself be outdone, either, and strove to maintain her linguistic superiority as determinedly as Tonomori sought to erase it.

That afternoon, since the weather was good, Diana and her small class sat on the main deck, but out of earshot of the crew.

". . . They had intended to find the shortest route possible to the fabled lands of Cathay and India. What they, the traders, found was a continent no one knew existed," Diana explained in Portuguese. "Before that, everyone thought the world was flat and that if you sailed too far out, you would fall off the edge." Diana paused. Oshabiri had raised an eager hand to ask a question in Portuguese.

"Excuse, please, but how do you know the world is not flat, that we will not fall off the edge?" This possibility had been gnawing at him daily, and Oshabiri needed reassurance.

"Put your mind at rest," Diana told him. "Many ships now have been around the world, which we now know is shaped like a globe. . . ."

"Excuse, please," Oshabiri insisted, "but if the world *is* indeed round, then why do we not fall off?" The possibilities of a round world were shaking his confidence.

"I do not know why. All the same, we remain fixed to its surface," Diana said rather shortly. "No one has fallen off yet."

Oshabiri appeared to be dubious. "If they *did* fall off, no one would know about it because they would be gone, so how can anyone be sure? . . ."

Tonomori, resisting an impulse to cuff him, interrupted. "Please continue," he said to Diana, who had just been reaching the interesting part—the wars for power among the princes of Europe, duels of honor, intrigue, rebellions, betrayals—and it was these aspects of life that Oshabiri was interrupting.

Diana bowed her head, smiled, and resumed. "Nevertheless, the fact that we do not fall off does not lessen the dangers of sailing around the world. There is much we don't know. Besides storms, reefs, and the like, we believe there are sea monsters. . . ."

Oshabiri started again.

". . . and, of course, pirates. Captain de Wynte informs me that these waters are swarming with pirates— many of them Japanese, by the way—but as you can see the ship is armed heavily."

"Excuse me again, please?" Oshabiri asked. "But if this is all so dangerous, why bother? Why not stay at home?"

"A good question, Oshabiri-san," Diana told him approvingly. Oshabiri preened, then subsided when he noticed Tonomori drumming his fingers in obvious impatience. "The answer is that enormous profits can be made in trade. And these profits make the risks worthwhile. One successful voyage can make many men rich for life. They would never have to work again."

Oshabiri and Yamahito looked at each other. Without work, a man had no purpose in life! The Europeans scurried around like a pack of despised merchants to make enough money to deprive themselves of purpose! A strange lot, yet decidedly warlike, these Europeans. How could people like that be explained? Oshabiri and Yamahito didn't even try.

"But what does all this have to do with war?" Tonomori demanded impatiently.

"I am getting to that, Tonomori-san, but your question is well put. The princes of Europe must have a lot of money to equip and pay their soldiers. Many extra expenses are involved—palaces, servants, jewels, velvets, and so on. Spain is very rich with the gold and silver plundered from the New World. If in addition Spain can control the trade with Cathay and India and Japan, the amount of money available for troops and ships would be . . . staggering."

"Your soldiers only serve for pay?" Tonomori asked in a voice that sounded contemptuous.

"You find it hard to understand, then? Well, it is an

accepted practice, without dishonor, in Europe,'' Diana explained. "And, I might add, the soldiers fight very well under this system, using their own code of honor, such as it is.''

This was the most difficult part. Diana was glad she had learned well as a young girl when, out of boredom, she had sat in on her brothers' lessons with their tutors. Her father had believed in the value of knowledge. But instilling in the Japanese mind the customs of the Western civilization was not easy. And the same was true for her comprehension of the Japanese way of thinking and of doing things.

Tonomori stood. "I mean no disrespect, but I think it would have been better if I had died with honor fighting Masanori's samurai on the beach.''

"I disagree,'' Diana said flatly. "If Spain is not stopped, then one day in the not too distant future, Spanish warships will be sailing in Japanese waters. You will serve your emperor well if you can stop them before they ever leave port.'' Tonomori had nothing to say now. Diana decided that she must keep reminding Tonomori of his purpose on the voyage. The farther he went from Japan, perhaps the less sure he might be.

Diana also stood up, relieved to stretch her cramped muscles. She had not caught the Japanese knack of squatting for hours, but her pride made her determined to try. Also, she did not want to overburden them with facts and customs. And besides, the young quartermaster, Carillo, had been paying far too much attention to their meeting, edging as close as he dared without being obvious. They would have to be on guard whenever he was around, and Diana made another mental note to tell Tonomori. She needn't have bothered. Tonomori was already suspicious of the junior officer whose thickening middle attested to his fondness for the stores he had under his charge. Carillo had all the earmarks of a paid informer—Tonomori had overheard him asking detailed questions of Hans and Volmer. Tonomori had already resolved that when it was conveniently possible, he would slide Carillo quietly over the

123

side with a weight attached to his ankles. He had decided not to upset his mistress with his suspicions.

Later that evening in the chartroom, when the captain was on deck, Tonomori watched as Toriko showed Diana how to pivot correctly with a spear, to counter the blow of one opponent when already engaged with another.

"That is excellent, Diana-san, you move well," Tonomori said, circling the room. Table and chairs were pushed against the walls, but the ceiling was too low to allow much maneuvering.

"Don't let this bother you, Diana-san. You may find yourself in tighter spots than this and you will have to make do. In a narrow alley or defile, for instance, choke up on the spear and use it to block and cut. Thrust mainly with the short sword drawn from the sash. A *tachi* is useless in a room like this." Diana felt a strong hand push at the small of her back. Then Tonomori took her hips in both hands, and settled her firmly into the proper position.

"There!" Toriko nodded in agreement. "Now you can move in either direction and keep your balance, no matter what. But do not move your arms so much. Twist your body instead. That is the source of your power."

Diana tried to make the move shown her by Tonomori, but nearly slipped.

"She has started a bad habit of making her arms do all the work. It is a difficult thing to break," Toriko remarked.

"Yes. I have seen samurai do the same thing, even when they knew better," Tonomori agreed. "Diana-san, you must practice and break this habit. You are sacrificing strength for speed, and you will achieve neither."

Diana set herself to try again. On the fourth try, she made it, slashing and counterblocking with perfection. She felt elation at the force she could generate just by moving correctly.

"But what about the samurai and the nobles of Japan?" Diana asked while they rested. "You have many wars. Don't the samurai also fight for pay?"

"Yes, the samurai are vassals of the lords they serve," Tonomori explained. "If their lord discards his honor by rebelling against his liege, then they must follow. However, they will not desert him if they are not paid.

"I find it curious, though," he added. "The knights of Europe have their code of chivalry, as you tell us. We have Bushido, the way of the warrior. There are obviously ideals. However, there are also the facts of plain reality. For me and the other samurai, war and fighting is a way of life, of honor. In Europe, it is more a business, like selling rice. But what I know of the daimyos, and what you tell me of your princes, persuades me that greed exists everywhere."

Tonomori gulped some cold tea and accepted a fresh bowl from Toriko. "I think the same pot boils in my country as it does in yours, or in France, or in Spain, or anywhere else. And the greediest and the strongest usually win the biggest pieces."

"Further complicated by the way that the world is so rapidly changing," Diana added.

"Yes, but not necessarily for the better. We dislike change. Look at the guns the Portuguese introduced into Japan only a few years ago. Many samurai fear the guns. It takes many years of training to become a samurai. But an *ashigaru* with a gun can kill a skilled samurai with only a few weeks of teaching. The shot goes through our armor like rice paper."

"My father said the same thing," Diana commented. "When they first began using guns in Europe, the captains of the lance companies used to hang or mutilate any gunners they caught. That happens no longer. Guns are cheap and effective and now everyone is using them, like it or not. I agree, though, everything is changing.

"Let me explain," she went on. "The merchants have gained enormous power, along with the guilds. With their wealth, they can afford—putting it bluntly—to bribe the princes who need money, in order to get the concessions they want. My father knew this when he quietly had ships built for trade. He risked his position. In France, they would have stripped him of his rank. Nobles are supposed to derive their funds from the lands they hold.

"In any event, money is power and my country is going

125

to need a lot of it. I expect to see a rebellion in my lifetime. My father was sure of it, but he tried to avoid it.''

"Well, if things are as you say they are, then what chance have you against the King of Spain?'' Tonomori inquired skeptically. "He is married to the Queen of England, is that not so? And he is king of all those other lands, correct? Then how do you think you can stop him?''

"I can't, really. But did you even bother to think about that when you swore revenge against two powerful lords in your own land?''

Tonomori's silence acknowledged her argument. Seeing that she had scored a point, Diana rushed on. "I can't stop his armies, but with my rank and my wealth, I can certainly cause a lot of trouble. *That's* what I can and will do.''

"I can understand that,'' Toriko said, settling gracefully into the lotus position. If they were not going to resume practice immediately, she wanted to be comfortable. "But I do not understand one thing. As you have explained to us, Europe is not so very much different from Japan in many respects—ambition, guns, war, changing times, these all seem very similar to me. But you said affairs in Europe are more complex.''

"Ah, yes, I was coming to that.'' Diana started to speak, but stopped to think clearly. The ship shuddered through the waves and their shadows moved as the bronze lamps swayed in the chartroom. "But perhaps I will save that explanation for later because it is the most difficult issue to understand. It is well that we have many months ahead of us, because by the time we reach Europe, I hope you will be able to understand.''

"This complicating factor, you mean?'' Tonomori asked. "Well, what is it?''

"In a word,'' said Diana, "it is called religion.''

Toriko's fingers found the beads of the crucifix at her throat.

Chapter Nine

"Are they all madmen?" Tonomori demanded angrily. He scowled at a crewman who had turned at the sound of his voice. The man scurried away. They were all edgy around Tonomori, the way a man might tread gently around a sleeping boar with razor-sharp tusks.

"They must be," Toriko answered. She kept her eyes on the greens and silvers of the water. The *Schoen* was hugging the coast, and a sailor in the bow was casting a lead weight to sound the depth. The weather was fair but the winds contrary, the clouds troubled in a brilliant sky of blues, yellows, and rich gold. The helmsman brought the ship on a seaward tack when the leadman warned that sand was coming up on the dab of tallow stuck to the weight. In these waters, a ship caught on a sandbar would be torn to pieces.

De Wynte was very cautious and would breathe easier when they were in blue water again. They were making good time and had been becalmed only twice. The captain kept a careful record of the journey in a chart, called a *rutter,* on which he engraved across thin copper sheets all details of coastline, currents, depths, condition of sea bottom, winds, and the myriad elements that another captain could use to retrace the voyage of the *Schoen.*

Tonomori and Toriko, leaning over the railing, watched the fish jump while they discussed what their mistress had said about the deep hatred separating Catholic and Protestant.

Thus, a man would torture his enemy, rape his wife and daughters, loot and burn his house, slaughter the servants, and raid his cattle and shipping—all in the name of religion. After listening patiently to Diana's explanations, it had seemed to them that Europeans were even bigger fools than they had imagined.

"If our priests caused that much trouble in Japan," Tonomori had said, when she had finished, "the shogun would have them all slaughtered."

Diana had looked shocked.

"It is true," Tonomori had insisted. "When the *yamabushi*—they are the Buddhist warrior priests of the mountains—get out of hand, as they do from time to time, then the daimyos ride in and burn the monastery and everyone in it."

"That is horrible," Diana had objected.

"Not really. I've killed a couple of them myself on occasion, when they got too arrogant," Tonomori had confessed. He had not looked repentant. "If priests want to meddle, then they can take their chances as the rest of us must. Our way is better, I think. It keeps everyone alert."

Diana had declined to join them on deck, preferring to catch up on entries in her journal. At the railing, Toriko pointed out the moss and barnacles encrusting the hull at the waterline. The ship would have to be dragged ashore and scraped once they reached India—if they did reach it. The journey was extremely dangerous, and was ventured only by the lure of immense profits to be made in trading.

Besides typhoons, the sudden squalls that came out of nowhere, uncharted reefs, submerged rocks, and sandbars, the perils included pirates, as ever-present and numerous as vermin.

A cry of alarm from a lookout on the mainmast shattered the calm. Tonomori looked up and quickly saw the cause—small, triangular sails, like shark's teeth, dead ahead.

The ship heeled suddenly with the groan of timbers, as the helmsman brought her hard into the wind. In the cabin she shared with Toriko, Diana slammed her journal shut as she heard a horn bray on deck. Men ran as commands were shouted, and she could feel the tension run the entire length of the *Schoen*.

"Pirates!" Toriko called out as she flashed into the cabin.

"I must get out of this dress," Diana answered quickly, reaching behind to untie her lacings, "and into proper clothing."

"The captain said specifically that you are to remain in your cabin."

"What about you?"

"The captain did not mention me, but it would not matter if he had," Toriko replied tersely. With amazing agility, she had shucked her kimono and replaced it with a plain one. With a thin cord, she tied back its drooping sleeves, then bent to wrap her lower legs with strips of dark cloth, so she would not trip on the billowing *hakama* into which she had tucked the kimono.

Toriko looked up to see Diana wriggling out of her dress. "What about the captain's orders, Diana-san?"

"*I* own this ship, and the captain can go boil his head," Diana snapped. "You know that I wouldn't miss this for anything."

Within minutes, she had donned her kimono and *hakama*, knotted the light armor into place, and adjusted her mailed *hachimaki*. Her hair was tied back out of the way with a black ribbon at the nape. The women hefted their weapons, sharp *naginatas* capable of cutting a man in half, and headed for the deck. There they found Tonomori and his two men already armed and armored and in position on the forecastle.

Tonomori turned his head as he felt Diana at his elbow.

"Here they come," he pointed. "They are too small to force us to stop, so they are going to have to try to board us." His quiver bristled with arrows and more were lying at his feet.

Many small boats, from twenty to thirty feet in length, were bearing down on them, their sails cupping the spanking breeze. They had swarmed out of the small green islands dead ahead to starboard, but with the wind at their backs and the *Schoen* tacking hard for blue water and deeper swells, the pirates were closing fast.

De Wynte interrupted them. "Didn't you hear, Countess? You are supposed to be below. I was in no position to save you from the gravest perils previously, but now that is my responsibility so far as I am able."

"I heard. I'm not going," Diana retorted.

"As the captain, then, I must remind you that I am responsible for your safety." His voice was rising.

"And I must remind *you* that I own this vessel and everything in her. And I intend to defend what is mine," Diana told him. She showed no sign of complying.

De Wynte threw up his hands in defeat. With the countess talking through clenched teeth, he might as well save his breath for the quarterdeck. He was going to need it.

"At least, go back amidships behind the mainmast," he pleaded. "There is not enough cover for all of you here."

To his surprise, Diana followed his suggestion. She thought that he was being reasonable, so she and Toriko took up their positions there and waited.

A shot puffed from a small cannon aboard one of the pirate craft and the ball hummed raggedly overhead, landing harmlessly far astern. They were aiming for the rigging.

The *Schoen*'s decks were cleared for action. All trunks, crates, and barrels had been dumped unceremoniously into the hold, to be sorted out later. Diana noted the precision of the gun crews; she had seen de Wynte drilling them relentlessly in practice. The artillery—bronze culverins and the smaller sakers—on the starboard side were being charged from leather powder buckets. Besides the ramrod, the men were also ready with sponges to cool the gun and snuff any embers left which might set off a new powder charge, and the "worm," a corkscrew to clear a ball if a charge became wet. Three men were aloft with muskets, and Diana could see the thin trail of smoke from their slow-burning fuses.

"They are *Wako*, Captain," Tonomori shouted.

De Wynte waved his hand from the quarterdeck to indicate he heard, but he swore aloud.

"Goddamit!" he exclaimed bitterly. That was all they

needed! The East Indies pirates were a thoroughly vicious lot at best, but the *Wako* were the worst, the scourge of the Asian coast from India to China.

Wako was the Chinese word for "dwarf," which they derisively applied to the small Japanese pirates who had been plundering their shores for centuries. De Wynte knew them to be the dregs of Japan, outcasts in their own country, which they also raided. Fearless, knowing no pity, the *Wako* wielded the same razor-sharp swords as the samurai.

The small cannon known as the bow chaser barked, and Diana jumped at the sound. The smoke from the gun smelled like rotten eggs. The boats were moving fast, difficult to hit on the fly. When they drew close enough, the gun crews would switch from solid ball to shovels full of musket bullets. Fired at close range, the culverins could rake the entire deck of one of the small boats with one burst.

Once again the bow chaser fired and the crew cheered. A hit. It was not enough. De Wynte knew that some of them would get close enough to use their grappling hooks, and then would be up and over the rail in seconds. Once on deck, the *Wako* would be slashing at his men and the rigging with their terrible swords. De Wynte had heard tales of horror and carnage from other captains who had fought the *Wako* and somehow survived. He could only hope his men were ready now.

Another cheer! A saker smashed a boat to splinters. Tonomori felt a bump as the *Schoen* ran over a *Wako* boat that had not come about fast enough. More cheers of defiance. The gun crews switched quickly to loads of musket balls. One boat that had come knifing in to intercept was completely engulfed in a hellish rain of lead. Tonomori saw that the inside of the vessel was sprayed with gore; the few men left alive were writhing in agony.

But then several boats thumped alongside and grappling hooks dug into the railings. Tonomori was already sending flights of arrows into the open vessels. Oshabiri moved higher onto the forecastle for a better angle, as the *Schoen* became a death ship with a trail of corpses bobbing in her wake.

The first wave of pirates came howling over the rails in a body, right into the blades and muskets of the crew. Diana slashed out with the *naginata* and cut the legs out from under one pirate before he even hit the deck, then fell back under the murderous press of another, fighting for her life. Toriko took a third in his chest with her spear, and was saved from the charge of a fourth by a crosscut from Yamahito, who had been sent aft by Tonomori to help the women.

Diana killed her attacker with a cut through his temple, and he rolled at her feet. She rejoined Toriko to stab and slash at the remaining pirates.

But more were pouring onto the deck and spreading out, despite the desperate efforts of the crew to throw them back. Tonomori and Oshabiri left the forecastle to join the fighting below.

The next few moments would be critical. The *Schoen* was slowing from the drag of the pirate boats clinging to her side. A few more minutes, and they could break through into blue waters, beyond the point where the pirates, accustomed to coastal fighting, could board her effectively.

If they made it through. The *Wako* were making frenzied attempts to kill the helmsman, who was protected by two crewmen's heavy swords and shields. Pirates' bodies were stacked bloodily in front of them, but they were getting weary.

When they were not slashing at the crew, the *Wako* hacked furiously at the rigging—anything to foul the sails and slow the *Schoen* so more of the pirates could swarm aboard.

Diana was almost overwhelmed by the savagery of the attack. She had no time to think through the horror of it all, the screaming, the blood, the numbing noise, inextricably mixed with the smell of gunpowder and sour vomit . . . only time to block, to cut, to slash like an animal.

Tonomori, seeing Diana and Toriko in the thick of the fighting, began cutting his way to them. When he was almost there, he saw Diana fall, and with a shout he bulled his way through.

One of the pirates was on her, but Diana stabbed blindly upward with the *tanto* torn from her sash, and felt its guard scrape his chin. The *tanto* point had gone all the way through the roof of his mouth into his brain. Blood flooded down her arm and into her face in thick ropes, and when she spit redly to clear her mouth, Diana thought she would retch convulsively.

Then Tonomori was astride her, holding attackers back while she crawled out from behind him, dragging her spear. With a deep sob of a breath, she lunged back in, skewering a pirate who tried to wrestle her to the deck with a knife.

The fighting was so intense no one had room to swing a weapon. Toriko had shortened the grip on her spear so she could stab at close quarters, and Diana followed her example. Tonomori shifted the *tachi* to his left hand, handle up, with the flat of the blade against his forearm to shield against blows, while with the heavy short sword in his right hand he slashed and jabbed at the twisted faces of the *Wako*.

Slowly, the pirates gave way, becoming more reckless with each step backward. Tonomori's armor held the point of a knife thrust from below. A pirate he had thought dead had treacherously lunged when a good target came close. Tonomori plunged the *wakizashi* deeply into the eyesocket, then wrenched it free and stepped carefully over the limp form. The heavy short sword was red halfway to the hilt.

"Hit them again!" he yelled. The crew's counterattack was faltering from weariness. The pirates, putting up one last gasp of resistance, began to press the crew back, giving ground now only when dead. De Wynte had joined from the quarterdeck, shattering one man's head with a pistol ball, and firing so closely at one attacker that the man's clothes caught fire and he threw himself into the hissing sea.

As Tonomori waded into the rest of them, the assailants reeled from the blows of the *tachi*, the two-handed killing sword his fury drove so deeply. Another went down. And another, this one with his arm and shoulder completely severed. The only sounds now were guttural and grunting, and the throaty rattle of dying men.

Suddenly, they were at the bloody railings and the *Wako* were no more. Gunners in the rigging fired a few sporadic shots at the fleeing vessels while crewmen chopped through the grapple chains with axes. The *Schoen* was in the clear, with blue water foaming beneath her bow.

Diana caught her breath in shuddering sobs. At any number of times, she could have been killed, and now that realization was sinking in. De Wynte was seeing to his men: Five were dead and three wounded, one seriously. If he recovered, he would eventually wear a steel hook where his left hand had been.

Those who were not busily repairing battle damage began throwing the bodies of the *Wako* into the sea. Their own comrades would be sewn into shrouds, prayed over later, and then slid into the alien waters, too.

The stench of battle was everywhere, but that would soon be remedied with some buckets of sea water. Tonomori wished they could do the same for the bilges, which he thought were far worse.

The survivors were numb from the shock—but they were alive. The fight just as easily could have gone the other way, and they knew that, too. The samurai had made the difference, he and his men—and the women. The crew would remember the name "samurai."

One of the crew approached Tonomori, who had retrieved his bow. No one aboard ship had ever seen anything like it. It was almost seven feet long, but Tonomori nocked his arrows on the bottom third of its curve. The Japanese, it seemed, did everything differently.

"Excuse me, sir, but I think the countess is not feeling well. Thought you might like to know."

Tonomori turned. "Thank you, Hans-san."

Hans stepped aside, pleased that the samurai remembered his name.

On reaching her side, Tonomori saw with relief that the blood on Diana was not her own, that she was only exhausted. She had suffered no wounds, only a few bruises forming. Toriko, too, had survived unscathed, as had his own men.

Diana maintained her composure until a crewman picked up the trunkless legs of the first pirate she had killed, then doubled up over the side and was violently ill.

The legs splashed whitely into the sea, then she heard the distressed voice of the crewman as he struggled to the rail alongside her. "Uh, excuse me, ma'am, you've got company."

Chapter Ten

"So this is what they call golden Goa. Well, well, well!" Diana exclaimed in considerable disenchantment. India's sights and smells assaulted her senses, and now her nine months aboard ship betrayed her feet; even the solid quay on which she was standing seemed to heave beneath her. Soon after feeling the merciless sun, she had agreed to use a broad-brimmed straw hat to protect her sensitive, fair complexion and to shade her eyes from the almost blinding glare.

In her shadow lay the *Schoen*, as her thirty crewmen swarmed over the rigging and the hull to repair the wear of her perilous voyage through Asian waters to the port on India's western coast. They worked hard and rapidly, for Captain de Wynte had informed them that no one would go ashore until repairs were completed to his satisfaction.

The captain now was locked in vociferous debate with larcenous port officials, who had anticipated a fat prize when the *Schoen* had dropped anchor. A Dutch vessel in Portuguese waters ordinarily could at best expect confiscation, with imprisonment for the crew for good measure. The port officers were more than a little disappointed to find de Wynte's license, obtained from the *Casa de India* in Lisbon, in good order. It allowed him to trade anywhere in the Portuguese empire.

Thus restrained, they countered by inventing taxes on the *Schoen*'s cargo. But de Wynte wasn't having any of their imaginary tariffs and so informed them in fluent, flamboyant Portuguese.

On the quay, Diana and her companions could hear him clearly as the port officials scuttled down the gangplank.

"You raggedy-assed shitpickers can try your extortion elsewhere," de Wynte yelled after them. "You're all vermin!" Portuguese workmen on dock stopped to listen in admiration. The captain glanced toward Diana, halted his tirade momentarily, and smiled as he doffed his cap in respect. Then he turned his attention back to the departing officials, cupping his hands for greater effect. "Assholes!" he screamed.

Their ineffectual rejoinder was lost as they hurried off, their departure encouraged by his raging vehemence.

At Diana's elbow, Tonomori did not display any emotion but was appalled, not by the captain's vigorously profane anger in his finely accented Portuguese—for he greatly admired the display and completely understood the language after months of tutoring—but by the port itself. *Golden Goa? A gilded cesspit was more like it*, Tonomori thought in Portuguese. He found it easier to understand a language by thinking in it.

Tonomori had been taught Chinese the same way, but he had not thought in Chinese in a long time. As a result, he had forgotten much of the Chinese language he knew, which was just as well because he thoroughly loathed the few Chinese he had ever met.

There were few men of China trading in India, this Tonomori knew, but they were not of the same rank as the courtiers from Peking who strutted in calculated insolence along Muromanchi Boulevard by the imperial palace in Kyoto. Only the express command of the shogun saved them from immediate decapitation by the insulted samurai. If Tonomori ever got one within a sword's length, the shogun's lamentable oversight would be immediately rectified. *The monkey eaters who deformed the feet of their women had the audacity to snub us as uncivilized*, Tonomori thought. He swore in Portuguese and immediately felt better. "Vá para o diabo!"

The reek of a nearby manure pile hit him like a blow, and Tonomori straightened. He supposed that, if he were forced to spend months in Goa, he could accustom his nose to the assault.

The *Schoen* itself had become vilely redolent in the months at sea. Here in port, they were merely exchanging one batch of smells for another. Oshabiri and Yamahito, standing alongside Lady Toriko, traded incredulous glances and significant nose-holding gestures. Even conditions on the ship—and the *Schoen* was cleaner than most—had not prepared them for this Indian dunghill.

The dock was piled with a variety of goods, which, Diana realized, would represent a fortune when delivered on the docks of Europe. Still, her nose also twitched with distaste. Behind her the bilge pumps of forty vessels were discharging their malodorous contents into the harbor. She recalled wistfully Japan's cleanliness and shook her head; no sense in dwelling on that.

As they picked their way carefully through the bales and bundles, she noted the amount and diversity of riches that the throng of cargo handlers were trundling along the quays. Great sacks of peppercorns from Ceylon lay in untidy piles beside bundles of cotton goods brought from the Gujarat region of western India. A thousand brightly plumed birds squawked their displeasure from within wicker cages. Dock workers swore lustily in a wild mixture of tongues, and everyone shouted to be heard over the din.

Seeing gourd-shaped ingots of Dutch steel awaiting shipment, Tonomori was surprised to be informed by Diana that they were destined for the frenzied preparations for war among Japan's feudal lords. Called *namban tetsu* by the Japanese, the Dutch bars would be hammered into

137

utilitarian samurai swords or even forged into guns. Pyramids of wootz steel—crudely produced in crucibles by Indian processors from an ancient formula—were also destined for Japan's battlefields in various shapes, though the Dutch metal was preferred. Although for centuries she had been an exporter of edged weapons to China and southeast Asian countries, Japan now needed all that her smiths could produce. Diana's curiosity had prompted an incessant barrage of questions that de Wynte patiently answered with full explanations. Privately, he thought he would go mad, but he answered with as much forbearance as he could muster while overseeing crewmen eager to leave tasks unfinished so they could squander their pay ashore.

The ship's guards, heavily armed, stood by the chests of Portuguese gold that had been carried from their country's fortified African ports. The gold would be used in exchange for goods sought after, back in Lisbon. Strongboxes of Japanese silver still in the hold of the *Schoen* would be added to those sold in exchange for such spices as cinnamon, nutmegs, and mace, whose scent was strong, almost overpowering, a help in countering the reek drifting over from nearby cattle pens. Dirt and filth seemed to be everywhere.

In fascination, Diana watched a Portuguese crew offload a terrified Persian stallion from a carrack—a large trading vessel with triangular sails—newly arrived from its route along the Red Sea. The horse, blindfolded, was carefully slung from the end of a crane. The crew deposited the valuable cargo daintily on the quay. The horse's flanks quivered, and his tail lashed away the cloud of flies that eagerly greeted him. As soon as the blindfold was removed, he tried to bite the nearest crewman. Tonomori laughed; obviously a horse of spirit and temper, it behaved exactly as he had expected. Tonomori regarded its golden color as lovely as a sunset.

"That is an Arabian stallion," Diana told him, as if reading his thoughts. "He probably will be the prized possession of one of the Hindu princes of Vijayanagar."

"You have learned much about the cargoes here, Diana-san," Tonomori observed.

138

"I thought it would be well if I did so."

As for the Arab-Persian horse trading in India, the captain had explained to her, the Portuguese had little trouble reconciling their dealings with infidels, whether Hindu or Muslim. They needed the goodwill of the Persian potentates to counter the ever-present menace of the Ottoman Turks in the Mediterranean. So, if the dark cloud blotting their religion had a Muslim whinny and a Hindu hand on the reins, it also offered a silver lining. Horse trading was highly lucrative.

Diana studied the Portuguese carrack with growing professional interest. Its single mainmast was thicker than five men, with two lateen-rigged sails behind and a square mizzen in front, and with a bowsprit sail to drop in front when the wind was up their backside. Six decks of cannon—three at intervals below the quarterdeck, a bank along the main deck, and two levels on the forecastle.

Six months ago, Diana would have been impressed by this towering fortress. At least one hundred and fifty guns. Ah, but looking closely she could see most of them were small-bore and not a one that could match the muzzle plugs on the *Schoen*. The carrack was massive, but shorter in length than the *Schoen* by at least twenty feet though much wider in the beam. "An undergunned washtub," Diana said and thought the captain would have been pleased. Tonomori spat.

Diana and Tonomori, together with Toriko, and with the *ashigaru* as an escort, continued on amid the chaos, past a number of bumboats that ordinarily shuttled to supply ships in the harbor but now lay in the sun for recaulking. They passed lines of iron cannon lashed to heavy wooden frames and open sheds where goods were somewhat protected from the frequent rains. These perishable items would be gone before the monsoon season.

"I don't think you really need to scowl at everyone as I notice that you do, Tonomori-san," Diana told him.

"They *are* moving out of our way, after all," Tonomori pointed out. The samurai wore his body armor, but no leg protection because he was not on horse. His black *hakama* were bunched at the knees, and his calves were wrapped in leggings. On rope sandals, he stepped carefully through the litter. His left hand rested casually on his long sword, but his gaze was alert and sweeping.

"Well, I doubt if any of these people intend to harm us," Diana rejoined.

"Anyone who is here has not come to study court protocol," Tonomori replied firmly, and Diana could see the force of his argument. The Portuguese of Goa had to be a hardy lot. Only the strong survived the long voyage out, and India's oppressive climate winnowed out any remaining weak. Goa attracted the dregs of Portuguese society. Pickpockets, thieves, whores, and charlatans rubbed elbows with adventurers and opportunists and with everyone else who had an eye to an easy fistful of Asian gold and jewels.

De Wynte already had lost two crewmen who had jumped ship to venture out to islands where they intended to pry up the golden paving stones with which the streets were said to be covered. For every truth, a thousand wild rumors spread, and for each of these plenty of dreamers were ready to chase over the horizon after golden rainbows.

Tonomori groaned as Diana headed for the bazaar, a rabbit warren of shops and stalls bordering the dock area beyond the storage sheds. Here they were assailed by more shouting, as everyone tried to outdo the competitors in lauding his own display of ointments, perfumes, saddles, and brass pans.

From his safe perch on Oshabiri's shoulder, Saru spotted a caged monkey and screamed insults. The target of this criticism responded by jetting a stream of urine while clinging to the bars. A passerby who happened to be walking through the arc shrilly demanded recompense from the owner for his soiled garments and injured dignity.

Saru, his honor assuaged and his courage unquestioned—if only to himself—seized the opportunity to help himself to the wares of a nearby fruit vendor while everyone watched the shouting match, marked by much arm waving.

Oshabiri retrieved his pet, and the shopping expedition hurried on—or, at least, tried to. Street urchins were underfoot everywhere, and the visitors were besieged on all sides by eager merchants. It was a market day, even busier than usual.

"Fresh betel nuts, sirs, madams!"

"Silver bangles, fit for a queen," cried a worker in silver. Diana passed along.

"Carved flutes. Carved flutes. Fine work. Who will buy?" Tonomori studied one of these, tried a few notes, found it satisfactory, and made a purchase. He tucked the instrument into his sash alongside his *wakizashi*. The fingering would be worked out later, at his leisure.

"Beans, the finest beans . . ."

"Knives, daggers, swords." The arms dealer looked hopefully at Tonomori, then saw how well armed he was already. The vendor spat as Tonomori walked on by.

"Saffron, golden as the lady's hair . . ."

While keeping alert to any potential threat to his mistress's safety, Tonomori examined the side streets for anything even remotely resembling a brothel. As with the flute, he would play at his leisure when the occasion permitted.

A swarthy gnome of an old man stepped from his shop and bowed deeply.

"Ah, good morning. It is a fine morning, is it not? We have a saying here that the thoughts of the young are always of love," he called in Portuguese with a toothless grin. His mouth was a hole punched in old leather. "And when love flags, what is better than to render it assistance? . . ."

With a practiced flourish, the merchant brought out for their perusal two artificial phalluses, one of wood, the other of ivory.

Diana stared, blinking, amazed by the brazenness of the transparent effort to annoy her.

"Not that *you* would ever need them, lady, but we also have powdered rhinoceros horn—the genuine item to be sure, to prolong a man's powers—and certain ointments to stir a lover's interest," he said.

"These, however," he paused for effect, caressing the ivory, "need no explanation."

Diana continued to stare at the dark rosewood carving,

which was completely faithful to the sizable original on which it was modeled.

Lady Toriko delicately took the stalk of ivory from the merchant, turning it slowly between her thumb and forefinger.

"This is very good work, Diana-san," Toriko assured her in a tone she might use to describe a back scratcher.

Diana's eyes widened, her cheeks burning.

A snort of laughter escaped from Tonomori, despite his effort to remain politely impassive. As the bobbing peddler held the rosewood almost under Diana's nose, Tonomori's mind was running to the practical: *splinters,* he was thinking and found the vision ludicrous.

"We go now," Diana blurted, and hurried away. "Please come!" she called over her shoulder.

Tonomori and Toriko dutifully turned to follow their mistress, though surprised and baffled at her discomfort. Such items, commonplace in Japan, were used by any man or woman who might feel a pressing need for them.

Behind them, the old merchant shared in the general laughter at Diana's obvious embarrassment and chagrin. The venerable scoundrel enjoyed outraging the occasional young women he encountered. It was one of his few remaining pleasures since his advanced years had placed him beyond the aid of his own merchandise.

Diana huffed along briskly in silence. What really galled her was that the display and the offer had been deliberate, to disconcert her. She ignored the blandishments of other shopkeepers, some of whom were still chuckling and smirking.

Tonomori and the rest of her escort eventually caught up with her. "I sympathize with your feelings, Diana-san," Toriko said as she hobbled along on platform shoes hardly designed for rapid walking. Diana felt a flush of gratitude; at least, someone seemed to understand her discomfiture and annoyance.

"The shopkeeper was totally outrageous," Toriko told her soothingly. "I cannot blame you for walking away like that. . . ."

Diana turned. "Thank you. I . . ."

Toriko continued, "I am sure, though, that you could have bought it at half that price."

Diana's chin snapped up. "I prefer not to discuss it," she replied evenly, exercising her prerogative of selecting the conversation.

"As you wish," Toriko said, still puzzled, failing to comprehend Diana's reaction to the merchant's crudity.

They paused at a shop that carried only gemstones; its reputation was for high quality. To pay back Tonomori for having laughed at her, Diana secretly vowed to take her time here, leaving no stone unturned.

The *ashigaru* squatted in a corner and played with Saru. Toriko remained with Diana. Tonomori passed the time by disrobing, within the realm of his ample imagination, every woman who passed in the street—even the fat ones. It had been a very long voyage.

The gem merchant, a pleasant man with heavy jowls and an impressive girth, was wealthy and his shop comfortable. His clients expected comfort and got it. Cushions were piled on the spotless floor. A slim woman, darkly beautiful and adorned with many bracelets and necklaces of gold, served strong, dark tea and stacks of sweet cakes. Armed guards, remaining discreetly out of sight, took a professional interest in Tonomori and his swords, in the way a fighting man sizes up another.

In turn, Tonomori had already evaluated and dismissed them with a glance. They could prevent a robbery or thwart anyone trying to break through the heavily barred window, but they could not match up against a trained killer. They had no balance, no poise.

Tonomori kept looking up the street. He had the impression that they were being followed: a face, a form, a movement receding too quickly into the shadows whenever he glanced that way. He was not positive, though, and he wished to be. Swallowing a bit of pride, he called to Toriko.

"Yes, Tonomori-san?" Toriko responded after excusing herself to Diana. She was glad for a diversion. The sapphires, emeralds, and winking rubies that Diana was examining so assiduously meant nothing to her. The Japanese did not wear jewelry, and she had no interest in gems.

"We are being followed, I think, watched out of perhaps more than simple curiosity," Tonomori explained. "The person is small and quick. I could not see the details of his face."

"No matter," said Toriko confidently. "If our mistress asks, please tell her that I am looking for a privy, and that I did not wish to interrupt the transaction." She slipped out the door.

Minutes passed. Toriko returned. "You are right; we are being watched," she reported quietly. "He moves with much sly speed. I did not see his features either, but that doesn't matter. I saw how he moves, and that was enough. I will recognize him anywhere. What we must decide now is what it may mean."

"I agree," Tonomori said. "It could mean nothing. Maybe the Portuguese are keeping track of us. Or our mistress may indeed have an enemy here who wishes her harm. We should assume the worst and take all necessary precautions."

"At this point, I do not feel it is desirable to inform Diana-san," Toriko advised. "She has learned much from me, but she still might betray our suspicions. Better to let her act natural, to put our shadow off his guard. If we are being watched now, then the ship is also being watched. I will slip out tonight and learn what we need to know."

"Very good," Tonomori said. "Are you carrying any arms now beside your *tanto?*"

"Yes, two *shuriken*," Toriko informed him, referring to the star-shaped throwing knives preferred by *ninja*. They were small, thus easily concealed, and very deadly, even when not tipped with poison. Because it would be rude to ask whether hers were tipped, Tonomori had no other questions before Toriko returned to Diana's side.

Diana and the merchant were finishing the customary haggling over a price. She had selected several emeralds, which she would have set in white gold in Antwerp. The rubies she had chosen were of excellent color and "water," or clarity.

"I must compliment you on your choices." The merchant's smile was an ingratiating smirk. "The stones are among the finest I have seen in a long time, and you got them at an excellent price. Should you wish to make further purchases, I will be most happy to assist you in any way."

Diana stood. "Thank you, and I will consider your generous offer." The gems would be delivered to the ship the following day and payment taken there in gold and silver. Diana could hardly believe the quality of her purchase, and the price. Just one of those stones would command a purchase price in Antwerp equal to what she had just agreed to pay for a small handful. Most of the stones in the merchant's trays would, in fact, eventually find their way to Antwerp, the clearinghouse for Europe's gem dealers and cutters.

Diana stopped outside, considering where to go next. They had forgotten a midday meal, but that was remedied quickly at a food vendor's stall with a spicy dish of rice and vegetables. Tonomori ate three bowlfuls, and Yamahito four, but Oshabiri and the women contented themselves with one steaming helping. For once, Saru did not pester them for handouts. He had just stuffed himself with sweet cakes filched shamelessly in the gem merchant's shop.

Feeling well fed, and reveling in her freedom after months of confinement aboard ship, Diana wanted to walk about, to explore, to find everything that was there to be seen, felt, experienced.

An idea had been forming in her mind, turning round and round like a cartwheel jogging in a much traveled rut. Diana wanted to learn much more about the Portuguese sea empire, about its ships, ports, cargoes, trade winds, and navigation, and about the daring men who made it fabulously successful and wealthy.

Her own rich estates were in Spanish hands. But her father's ships had represented wealth even greater than the estates, and now they were hers. Diana saw them as a promising beginning for what she had been planning. That

145

she would personally kill the Duke of Alvino, Diana had no doubt, but that would not be enough. She wanted more—revenge on a grand scale against a king and his nobles who ignored the reign of terror of the assassins and robbers whose plundering of nations meant enslavement for the helpless subjects.

Every cargo carried by her ships would be trade pried from Spain, and Diana intended that the repayment would be in bloody coins. Diana would form her own sea empire, and with its gold she would wage private war against the King of Spain, in the marketplace, in the alleys, on the battlefield.

With the fast ships that she intended to build, Diana would cut into Spain's vital monopolies of trade from the New World. She would finance a network of spies through her commercial agents in Europe's most important trade centers. Her gold would be transformed into enough lead and steel to arm the king's enemies.

And in the midst of her manipulating and plotting, Diana intended to show herself only as one of the king's most loyal peers, without his ever learning that she was as deadly as she was seemingly devoted.

That was the scheme of things. The outcome would depend on whether she could remain in command. Her first battle would be that of survival.

Diana intended to retain control of her ships through her father's agents. Everyone would expect her to sell the ships, to seek the protection of a husband in an alliance with a powerful and noble family. Let the husband attend to details, they would say; do not concern yourself.

But Diana also had the spirit of independence so typical of her Dutch ancestors. The male side of the line had all been men of the sword, holding against all opposition what they had taken. Their blood sang in her veins. To surrender herself to a husband would be to lose her freedom. Her body and everything she owned would become his property to use as he pleased. Having already breathed the air of open skies and sailed across strange seas, Diana would never give up that precious freedom. She owed it to herself, to her father's memory, to her own people.

All her scheming could be made possible; Diana was confident that she could bring it about. In this, she had reason for hope. Her father had been a foresighted man who employed competent and loyal men, like Captain de Wynte, in key positions and assured their loyalty by paying them well. His shipping interests were not generally known, or, as de Wynte had pointed out, the Spanish authorities would have confiscated the lot. They had no reason to suspect the existence of the ships as an essential part of his holdings.

In most lands, noblemen relied on their estates for their income and looked down on those who engaged in any form of trade; codes of behavior were rigid and, in the Netherlands, for those who broke them, unforgiving. On the other hand, people tended to be practical; they had to. Life was a constant struggle. The very ground on which they stood had been torn from the relentless North Sea. Their very existence was ignored by an indifferent monarch except when he wanted more money.

If the king underestimated the new Countess de Edgemont, that would be all to the good. He might not know her wrath, but he would feel it. There would be her reward!

Diana had already persuaded two samurai to serve her, and they were no less proud than the stubborn Dutch. She could enlist others. It was a promising beginning.

Her thoughts actively engaged, Diana hardly spared a glance for her surroundings, the whitewashed homes with their tiled roofs and carefully tended gardens. Here and there, churches squatted with their Latin crosses that proclaimed the Catholic faith the Portuguese had carried, along with the cannon, across the stormy seas. They neared the old red brick wall, which at one time had protected the main colony but now was unnecessary because of the large fort guarding the sea entrance. From a hillock, she could see the tidy orchards and the patchwork of fields with their row crops along Goa's undulating northern coastline. While she stood watching, two masts separated themselves from the harbor's wooden forest as a caravel put to sea. The smaller, more lightly armed caravels carried less cargo but were more seaworthy, perfect vessels for hugging a coast or crossing unknown seas. Columbus had discovered the New World in a caravel—for the Spanish, after the Portuguese king had turned him down. Diana gritted her teeth at the ill fortune that had dropped the New World into Spain's grasping hands.

At her side, Tonomori's thoughts were steeped in conflict. Diana had been urging him to plunge his gold into the Goa marketplace, to buy spices and gems—whatever extra cargo the *Schoen* would carry—and then to sell them in Antwerp for a hundred times their present value.

He had resisted. Tonomori was no merchant. The very thought was repugnant to him. But in the end, his pride had buckled under the loyalty and devotion he retained for the memory of Lord Betsuo. His pride remained a seething lump in his belly, but Tonomori knew Diana was right. He realized now that in the Netherlands, with enough gold, he could expect to outfit a ship with a load of guns and cannon, and then to claw his way back to Japan. With the guns and an army of picked men, Tonomori could blast Masanori and Atsuhira into eternity. He would piss on their graves and be done with it. Lord Betsuo's spirit would at last know peace, and Tonomori would be free to seek his own destiny. For this goal, he was willing to suffer any indignity, endure any hardship.

And afterward, who could tell? He could offer the guns and his services to the shogun, win his own lands, and perhaps one day find the answer to the riddle of his own origins.

Tonomori's thumb rubbed along the edge of his sword guard, the *tsuba* that bore the hidden carving of the sixteen-petaled chrysanthemum, the imperial crest—and the key to everything that he was. Or could be.

Tonomori filled his lungs and stretched his muscles. The breeze was fresh and clean, a marked improvement over the crowded shops and streets, not to mention the choking hold of the *Schoen*. The sky was completely alien, shot through with gold and pinks so different from anything he had ever known in Japan. The world was revealing itself as more immense than he could possibly have imagined.

To the west, he was told, beyond the vast expanse of sky and sparkling ocean lay Africa, the unfathomable giant. Past the Cape of Good Hope, and beyond the Sea of Darkness to the north, lay Europe and more unknowns.

The sun was an orange ball dwindling on the horizon. Shadows grew long and thin. "It is time, I believe, that we returned to the ship," Diana said. She looked around, her thoughts turning now to practical matters. Her brow creased in irritation. *We're lost.*

Toriko sensed her predicament. "Allow me to lead the way, Diana-san."

Diana responded with a slight bow and a smile. "I had lost my bearings, you know."

"I thought it might seem impolite to say so," Toriko remarked.

"What difference does it make?" Tonomori asked rudely.

The women had nothing to say in reply. He could be overly brusque at times, but lately he had been even grouchier than usual.

They walked slowly, taking their time, but Tonomori was at pains to conceal his impatience. If he tried to hurry the women along at a more reasonable pace, they might balk; they could be so touchy.

Squadrons of gulls were beating in with the rising wind. Perhaps rain would come by morning.

Toriko was wrapped in introspection while admiring a field of swaying red poppies. *So beautiful,* she thought. *There is beauty in every land we meet.*

A poem was forming, an almost tangible presence. She would put this one down on paper later, but her mind already was applying the brush strokes.

> *O foolish, happy flowers,*
> *nodding in strange dreams,*
> *in the hand that has picked them.*

Perhaps she would offer the verse to Tonomori when she had finished. Toriko was pleased that he had a taste for haiku. Most samurai didn't know a poem from an earpick. Toriko was feeling content and complete.

Two sparrows, darting up from the field, flew low and away into the sun. Even as Toriko narrowed her eyes against the glare, she spun to cry out a warning.

Diana heard the heavy roar of the gun only at the moment she felt herself being flung backward through the air into blackness. . . .

Chapter Eleven

Diana regained consciousness with a groan. She ached all over and felt grit in her mouth. Gingerly, she touched her fingers to her cheeks and then brushed them through the tangles of her hair.

She realized that she was being cradled. "He missed," Tonomori murmured close to her ear, sensing the darting concern in her eyes.

"Missed? It doesn't feel like it," Diana exclaimed thinly. Tonomori held her down as she tried to struggle to her feet, and she decided not to resist. Yamahito stooped and offered an earthen bottle of water. Diana rinsed her mouth, turned her head to the side, and spat widely into the dusty road. Then she drank deeply and gratefully.

Toriko and Oshabiri were returning. Oshabiri was carrying a heavy musket as well as his bow.

"I can get up now," Diana protested. Her head was clearing. Tonomori consented to help her stand.

"The assassin got clean away," Toriko reported in evident disgust. Tonomori said nothing but was cursing himself. They should have anticipated such an attempt, he knew, and taken more precautions, instead of parading as though on a festival holiday.

"What happened?" Diana asked, her eyes narrowed. Her temper was raging. Already, it seemed, her father's enemies were trying to kill her off, the last of the de Edgemont house.

Toriko took a deep breath and explained. The beauty of the field of poppies that had drawn her attention was responsible for saving Diana's life. Otherwise, she would now be the assassin's victim. It was when the birds flew out of the poppies to safety that Toriko's *ninja* training had screamed danger. At almost the same instant, Tonomori had seen Toriko tensed to spring and had swept Diana out of the way with his arm even while moving in the direction where his instinct told him the ambush would originate.

In less than a heartbeat, the bullet had torn through Tonomori's kimono sleeve at the very spot where Diana had been. Diana's misfortune was limited to being knocked unconscious by the force with which Tonomori had thrown her to the ground.

With her mistress lying senseless in the dirt, Toriko had kicked off her *geta,* the wooden platform shoes, hiked up her kimono, and raced after the would-be killer, with Oshabiri flying after her, arrow nocked. Tonomori and Yamahito had stood over Diana in case the road had been bracketed by other guns.

"The plan was well conceived," Toriko said as she slipped back into the *geta.* "The sun was in our eyes, his position hidden at the end of a drainage ditch. From there, the assassin easily made good his escape. He was too far away, and dodging between those houses nearby, for pursuit to be possible. But, because of the way he looked as he ran, I know who he is—the faceless one who was watching us at the shop of the gem seller."

"Someone was watching us?" Diana asked in surprise. "How can you be so sure it was the same person if you had not seen his face?"

"Experience, Diana-san," Toriko replied. "Everyone walks, stands, and runs differently, as we have been taking up in your lessons. When one learns the extent of the difference, it is even possible to identify someone in the dark.

"The weapon was left behind as he fled from us," Toriko went on. "From what I am able to tell of its make, it seems to be a very expensive musket. Someone must want you dead very badly."

Tonomori was carefully examining the gun, a wheel lock, well made, with dark stock and black barrel. All brass fittings had been removed to help in its concealment. A killer's weapon for just the kind of ambush they had experienced.

Awareness was dawning on Diana's face. "The gem seller's shop? . . ." she asked. "Then you suspected? . . ."

Toriko bowed deeply. "Yes, but we were not sure. . . . This is my fault. I should have been more careful. It was my responsibility."

"And mine!" Tonomori was furious with himself. His mistress had almost been killed because of their carelessness—and he dared still call himself a samurai? Tonomori prepared to face Diana's anger.

"We were all stupid, I think," Diana told them. "I am not displeased with you. On the contrary, your concern for my safety pleases me very much. But I now see that I have been underestimating my enemy. We return to the ship at once.

"Tonight," she added with firm decision, "we hold a council of war!"

At the ship, after informing Captain de Wynte of what had occurred, Diana sat humbly in his cabin while she endured a thundering lecture on her stubbornness, her foolhardy disregard for her own safety, and the concern of more experienced people trying to guard her from those with murderous intent.

Diana shifted uncomfortably in her light gown. It was very warm in the cabin, and the hot season had not even begun. She was thankful that they would be hauling close to the African coast when it did. The heat would not be less, but at least they would be a few thousand miles nearer home.

152

". . . and furthermore, if you were my daughter, I would take you over my knee, give you the thumping you deserve, and then lock you in your room," de Wynte declared at the conclusion of his tirade.

"I understand your worry," Diana replied. "But I am not your daughter. If I were, I would not be in this pickle. I am my father's daughter. I will be more careful in the future, I promise you."

"You will remain aboard ship, then, under guard, while we are in port?"

"Hardly, Captain, but I *will* be cautious," Diana conceded.

"Aaaaagh!" de Wynte almost shouted, throwing up his hands in exasperation. "At least hire some natives and take a sedan chair like a Christian woman."

"I will, Captain," Diana said, hiding a smile. She was very fond of de Wynte. And when he talked to her like a true Dutch uncle, she knew that she deserved it. But she was not going to change—and he understood that, however reluctantly.

In the flickering candlelight, de Wynte studied Diana's determined countenance. In it, he could see her father—the somewhat triangular face, the high cheekbones, the almost patrician nose, and the downswept mouth capable of relenting in an enchanting smile.

That smile now was disarming de Wynte against his will. Diana could hide it no longer, and hoped that the captain would take no offense. He was capable, tough, and somewhat ruthless—as a captain had to be—but de Wynte, as her faithful servant, must bow to her wishes.

"Very well, Countess, but if you will permit me I will have a word with the samurai Tonomori," the captain said, and left, taking with him a pair of pistols he had concealed within a cloth. At the door, he paused to look back at Diana, who raised a wine glass with which she had been toying, and saluted him.

De Wynte was distraught at the thought of her lying dead alongside a road somewhere, as her father had, knifed to death by murderers. The Spanish authorities had been very apologetic, according to the private intelligence de

153

Wynte had received. There were cutthroats everywhere, the authorities had said. *Especially in the halls of the king,* the captain thought.

Diana listened to his footfalls recede, and then was lost in contemplation. She must continue her training with Toriko, that much was clear. It was equally plain that the rulers of Spain were reaching halfway around the world for her throat. But Diana had escaped the Duke of Alvino before, in fleeing the Netherlands as a girl, and she was confident of prevailing again. She could not prove that Alvino was responsible for the murder of her father, but she nonetheless felt certain of his guilt. She and her samurai would have to lay their plans carefully. Tonight.

Floorboards outside the cabin creaked softly. The door opened slowly.

Diana took a sharp *tanto* from her sleeve and began peeling a piece of fruit with it. "Yes, Señor Carillo?"

"Excuse me, Countess, I was looking for the captain. I did not know that you were here," the young quartermaster said, whipping off his cap and bowing. Diana was very aware of the large knife with its ivory handle hanging from his belt.

Liar, she thought, *you knew I was here. Alone.*

"You only just missed him," Diana told Carillo. "Shall I ring for a crewman to find him for you?" She reached for a silver bell with a black grip.

"That will not be necessary." His pale blue eyes flicked from the bell to the dagger in her hand, weighing his chances. It was not the time. "I will find him myself."

Carillo paused, licking his lips nervously. "Allow me to say that I am very happy that you were not harmed in the unfortunate incident in town this afternoon. If you should require any assistance in the future, perhaps I could act as your escort. . . ."

"Your concern is touching, señor, but tell me, how did you know about it, since I told no one but the captain?"

Carillo, unnerved by her level gaze, nevertheless kept his head. "I overheard two of the crewmen talking," he explained briefly, twisting his cap in front of him.

"Do you recall which ones?"

"Alas, Countess, I do not. It was dark, and I did not think it an important matter at the time. If it pleases you, I could make inquiries. . . ." He was thinking fast. "We could meet later somewhere. The information might prove useful."

"It might, at that. Let me know when you have found out something," Diana agreed.

"I will, Countess. Your servant . . ." Carillo bowed his way out.

Diana breathed a sigh of relief when the latch dropped. She was sure that Carillo would have killed her had there been the slightest opening. She would wait for de Wynte's return. She did not intend to walk alone through the ship, with a knife waiting somewhere in the shadows.

"I think I should kill him at once," Tonomori growled to Diana after the captain had escorted her to the small cabin she shared with Toriko and had returned to his duties.

"Not yet," Diana said. "We need to know who he works for. I want to know everything he knows."

"There is still the risk," Tonomori objected. "Killing him would eliminate that."

"Yes, but who are his masters in Castile?"

"What does Castile have to do with it?"

Diana tried to explain. "Spain is ruled by the king, but it is made up of many old kingdoms, which were vanquished long ago or swallowed—Aragon, Navarre, for example. Castile is the strongest, and it is from there that the king exerts his control and rules Spain and its dominions elsewhere."

"I see. Very well, but one of us must be with you at all times."

"I agree to that. But speaking of all this, where is Toriko-san?"

"We quarreled. She won," Tonomori told her. "She argued that she was better suited to search the docks tonight for our friend from this afternoon."

"Alone?"

"Yes. I had planned to slide out there and cut him in

155

half." Tonomori seemed to be discussing the carving of a roast. "Toriko-san felt she could better make him talk before booting him into eternity."

"Do you think he will talk?"

Tonomori looked surprised, then smiled. "Oh, yes, Diana-san, he will talk freely. And then he will die." Tonomori's smile drew an icy finger down Diana's spine, and she shivered despite the warmth of the cabin.

It was impossible to know how long Toriko would be on the prowl, and Tonomori could not remain closeted with Diana indefinitely without arousing idle speculation among the crew. They left the cabin for a welcome respite on deck, where it was, in any event, cooler.

To confound eavesdroppers, they spoke in Japanese. Tonomori's eyes probed the shadows, and his ears weighed every sound that did not match the rhythm of the ship's slow roll at the quay. Except for the watch, most of the crew was ashore. The glow of Goa's lanterns stretched far away, and they could hear sounds of roistering and laughter from the taverns just off the dock area where the rougher element diced, drank, or whored away their pay.

"I see the captain gave you the pistols," Diana remarked. "A very good idea."

"A loan," Tonomori amended. "He also showed me how to fire them. Tomorrow, weather permitting, I will begin practice." His sword hand brushed the pistol butts protruding from his sash. Clouds were bunching across the bright moon, and by morning rain could be expected. No hard storm, though, which was fine because the *Schoen* was due to be hauled a half mile away to the docking facilities, where she would be careened and her bottom scraped of barnacles and seaweed. Goa was the only port in Asia capable of refitting a ship with the tonnage of the *Schoen*.

The Portuguese preferred the smaller carracks and the broad-bowed caravels for the coastal trade. Compared to these, the *Schoen* was a hungry hawk among a brood of fat pigeons. More than a hundred feet from prow to stern, not including the jutting bowsprit, she sat lower in the water than most in the galleon class. Her cannon were capable of tearing apart anything in Asian waters, including the formidable Chinese war junks. Hence the nervousness of the port authorities and their careful scrutiny of the ship's license to trade. The short step from trader to pirate had been taken too often in their experience.

But the *Schoen* was built to fly, not to fight, unless lacking an alternative. The Dutchmen who had cut her spars and laid her keel in Amsterdam had lowered the forecastle and the quarterdeck, and had eliminated the narrow fighting deck that usually connected both ends of the ship in Spanish galleons. When the Spanish fought at sea, they grappled and boarded, clearing enemy decks with steel, not cannon. The *Schoen* could outrun any galleon she encountered, so frequent chiseling off the marine growth clinging tenaciously to her hull was vital. Drag increased with each barnacle.

Diana leaned over the rail, peering at the moonlight on the water. All aspects of the harbor were prettier at night. One did not so easily notice the floating refuse—garbage, dead dogs, chamber pots' contents, and, not infrequently, a bloated corpse.

"If you wish to practice with the pistols, you could always rig a canopy on deck and shoot from beneath it," she suggested as Tonomori continued to fondle the pistol butts thoughtfully.

"I probably will. It smells like rain. Yamahito has the gun we retrieved this afternoon, and is becoming familiar with its mechanism. Tomorrow, we can get a new bullet mold made and obtain a powder flask. The excellent condition of the musket indicates to me that the assassin was no Portuguese."

"How do you mean?"

"Take a look around you the next time we go out." Tonomori hoped that Diana would not be offended by his intimation about her powers of observation. "You will see that half the Portuguese soldiers are carrying guns so rusted as to be unusable. It is unthinkable that such a motley crowd could win an empire by force of arms."

"Yet they did it!" Diana observed.

"Yes, and so you must wonder at the capabilities of

their enemies. I heard someone describe a Portuguese charge as like a bucket of apples being dumped down a stairwell. Each soldier is trying to outrun the rest.''

"Disorganized, perhaps, but also tough," Diana objected. "The Spanish have won the route to the Indies from the West, but the Portuguese have taken the route to the East." *For now*, she thought. A nation with imagination and daring, coupled with efficient organization, could take it all away from them. A people like the Dutch! The trade was too rich for Dutch seafarers to sit by, content only to haul barrels of salted herring from the North Sea to Lisbon—or even timber, cordage, and tin from other ports—in exchange for mere scraps.

Diana gazed into the darkness. Toriko was prowling out there somewhere amid the bales and stacks of goods.

The *Schoen* was a dark outline against the sky, with small points of yellow indicating the few lanterns that had been hung out.

Crouched between two rowboats, a shadowy figure watched intently, waiting for a signal. Two quick flashes from a light and he would be across the guylines and over the rails within a few breaths. He had failed this afternoon, and could not afford to fail again. It was dangerous, but that young ship's officer had paid him the ten newly minted *Saõ Vicentes* that now hung heavily in the purse at his belt, with ten more to come when the job was done. Twenty pieces of gold for the life of a young girl—a countess to be sure, but what difference did that make? Was he not rightly known as Alfredo the Silent? A hand over the mouth, a thrust . . . Alfredo would become a rich man, his reputation enhanced, the men requiring his future services ready to pay even more.

In the captain's cabin, the ship's quartermaster fretted. He would be delayed long past the time for the signal, but he could not be disrespectful to the captain, who seemed unduly interested in reviewing certain obvious details of his duties. At Tonomori's request, de Wynte had agreed to summon Carillo for an interview that was to be as prolonged as need be, until word came that he could terminate it.

No sign, goddamit! Alfredo thought furiously. The guard at the large lantern illuminating the gangplank had been relieved and not replaced, but still no sign. Only a lousy cat moving around, searching for fishheads or rats. Alfredo had tossed a couple of pebbles in its direction, but the cat had not gone away.

Something was amiss. It was too quiet. Alfredo felt a lump of apprehension beginning to grow solidly at the pit of his stomach. From nowhere, a rough stone landed near him and bounced. Alfredo whipped out his dagger, a silvery fang, and in the same motion started back. Then light exploded in his head as a club hit him from behind.

A muffled figure secured Alfredo's hands behind him expertly with thin, tough cord. A touch against the pulse. Good! He would be conscious in less than ten minutes. And shortly after that, with the razor edge of a *tanto* at his genitals, Alfredo would be telling an interesting story. Toriko knelt to wait, and carefully began cutting away his puffed slop breeches and hose. When she was done, he would hardly have further need for them.

The candles were guttering low in the chartroom lamps, and Diana was concerned. It must be past midnight, and still no sign of Toriko.

Tonomori read her expression. "Do not worry. She will return."

"I must learn to control my emotions better," said Diana. "You are so good at it. I can seldom tell what you are thinking."

"Practice is what you need, Diana-san. Emotions can be a weapon turned against you," Tonomori advised. "Show nothing. It will be more difficult to manipulate you."

"I will try harder," she promised. Toriko was female, even though a samurai and *ninja*, and Diana frequently could discern her moods. But Tonomori's slightly forbidding face was like a mask, his eyes black as jet always probing, sifting, giving away nothing.

She recalled his reaction when told that he should become a Roman Catholic—if only to pay lip service—so that the Portuguese or Spanish would not arrest him as an infidel.

"I should have thought of this earlier," Diana granted. "I had thought we would have plenty of time. But the Jesuits here have missionaries in Japan, after all. There is a real possibility that they have someone here in Goa who understands Japanese. If they were to question you, we could all be in trouble—you for being an unbeliever, and me for taking you in my employ."

"Very well," was all that Tonomori had to say when Diana gave him a golden medal of Our Lady to wear on a thin chain around his neck. His real reaction would have been startling to her: Tonomori wanted to laugh. He found Europeans so concerned about appearances, just like the Japanese. When they met a genuinely good man, which was rare, they were sure to suspect his motives. Meanwhile, he could see no harm in acting out a fiction. And, besides, he could always sell the medal later.

Toriko slipped soundlessly through the chartroom doorway. Not one board outside had groaned. Diana raised an eyebrow in appreciation of how she had managed that.

"Good evening. *Konban-wa.*" Toriko's kimono of cream-colored silk was decorated with red birds, and she looked as fresh as a spring flower, not at all like an accomplished murderer who had just successfully completed a dockside tour of Goa in pursuit of a professional assassin. Diana noticed that her hair was damp.

"I would have returned sooner, Diana-san, but I took time to bathe and wash my hair. Everything about the harbor is filthy," Toriko explained. Diana tried to discern the night's events from her expression. Tonomori already knew the most important: The assassin was dead. Toriko's look was that of a cat after catching an elusive bird.

"We had a talk," she continued. "Rather, he talked and I listened, with only an occasional prompting required. Before he died, he told me that he was hired by an officer from this ship. He did not know the man's name—I believed him. But it may be that many people are looking for you. We must be very careful!"

"And where is the body, Toriko-san?" asked Tonomori,

ever practical minded. He would have thrown it into the harbor for the fish.

"Where it can be found, Tonomori-san. As a warning."

Diana, sitting on the floor, her back to the wall, hugged her knees. She wanted to drum her heels on the floor in excitement. She suppressed the impulse. But they were winning. They would continue to win. Diana was feeling confident enough to take on the Duke of Alvino as soon as the *Schoen* docked in Antwerp. *I just wish I could kill him now!* The peril of the afternoon seemed far away, remote.

"We are running out of time," Tonomori cautioned. "What do you propose to do now?"

"To present as small a target as possible," Diana said. "But I may make one more trip into the town, under your close guard, of course. Perhaps my enemies would think I grow careless, and then you can take care of them. What I do feel is confidence. Many times now, my life has hung in the balance and I have won."

"It is not good to be overconfident," Toriko told her sternly. "This lord you wish to kill should not be underestimated. So far from home, yet he is a danger to you even now. What happens when the ship finally reaches your homeland? He will be a greater danger then."

"Something will present itself," Diana predicted.

"Not necessarily the best course of action. You cannot just simply walk up to a duke and stab him to death. The captain tells me the duke commands ten thousand warriors. If you do not do this thing correctly, then you will be killed and many others slaughtered. And the duke might still be alive."

"A good plan of action is the best," Tonomori suggested.

Diana licked her lips, lost deeply in thought. "I had thought to take a small house and then bide my time. . . ."

"That won't do. I suggest boldness," Tonomori urged. Diana and Toriko looked at him questioningly. Obviously, he had been considering the problem and could propose a possible solution.

"This duke has the confidence of the king, does he not?" Tonomori asked. "We have to dock in Lisbon anyway, do we not? Afterward, can we divert the ship to a

Spanish port? Can you not obtain an audience with the king? Gain his support. Secure your lands. Get him to sign the papers.'' Tonomori paused, carefully choosing the right words. ''Above all else, approach the king in high style. You will have arrived from the other side of the world. He and his warriors will be eager for news. I understand the Spanish have a taste for display, as we Japanese do. And when you are alone with the king, be bold in all things. You are his subject, but a daimyo from another land whose people offer only tenuous allegiance. He will be eager for your support.''

''Yes, Diana-san, it would work,'' Toriko interjected eagerly. ''You would gain the protection of the king. Anything that might happen to you would become his concern. The duke would have to tread carefully. It would become difficult to eliminate you because the king himself would take an interest in the matter. Tonomori-san is correct. Boldness is the best course here. But also stealth and cunning.

''If the king is dazzled by the appearance of your retinue, then he will not notice how adroitly you are manipulating him,'' Toriko continued. ''You have no army to challenge the duke's position. You can help your country in other ways until the time for armed resistance arrives—if that is what must happen, as you seem to think.''

''Yes, it must!'' Diana declared forcefully. ''When Alvino is out of the way, we can bleed their forces and quietly strengthen our own.'' She looked from Toriko to Tonomori. ''You are my good friends. You have saved my life many times. When my father's murderer is dead, my family will know honor again. I am proud to learn from such samurai.''

Toriko and Tonomori bowed their heads, pleased with the praise.

''It is our duty to think of such things and suggest them to you, Diana-san,'' Tonomori pointed out.

''Nevertheless, I am honored and well served.''

Diana poured tea while they formed a plan. After the *Schoen* ported in Lisbon, and the *Casa de India* authorities checked and verified her cargo and deducted their shares, Diana would seek out the king. The people would enjoy the show, and the details of her progress from Lisbon would have been reported to the king. Tonomori was samurai and also of daimyo rank—without lands, to be sure, but the Spaniards would not know that, and he could be presented to the king.

Toriko's samurai rank, the equivalent of knighthood, also made her of suitable rank to add prestige to the delegation with the countess. She would wear her finest silks, Tonomori his armor.

Diana's mind was already adding imaginatively to the procession—black slaves with fans of ostrich plumes, grotesque dwarfs, and anyone else who might awe the Spanish court.

"A letter from the king would be a safe passport in your country," Toriko mentioned. "Ask him to order the duke to extend his protection to yourself and your friends. The duke will be watching you closely—but we have escaped notice before, eh, Diana-san?"

Diana smiled. She longed to go prowling again with Toriko, like a wild thing escaped from its gilded cage.

"Yes, it could be easy," she agreed. "Even the Duke of Alvino could hardly take action against a favorite of the king, one who has brought expensive presents to her sovereign as a token of her esteem."

Tonomori entered into the spirit of the conversation. "Then, when all seems well, you can have the duke's guts on a plate."

"Very well put, Tonomori-san," was all Diana could think of in response. But she was satisfied. And sleepy. Her yawns were an excuse for Tonomori and Toriko to escort her back to the cabin. While she undressed and collapsed gratefully into her small bunk, Toriko and Tonomori conversed quietly outside her door.

"That officer, Carillo, must be killed," Tonomori whispered.

"I agree, Tonomori-san, but not now!"

"Why not now?"

"Because there is already one body outside, which will be found in the morning. Carillo would be one more corpse, a trail leading right back to this ship and to us,"

Toriko said. "The Portuguese authorities are one thing, the Jesuits are another. Already they are asking questions. They would be asking even more."

"So what?"

"The Jesuits are a power in Spain and everywhere. We cannot afford to make enemies of them or to arouse their suspicions. They have missions in Japan. So far, the Spanish are ignorant of the capabilities of samurai. I think it good that they remain that way. If the Jesuits become too suspicious, they might request a report from the fathers at the missions. That report could eventually find its way to Spain and to Diana's enemies, to be sure, even though of course we would reach there first. We would no longer be merely a novelty. They would understand how dangerous we really are. I think it better that we eliminate Señor Carillo at sea."

"Good," Tonomori grunted. "I'll take the first watch. Oshabiri and that blasted monkey of his can take the second."

Toriko raised an inquiring eyebrow.

"Saru ate my last cake of ink, thinking it was candy, and was violently ill all over the latest poem I had written," Tonomori explained.

"A critic, then? I did not know that your poetry was so bad, Tonomori-san," Toriko said impishly.

"Ha!" Tonomori's voice was stern, but his face betrayed amusement, as Toriko was quick to note. They parted on good terms, and Tonomori took up his position outside the cabin door. Oshabiri and Yamahito would be rolling out their sleeping mats in the chartroom, Tonomori thought. His own pallet had been used little of late. The mats were kept in a storage chest when not in use. And until they left Goa, Tonomori knew he would be getting even less sleep.

At the first morning light, the *Schoen* was warped into drydock by two hired longboats. Under other circumstances, Diana would have gone, carefree, into the town. Instead, she took refuge from the light drizzle under a nearby shed, with Tonomori and Toriko in attendance, and watched while the ship was hauled over on her side with lines of block and tackle. If she was to command her own sea empire, Diana realized that she should know everything about maintaining ships. This seemed as good a place as any to start—from the bottom.

Swarms of natives began chipping off barnacles and marine growth. De Wynte walked and crawled among them, examining every plank of the hull painstakingly. If any boards were damaged, now was the time to find and replace them.

The *Schoen* already had been moved from the quay when Alfredo's body was discovered. A stevedore, hearing the sound of a dogfight, had gone to investigate, only to find Alfredo's eviscerated corpse, with two mongrels fighting for possession of its entrails. The Portuguese officials were summoned, but their concern quickly wore off when they discovered the dead man's identity. Alfredo was well known to them, and his end had been regarded as overdue. The subsequent investigation was pigeonholed. Among the crew of the *Schoen* the gossip created almost no stir.

Diana spent the remainder of the day sipping cold tea and selecting from a fine repast of spicy lamb and native fruits provided by the harbormaster. She had charmed him, and then bombarded him with questions on harbors, ships, and the handling of cargo.

At his invitation, Diana and her retinue spent the night with the harbormaster and his family inasmuch as they could not return to the ship while it was careened.

In turn, Diana regaled her host, Senhor Avilar, and his wife, Teresa, with stories about her sojourn in Japan. Her hosts were completely captivated, having never had so exalted a personage beneath their roof. Her visit would provide the Avilars with conversational gambits for months. And Diana repaid their generosity with some splendid presents.

Except when relieved by the larger of his two uncommunicative servants, Tonomori remained outside the door of Diana's chamber during the night. Avilar's own servants were naturally curious about Tonomori, but they gave him a wide berth, as one would a large, snarling hound guarding a bone.

165

A day later, the *Schoen* was back in the water, her hull clean as a whistle, and her crew filing aboard. Tonomori thought that Carillo was avoiding his presence. The quartermaster did not realize that Toriko was keeping an eye on his every movement. It was possible, Toriko thought, that he would try to kill Diana and then jump ship.

After the *Schoen* hoisted sail on the tide of the following morning, Carillo would have to await an opportunity when he would not be likely to be caught or suspected. Tonomori was determined that Carillo would not live to see the African coast.

So Captain de Wynte was not the only one who was pleased when the *Schoen* slipped into the channel, dropped her topsails, and eased past the small islets dotting the entrance to Goa's harbor. De Wynte was not a landsman and never liked dealing with merchants: One had to check every barrel for spoiled wine or brackish water and every bale for correct weight.

The rain clouds were gone, and the shifting land breeze was welcome. Small seabirds hurried by on morning errands, and the sun was rising at their backs, golden with promise. Standing on deck near the prow, with Tonomori close by, Diana did not look back. Ahead was the future. Stormy seas. Strange lands and even stranger people. When Diana had been sent to the other side of the world—so many lifetimes ago, it seemed—she had taken notice only of the here and now. With a hundred knives at her back in the dark, a thousand treacheries, she had been a frightened young girl running for her life.

Now, it was different. *She* was the knife in the dark. The storms might rip at the ship with strong claws, but she was not afraid. Ahead, for many days, was the Arabian Sea, with Cape Guardafui at its western jaw—their first contact with Africa. To reach it, they would have to beat hard against southeasterly winds, but the ocean currents would be sliding beneath the keel in their favor. Then south down the African coast, past fabled Zanzibar, then Mozambique and beyond, to the crashing waters of the Cape of Good Hope. Diana took a deep breath. She would meet each challenge as it came, as would the *Schoen*.

Behind her, Tonomori stood guard, his eyes everywhere, on the deck, in the rigging. Accidents could happen easily at sea: rigging could be cut, tackle dropped from above. He was taking no chances: Tonomori knew he could not afford to daydream, to think of his own vengeance—not with Carillo alive and somewhere aboard ship. Let his mistress think she was ready to take on any enemy—Tonomori would not dream of telling her otherwise. In time, she would learn. Meanwhile, he would watch for her.

The mainsails unfurled and swelled to their fullest.

"The sea is so beautiful," Diana exclaimed appreciatively.

"So desuka, neh?" It is, isn't it? Tonomori concurred.

"I am fine, right where I am. You needn't dance attendance on me all day," Diana told him. She was young and in high spirits, momentarily forgetful again of the dangers surrounding her.

"As you wish." Tonomori bowed. But he did not move.

From his position on the quarterdeck, Carillo swore silently. The samurai apparently was going to continue to shadow her every move. Carillo swore again and went below, unaware that Toriko was following him. His curses embraced the miserable Alfredo, who had fumbled glorious opportunity and left the onus to Carillo himself. Professional assassin, indeed! But, in any event, the rewards now could be his own, with only the loss of Alfredo's ten gold pieces.

Tonomori saw Toriko on Carillo's trail and grinned. They would deal with him soon enough.

The *Schoen* sailed across the deep blue waters into the new day.

They maintained constant vigilance, never for a minute leaving Diana unattended. She began to chafe occasionally under their scrutiny, but understood the need for caution, and cooperated well. One slip and she could be wearing a shroud.

Three weeks out, the storm broke, a sudden but vivid squall from the north. The ship plunged heavily in green-gray water, its salt in every crewman's teeth from the wind-whipped waves.

The captain shortened sail to ride out the storm, trusting to his compass and dead reckoning as to where the winds were blowing them.

In two days, the squall blew itself out, but the exhausted crewmen slept below decks where they dropped, clothes streaming into widening pools beneath them. It did not matter to them where they slept, because all their bedding was soaked through.

That night, as the wind began dropping but still sang in the lines, Carillo was ready to make his move. He knew that the samurai and his men were on deck, along with the Japanese woman. Carillo made doubly sure of that, and then bolted below. The countess was alone in the cabin she shared with the Japanese woman. This was the moment he had been waiting for. The promise of gold for her life was a lodestone, drawing his knife to her beating heart like the point of a compass. He even felt grateful that Alfredo had failed. And the Japanese could be blamed for her death. After all, they were foreigners.

He slipped inside the small doorway quickly and, knife in hand, closed the latch quietly behind him. A candle's flicker showed the blanketed form in the bed, her back to him. Well and good—she would never know what was to claim her life. Carillo did not think himself a cruel man. This was purely business, with full payment promised in Spain.

With three quick steps to the bed, he started his lunge. The form twisted like an eel and exploded at him in sudden fury. A small, hard foot kicked the blade from his grasp, and another hammered into his testicles. Carillo doubled onto the floor, helpless, with a *tanto* gleaming at his throat.

"You have been expected, señor," the voice at his ear told him.

It was the Japanese woman. In his agony, Carillo's mind reeled with sickening awareness. He had been duped. When the samurai entered the cabin moments later, Carillo had no more thoughts of his chances of escaping.

168

"When you are ready, we will talk," Tonomori informed him.

"I . . . I know nothing," Carillo groaned. Thin cords cut into his wrists and ankles, but the pain was nothing compared to the heavy throbbing in his groin.

The samurai laughed softly without a trace of humor. "Ah, Señor Carillo, before long you will be surprised by what you know!" Tonomori balled a filthy rag into the gaping mouth and bound it in place with a strip of cloth. Then he began applying pressure to the scrotum.

Carillo's screams were completely muffled. After he fainted dead away, Tonomori rocked back on his heels and waited.

When Carillo edged back to consciousness, drenched in sweat, his darting eyes indicated a frantic eagerness to cooperate. Tonomori removed the gag and the wadding with caution.

"Talk, and you will be released unharmed, on your promise not to endanger my mistress again," Tonomori gently assured him.

"I promise! I promise!" Carillo sobbed. He had no such intention: Once free, he would steal a gun from the captain's cabin and shoot not only Diana but the samurai at the earliest opportunity, after denouncing him to the captain. Also, the Japanese bitch—she would pay, too.

First, though, Carillo spewed out his story in ragged gasps.

He was employed, *sub rosa*, by a Spaniard named Martin de la Cruz, with headquarters in Seville. De la Cruz subsidized many men looking for weaknesses along the Portuguese trade routes, which Spain coveted. He reported to a nobleman named Mendoza, spymaster to the King of Spain. It was Mendoza who had offered a reward for the death of the countess, with a bonus promised if it were arranged to seem to be an accident. The catch, of course, was that no one knew where she was to be found. Carillo had joined de Wynte's ship in Portuguese Macao, off the China coast, after having shipped there on another vessel that had become unseaworthy en route. He had not known that Countess Diana was in Japan until she set foot on the *Schoen*. The meeting was unexpected and, for him, fortuitous. Except for Alfredo in Goa, he had told no one of his good fortune.

"No lies, now," Tonomori growled.

"The truth, I swear it! Mother of God, I swear it!" He was almost screaming again, but Tonomori threatened him with the gag and a squeeze. Carillo could not bear the thought of the torment, and would have denounced his own mother to the Inquisition to avoid enduring more at Tonomori's hands.

"Very well then," Tonomori said, hauling Carillo to his feet.

"Your promise, señor, to release me," Carillo reminded him, weak with relief as well as pain.

"As I said. This way." Tonomori sliced through the bonds at Carillo's ankles and wrists and propelled him toward the door. The hallway was deserted, and only a few steps took them to the hatchway leading to the catwalk below the quarterdeck at the stern.

Carillo looked around. The woman had disappeared, but suddenly a loud, unintelligible argument erupted amidships.

"What the? . . ." Carillo began, then felt two strong hands grip him and hurl him outward into the darkness. Foaming sea water stifled his screams. Carillo flailed in the troughs, coughing, as the dark outline of the *Schoen* disappeared into the night.

Tonomori listened carefully. The officer's thin cries for help could not be heard above the prearranged quarrel raging between Oshabiri and Yamahito. When Tonomori could hear Carillo no longer, he made his way back to the main deck to play out his part.

"Enough!" he commanded his men, who had been shouting at each other in Japanese. As they had planned, the crewmen on deck had been diverted by the argument and did not notice when Tonomori threw Carillo overboard.

Oshabiri and Yamahito immediately fell to their knees with their heads touching the deck. They had been enjoying themselves immensely, shouting epithets.

"All foreign devils eat rat dung."

"No, all foreign devils *are* rat dung."

The event had given them a chance to vent their spleen. They did not like the sea, but they liked smelly foreign vessels even less. Unfortunately, the argument sounded too realistic, and Saru, fearing for his master's life, had bitten Yamahito. The victim rubbed a hand gingerly. As Tonomori approached, Saru clung to Oshabiri.

Tonomori drew his sword. The crewmen held their breath, wondering what the bloody savage was going to do now.

"If you dare to disturb my peace again, your unworthy heads will roll," Tonomori shouted in Portuguese for the benefit of the crew, some of whom looked disappointed.

"Yes, Tonomori-sama."

The two *ashigaru* bowed again and left quickly. Tonomori sheathed his sword, and grabbed a line for balance as the ship shuddered through another wave.

The weather was still foul, but the air at least was clean. Tonomori greatly preferred it to the stench from the bilges permeating every part of the ship. He went below decks only when necessity required it—to eat or to protect Diana.

Tonomori could rest easy. The danger of the assassin was past—for now. The night closed around him like a cloak, but Tonomori was content. His mistress was safe, his duty accomplished, and he was samurai.

Chapter Twelve

"There it is, just as I told you, the Straw Sea!" Diana exclaimed, exhilarated. With the prevailing winds from the Atlantic at her back, the *Schoen* cut into the bay. Ahead, to starboard, lay Lisbon, shining and golden in the setting sun.

"Truly a pleasing sight," agreed Tonomori, who hugged the starboard railing with Diana and Toriko. They were all eager to touch land again.

The waters of the bay shone with the luster of fresh straw, hence the name. Passing to port, their triangular lateen sails filled, were low-masted fishing smacks on their way to the Atlantic in pursuit of sardines and mackerel or anything else that would swim into their nets. The crews waved and yelled out greetings, then scrambled to come about in the wake of the *Schoen* to tack their way against the wind.

The surrounding hills were green and rolling. Diana felt secure. Lisbon was a safe haven after rough seas over so many leagues.

Gulls screamed overhead. Diana blinked. Lisbon represented safety, but she would watch her every step nevertheless. She did not intend to repeat the mistakes of Goa. Tonight she would sleep soundly with the *Schoen* snug against the well-patrolled quays of the Lisbon waterfront.

"We'll post our own guard," Tonomori announced.

"As you wish," Diana replied.

Captain de Wynte's voice ripped through the rigging. "Prepare to shorten sail!"

Dawn arrived quickly with the clamor of a thousand strident voices.

Diana rubbed the sleep from her eyes and reached reluctantly for one of her trunks. The day of the kimono and the loose gown was over. The item she retrieved was unyielding in her grasp.

Toriko, busily tying the points of her underkimono, clucked her tongue reprovingly at the sight of Diana's corset, with its cast-iron strapping only slightly disguised by its canvas cover.

"That looks terrible," she observed. She tied the overkimono into place, adjusted the *obi*.

"It feels even worse," Diana lamented. The back and front pieces were hinged together at the left side. The hinges creaked as she closed the halves together. She twisted to check, in her small and clouded mirror, the resulting effect on the bottom line.

Corsets, though a torment, were absolutely necessary to maintain the smooth lines dictated by European fashion, a harsh mistress.

Diana struggled into her dress—at least five years out of style—and Toriko tightened the lacings up the back. Diana spent only another half hour on her hair—some women took half the morning—so she felt the very soul of alacrity. With a flat velvet cap adjusted rakishly to one side, she pronounced herself ready.

"Once we are done with the customs house, the first thing we will do is get some suitable clothes," she told Toriko. "I do not want to look like an old-fashioned frump."

"Yes, Diana-san." Toriko eyed the dress dubiously. Her turn would be next, and soon enough. They already had discussed the dress at great length. Toriko's kimonos would do for festivals and formal occasions, when they wished to make a certain impression. But for daily wear

173

and to avoid drawing attention to themselves, Toriko would have to conform to European tastes.

She felt privately that she must have committed an unspeakable evil in an earlier life to have merited such a punishment.

As for Tonomori, he knew that his fate also was sealed, but he had merely shrugged his broad shoulders. He would look no more ridiculous than anyone else. At least he was not required to wear a corset.

By the time Diana and Toriko appeared on deck, he was already sauntering back up the gangplank with a pleased look on his face.

"Good morning, Diana-san, Toriko-san," he greeted them jauntily.

Diana fixed him with a jaundiced stare and replied mechanically if not politely.

"A fine day," Tonomori added. He jerked a thumb in the direction from which he had come. "The fishmongers are bargaining for the morning's catch. I met a vendor, a wrinkled old crone who can swear better than all the crew put together. She was selling shrimp dipped in batter and fried. Delicious! I ate ten big ones." He rubbed his flat stomach in satisfaction.

Wonderful, Diana thought. *There stands a man who is not wearing a corset, who does not need to wear a corset, and who has enjoyed breakfast.*

Tonomori had practiced reading her moods, and usually avoided Diana in the mornings because she almost always was grumpy for an hour or so. This morning, however, he was in an excellent temper and inclined to humor her.

"Come," he said. "The old woman probably will still be there. She had plenty of shrimps left. And a lobster or two. I will buy breakfast—no Dutch treat!"

He smiled again and looked from Diana to Toriko and back to Diana.

Lobster! Diana's morning clouds vanished. With Tonomori elbowing a wide path through the fish buyers, Diana and Toriko soon were enjoying a meal of fried lobster. Tonomori reappeared from a nearby stall with earthenware beakers of a lemon drink sweetened with honey and spiced with nutmeg.

Diana swallowed and smiled. Tonomori was forgiven for not having to wear corsets. And for having already had breakfast. And even for being cheerful.

The noise did not bother her now. The fishmongers were busily packing their purchases in carts lined with dripping seaweed, then everyone seemed to head for the gates at once, swearing, scraping wheels, shouting at the top of their lungs. It was Friday, and everyone would be wanting fresh fish for the table—fried, grilled, or broiled.

"You are in a better frame of mind now, Diana-san?" Tonomori asked. He cracked open a lobster claw and picked out the meat.

"Oh, yes, thank you. Fresh lobster always puts me in a good mood." Diana wiped oil from her mouth with a linen handkerchief and tucked it back into her sleeve. Toriko looked away from this display of bad manners. The Japanese carried packets of soft tissue made for wiping the lips or blowing the nose. Rather than carrying a soiled cloth about on one's person, the tissues could be cleanly disposed of. She supposed she would get used to the practice. It *could* be worse; the crew used their sleeves!

"Very good, Diana-san," Tonomori told her cautiously. "You will need full control of your emotions today. I have just observed a group of customs officials filing aboard ship."

He might as well have announced that pickpockets were rifling her purse; the effect was the same. Diana lifted her skirts and took to her heels, hurrying toward the ship, with Toriko following close behind.

Tonomori dodged and twisted from the grasp of streetwise urchins, some of whom could lift a wallet with professional ease, as they plucked at his kimono sleeves.

"Bugger off!" he bellowed and made as if to draw his *tachi*.

It was language they understood, and the urchins scattered while making horns against the evil eye.

Tonomori had kept Diana constantly in sight. By the

175

time he was back aboard the *Schoen*, Diana already was having an intense discussion with de Wynte.

"How much are the thieves going to hold us up for?" she was demanding.

The captain was rubbing his chin. "Since we already have our *cartaz*, the license that permits us to trade in Portuguese waters, and allowing for import duties and *propinas*—the rakeoffs we are going to have to pay—it should not amount to more than a fifth. . . ."

"A fifth! The leeches!" Diana howled.

But the duties officers were deaf to any such outcry. It was only expected. They were all over the ship, poking their experienced noses into jars of powdery red cochineal dyes, fingering the weave of bolts of silk. At a glance they could tell the peppercorns were from Ceylon, not the inferior variety from Malabar.

Banda nutmegs and mace, Ternate cloves, Ceylon cinnamon. The lists grew and the duties officers calculated the cargo down to the last *real*.

"Those are *my* emeralds, *my* rubies, *my* pearls!" Diana declared through clenched teeth to a grim official who was examining her jewelry chest.

"At least we know who to assess, Countess." The captain had informed him of Diana's rank.

"Maybe you would like to examine my teeth, senhor?"

"That will not be necessary; a countess is not taxed," the official assured her in an effort to lighten the situation with a bit of levity.

"Only robbed," Diana shot back. She went to find de Wynte, who had disappeared.

"They are going to loot this ship," Diana told the captain after finding him arguing over a list with two officials.

"Not entirely. Duties do have to be paid. . . ."

"Let me see that," Diana demanded, snatching the list. She pored over each item, muttering.

"There," she said, pointing an accusing finger. "They are assessing me for my personal jewelry. Jewelry is not taxable." She held the list up triumphantly.

The officer who had examined her necklaces and rings appeared on deck.

"Jorge Escamillo, at your service. That is true; jewelry is not taxable. However, your gems are unset, and therefore are assessable." He bowed and quickly made for the gangplank, followed by his underlings.

"I'll glue them all to my backside or throw them into the sea before I pay you a *cruzado*," Diana yelled at their departing backs.

De Wynte laughed softly and applauded.

"How did I do?" Diana asked.

"You deserve a standing ovation, a shower of silver at least."

"How much did they miss?"

"A great deal, I am glad to report."

"The false decking? . . ."

"They overlooked it completely. They must be slipping," the captain said smugly.

"Why do we do this?" Diana wondered. "They overcharge us to make up for the cargo they know we have hidden but can't find. Why can't we just be honest with each other?"

"And spoil the fun?"

The next delegations arrived in twos and threes, representatives from the various guilds eager for new merchandise and the foreign bankers who maintained resident agents in Lisbon.

De Wynte met these, courteously, but sent them away empty-handed. Most of the cargo was destined for Antwerp and the rich marketplaces of the north for a profit higher than could be gained in Lisbon.

Then, at mid-morning, a sedan chair arrived, carried by four immense black slaves, all heavily armed. A gentleman of distinguished appearance emerged, leaning on a gold-headed walking stick. De Wynte estimated that he would be in his sixties.

"I am Lucas Giraldi," the gentleman announced on board before they exchanged pleasantries. The captain had heard of Giraldi. An immensely wealthy merchant, he owned the monopoly on all the crown's sugar tithes from the Indies. Giraldi was not one to send agents when he sniffed a potential fortune in the winds.

"You are well known to me, sir," de Wynte said. They went below to make themselves comfortable in the captain's cabin. There they were joined by Diana at the captain's summons.

"To bring matters to the fore, I would like to contract for all or part of your cargo," Giraldi said briskly.

"I am afraid that is impossible," Diana responded flatly.

Giraldi had expected that the captain would speak; he took on a thoughtful look. "Impossible is a large word. Besides, you have not heard my offer," he continued smoothly. The fluency of his Portuguese contained only the slightest stridency of the accents from his native Italy.

"Rather, I would like to extend an invitation to visit my home this afternoon, at your convenience. Afterward, we could perhaps dine together. I am always eager for news from the Indies. Talk costs nothing and may prove to be mutually advantageous in the long run." Giraldi's dark eyes sparkled youthfully in a gaunt face wrinkled by sun and salt air.

De Wynte saw him weighing the advantages and disadvantages of dealing with potential competitors, and was intrigued by the possibilities.

"Your offer sounds interesting and at least entertaining," Diana conceded.

"Ah, then I can expect you? Three is a good hour. You will want to see the city. I will send sedan chairs. After such an exhausting journey, no need to fatigue yourself further. When you feel up to it, I would be happy to act as your guide."

When the merchant had taken his leave, Diana and de Wynte held a strategy conference. The merchant needed merchandise, which they had in plenty. In turn, they needed information that Giraldi might be able to supply.

Where was the King of Spain? What was the fastest and safest route to get to him? What was the latest news from the Netherlands? Diana needed to know myriad other details before committing her plan to action.

Word was spreading throughout the city about the beautiful countess and the exotic foreigners on the Dutch ship newly arrived from the Indies, and it seemed that the entire city was eager for at least a glimpse. But the city could wait; Diana took a nap. The meeting with Giraldi could be important, and she wanted to be alert for it. When the sedan chair arrived, she felt much refreshed, though sleep had not come quickly. She was excited, but finally had muffled the dockside din by pulling a pillow over her head.

By the time Diana came on deck, Toriko was assembled with Tonomori and the two *ashigaru,* armed as usual.

One sedan chair offered space for two, so Diana and Toriko rode in it, de Wynte in another. Tonomori chose to walk with his men, carefully noting the route.

Giraldi's house was not far from the warehouse district, just to the east of the tumultuous fruit and vegetable markets, where the merchant could keep an eye on his goods and conveniently be on hand for the arrival of ships.

Servants, on the lookout for their arrival, ushered them in silently. A stout gate sheathed with gilded bronze pierced the thick walls surrounding the villa. A fountain bubbling in the center of a tiled terrace made the rattle of carts and murmur of outside voices barely discernible.

"Welcome! It is so good of you to come." Giraldi was posed by comfortable chairs placed around an ebony table inlaid with ivory and mother of pearl marquetry. Servants stood discreetly in the background. Tonomori breathed easier; the servants were unarmed, but he kept his ears open for the clack and scrape of armor. He did not suspect an ambush, but he intended to take Giraldi's head off his thin shoulders if there proved to be.

Once seated, Giraldi opened the conversation. His discreet inquiries indicated to his shrewd mind that a slice of the goods could be his for the buying. And if he played his hand correctly, he might get even more in the long run.

"You are experiencing difficulties with the customs officials?" It was more of a statement than a question.

"Customs bandits would be more like it," Diana

answered, sipping a fine Manzanilla, shining through the hand-blown Venetian tumbler like liquid gold.

"Cream rises to the top. Also scum. You will find both in the *Casa de India*. I can be of assistance to you there," Giraldi assured her. He had decided not to underestimate this attractive young woman whose loveliness now graced his home. A countess from the Far East, on a Dutch ship under Portuguese license. An enigma, and possibly dangerous.

"I would value your help," Diana told him.

"Value is many things to many people," Giraldi mentioned with a casual wave. He decided to take the risk. "To a businessman like myself, merchandise, ships—these things have value. To the Dutch, hard work and thrift are virtues of value and bring their own reward. To the Japanese, loyalty and honor are treasured more than gold."

Tonomori's gaze turned hard. The old merchant was up to something and knew more than he was revealing.

Giraldi's eyes flicked rapidly from Tonomori, to Diana, to the lovely madonna with the almond eyes. And back to Tonomori; in all probability such a man was more than a match for the *Ashanti* warriors who served as his own bodyguards.

"What do you know of the Japanese, senhor Giraldi?" Tonomori interjected. The merchant had thrown some feints, he knew, to test their reaction. *What is the game?*

Giraldi gestured with his hands openly. "Perhaps I should preface my remarks with a short lesson in our history. A decade or so ago, our monarch King João the Pious, so recently departed from us, invited the Jesuits and the Inquisition, for reasons of his own. They have been here ever since.

"The Jesuits have missions in Japan. I have agents who have been to Japan. Therefore I know something about the Japanese and what they are capable of. The Jesuits do not—not completely. They have seen only a few faces of the Japanese. On the other hand, the Society of Jesus is not to be crossed, even lightly. When their curiosity is aroused, the Jesuits have the tenacity of ferrets in digging out information."

Tonomori had seen the black-robed Jesuits in Nagasaki,

in Goa, in Lisbon. They seemed far more intelligent than the other priests he had seen in Goa or in Lisbon, whose purpose seemed to be frightening superstitious peasants. *They would have to be even more careful. This was a warning.*

"Then there is the matter of Spain. The Spanish always have cast covetous eyes on my adopted country. Our king, Sebastião, is only four years old, may God preserve him. Much can happen before he reaches maturity. Não há remédio.

"That brings us to my situation. Trade is changing rapidly. I see great power in this, more than most people realize. I intend for my descendants, for the House of Giraldi, to have part of it. The Spanish believe that power exists only in swords, in guns. They ignore the possibilities of their own commerce, because it is beneath them. Their mighty armies are bleeding them to death in their vain quest for glory."

Tonomori followed his words carefully. The man had valuable knowledge—better even than cannon.

"You have valuable contacts in the Netherlands. I already have agents in Antwerp, the queen city of the north. Your assistance would be priceless to me. In return, Dutch ships could find favorable trade agreements here. I think the trade route to the Indies will be closed to you soon. The crown regents want it for themselves.

"However," he added after a brief pause, "of course we all know of other ways of cutting up a pie. . . ."

"Excuse me," Tonomori interrupted. "Knowledge is valuable but it also is dangerous. Are you not risking much by confiding in people you do not know? In Japan, when a secret is shared, it is no longer a secret."

"True, but I had word of your coming. My couriers traveled by dhow through the Arabian sea, across the desert by caravan, then by fast ship through the Mediterranean. So I knew two months ago of your prospective arrival. I have made careful inquiries, and I am willing to take the risk.

"I am an old man, with not many more years left. As you can see, my family is away on a convenient holiday,"

Giraldi went on. "They are in the company of reliable witnesses should it ever be required. No one else is present to overhear us except my servants, and they only understand *Ashanti,* which I also speak. Not even the Inquisition's instruments can pry out information that is not known."

He leaned forward, intense. "My heirs can carry on without me. The enormous possibilities of the future are worth risking what time I have left." He paused again for effect. "The philosophers' stone has been found—that alchemists' dream of the centuries for turning dross metals into gold."

Complete silence fell upon the room.

"Few people realize this, and most would not believe it if you told them. What is the philosophers' stone? It is trade! Lumps of lead into gold. German grain becomes Spanish silver. Flemish cloth turns into Italian glass and pottery. Pigs' ears—nay, the whole animal, gutted and salted in barrels—become silk purses—lined with precious metal—in the right market. Do you understand now?"

Diana and de Wynte exchanged small, expectant smiles. "We understand completely, senhor," she said with open delight. What Giraldi had described was similar to what Diana already had been contemplating as far back as Goa, but with all the fine detail now ready to be filled in. She could arm the king's enemies and bleed the Hapsburgs white at the same time!

Tonomori was turning over the possibilities in his mind, and dismissed them. A samurai did not trade for a living. If he could no longer use his sword, the code of Bushido allowed him to make paper fans or parasols and sell them, or perhaps to raise crickets to be kept as house pets in little cages.

Tonomori would trade and work for the guns and ship he needed, no more. He would pull a *tanto* across his belly before he would stoop to commerce. But he saw nothing wrong in Diana's pursuing her own vengeance in this fashion; he would continue to assist her so long as he could live and breathe as a samurai. He could see that she was excited. Giraldi had just shown her the path to outflank Spain and also whoever else might come after the fall of the Spanish.

"You have my assurances for help in the north, and a third of the cargo in the *Schoen* now. We can work out the details later," she told Giraldi. "Much of what you say intrigues me. I accept your help gratefully. What I do need for the present is information. When my father was killed, the Spanish crown seized my estates because they couldn't find me. I need to be able to approach King Philip."

"That can be arranged." Giraldi was used to dealing with the nobility, having loaned money to ambitious Portuguese diplomats and Italian ecclesiastics whose spending habits far outstripped their benefices. They often accompanied repayment of their notes with useful information by way of further sweetening the useful relationship. "The king is in Seville," Giraldi told them, "to quiet down some rumblings among the nobles and to attend an *auto-da-fe,* an act of faith. The Inquisition is about to deliver some heretics up for burning, and the king would not miss it for the world. So he is now carrying out the affairs of state in the royal palace of the Alcazar.

"You must be aware and alert," he continued, "to the possible complication of the presence in Seville of the king's spymaster, Mendoza. That is his base. He and his henchmen are tireless, and employ great imagination as well as zeal in tracking down all persons whom they conceive of as sources of trouble for the king and his policies. Have a care and be on guard for this man and his agents, especially one named de la Cruz. In one way, which you will understand, it is unfortunate that King Philip will be in the same city with these hounds of his. Their access to him might turn him against you at an unexpected hour."

They continued planning at length, halting only for dinner. Tonomori passed up the roast lamb and capons for saffron rice, slices of roast fish, and black olives, which he found to his liking. He declined an offer of wine, preferring to cup his hand in the ornamental fountain.

* * *

At least two weeks would be needed before they could leave for their overland trip across the mountains and southward into Spain. Diana required clothes suitable for presentation at court, Tonomori had to be fitted with European armor, and they needed a pack train of horses and mules. Even more important, they needed an experienced guide to take them safely to Seville. This turned out to be Juan Contreras, a man well experienced with Seville and the route from Lisbon. He could steer them around the many possible pitfalls awaiting unsuspecting travelers. His first act was to arrange for them to be attached to a caravan from Lisbon for the tortuous journey.

Giraldi lent them other assistance from among his own workers. A former man-at-arms took Tonomori to a reputable dealer in armor, and an expert on material of every kind escorted Diana to the best dressmakers in the city.

And while the horses were being assembled and pearls were sewn onto Diana's new gowns, Giraldi took pleasure in showing Diana and Toriko the city he greatly loved.

"There," he said, pointing, "lies the castle of Saõ Jorge. It has withstood many sieges. Over there, with its turrets and battlements, is the Tower of Belem." The fortress rose five stories in the middle of the mouth of the Tagus River, commanding all approaches.

"You should not exert yourself, taking us everywhere," Diana chided gently.

"Ah, after all, it is my servants who are carrying our chairs. They get the exercise and I get my fill of fresh air," Giraldi laughed, "not to mention the pleasurable company of the most beautiful ladies in the city. I am to be greatly envied."

The townspeople were eager to get a look at the foreigners, but kept a respectful distance. Tonomori accompanied them and was now wearing a three-quarters suit of Innsbruck armor. His heavy sword was rehilted with a Spanish guard and scabbarded in black leather with silver furnishings. Straight blades were the rule, but curved swords like Tonomori's *tachi* were not unknown. Everyone simply assumed that the scowling Jappo was carrying a falchion, a very heavy curved sword resembling a scimitar. And he looked deadly enough to make it advisable to avoid provoking a test of his skill with it.

Rumor had it that he had killed a two-headed giant with it in defense of the countess, and had slain some man-birds off the coast of Cathay, and that his pillow was a fabulous pearl that he had looted from a bloody temple in India, after slaughtering the ogres who guarded it.

Behind the rumors were crew members of the *Schoen*, who had discovered in the many taverns of Lisbon the free wine and ale that the gullible provided for the telling of these stories, the wilder the better. When demand exceeded supply, the seamen quickly invented others.

"We should leave soon, Diana-san," Tonomori cautioned. "The Jesuits are beginning to become curious. They have watched me three times this week when I went to mass. I am beginning to run out of sins to confess."

"That really should pose you little problem, I believe," Diana replied with a knowing smile. "In two days we should be ready." She cast an admiring glance at Tonomori. "The armor becomes you. Is it very heavy?"

"Slightly more than my Japanese *yoroi*, the one I wore when we first met, but the steel is tough. It will do; it is comfortable enough. I do not see why you complain so about your corset."

"Aaaagh!" was Diana's only acknowledgement.

Chapter Thirteen

"After the disappearance of the lady in question, Lady Diana de Edgemont, close scrutiny was maintained over her father, the late count. We determined that the count met numerous times with men who were suspected as rebels or heretics. . . ."

The reader had been droning on, a sheet of unrolled parchment placed in front of him. The scroll, however, was strictly for official effect. As secretary to His Most Catholic Majesty, Philip II, inheritor of the kingdoms of Spain, Naples, Sicily, and the Netherlands, he was required to know these things from memory.

The reader, Pedro Utraca, paused, having noticed that at the mention of heresy his royal master at last had shown an interest.

Philip shifted in his chair. He had, in fact, been daydreaming. A cloud castle was taking ethereal shape on the slopes of the Sierra de Guadarrama, far to the east, overlooking the splendor of Madrid. The king found it difficult to pay consistent attention to his advisers, even to his most faithful servants. The trait was inherited from his father, who had abdicated his earthly crowns and glory as Charles V for monkish solitude in a monastery. But now the dream popped like a stretched bladder.

"You have proof of heresy, Don Pedro?" the king asked sharply. Philip had developed a distaste for war, having viewed the carnage of the battlefield at St. Quentin, where he only recently had beaten the French. Further, he was repelled by crowds and strangers and particularly by the factions that plucked at his sleeve ruff to settle their disputes. In the matter of religion, however, the church had found a champion. All his other interests—even the condition of the royal treasury—were secondary.

"No, Your Majesty, we have not," Utraca conceded. "We do, however, have reports from our agents that suggest potential problems."

"Agents' reports?" the king interrupted. "Or the slander of paid spies against a man, a noble known to me? In this matter, I will trust my own judgment."

Philip tugged at his beard. The famous Hapsburg lip jutted out even more than usual; Utraca could see his lower teeth. The secretary suppressed a sigh. His task of persuading the monarch was not going to be an easy one. The king was, on the one hand, aflame with the desire to expunge heresy and cut down all heretics, such as de Edgemont was reputed to be, but on the other, he had been highly embarrassed and chagrined that a visiting nobleman had died violently while almost literally under royal protection.

"The agents are loyal men in Your Majesty's service, sire," Utraca countered. He rolled the parchment. The king had also inherited the pathological tendency—distrusting his own retainers—that his father had so often displayed, to the retainers' annoyance. They were distressed, too, by his readiness to prejudge issues and make quick decisions that were not always in Spain's best interests.

Utraca had a sinking feeling that Philip already had made up his mind about the rich de Edgemont estates, and that none of the present discussion would change it.

"What about the daughter, the new Countess de Edgemont—is she devout or is she tainted by rebels and heresies?"

If Utraca detected a note of frustration in Philip's tone, he was indeed correct. The king needed revenues from the de Edgemont estates—and anything else of value that the crown could lay its hands on—though sometimes he wondered why more riches were not forthcoming from the low countries. In addition to the crown, Charles had passed along a staggering debt of twenty million ducats! The interest alone was shattering. With Spain's vast soldiery consuming gold and silver like regiments of armored locusts, the crown was mortgaged to its topmost jewel.

"We are aware of no taint on her part." Utraca paused. "Your counselors, however, believe we have no need to return the estates at this time. When the count died and no heir could be found, the crown in good faith legally took the property, to be administered for the benefit of the people."

Utraca passed quickly over the death of the count, for it was still a sore point with Philip that a nobleman had been waylaid like a commoner in his country.

The royal throat was cleared emphatically. "Well then, sir, the true heir now having been located, the crown will return the property in good faith. Immediately!"

Utraca bowed to the inevitable. "Yes, sire, it shall be attended to at once." He ventured to look directly at the sovereign. "Should you think it over, Majesty, our troops are in dire need of money."

"No one"—Philip insisted, raising his voice—"no one knows that better than I. We have war with the French to finance. Though I have genuinely attempted to deal effectively with the English through my wife, she and her English lords are proving to be even less hospitable than their foul climate. Not a penny will they send, even though we are fighting their own enemies. The queen seems determined to wallow in her own misery, and that is her affair. Since I am able to effect nothing in the way of a remedy, I have turned to other matters."

Utraca knew all this but remained patient, a virtue needed in dealing with the king. Mary remained in England while Philip saw to his own kingdom. *Long may she live,* Utraca thought, because the marriage was a thin mortar binding England to the schemes of Spain.

Philip continued, "And the fact is, sir, that, whatever the need, I hardly can afford to antagonize the Hollanders by keeping a property that does not belong to me."

"Yes, sire."

"The Dutch are as rebellious as they are dilatory—a

pesthole of heretics. I have been there, as you know, and I will need to go again soon. A penance, as I view it."

Philip inserted a finger into his neck ruff and pulled. It was much too stiff. Like the stiff-necked Dutch.

"When I have settled with the French, be sure that I will attend to the heretics in the Netherlands. If need be, I will bind them to the stake myself and pile the wood around their feet. I will *not* rule over heretics!"

Philip did not invent the Inquisition, that cadaverous arm of the church responsible for rooting out heresy and apostasy, those who lapsed back into Jewish or Moorish practices, or who secretly followed the teachings of Martin Luther. But he was its most staunch adherent, no less than the fathers in the Holy Office themselves.

The king paused and studied the table before him, which he particularly liked. It was of dark polished wood and unadorned, in stark contrast to everything else in the room, which he found overly large and unnecessarily ornate. The draperies were, for his taste, a hideous green, and there was even too much gold leaf, a contribution of the New World's distant riches.

The doublet he wore reflected the king's simple tastes— fine dark velvet, black as night, and well cut with a few pearls added for contrast. The puffed and slashed breeches shone with a soft luster. He refused to accede to the general custom of wearing padded hose to make thin legs more impressive. White leather slippers, deeply slashed in the German manner, represented almost his only deference to fashion. He thought, however, that few people would pay much attention to his feet, even when they bowed so deeply before him.

"But until that time, do try not to stir up the Dutch," Philip added, looking up. "And please inform me when we are to meet the countess."

"Today, sire. A private audience at your convenience, and with a formal presentation at court tomorrow," Utraca replied. He had other business to present, but the king was becoming bored.

"Must it be today?" He did not like to have his musings interrupted.

189

"Yes, sire. It would be most advisable."

"Do we have an interpreter? I have difficulty with the tongue that the Dutch speak. . . ." Philip's unease in any language other than Castilian Spanish was well known. His deep, natural reserve, coupled with the formality that resulted from the use of interpreters in other lands, had done little for his popularity.

"No need, Majesty, the countess speaks Portuguese fluently," Utraca told him.

"Ahhh, well, then, close enough. We shall have no trouble making ourselves understood. Will any others be present for the audience?"

"Only the Japanese man, sire," Utraca sniffed with distaste.

"The warlord, yes. We have had reports of their progress from Lisbon. The people there and all along the route have been astounded, I understand." The Hapsburg postal service, begun in Austria, had been expanded throughout the Spanish empire. Philip received dispatches daily from all corners of his far-flung domain. In turn, he kept couriers constantly in the saddle with correspondence from his busy pen.

"The people are like children, sire, easily impressed," Utraca commented.

"I must confess that I, too, am interested in meeting this foreign lord," Philip remarked. He frowned suddenly, a dreadful thought having struck.

"This warlord must be an infidel?"

"No, Majesty. He has embraced the faith and is now a son of the true church," Utraca assured him. "You need not fear contamination."

"Very good. I am pleased. I could not believe that a countess would actually include infidels in her circle."

Philip stood and adjusted his cap, a small, flat circle of black velvet, pinched in by a thin silver chain and flaring out slightly again to make a narrow brim. He nodded to Utraca, who left to usher in the Countess Diana.

*   *   *

At the sound of his approaching footfalls, Diana lifted her head and composed herself, trying to will away a churning feeling in the pit of her stomach.

"Good day, Countess," Utraca said, bowing deeply. "His Most Royal Highness awaits you in his private chamber."

He thought she looked pale, and forced a smile to put her at her ease. Since the king had refused to listen to reason and was willing to throw away a fortune, one might as well be magnanimous. Besides, the countess was now a rich woman again, and Utraca thought it well to cultivate her as an ostensible friend.

Diana returned a curtsy, and extended a hand that sparkled with jeweled rings. "His Majesty is so kind," she responded. It was her turn to force a smile.

"Not at all, Countess. The king is most eager to meet someone of your station who has been to the fabled Japans. An amazing feat," Utraca told her obsequiously. "As for what we discussed earlier, I am delighted to be able to inform you that the king has listened to our persuasions and is receptive to granting your petition. Naturally, he is ready to right any wrongs that may, unknown to him, have been committed in his name."

"I am most grateful for all your efforts on my behalf." Diana spoke humbly. "Be assured, I will remember you."

Utraca smiled freely; such an innocent, so gullible!

Diana did her best to look demurely impressed. The door between the anteroom and the king's chamber was thick, but her hearing was excellent and she had not hesitated to eavesdrop. She would remember Utraca very well—as a pious hypocrite.

"One word of advice, Countess," Utraca urged. "The king is comfortable only if speaking in Castilian Spanish. He has much understandable difficulty with your native tongue."

"I understand completely, señor," said Diana, switching quickly from a soft Portuguese dialect to the complexities of the Castilian lisp.

"Excellent! His Majesty will be greatly pleased." Utraca could not know how diligently Diana had worked on her accent. A hired tutor had accompanied them on the long, tiresome journey from Lisbon to Seville.

A soft rustle of silk reminded Utraca that the warrior of Japan must be recognized. Tonomori's silks were a rich brown with a pattern of silver ravens woven in. Utraca found the costume to be of a strange fashion, but oddly not out of place. He felt a pang of envy; the court sword tucked into Tonomori's sash appeared to be of a delicate workmanship.

"A good day to you, señor," he acknowledged now, bowing stiffly.

"And good day to you," Tonomori said in Japanese, returning the bow. The strategy was for Tonomori to feign ignorance of the Spanish tongue; people talk more freely in the presence of those who presumably cannot understand them. *They talk like they have rocks in their mouths,* Tonomori thought. Castilian speech was difficult to master, and Tonomori had not deigned to trouble himself with it.

He pursed his lips. Everything in the palace he found ostentatious and overdone, and the servants officious and haughty, no less irksome than the peasants milling in the streets. He considered the Portuguese, for all their strange ways, to be more civilized than these lisping Spaniards.

"If you will step this way, please—His Majesty is very busy," Utraca invited, extending an arm to Diana.

Philip was standing in a formal pose when they entered soundlessly across the thick carpeting of Persian design.

"The Countess de Edgemont of the Netherlands and the Lord Tonomori of Japan," Utraca announced, then scraped himself away into the background where he could watch and listen with unobtrusive care.

"I am pleased to be able to receive you, Countess." Philip stepped forward to take her hands as she bobbed up from a deep bow. The king's suggestion of a smile was, for him, an effusion tantamount to warmth. "And you, Lord Tonomori."

Diana smiled shyly. "You are very gracious to arrange this audience, Your Majesty."

"Not at all, Countess. I must confess to a certain amount

192

of curiosity about one so young and fair who has traveled so far.''

Philip was not the womanizer that his father had been, but he admired what he saw: a lovely young face with a sensuous mouth and clear blue eyes, golden hair pulled back into a thick bun and capped most attractively by a black velvet hat much like his own.

Spanish fashion for women tended, except for the full skirts, toward the masculine, and Diana's garments were designed to reflect this. The gold trim on her full-length skirt touched the carpet. A partlet of thin fabric, which sheathed her shoulders and the upper part of her breasts, otherwise left uncovered by her bodice, was tied at the neck with a thin black ribbon. Above this flared a small ruff supporting her chin. Undersleeves puffed through the slashes in the oversleeves of the bodice. Except for her rings, Diana wore only simple but exquisite jewelry: a belt of pearls and gold, from which dangled a single strand ending in a richly worked pendant of rubies and fine gold.

''The lure for travel is very strong, Your Majesty, something I have come to like,'' she explained. ''But the pull of my homeland is also felt very strongly, and I must return. Before I can do that . . .''

''Permit me to interrupt you, Countess. We know of your petition and find it full of merit, as is your own fair person. We will deliver our decision to you this afternoon, in writing, with copies sent north to the proper authorities as soon as possible. Well pleased we are in being able to grant your request. And, in addition, as a further expression of our esteem, we will send to the governor-general a suitable notification of our wish that you receive his protection as you enter your homeland and pursue your chosen activities there. God grant you good health in all your undertakings.''

Liar! Diana thought as she began to express her gratitude. *If he did not need peace in the Netherlands now, he would have found a pretext to keep it.*

''No need for thanks, Countess,'' Philip said. ''It is our wish that all our loyal subjects receive justice for any wrongs. We do regret any inconvenience that may unhappily have been caused by your property being placed temporarily in trust of the crown.''

Theft, murder—that is Spanish justice, Diana wanted to scream. She bowed again. Philip looked wistfully down at her. His wife was eleven years his senior, and their bed—on those rare occasions when they could share it—as cold and cheerless as an English winter. Another penance! His people did not realize what he was required to endure for their sake. His ambassador had only recently informed him that his queen was with child. A child certainly was needed, to assure continuance of the Hapsburg dynasty. And, perhaps, to bring some happiness at last to the queen. When he was present, she railed at him for alleged infidelities, and in his absence she was miserable. Philip considered that she almost surely would be unhappy anywhere.

Diana looked up, murmuring again, ''We are indebted to Your Majesty.''

He nodded and turned his attention to Tonomori, at a loss as to what to say.

''Lord Tonomori, you must be astonished at what you find here in Spain after your journey through so many foreign and barbaric lands,'' the king suggested, without intention of being condescending. No less than Utraca and all other Spanish subjects, he considered other nations and their peoples foreign and therefore barbaric, making allowance for the French and Italians, who at least had the decency to be fashionable.

''Lord Tonomori has difficulty in understanding other languages,'' Diana told him. ''He knows a few phrases in Spanish but is only learning. I will translate, if Your Majesty pleases.'' She repeated the king's remarks in Japanese.

Tonomori listened, keeping his gaze on Philip, who seemed almost tiny as he teetered on remarkably bony legs.

''Thank you, Diana-san,'' he said, formally hissing Japanese when she had finished. ''Tell anus-face that I am astonished that he is proud to rule over such a widespread dunghill.''

Diana's knees turned watery. She wanted to strangle

194

him! If the king or his secretary had even a hint of what Tonomori was saying . . .

She turned to face Philip. "The Japanese lord says he is proud to meet such a mighty king. He is indeed astonished by the size of your kingdom. Japan is an island, many islands, much smaller than Spain. He will always remember his visit here and Your Majesty's hospitality."

Philip indulged a smile when Diana had finished her "translation." It was a ghastly thing to see—a thin sword slash on an effigy of a face, remarkable chiefly for its scruffy beard over the jutting jaw, and red-rimmed eyes watering from too many hours passed at reading.

"I am eager to hear more, Countess, but I have many duties, so you must hold me excused. I look forward to your formal presentation at court tomorrow. We will talk at length later."

A formal presentation would mean gifts. Anything that did not immediately catch his fancy for inclusion in his own art treasures, Philip would convert into ready cash, which was always in short supply. Though Spain was on the verge of bankruptcy, that did not deter the king in his pursuit of more priceless paintings and sculpture. He idly wondered what the countess was going to give him and, because of his recent favor, felt confident that it would be expensive, whatever form it might take. His thoughts returned to the castle he hoped to build in the mountains, there to establish the new royal seat.

The audience was over. Tonomori and Diana bowed their way out. Utraca saw them through the door and left them in the hands of a majordomo who would guide them out of the maze of palace corridors. A young boy, in his early teens, was standing nearby when they emerged, and Utraca scowled.

"If you please, I want to see my father," the youth faltered. His disheveled appearance suggested that he had slept in his clothes for several days. The strangely twisted face was petulant.

"Not today, Don Carlos, as I already told you—three

times," Utraca insisted. Men were coming up behind the boy. Ostensibly his tutors, in reality they were his guards.

Don Carlos looked at Diana and Tonomori with a faraway look of puzzlement. Diana held her breath. The rumors of insanity in the family were true! Dark fires of irrationality burned in those eyes. His grandfather, himself one of the ugliest men in Europe, never could stand the sight of him, as repulsive as he was in his almost obscene madness. Don Carlos reportedly was the source of Philip's deepest despair—and he still stood first in line for the throne of Spain. The king needed another son.

The tutors took the boy by his thin arms. "Come along, sir. You are truant in your studies," one of them reminded.

"I don't like my studies," Don Carlos mumbled. "I don't like either of you. When I am king, you shall be whipped!"

Their mouths compressed, the tutors forcibly marched the boy away at a nod from Utraca.

"The boy has been ill. He has not been himself," Utraca told Diana, sweating. *El Infante*, as Don Carlos was also called, had been provoking incidents of late. He liked to flog pretty girls. *God be thanked that he had not tried to molest the countess.*

"I understand," Diana assured him. She remembered that the boy's grandmother was called Joanna the Mad. "I have already forgotten it. Come, Lord Tonomori!" They bowed again, and Utraca left to attend the king.

Tonomori retrieved his *tachi* from a palace guard and tied it in place. Long swords were permitted in the presence of the Spanish king, but Tonomori, following Japanese practice, had worn only the short sword as a mark of the respect he did not feel.

The majordomo led them silently through the wide halls, his staff of office tapping the marble floor. Diana, her thoughts in a whirl, nodded absently to the courtiers she encountered, gathered in knots of twos and threes. The palace vultures, always up on the latest gossip, would know who she was and what she wanted. They would remain aloof until the settlement of her suit with the king was known.

A landless countess might prove to be a hindrance in their climb over wrecked careers, and need not be acknowledged except with a bow or gesture. But a countess with vast estates would be welcomed everywhere, especially if she enjoyed royal favor, another lever they might press to move a stubborn monarch.

Relieved that the interview was over, Diana was eager to return to her rented villa. She was also furious with Tonomori for his vulgar remarks about the king, even if Philip could not have understood. She had been caught off-guard. And her seething hatred of the king and what he represented boiled anew.

Their horses were ready for them in the late-morning sunlight of the courtyard, which already was growing hot. Young servants held the reins, and Tonomori dismissed them with a toss of small silver coins that they deftly scooped out of the air. A guard returned Tonomori's pistols to him. These were forbidden in the palace. Tonomori boosted Diana into the sidesaddle, a recent invention made popular by the de Medici queen of France.

Once out of the gate, they spurred their horses to a brisk trot. The overhang of olive trees, dappling the shade, made for a pleasant ride. Diana chose to take the long way around the town in order to avoid the market crowds.

"Seville is a world all its own," Contreras, their guide, had warned them, and he had proved to be a master of understatement.

If Seville was the port of entry for the New World and its floodtides of gold, then it was also the capital for most of Spain's hardened rogues and cutthroats, who strutted and swaggered along its narrow streets and alleys.

The beautiful women kneeling in the cathedrals, Contreras had told them, probably were asking penance for sins committed in the same position only an hour before in one of the many *puterias* in the La Lagune quarter. With municipal sanction, these perpetually did a thriving business.

But despite Seville's more unpleasant aspects, Diana had been fortunate in one important respect. It turned out that the spymaster Mendoza and his henchmen were off on an errand in the eastern portion of the country, hunting heretics and witches there. Thus, they were not in a position to menace Diana at close range, as Giraldi had feared, nor could they seek to influence the king against her. Fortune had once more played into her jeweled fingers.

Giraldi's resident agent had found a villa for Diana, to make sure the countess would not be unduly fleeced. When Tonomori was not booting bogus cripples out of her way, he and his *ashigaru* were making sure that no opportunists had a chance to slit the panniers on the pack mules and make off with valuables.

The villa was thickly walled so as to be easily defended. And for good reason. Tonomori learned quickly the tricks of the specialists in thievery. He had to contend with the *grumetes*, the ship boys skilled in climbing rope ladders when looting houses, and the *apostols*, who were reputed to have more keys than Saint Peter. On the other hand, he did not trouble himself with the morals or practices of the cape and mantle snatchers or the *devotas* adept at levering alms out of church boxes and stripping rings from statues of saints. Such thefts occurred not only away from his line of vision, but mostly at night, when the countess and her entourage remained indoors.

And after the headless bodies of known thieves were discovered outside the walls of the villa, the countess was not threatened again by thieves seeking an entry into her home.

At night only the brave went forth—and the agile. It was then when the citizenry emptied the day's collection of the chamber pots into the already redolent streets. . . .

"You take too many chances," Diana said to Tonomori, breaking an extended silence.

"How so?"

"What if the king had someone hidden who understood Japanese?"

"It certainly would have made for a lively morning." Tonomori's tone held no remorse.

"We would be cooling our heels in a dungeon somewhere, awaiting the royal displeasure, that's what we'd be doing."

"You give the Spanish too much credit," Tonomori retorted. "They are so puffed up with self-importance that they could not possibly imagine that anyone might figure them for the bumbling idiots they really are."

Diana began to rein in her mare so she could stop and argue, but Tonomori reached out with his riding crop and stung the horse on the rump.

"Keep going! A moving target is a more difficult target," Tonomori cautioned. He had checked the loading and priming of his pistols after retrieving them.

"No one would be foolish enough to try something at this time," Diana objected.

"*Now* look who is taking chances," Tonomori pointed out with a malicious grin.

Diana laughed. He was right, of course. Tonomori had maddening ways sometimes, but she could never stay angry with him for long. "I won't take chances if you won't. Promise me."

"I promise," he lied cheerfully.

Diana knew he was lying, and she also knew that he would not change his ways. They played a charade for the benefit of each other: When he broke a promise, she would not remind him of it—unless he goaded her—because she was also lying.

They found the villa a scene out of a madhouse. The first hint of what awaited within was the sight of two unconscious forms lying in a heap outside the walls. These proved to be servants who, Diana learned later, had breached their trust by tapping a cask of ruby wine before breakfast. On discovery, they had been sacked immediately and deposited beyond the pale to sleep off their binge.

Liveried pikemen in silver and blue, the de Edgemont colors, stood about arguing while seamstresses made final adjustments. A small boy was straining at the leashes of two wolfhounds that were panting from the exertions of chasing a clutch of peacocks now being rounded up by several swearing dwarfs. The monsignor who had been hired to serve as household confessor was displaying a quite worldly interest in a pretty chambermaid. She appeared to be in need of four arms, two to hang out the linens and at least two to fend off the monsignor.

Everyone was talking or shouting at once, demanding to know where now was their position in line for presentation at court, please; when was lunch going to be served, please; what were they going to eat for lunch, please; when were they going to be paid, please; and would the grand lady of the Dutch be giving them any presents?

While Tonomori and Diana surveyed the chaos, the wolfhounds slipped their leashes at the exciting prospect offered by a gaggle of geese, which had been honking at them in irritation. The horses shied and kicked as the dogs disappeared through the gate amid a small snowfall of white feathers.

In the middle of all this calmly stood Jose Montejo, pensioner of the crown and a former chamberlain and master of ceremonies. He had remade the procession list five times so far that morning. Royal presentations were nothing new to him. Montejo looked up at the countess, smiling.

"Good day to you, Countess," he lisped.

Diana returned the greeting and dismounted, assisted by Tonomori, who searched the seething throng for his men. He found Yamahito and Oshabiri squatting in the shade of a large olive tree by the water fountain. Toriko stood at the fringes of the uproar, fanning herself.

"Will we be ready in time, Señor Montejo? The presentation is tomorrow," Diana informed him.

"Tomorrow?" Montejo's question was more of an exclamation, but his reply was calm. "All will be ready, Your Ladyship." Mentally, he crossed himself.

"Very well. We are depending on you." Diana disappeared into the villa to change from her clothes into something more simple. Her back ached. After years of freedom in kimonos, she was back into a canvas-covered iron corset. Despite discomfort, however, she kept in mind that it could help bring her closer to avenging her father. Toriko was dressed similarly, though she would wear a kimono for the court presentation. The clothes would simply not fit properly without the corset, no matter how trim the figure. Toriko did not complain, however much Diana might moan loudly with every pinch of her stays. *To each her own,* she thought.

Tonomori, having tried on his hose and doublet once, had said nothing, though his face thundered volumes. He would wear the Japanese court costume of a samurai for the presentation. After that, they all would dress in the European clothes that befitted their station and rank, like it or not, except for certain few special occasions when their native garments would be appropriate.

"How do they progress, Toriko-san?" Tonomori asked after turning his mount over to a groom.

"Slowly, Tonomori-san," Toriko replied, fanning herself. Tonomori did not remark on her dress. Their clothes apparently had been designed without comfort in mind, and his turn was next. Because it would be bad manners to complain, they completely avoided the subject.

Yamahito and Oshabiri, however, had been loud on the subject. It was too much. Could they not go back to Japan? The Spanish were barbarians, the clothes Diana-san had bought them were ugly.

Tonomori had informed them calmly that they could wear the clothes quietly, or he would personally sausage them into their doublets with the aid of a bung starter before stuffing them down the nearest privy, which would serve as an appropriate tomb. The *ashigaru* watched him in sulky silence. Tonomori expected that their mood would change once they saw him in his new finery. He spat.

"And to think that the Spanish have conquered the New World and now have most of Europe shaking in its boots," he observed wryly to Toriko.

"I saw the pikemen practice this morning. They are quite skilled. Not as good as our *naginata* men, but not greatly inferior."

Tonomori grunted. Just then the dogs reappeared, followed by a red-faced fat man. They had abandoned the geese in favor of a herd of squealing porkers being escorted to market. Shrilly demanding recompense for his wasted time, the pig herder was brandishing a cudgel at the dogs, who had waded into the fountain to drink.

Galloping after geese and pigs was hot work, and they flopped down in the shallow water.

Montejo was equal to even the most unpromising social situation. He raised a finger at the captain of the pikemen. "Eject the buffoon!" he directed.

At the captain's determined approach, the herder fled. Their thirsts slaked, the dogs padded wetly into the villa seeking a cool corner to sleep. There, they were no match for the maids, who broomed them out the door and into the boy's waiting arms.

Another half hour passed before Montejo finally got most of the people lined up to his satisfaction. The dwarfs here, the pikemen just so . . . Tonomori and Toriko stepped into their places, just behind a chambermaid who was filling in for Diana.

Then the bell rang for the noon meal and everyone scattered, the empty courtyard echoing to the sound of scampering feet.

Montejo did not even look up. Tonomori watched, fascinated, as he crossed out several lines and began writing new directions.

Chapter Fourteen

By even royal standards, Diana's presentation at court had been a popular success. It had gone better than Diana had daydreamed in planning it aboard ship months before in Goa.

The court had been dazzled by the parade of blackamoors,

in turbans and silks and carrying giant fans of ostrich plumes; an honor guard of strutting pikemen resplendent in their new livery; exotic Japanese in their brilliant costumes; and preening peacocks followed by scurrying dwarfs carrying small silver shovels to scrape the marble floors after the birds.

And, of course, the countess herself, breathtaking in a dress of dark purple velvet and gold silk encrusted with pearls and sapphires. Seven Lisbon jewelers had worked furiously for a week to turn out a stunning necklace of white gold set with two dozen emeralds, now reposing seductively between the impressive swell of her breasts.

And the king had been pleased with his presents—coffers of the finest spices; strange, horned animals made of pure gold (which he later had melted down); fine lacquer work; bolts of Chinese silk in his favorite colors of yellow and silver and black; and some exquisite porcelains. These he would keep for his most private collection.

Philip had charged Diana with messages of goodwill to the nobles of the Netherlands, and promised another royal visit as soon as certain duties at home would allow.

These assurances and promises Diana had accepted with grace, though she thought an announcement of impending plague would be better received at home.

She took her leave from Seville quickly, disappointing the sudden surge of well-wishers. The *auto-da-fe* which had brought Philip to Seville would occur soon, and she was intent on departing first. Those who had hopefully anticipated the largesse of a wealthy woman now restored to royal favor found, instead, the brass knocker tarnishing at the deserted villa.

Only one unpleasant incident occurred as they rode through the cobblestones. Early that morning, they had heard cannons booming in salute. Two galleons had arrived from the New World, and much of the town had turned out to line the banks of the Guadalquivir to watch the ships put into port. For most, it was an opportunity for a holiday; for others, a chance to pilfer goods.

Having omitted breakfast in her haste to leave, Diana

was ravenous. At a crossroad where a vendor was doing a lively business selling meat pies, she reined in her horse.

"Please do not, Countess," Contreras urged, laying a restraining hand on her arm, his round face set oddly.

"But we have plenty of time, Senhor Contreras, and the pies smell so good." Diana smiled, poised for a bite.

Contreras did not remove his hand. Diana began to feel annoyed.

"Please excuse my caution, Countess, but three days ago several condemned criminals were executed and their quartered remains hanged in prominent places throughout the city," Contreras explained. He cleared his throat and continued. "I have observed that many of these remains are no longer in place, as they should be according to law. And since it is not generally known to travelers that unscrupulous men in the city will mince the meat from these remains and bake them into sausages and meat pies . . ."

The pie dropped from Diana's fingers and plopped open on the ground, the sauce and meat splattering through the crust. A small, spindly cur dashed in and began wolfing down the scraps, its thin flanks heaving with the exertion. Diana leaned over in the saddle and retched dryly. Tonomori turned to lash the vendor with his riding crop, but the man had scrambled over the nearest fence, pausing only to call out curses on Contreras for interrupting the business of an honest man.

After that, Diana and her entourage rode at a brisk pace. Tonomori was glad to be leaving. He had thought Seville was the rankest city he had ever had the misfortune to encounter, despite its obvious wealth from the New World. Its people were dispirited and wary; most were poor. The arrogant rich treated their horses better than they did any beggars who might not be fast enough on their feet to escape the horses' hooves. The Portuguese, he had noticed, had a more efficient plan for dealing with the impoverished: When the beggars and vagabonds could be caught, the crown simply transported them to swell the populations of Portugal's burgeoning colonies.

Tonomori tugged at his tight, binding garments, longing for his comfortable kimono. Behind him, despite their saddle sores, Yamahito and Oshabiri were restored to relative good spirits by the sight of their master sharing the pain of their accursed Spanish clothes. Saru clung tightly to his master's saddlebow. Oshabiri had shrugged aside several lucrative offers for him. The offers had tripled after the little monkey had bitten the Count of Olivares, a most unpopular man, but Oshabiri had not wavered.

As they reached the Lisbon waterfront and paid Contreras appropriately with lavish thanks and pieces of gold, they found de Wynte relieved by their return and eager to sail. He had been pacing the deck impatiently for days.

"It is with relief that I see you back safely," he told Diana while crewmen struggled with the travelers' luggage.

"It is well that we be gone soon now," she agreed. She felt depleted in body, though as vital as ever in spirit. They had been on the road for a week. Tonomori and Toriko stood by her side in the chartroom's relative comfort as de Wynte explained his woes.

Lisbon also had its share of thieves and robbers, not all of whom toiled in the *Casa de India*. Two of de Wynte's men had been stabbed ashore. The miscreants escaped, so the authorities seized the victims and forced de Wynte to pay their fines for disturbing the peace.

Giraldi had sent a message wishing the *Schoen* a safe voyage and urging the captain to weigh anchor as soon as was convenient. They waited no longer. Their longboat warped them out of the harbor with the tide, and the *Schoen* rode the swells, ready to fly with the first puff of air. When it came, de Wynte had the crew set the mizzen to bring the ship about. They would go past the chalk cliffs of England to the Netherlands.

Tonomori picked out familiar landmarks he had noticed three months before when they had put into Lisbon. He had meanwhile paid careful attention to everything, from the amount of the rake-offs paid to crown officials at the *Casa de India*, to the arms carried by the Spanish soldiery, to the handling of ships and the ways of the sea.

He wanted to learn all that he could on every subject, and in his mind he projected future occasions to observe the construction and operation of powder mills, and the forging of arms and armor. Especially guns. Tonomori liked to think of these things as he leaned against one of the ship's cannon.

The waves were a dirty jade green after recent winds. His experienced eye roamed the skies, looking for significant clues. He could detect no likelihood of more storms for a while. Only with reluctance was Tonomori growing accustomed to the sea. He had come to realize that his mistrust of it was wholly natural; as de Wynte had said, anyone who grew careless aboard ship could be swallowed in an instant. Tonomori understood this well, but he could not comprehend why men were willing to voluntarily undergo the hardships of life at sea.

As samurai, he had a rigorous life, to be sure, but Tonomori had begun to think that, compared to sailors, samurai had it easy: a quick death for the samurai, a lingering agony for men whose lives ebbed away on the oceans.

A quick death . . . The life of a samurai was one headlong rush toward death. His was no different. Death might be waiting for them in the Netherlands. The real enemy was there—and must know they were coming.

Tonomori looked toward his mistress at the rail. They were only a few against many; no matter. Diana was an untried blade—but already she had been forged and tempered. Her initial tests were against ronin and pirates. Europeans were another matter, as yet an untested factor. But then so are we, he thought, now so far from his beloved Floating Kingdom.

"You are late!" The voice was heavy with contemptuous reproof, and the uniformed man standing stiffly before the seated nobleman plainly was nervous. He cleared his throat, and fumbled for the right words.

"It was unavoidable, Your Grace. The crowds were so heavy. . . ." Captain Hernan Nunez stopped, groping for words.

"Unavoidable, Captain? You should have anticipated all possible problems and made contingency plans." His Grace, the Duke of Alvino, governor-general of the Netherlands, sat casually enough in his chair, inspecting a finely manicured nail, but his attitude bespoke an urgency. ".I do not like to be kept waiting. You may begin."

"The Dutch wench received a hero's welcome here in Antwerp. The entire city seemed to turn out to meet her. Frankly, I've never seen anything to approach this reception. A two-headed elephant wouldn't cause this much excitement. . . ."

"I'm sure the countess does not suffer in the comparison," the duke interrupted. "And remember, please, that we are in the Netherlands. She is noble born. You will refer to her as the countess. Do I make myself clear?" It was desirable not to needlessly offend these lowlanders.

"Yes, Your Grace. . . . Then there were the foreigners, the Japanners. Three men, a woman, and a monkey. All of a kind. This city is agog. If they had come from the moon . . ."

"Spare me," Alvino said abruptly. "Just the facts, if you will be so kind."

The captain's feet shifted uneasily. On the duke's handsome face he discerned the expression of a cat contemplating the pleasure of swallowing a mouse.

"They have arranged a celebration for tonight at the Hall of Burghers. Almost all the nobles are to be in attendance. I am sure that if the burghers had a king, he would be there too. I am thinking that you might wish to forbid this affair?"

"No!" Alvino snapped. "Let them have their stupid celebrations. For now." He leaned back in his chair, reviewing the events that had led to this state of affairs.

The lady certainly led a charmed life. A written report from his agents, received weeks before, had contained useful information, scant and frustrating though it was, about the bungled attempt on her life in Goa. The Countess Diana had gone on to survive a long sea voyage and had stood before the king and persuaded him, by God, to relinquish the de Edgemont estates.

He recalled a cross-reference to the Japanese, copied secretly from a report in Jesuit files. That report was now five years old; the duke could recall it from memory.

They carry a sword and dagger both inside and outside the house and place them at their pillows when they sleep. Never in my life have I met people who rely so much on their arms. . . .

So ran the letter of Francis Xavier of the Society of Jesus. Alvino was annoyed. Why had not the missionary in Japan included more details? It would have spared the duke much trouble. Now he would have to be at great pains to take the measure of his opponents, and he felt the pressure of too little time available to carry this out effectively.

"What else?" he demanded of the captain.

"The Japanners appear to be nothing more than dumb savages, as one would expect. At your orders, one of my men tried to draw them into conversation, but they did not seem to understand what he was saying."

Of that, Alvino was not so sure—and he needed to be sure of every element that related to his scheming. The estates had slipped through his fingers, and his ambitions had been dependent on them. Having just now vacated the de Edgemont mansion—after emptying it of every article worth selling—the duke was forced to reside uncomfortably in his military headquarters. Here, on the outskirts of Antwerp, the guns of his fortress commanded the broad River Scheldt and its seaward approach to the city. Like Seville, Antwerp was a major European port located along a heavily trafficked river that emptied into the sea many miles distant.

A spot over his left eyebrow was beginning to throb; his headaches were becoming worse lately.

"What about the banquet we are to hold in honor of the countess?" he inquired of Nunez.

"My men have attended to it, Your Grace. She has accepted, and will confirm it in a note she is to send later."

"Excellent! I think we can show the Dutch how to stage

a banquet, one that they always will remember. You are dismissed.''

Nunez bowed and withdrew. Alvino listened as his departing footfalls grew fainter, and returned to his innermost reflections.

Candles had been newly lighted and a small fire laid in the hearth despite the warmth of the early evening. Alvino was always cold. He hated the winters of the Netherlands, but found the summers just as unpleasant. He suffered from night sweats and often awoke with a rude start, the bedclothes damp, his skin as cold and clammy as that of a corpse.

For a brief moment, it even seemed a pity that the countess would not live to enjoy the banquet he was arranging, ostensibly to honor her. Preparations would continue, of course; otherwise, people might become suspicious when it turned out that there was neither banquet nor guest of honor.

But Alvino needed her land. He was deeply in debt, despite the ton of gold and silver extracted from heretical victims of King Philip's Inquisition and from those unhappy Dutchmen suspected of harboring rebellious ideas. Only a fraction of the gold had been making its way south into the crown's treasury. Even so, Alvino needed more—and the moneylenders were so crass and bold as to demand payment. The immense cost of building his private cache of armaments and of paying bonuses to a thousand soldiers who would be loyal to him instead of the crown was a continual, nerve-racking drain on the duke's emotional as well as financial resources.

Sale of the de Edgemont estates would have satisfied the creditors until he was far away from these provinces. Then the creditors would be left holding a very empty gunnysack, and with exactly nothing that they could do to recoup.

A bronze bull, frozen in an eternal charge on a low table by the hearth, was burnished by the firelight's gleam. It was the duke's most prized possession. Once owned by Cesare Borgia—son of that most notorious pope, Alexander VI; and himself a warring and murderous cardinal, the model for Machiavelli's Prince—the Borgian bull symbolized a dead age and an extinct family. Or so everyone said; everyone except the present Duke of Alvino.

Cesare Borgia ultimately had been forced to flee from Italy to Spain, where his family had originated. Though he had suffered imprisonment, he later had won new distinction, eventually to fall in battle while fighting for Henry, King of Navarre.

There were those who whispered that the Alvinos were tainted by Borgian blood as the result of a clandestine affair between Cesare and the first duchess, Alvino's grandmother. As a small boy, Alvino had innocently repeated this servants' gossip to his father, who had laughed his brittle laugh—and then had ordered three of his wife's maids whipped to death.

Except for his father's rages, Alvino could hardly remember him. During one of these wild tirades, the duke had stabbed Alvino's mother to death. He remembered finding her naked body and how her thickening blood had darkened his small hands. Much within him had died with her, but not his dream of becoming a successor to Cesare Borgia. She had not laughed when he had told her of that dream, but had, with him, relished the romantic and rousing concept.

And when the old duke had died only a few years later after falling down a flight of stairs in the palace, the bronze bull had been found beside him. Had he merely admired its striking, forceful beauty—or had he actually been proud of the Borgia strain? The new duke buried his father with proper honors, and kept the bronze as his own talisman.

The fire burned redly, but Alvino shivered. His mother had been this cold when he had found her.

He shook himself; he could not afford to waste time traveling down dusty corridors, dredging up old horrors. Best to contemplate what will be, rather than recalling what was.

An orderly slipped in with a large tumbler holding the duke's first cordial of the evening, stirred the fire, added a few more pieces of split oak, then left unobtrusively. Not a word was exchanged.

Alvino's flight of thought rose with the flames. Three ships at anchorage were ready to be loaded. They would receive guns, cannon, powder, and shot, as well as armor—enough to equip an army—from his warehouses within the shadow of his fortress, when the time was ripe. The time was approaching.

Within a month, he expected to have in his hands the papers appointing him governor-general of Naples. He would take with him his thousand picked men to form the solid heart of his armed forces. They would be augmented by others he would sign on in Naples and arm from his secret cache. The crown of Naples would follow; Alvino would seize it for his own, rallying supporters beneath the charging bull of his new banner. He would be no governor-general; he would be king!

From that stronghold, Alvino's forces would strike out and reclaim all the vast lands once held by Cesare Borgia, whom Alvino was proud to claim as a forebear. Those lands and more . . .

Most men might consider him mad for conceiving such a bold design, but they did not yet know his full genius; of that Alvino was sure. The plan was bold, yes. But with the proper timing, it would work. And Italy would have a new king in a new and golden age.

The countess had to die as the next step in his path to power—as her father had had to die; the duke's agents had silenced him in Spain before he could reach the king.

Alvino rang for his orderly and called for another cordial, red wine thickened with a sweet syrup and opium. His headache was worse, and he needed the cordial to help him relax, to think more clearly. Cesare Borgia himself must have been possessed by such visions, he reflected. Sipping the cordial, he called for the commander of his network of spies in the Netherlands, Captain Rodrigo Gutierrez.

"Your Grace commands," Gutierrez said with a sharp salute ten minutes later.

"You are prompt, Captain," Alvino told him. It seemed only a few seconds since he had dispatched the summons for Gutierrez. The room appeared dreamy in quality now, almost as if he could reach through the walls and beyond, to distant horizons.

"You are of course maintaining a constant watch on the countess's every movement," he went on. "Where she rides, with whom she speaks, everything she does, on her estate, in the city, and in the countryside."

"I have established all possible surveillance, and will keep you informed, Your Grace," Gutierrez assured him. The captain was concerned. He had his own ambitious dreams, and had long since hitched his own career to Alvino's ascent.

The duke's eyes glistened with a sheen produced by the opiates. At first the drugs had not alarmed the spy. He also was aware of Alvino's headaches. But lately, the duke seemed increasingly dependent on his cordials, as he preferred to call them. They were engaged in a dangerous game, and Gutierrez hoped the duke did not make his moves recklessly. But he recognized that it might be even more dangerous to mention the drugs. Alvino then would know that Gutierrez was aware of a weakness within him— and that could prove fatal. So he kept his counsel watchfully.

"Excellent," Alvino said. "You anticipate me. I want you to arrange a meeting for me with the countess. It must appear to be by chance. I wish to see for myself what kind of woman it is I am to vanquish."

"Consider it done, Your Grace."

"We will talk later. See me when you can bring me news." The duke dismissed Gutierrez with a wave of his hand. The captain was a good man, loyal and reliable. It was to him, after all, that Alvino had felt able to entrust the sensitive mission of killing de Edgemont on that roadside in Spain, far from a place where the duke could logically be connected to it.

When Gutierrez had departed, Alvino turned to watch the patterns of the flames. The coals were glowing orange and white; small chunks broke off and bounced below the grating. The duke stared at the coals, and through them. And stared. And stared.

Chapter Fifteen

The great house seemed smaller somehow, the trees larger. Could five years have made such a difference? No, six actually, and a little more. Diana was beginning to feel a stranger in her own land, her eyes rimming wetly with memories.

A voice: *"She is here!"*

The servants began flooding out onto the front steps, eager, excited, no less than their new mistress.

The faces were older, more careworn, a few unfamiliar, but most had been known to Diana from earliest childhood. She dismounted quickly.

"Amalia! Christina! Frans!" she cried. Formality was briefly forgotten. Their mistress was a countess, but most of them had known her from the cradle, and their affection had grown during the years, increasing with the death of her father, the Spanish occupation, and her banishment to a heathen land.

And there was old Willy, the estate carpenter, in his leather smock. Willy had made her her first doll. Amalia had taken out the splinter her small finger had drawn from the doll, and had tongue-lashed Willy. Frans, the steward, now beaming indulgently, had watched Diana take her first steps. Pieter, the groom, had saved her from tumbling down a well as a child while playing with the bucket.

"I have missed you all terribly," Diana said when the jubilation had died down to a babble of questions. "We have a lot to catch up on. Be sure that I will tell you about all that I have done and seen. And I have much to ask you. Please be patient with me, as I will be with you."

Diana noticed a few small children peeping around threadbare skirts and realized she would have to learn some new names. She would have all the personal idiosyncrasies of her servants to relearn also, but she knew she could rely on Frans, who, she remembered, ruled the house with a firm but fair hand. His slightly agitated manner—amounting to a show of hysteria for the usually unflappable Frans—indicated to her that something was amiss, but she would do him the courtesy of discussing it with him later, in private.

The manservants began unloading the baggage cart Diana had brought with her, but were pausing to give Tonomori, Toriko, and the *ashigaru* questioning looks. Tonomori's composed countenance had a predatory look that did not invite efforts at conversation.

Diana was led into the house by Frans as the rest of the servants went back to their work. "What happened?" she asked with barely controlled anger. Its emptiness echoed her voice. Perhaps she had been wrong to come to the estate first rather than to her town house.

"The Spanish, they took everything," Frans explained dolefully. He had not known how to prepare her for this shock.

Except for a few heavy tables and chairs, in the family for generations and too old-fashioned to be marketable, the house was devoid of furnishings or decoration. Light patches on the walls were vivid where paintings once hung.

"Most of the servants were turned out when they came," Frans said. "Only I and a few others were kept on." He coughed apologetically. "And even we have not been paid in nearly four years now. When word of your imminent arrival was received, I took it upon myself to rehire the servants. Most of them came back, but a few were afraid."

"What about the household accounts?" Diana inquired, remembering dimly the placement of tables, chairs, urns, candlesticks, carpets—everything that no longer was there.

"Nothing left, I'm afraid," Frans replied sadly. "The

Spanish ate every bird, slaughtered every last animal to feed their troops, which they quartered around the house. This was the headquarters of the governor-general, you know. We served him. Outside, our nearest fields have lain fallow. I was able to hide a very few casks of wine from the cellar. The Spanish drank the rest. We would have starved these last months except for the generosity of your neighbors. They are responsible for the hens we now have, for the seed that is to be planted, and for the few animals we have to work the land.''

''I will remember their generosity,'' Diana told him. ''And I will remember the Spanish for what they did. I will also remember your loyalty.''

Frans bowed.

''Now then,'' she continued in a mixture of anger and pride. ''I have money of my own. The house will be what it was. You may hire what servants you see fit. I suppose the duke's men confiscated all the family plate?'' She referred to eating utensils, candlesticks, and art objects cast or hammered out of solid silver.

''No, Countess. They were very angry about that. They assumed that your father, the late count, had run into debt and sold it all. None was to be found. But I know that not to be true. There *was* money, but no one, myself included, knew where it was. And before he left, your father removed all the silver.''

Diana's eyes lighted. ''Ha! I think I know where it may be. Go to the stables, the third stall. Pry off the boards at the rear after having Pieter or someone shovel out the manure pile that has always been there. Bring me what you find.''

''At once, Countess!'' Frans left on springing steps.

Diana looked around. She had been a young girl when she left. Her father, his face drawn with grief, had bundled her down the stairs in the dead of night after her brother had been found beaten to death in an alley brawl. Her eyes had been heavy with sleep, and she had shivered with fear and cold. In the dark, Diana had ridden behind her father, with several heavily armed friends at their side. In the city, at the waterfront, the count had kissed his daughter good-bye and placed her in a small boat with Captain de Wynte. He was to command a Dutch trader anchored downriver in Flushing. So had begun her odyssey around the world in flight from the tragedy that stalked her family. And during much of the time that she had been away, her deadly enemy, the Duke of Alvino, had been occupying this house. Diana wanted to weep in rage and in sorrow, for her family, for her own lost years, for horror and tragedy.

Diana recognized Tonomori's footsteps behind her. Toriko padded in silently behind him. Diana turned from them momentarily to swallow her tears and control her face.

"Except for the wall hangings, this is as bare as a Japanese house," Tonomori observed.

"It was not always so," Diana said in Japanese. "And we must be careful how we speak. I do not know all the servants who are here now, and so I cannot be completely sure of loyalties."

"That will be fine with me," Tonomori responded in his native tongue. "Well, what do you propose to do now?"

"I will return to the city tomorrow to see my father's bankers," Diana told them. She looked up the dark stairwell and began taking the steps slowly. Tonomori and Toriko followed her. "If they are men of trust," she said over her shoulder, "my funds will be safe. If not, I will have to make do with what I brought."

Diana looked into what had been her own room, at faded yellow paint. She could see the marks left on the door-jamb where her nurse had measured her as a child. The rooms were full of ghosts.

A few doors down the corridor was the master bedroom, hers now. A large solid bed, fully canopied and heavily carved from oak, jutted out from the far wall. It remained because it had been built into the room. It had been her parents' bed—and that of the Duke of Alvino.

The Spanish grew careless, Diana thought. *They left me the mattress. It is just as well I brought sheets and pillows from the Schoen.*

The family's silver had been where Diana said it was, in a hiding place that had eluded forays by the Count of Flanders and Burgundian troops in ancient times. By the evening meal, the tarnished silver had been burnished to its former glory, even if there was no place to set it.

She would have much to do, Diana discovered after a quick inspection. The servants had cleaned and polished everything to her satisfaction, but the house, inside and out, was in need of paint and plaster. The groundsman, father of the two little girls Diana had seen earlier, would need help to whip the garden and hedges back into shape after years of neglect. Unless a military reason required it, not a florin had been spent on upkeep of the estate.

Tonomori and Toriko seemed to wander aimlessly around the grounds. In actuality, they were taking stock of the defenses.

"Too flat. No walls. Twenty samurai could storm the house easily," Tonomori commented.

"Or one assassin," Toriko added. "Everything is overgrown, too much cover. But I have the feeling that Diana-san would not approve the removal of the hedges."

"I'll have them clipped, but not cut down," Diana decided after they informed her of their assessment. "The hedges have been there such a long time. I thought of having the house enclosed, but I'm of the opinion that if the Spanish want in, they'll get in. I'd rather make a run for it, if the need ever arises."

"As you wish," Tonomori said shortly. Then Toriko began her own arguments.

In the end, Diana agreed to have one line of hedge pulled and an ornamental border of gravel put in. Tonomori had explained the difficulty in walking across pebbles without being heard; his main concern was in foiling cutthroats.

At a knock at the utility room door, Toriko admitted Diana's personal serving maid, Lucia, a large woman with iron gray hair, wrinkles around her eyes, and round and rosy cheeks.

"Spiced wine, Ladyship," Lucia smiled, setting the

tray down on a broad window ledge, finding nowhere else to put it.

Tonomori sniffed the wine suspiciously after Lucia had left. Three cups were on the tray, but he and Toriko declined Diana's offer of wine.

"I do not care for all these spices. I will have to try to get used to them," Tonomori said pleasantly enough. He had subsisted on rice and fish, plus fresh vegetables and fruit whenever he could get them, ever since they had left Japan. He had declared Spanish food to be barely tolerable, and would withhold his verdict on the horrors he was sure were awaiting him in Dutch kitchens.

"Your own spices from India have given you a tidy nest egg," Diana reminded him.

"I don't eat eggs, either," said Tonomori with a straight face, adding, "I think we should take out the hedge along the south wing."

"Tomorrow!" Diana told him, sipping her wine. "I'm heading for bed now. We'll discuss it tomorrow."

Tonomori lifted his shoulders. For this evening, he would enjoy the freedom of his Japanese silks, the familiar clothes that had caught the eyes of the eager Antwerp crowds that morning. Tomorrow, it would be back into the ugly doublets he was forced to endure. He would be up to greet the dawn, and after breakfast, he would work on Diana some more. For her own good.

They rode along the *Talverstraat* at a leisurely pace. The thoroughfare was congested, despite the early hour. Diana returned many hearty greetings. Her father had been liked and respected, and her arrival was like the resurrection of a loved one. That the governor-general was forced to disgorge the de Edgemont estate added sauce to their pudding.

"Good day to you, Countess Diana!"

"And to you," Diana acknowledged for perhaps the thirtieth time that morning. She had lost yet another argument to Tonomori on the subject of the beautiful hedge along the south wing, and her mood was pouty. Tonomori could be tenacious at times, like a small boy inquiring about a promised picnic, and he had worn her down finally. The knowledge, though, that he hated his new clothes as much as she hated her corsets did much to elevate her spirits.

"You look dashing in your doublet, Tonomori-san," she teased airily. "You do have good legs."

Tonomori, who was constructing an argument for the removal of the hedge along the vulnerable north wing, merely ground his teeth and refused to give her the satisfaction of replying. It was a game they both played.

At the Exchange in front of the Town Hall, a delegation of burghers was waiting for Diana, as an official escort. The conditions of Antwerp—mild weather and a strategic location—made it almost ideal for a year-round marketplace of international flavor. Urbane Venetians, sharpeyed with the shrewdness of centuries of hard bargaining, rubbed shoulders with pragmatic German traders, cheerful English merchants, loquacious French entrepreneurs; and doleful Spanish business agents.

Only in Antwerp could Tonomori walk and prompt only a second look by those unaware of his national origin.

Diana told Tonomori to enjoy himself and was swept away with Toriko by the assembly of bowing businessmen. Because the de Edgemonts were known as a power in the land, the burghers could hope to use the countess as a prospective buffer against the Spanish levies. Very few knew who really owned the cargo of the *Schoen*, now being looked over by port officials and by priests of the Inquisition, sniffing out banned books.

Left to his own devices, Tonomori turned to his men. "Yamahito-san, do not piss in the public street. Duck into an alley when you feel the need."

"Yes, Tonomori-sama."

"Oshabiri-san, do not allow Saru to play with himself in front of the children. It is a disgusting habit, probably picked up from his master."

"Yes, Tonomori-sama . . . I mean, no, Tonomori-sama."

"You will meet me back here when the hand on the time device on that building over there," Tonomori ordered,

219

gesturing at the Town Hall, "points to the number three." He anticipated Oshabiri's next question by adding, "That is the number that looks like a seagull flying sideways."

"Ah, Tonomori-sama, so it does," Oshabiri agreed.

The *ashigaru* disappeared into the crowd, their heads twisting in all directions. The clock, newly installed and a mark of growing prosperity, was but one of the wonders of Antwerp. Tonomori felt almost overwhelmed by the many accents and foreign tongues being spoken. Business was literally booming: The signal cannon on the northern approach of the Scheldt had been fired three times already, announcing the arrival of as many ships.

The prosperous Dutch were everywhere a florin might be pocketed in honest trade. The day before, Diana had pointed out a series of covered tables in the Exchange, representing the grain basket of the western world. The wheat and barley stackers of Antwerp had discovered that by storing their grain and selling it when failed harvests or famine drove up prices elsewhere, they could reap enormous profits. Pieces of paper changed hands, and fortunes were made. The Dutch did not invent the middle-man, but they improved on him.

And thanks to the flotillas of fishing boats, the Dutch could never be starved. They might grow sick of herring, but their bellies would be full enough.

Tonomori strolled away from the Exchange to take in the sights of *Francstraat,* where shopkeepers displayed the finished products of the Exchange, or goods imported from the ends of the earth—Nuremburg timepieces so small they were made into rings, French cosmetics and perfumes, crystal from Venice, and clothing made to the latest fashion, slashed and paned in a riot of color. In the adjoining *Liedestraat,* paralleling the *Herengracht* or Lords Canal, were the shops of the artisans, the armorers, gunsmiths, cabinet makers, and embroiderers, elbow to elbow.

Tonomori saw a sign made in the outline of a ship, indicating that the shop over which it hung offered navigational equipment for sale, such as sextants and maps. It reminded him of Captain de Wynte and the *Schoen,* and also the crewmen, Volmer and Hans, who had been so friendly once they had lost their fear of him. He wished them all well, wherever they might sail on from Antwerp. With any luck, they would be returning from their venture to the distant north land of Norway to exchange the last of Diana's spices for furs, amber, and fish oil.

He thought the Dutch people's mood pleasant, different from the public formality of the samurai, but rather like what he was used to among his old drinking companions when he was the Betsuos' undefeated champion.

Tonomori would never get over the tallness of the northern men. He was considered big for a Japanese, and Yamahito exceptionally tall. But here, among the Dutch, and among the Swedes and the German mercenaries, his height was only average.

With so much to see, the time passed swiftly. Before he knew it, Tonomori was ambling toward the Town Hall, where his men were already waiting. Yamahito was eating a pomegranate, a taste he had acquired in Spain, and spitting the seeds onto the plaza.

"An unattractive practice, Yamahito-san," Tonomori scolded by way of greeting.

"We only follow local custom, Tonomori-sama," Yamahito replied.

"Nevertheless, your manners should be better than theirs. Have you kept out of trouble?"

"Yes. It was most amusing. A trader of strange wares offered Saru twenty florins for Oshabiri-san."

"Too much," Tonomori replied swiftly. "The monkey should have taken the offer."

"That is not true, Tonomori-san," Oshabiri told him indignantly. "It was I who was offered money for Saru."

"He would have gotten a bad deal either way," Tonomori said. "How much did Saru steal today?"

"Only a little." Oshabiri wrapped a defensive arm around his pet.

Tonomori smiled indulgently. The weather was good, his mood excellent. "If there were only a market for idiots, I would be a rich samurai," he mentioned.

"Think of the trouble you would have breaking in new retainers, Tonomori-san," Yamahito said, bowing.

"I am thinking of the trouble I already have keeping the ones I've got." Tonomori nudged Oshabiri. "Smarten up. Here comes our mistress. I don't want her mistaking either of you for a couple of apple sellers."

Diana said her good-byes to the escort of cheerful burghers and turned to Tonomori.

"So far, so good," she said in Japanese. "I have been followed all afternoon. Discreetly . . ."

"And I . . ." Tonomori agreed.

"However, I managed a word with my father's banking interests—undetected, I think—and my funds are safe. We have a firm foundation on which to build."

"That is good news." Tonomori was pleasantly surprised. "We should begin making plans."

"We will start this afternoon. While we are riding. I want to ride every day," Diana said decisively.

The jaunts on horseback became a daily occurrence for Diana. Tonomori urged caution, arguing that she was setting a predictable pattern.

"I do not think my enemy will have me attacked in broad daylight while I am under armed guard," Diana replied. Besides, she was eager to be gone. On the way, she would call on some neighbors whose acquaintance she wished to renew. At home, the house was in an uproar. Wagon loads of new furniture, tapestries, and fixtures were arriving daily. Diana left detailed diagrams of where she wanted everything. When she returned from her outings, and found her house in order each time, Diana took great pleasure in the efficiency of her servants.

"This is a needless gamble," Tonomori said for at least the fifth time in as many days. A groom helped Diana into the saddle, and she arranged her skirt before replying.

"I will not live a prisoner in my own house," she declared. "Your fears for me are appreciated. But I think you worry too much. Again."

"I usually am right, if you remember, Diana-san,"

Tonomori reminded her. "You have much courage. I am not afraid to die, either. My whole life has been spent preparing for the perfection of the moment. If they kill you, they will have to kill me. If I survive, if I cannot take revenge, or even if I do, I will open my belly for my failure. Either way, I will follow you, and we will have come all this way for nothing."

"I will consider what you say," Diana conceded. But she did not dismount.

The day was too perfect to remain indoors and direct the energies of servants. The sky was puffy with white clouds, but the air did not hint approaching rain.

Golden clover bells nodded their heads along the roads, and the fields were lined with row crops of turnips, carrots, and lettuces.

"Farther to the north and the east, you will see the polders," Diana told Tonomori. "That is where our people claimed the land from the North Sea. The dikes must be constantly maintained, or we would lose all that we have taken from it."

She was happy. The white plume of her gold-accented, purple velvet cap fluttered jauntily in a light breeze. Tonomori rode alongside her, while Yamahito and Oshabiri, armed with carbines, brought up a watchful rear. Toriko had remained behind for private purposes: She needed *ninja* practice sessions.

Tonomori had been given a new brace of pistols—those he had been carrying belonged to de Wynte, who did not want to part with them—but he also had brought his great bow with him. The horses clattered over a wooden bridge spanning a canal, and they headed left down a dusty road past spreading trees on the last leg for home.

"Your people work hard," Tonomori observed. He meant it as a rare compliment. He liked what he saw in the Netherlands—its trim houses, the order of crops carefully ditched and tended, the fullness of color in its cheery yellows and deep browns, and the greenness that dominated everything. Antwerp, to his mind, could not compare to any Japanese city but in contrast to what he had seen elsewhere in Europe and in India, the Dutch were industrious and, above all, tidy. Almost as neat as the Japanese.

"Yes, and they prosper," Diana responded. "When the Spanish let them alone, that is."

She explained briefly how the Spanish had managed to take over the Netherlands, relating how the House of Burgundy had married its way into Flanders and then elbowed its way even further.

Less than a hundred years before, Diana continued as they rode, the last powerful Duke of Burgundy, known as Charles the Good, had the misfortune to drown in an icy pond during an engagement with the recalcitrant Swiss. His daughter later had married the Archduke Maximilian of Austria with the aim of acquiring resources to counter French forces marauding in from the south. The result was that, ever since, the Hapsburgs had been in the saddle, trying to curb Dutch aspirations for self-reliance and religious freedom, and to retrieve rights and privileges granted the Netherlanders earlier by treaty.

"But they bit off more than they could swallow," Diana commented with vigor. "We are a fairly tolerant people. We were able to get along with Philip's father, King Charles, who at least was willing to compromise, even if the church didn't want to let him.

"But Philip is impossible, as you can understand from having seen him in action. The Protestants and the Catholics here had finally managed to find a more or less peaceable way of existing side by side. Then the Inquisition came to us from Spain. I am a daughter of the church, but my family has many Protestant friends, and I do not want to see them burned or strangled." The horses had slowed to a walk. Diana kicked her mount into a trot.

"What do you think will happen next?" Tonomori asked.

"That really is up to the king. He can't disrupt trade with us, because the crown needs the revenues from it. His troops are expensive to maintain, and he needs them here to keep the French out. But if he decides to continue to press the Inquisition here, he can expect to bank nothing but deficits. Spain badly needs our trade. We can survive without theirs. I can imagine. . . .''

For the past half hour, Tonomori had been taking the lead. Small groups of horsemen were coming up on parallel roads and remaining just behind them, maintaining a respectable distance.

"We are being driven. The men behind us are the beaters, we the quarry," Tonomori said finally, stringing his bow as they rode.

"Side roads?" Diana asked, as she turned in the saddle to look.

"Blocked! We are going in the direction they want." He could not refrain from adding, "I did warn you. . . ."

"And I was a fool not to listen," Diana agreed soberly.

As she spoke, a troop of horsemen appeared from a grove of trees and straddled the road nearly a hundred yards ahead. Tonomori instantly nocked an arrow, and his men hefted their carbines.

"Wait!" Diana ordered, laying a cautioning hand on Tonomori's bow arm. Yamahito and Oshabiri flared out alongside.

The lead figure in the menacing group had detached himself and was walking his horse slowly toward them, a hand upraised. The soldiers all rode black mounts, but this rider's roan was a horse of a different color.

"Good morning to you, Countess. This is for me a most pleasant happentance." The rider removed his cap and bowed low from the saddle.

"You have me at a disadvantage, sir. We have not been introduced, I believe," Diana quickly responded, frowning. They were in mortal danger. She had immediately guessed his identity, but was damned if she would admit as much.

"Then pray forgive my boldness, but you have been made known to me. Hearsay proclaims that there is none so fair in the land as the Countess de Edgemont, and that hearsay exactly describes yourself. I am Enrique Maria Manuel Alleara, Duke of Alvino. At your service!"

Diana examined him critically and found him, to put it mildly, a beautiful man, with a face sculpted by Michelangelo and framed by golden curls, cropped short. His rich riding attire of black accented by silver molded his lithely robust frame perfectly. The light blue eyes held her gaze; his teeth were even and small, she noticed as he smiled at her. Despite her rancorous feelings toward him, Diana's heart fluttered like a startled bird. The duke, for all his terrors by night, was a gallantly winning performer by day.

Alvino had fifteen well-armed men at his back. As if reading her mind, the duke signaled with a commanding gesture, and they wheeled their horses to ride off another fifty paces before turning to confront Diana and the duke again.

"I did not mean to alarm you, Countess, but when I learned that you enjoyed a daily ride, I simply could not wait for an introduction until our banquet. I beg your forgiveness!" Alvino rode closer, took her hand, and kissed it.

Diana's tongue was dry. They had been watched all along! She should have known better than to be trustingly careless, and she had diverted Tonomori's usual acute perceptions.

"You are forgiven," Diana told him calmly, though her mind was in turmoil. *Did the duke insist on being at the kill, or was he merely out to sample the thrill of the chase?*

"I am absolved, then? I am pleased." Alvino studied her face. *Intoxicating,* he thought. *Diana, the chaste huntress of Greek mythology. The hunt is almost over, but she does not know that. Good. That lovely brow need not be unnecessarily creased with worry. Her end will be mercifully quick, and without blood tracing back to me.*

"This is lovely, isolated countryside. Do you ride here often, Duke?" Diana asked.

"Not usually. I do not have much time for such pleasures." Alvino noted that the stern foreigner had not relaxed the pull of that ridiculous bow with the arrow nocked along the bottom. He also saw the quality of the carbines carried by the men behind the countess.

"A pity," Diana remarked.

"Yes. I understand that, like you, your late father enjoyed riding. My condolences to you. He was a fine man. I admired him.''

Admired his lands and wealth, you mean, Diana thought with fierce anger.

"I shall always do my best to honor his name," she said evenly. *And dishonor yours.*

"I believe you will," Alvino acknowledged.

"The morning grows late. I must take my leave, Your Grace," Diana said.

"I look forward to our next meeting," Alvino replied, replacing his cap and tugging at its brim.

"And I, Duke. Good day!" With a salute of her crop, Diana galloped on. Tonomori and his men were hard pressed to remain close behind. She could no longer endure the overpowering odor of evil that surrounded such a man. She must remove herself from its aura as rapidly as possible.

When they were only dwindling specks in the dust, Alvino signaled to Gutierrez. "Tomorrow night!" he instructed when the captain had reined in beside him. "Pick your best assassin. I'll leave the choice to you. No knives! I want no blood. Just hands, or a pillow. As for the Japanners, they are no concern of mine unless they interfere and get in the way. Kill them, of course, if they do.''

"After that, Your Grace?"

"Continue stacking the arms and making purchases as before. But take your time. Use extreme caution. Our fellow countrymen are always suspicious, as you know, ready to smell treason at the slightest provocation. Make sure that you give them no cause! We are too close to the goal to make a mistake now.''

But despite all the precautions that Gutierrez might be advised to take in stocking Alvino's warehouses on the waterfront, there was no disguising the fact that all of the duke's stealthy preparations—accomplished at such devastating cost—were indeed treasonous to Spain and King Philip. When his appointment to Naples arrived, he would soon be ready to depart—and ready for his conquests to follow!

"Yes, Your Grace, I will exercise great care, as always.''

"Oh, and I must be sure to talk later with you about the *other* arrangements."

"Your Grace?" Gutierrez did not follow his reasoning.

"The de Edgemont estates will go on the block again. I will sell them to the highest Dutch bidder. For the glory of His Majesty!" The duke chuckled to himself. He had not specified exactly whose glory would be served.

Chapter Sixteen

Something was coming. Something large enough to be *someone*—a man! Tonomori snaked his way under some of the ornamental shrubbery that still bordered Diana's mansion in a geometrical fretwork pattern.

He searched the impenetrable night. It wasn't a dog, he was certain; they invariably made too much noise. Diana had insisted on acquiring several for the mansion's kennel, and Tonomori had reluctantly agreed. He considered that Europeans placed too much trust in their dogs, even these huge brindled mastiffs, which were capable of tearing the throat out of a man.

The night was warm, the darkness a thick blanket. Heavy clouds obscured a waning moon.

An hour before, Tonomori had listened intently to some living thing's approach across the fields and canals toward the dark and inviting mansion. The crickets and frogs had gone still then, erupting again in their night music only when they sensed that the danger had passed on its not-quite-silent path. Tonomori waited.

The dogs had bounded out to investigate, growling low and throaty, and strangely had not returned. It was totally unlike them to quickly forget their mission and go off larking elsewhere. There had to be a more dire reason. But the thing that had stopped was now moving again. Slowly. Ever so slowly!

Tonomori, carefully concealed, waited patiently, alert to every minute sound and to each shadowy stirring, which might be a bough or a being.

Why isn't he moving in? Tonomori wondered. *The conditions are perfect. Maybe too perfect?*

He would wait. Tonomori wanted his quarry alive and able to talk.

He would wait all night if need be. Whoever was out there could not get past him. *Too perfect?*

Doubt trickled into his mind, like the beads of sweat oozing along his broad back. *While I am here, she is alone!*

Danger screamed in his mind.

Tonomori broke cover and began running across the newly mown grass, dodging to the left, to the right. . . . A shot rang out from behind him. The bullet crinkled through a pane on the double doors that opened from a drawing room onto the garden. Tonomori went through the doors at a jump, through the shards, feet first, rolling and skidding on the marble, then running, taking stairs three at a time. . . .

By all the gods that ever were, let me not be too late!

The dreams were bad, formless things that seemed to engulf her. Diana awoke once, her limbs and head heavy with fatigue. She had left a candle burning, and it was flickering low by her bedside. She replaced it with a fresh taper and lay back on her moist pillow.

To Diana, it seemed she had not rested for even a moment. She closed her eyes again. The lids felt hot. The need to sleep pressed on her like an unbearable weight.

Then her eyes opened suddenly, and she found herself looking through the candlelight at her maid Lucia, her round face lined with apparent anxiety. She was holding a pillow in front of her.

"Oh, you startled me, Lucia," Diana exclaimed. Her mind was buzzing, and she struggled to clear her thoughts.

"I thought I heard Your Ladyship cry out, and came to see if I could be of help," Lucia murmured softly. Her smile was sweet, full of concern.

"But your room is on the third floor, in the servants' wing; how could you? . . ." Diana began. Her eyes went to the pillow, and to Lucia's face, the lips now thinning, the teeth showing yellow, the eyes hollow shadows in the candlelight.

Diana felt the flesh begin to crawl on her neck and shoulders as nightmare became waking reality. Lucia was going to try to kill her. Here! Now! With a pillow.

"I couldn't sleep, either, Your Ladyship. I was walking by . . ." Lucia moved closer with the pillow, and Diana rolled away across the feather mattress, trying to kick free of bedclothes that threatened to become her winding sheet.

Lucia scrambled around to the far side of the bed, holding the pillow in front of her. The eyes never wavered, her lips now twisted obscenely. Diana moved back in the opposite direction. Lucia climbed onto the bed.

"Your Ladyship is upset," she puffed. "You have not been yourself. You need rest. Let me help you."

The wine! The wine must have been drugged, the spices and honey cloying its bitter taste. Diana had drunk it to the lees, had encouraged Toriko to drain her own cup, to try a German wine.

"Toriko! Help!" Diana cried and fell from the bed. Lucia crawled across and swung her legs down.

"Now we can have a nice long rest," Lucia was saying, descending on Diana, her massive form blocking out the candlelight.

Diana tried to struggle, but she was too weak; her limbs were leaden. The thought of her *tanto* flashed into her mind, but it was no longer in reach. Then the pillow was covering her face, smothering out everything. Diana groped for the thick wrists that held it as Lucia bore down with all her weight.

230

The door between Diana's room and Toriko's flew open, and a slim figure weaved across the floor toward Lucia, a blade in one hand. Toriko looked uncertain, dazed, moving in to attack with agonizing slowness.

"Oof!" Lucia bleated as a calloused foot struck her side. Lucia's meaty arm swept past Toriko's shaking knife hand, knocking her to the floor. She began staggering to her feet, but a heavy chair crashed into her head and shoulders. Toriko fell limply.

Diana, trying to crawl under the bed, felt a fleshy hand grab her ankle. She cried out as Lucia began pulling. Her thin nightgown caught on something sharp, ripping. Now both ankles were grasped. Diana tried to hold onto the carpet, a bedpost, but Lucia's grip was much too strong. The nightgown tore away completely.

Naked, she was dragged out from under the bed. Her hands were scraped raw. Lucia, breathing heavily, was lunging out for the pillow that Diana had managed to kick beyond her reach.

"Your Ladyship has been unwell, your mind under too much strain," Lucia said, preposterously maintaining her fiction while coiling a hand in Diana's long hair and yanking her across the floor. The pillow was a sinister blob on the polished oak.

"And now, you Dutch bitch, you will trouble no one anymore," Lucia grunted grimly, the mask of servility finally off. Diana twisted as Lucia kneed her in the ribs.

The hallway door splintered open, and Diana felt Lucia's weight snatched from her aching legs, saw Tonomori seize the woman by the throat, lift her off her feet, and pin her against the wall.

Tonomori looked down at the small figure curled on the floor into a protective ball.

"Diana-san . . ." His heart was racing, but with relief he saw life as her hands moved to cover her mouth.

"She tried to . . . kill me," whispered a small, far-away voice.

Lucia tried desperately to tear at the iron fingers biting into her throat.

"She . . . lies. She . . . ah . . . lunatic," Lucia

231

gurgled, her legs thrashing. Tonomori held her fast with one hand. In the other, steel flickered yellowly in the faint light.

For the rest of her life, Diana thought fleetingly, she would never forget the triumphant malice on that woman's face as she had retrieved the pillow.

Diana shuddered.

"Kill her, Tonomori-san!" she ordered harshly. *"Kill her!"*

Lucia lashed out futilely with a foot as Tonomori tightened his grip. Her face mottled purple above his hand, and her heels drummed a death rattle against the wall.

When it was done, Tonomori quickly carried the bulky body out of the room and down the hall. Pausing only momentarily to search Lucia's pockets, he hurled her down the blackness of the stairwell.

Querulous voices were approaching from other parts of the house. Tonomori hurried back to Diana's room, picked her up, and gently put her back in bed. Frans entered the chamber just as Tonomori covered Diana with a sheet.

"What has happened?" Frans demanded excitedly. His hair was disheveled, and he held his candle high to peer into the dimness.

"The maid. She went insane, struck the countess, and then threw herself down the stairs. I think she must be dead," Tonomori replied. He wanted to keep the man busy, keep him from asking too many questions until they could think of suitable answers.

"Is the countess injured?"

"I am bruised, nothing more," Diana was able to answer from deep within the large bed. "Please attend to poor Lucia."

Tonomori escorted Frans firmly through the doorway and cautioned him. "Remove the body. Have it buried in the morning. Keep the servants calm. There is no need for alarm."

"But the shot?" Frans sputtered. "I thought I heard a shot."

"One of my men shooting at a fox. They are busy again now that we have hens," Tonomori smiled. He would have to find an explanation also for the door he had smashed downstairs. Later.

"You can count on me," Frans assured him. The steward hovered for a moment, apparently unaware of Toriko on the floor; then his sense of duty won out over his curiosity, and he busied himself in shooing the other servants away. A small female shriek was heard from the foot of the stairs. Lucia had been found.

Tonomori closed the door and went over to lift the chair from Toriko, who was trying to pull herself shakily to her feet.

"Easy, Toriko-san. You must have taken a hard blow," Tonomori said with unusual gentleness. He uprighted the chair and set Toriko down on it.

"I hit her perfectly. But she did not go down. I did!" Toriko exclaimed dazedly.

"Do not blame yourself. That one would have been accounted strong had she been born a man!"

"How did you kill her?" Toriko wanted to know. Her head and shoulders throbbed. She thought she was going to faint, and steadied herself until the room stopped turning.

"A crushed throat," Tonomori reported briefly.

"Diana-san, are you badly hurt?" Toriko asked. A pang of remorse. She should have asked that first of all.

"I am alive, thanks to both of you," came a shaky voice from the bed.

"It was a close thing," Tonomori said. "When I finally figured out that the man outside was a lure to keep me occupied, I was afraid that I would be too late. We should have suspected treachery. . . ." Tonomori's hands flailed the air. He was angry with himself.

Diana sat up, remembering belatedly to pull a sheet over her breasts. "I think Lucia used only a little bit of her drugs at first, then added a little more each day until we became used to the taste and could receive a large dose. She was very clever. Or whoever was instructing her was that clever."

Tonomori went over to Toriko, who looked as if she was ready to topple, and helped her walk slowly from the room to her own bed.

"I believe she will soon be fine," he told Diana when he returned. "I also think that whoever was out there in the darkness, playing me for the fool that I was, will be long since gone. But I will remain on guard, just to be sure." He turned to leave.

"Wait! Don't go," Diana asked. She pulled at his sleeve. Tonomori saw that she was regarding him thoughtfully and with warmth.

Diana's fingers stroked his cheek. "You are hurt!" she said in surprise. The sheet slipped from her grasp.

"The glass from the doors I broke downstairs. It is nothing," Tonomori explained. Diana moistened a corner of the sheet at her lips and wiped dried blood from his face. Tonomori felt her wetness drying on him, from her own pink tongue, and desire flared hotly.

It was madness. Tonomori began backing away.

"I will not be far from you," he promised.

"Stay with me? *Please!*" she added.

"You wanted to be samurai. Death is part of it," he reminded her, desirous of smothering the emotion of the moment.

"I am not afraid of death! I am only afraid of being alone, waiting alone."

"This is too dangerous," Tonomori interjected. He was still very close to her bedside. "I do not know all of your customs, but I do know we cannot remain in the same room together all night. Even if nothing happens between us, your people would talk. You would become an object of gossip; your reputation and your ability to do your duty would be damaged. That must not be!

"And if I stayed, I could not promise to remain immune against your charms. You are a lovely woman, golden as the sunlight on the Inland Sea. Your spirit has touched mine. Even as we speak, my heart is beating fast. . . ."

"And mine!" Diana whispered, placing the flat of her palm against his cheek. She pressed his hand against her breast, over the fluttering heart. "Mine also is beating!"

Tonomori leaned over her, almost touching. Her mouth

234

was slightly parted, eyes wide and questioning. Then Diana put her arms around his neck and drew him down beside her.

"Good day to Your Grace!"

The duke's horse reared and whinnied sharply at the sudden appearance of the Countess de Edgemont standing at the edge of a clearing in a grove of scrub trees bordering Alvino's own lands. Alvino fought for control of the bucking brute. The two mounted retainers behind him had drawn their blades, but the duke angrily waved them back.

The countess seemed to have materialized out of the ground. Blood of Christ!

"Your Grace looks as though he has seen a ghost," Diana said. Her riding dress was purple edged with gold trim, and the countess was very much flesh and blood. She not only was alive, but it seemed to him that she looked healthier, more vibrant than ever.

"You gave my horse a fright, Countess," Alvino replied with an attempt at airiness. Inwardly, he was boiling. The woman was supposed to be dead; last night finally was the night for the awaited deed. For a moment, he thought he had seen her specter, come to haunt him. Was he surrounded by nothing but incompetents?

"I must apologize, then. It is just that I know you enjoy riding, and I hoped you would not think it presumptuous of me to join you. Was I wrong?"

Farther along the edge of the clearing, Alvino could see the foreign lord walking two horses. The foreign lord appeared to be well armed. Killing the countess here and now would be too risky. The Jappo Tonomori was an unknown, his abilities untested. Alvino wanted only a sure thing.

He smiled pleasantly. "I am afraid it is not possible today, Countess. Most unfortunately. I must ask that you forgive me, but I am on my way to an important meeting, a tedious affair, but necessary nonetheless."

"One day soon, perhaps?" Diana raised an inquiring eyebrow.

"I would be honored, of course."

"Then you *are* forgiven. To be honest, I also have pressing business in the city."

It was the duke's turn to look questioningly.

"A domestic crisis of small proportions," Diana explained with a smile at one corner of her mouth. "One of my servants proved unreliable. We go to fetch some new people. It seems there is always a problem with servants."

Alvino raised his velvet cap. "You should try a touch of the lash, Countess."

"I'm afraid that it wouldn't do, Your Grace." Diana curtsied. "One cannot whip a corpse, can one? Good day to you again." She turned and walked toward Tonomori, who had remounted and was leading her horse. Diana stood on a dead log and eased gently onto her sidesaddle.

Alvino and his men were already spurring away rapidly. As if devils were after them.

"If you are determined to commit self-murder, Diana-san, I can show you an excellent ritual, beautiful and full of honor." Tonomori's greeting was a rebuke.

"I am not going to commit self-murder—"

"A small platform, a sharp *tanto* . . ."

"—I am going to bring that bastard to his knees," Diana finished.

"I stand beside you with a sword; you make a tiny cut at the throat with the *tanto* and . . ."—Tonomori made a cutting motion with his hand—". . . I ease your passage into the next life."

"I *am* going to beat him! I am!" Diana insisted. They headed their horses back toward the estate. She had no intention of going into town.

"You are going to provoke him into doing something unpredictable," Tonomori warned.

"He is unpredictable now."

"The duke could have struck you down where you stood."

"Not with you so close by."

"He might have more men next time. Don't take foolish chances." Tonomori was determined to have the last word. They rode silently for a while.

"What are you thinking?" Diana asked finally.

"I was thinking about last night," Tonomori said. His face held no expression. Diana knew he was on the lookout for armed interception. "I almost lost you!"

"And I you. Instead, we found each other."

"And so we shall risk everything else?" Tonomori was as implacable a lover as he was an enemy.

"It is worth it to me. And to you?"

Tonomori turned in the saddle. "We each have our duty to perform, as we see that duty. That must come first. When that is done, we can think about ourselves later. I am sorry that is the case, but you know this to be true."

Diana's eyes welled with tears. "Yes—but I still want you. I want the best of both our worlds. I won't go back to what I was or to being what other people expect of me."

"We must be careful or we will quickly have the worst of both our worlds. For your sake and for mine, I can't permit that. I must honor Lord Betsuo's spirit or lose my own. I also want you. I want you right now. If it were not dangerously foolhardy, I would lift you off that horse and pillow you under the nearest tree."

"Not today you won't," Diana objected with a smile. "My ribs and legs still ache from where that dreadful woman hit me. And then there is a certain stiffness that I believe may be a result of your own activity. . . ."

"Was that not your own idea?" Tonomori countered.

"Yes, and one you certainly seemed to accept readily enough!"

They trotted along silently again for a while. The road was now cutting through her lands.

"Tonomori," Diana spoke hesitantly. "Toriko tells me that you write poetry."

"It has happened."

"Would you satisfy a whim of mine and write one for me? No one has ever sent me a poem. I think perhaps the occasion calls for it, if one ever did. Hmmmmm?"

"I already have, Diana-san."

"Ha! When can I read it?" Diana demanded, brightening even more.

"You can't. It is meant to be spoken. It is a haiku, just

the three lines. I will tell you in Japanese, since I think it suffers in translation."

"Say it now!"

Tonomori cleared his throat and began:

> *Golden butterfly trembling*
> *on the rose of the morning—*
> *Love's first embrace.*

Ah, Diana thought, touching his arm, for a samurai life and beauty and death are ever mingled, like lovers entwined in their sheets.

When had she begun to love him? Not at their first encounter, when Tonomori literally swept her off her feet. Diana almost laughed at the thought. With wonder and fear she had seen him send two fishing boats full of samurai to their doom in the depths of the sea. Again, he had saved her on the *Schoen*, straddling her, cutting down men like straw dolls, while she crawled to safety on a heaving deck slippery with blood.

Then he had cradled her in his arms on that dusty road in Goa after stepping in front of the assassin's bullet. Again and again, she had stood in the safety of his shadow, his body facing the knife in the dark. Yet that same hand had written poetry, had described in waving arcs the old legends when demigods and men fought together. His hands had now touched her most secret places, and his words and the notes of his flute had plumbed the depths of her heart.

In return, she had surrendered to him not only her body but her innocence, her honor. The samurai understood honor. Hers would be safe, would remain secret—if they were careful, and refused to let passion displace discretion.

"If you do not like the poem, I will write you another," Tonomori offered with an unusual tentativeness.

Diana shook free of her reverie. "No—it was beautiful! I know how the rose felt, with the touch of the butterfly's wings. I'm just thinking—there are so many things. . . ."

"Oh?" Tonomori was puzzled but not unhappy. Women were a mystery to him. *They are a mystery to themselves,* he thought as he automatically scanned the road and countryside for signs that peril might lie in wait.

Diana understood another danger: Hers was a separate world from his, one that was sensuous and immoral—and hypocritical. She could never marry Tonomori, even if she decided that she wanted to. Surely, Tonomori must also realize as much. A child of theirs would be rejected by both their peoples. But, in any case, Diana intended never to give herself in marriage.

To give herself to Tonomori was another matter. She wanted him as much as she knew he wanted her. They always would need to be cautious. She understood that people tended to assume the worst, and to fill in from lively imaginations all the lurid detail. Diana smiled. If she and her samurai could only be infrequent lovers, at least they could be bolstered by being enduring friends. She was aware of the power in friendship, power that would grow with the years. And their constant companionship was a natural aspect of the samurai's need to be on hand to protect her.

They could see the mansion now. "I'll race you to the stable," Diana called to him suddenly, and cropped her horse into action. Tonomori spurred his horse, and neck and neck, they galloped forward into the wind.

Chapter Seventeen

It was after the Duke of Alvino's summer gala, held in her honor, when Diana began to worry. That he would be up to something, she had no doubt. But what?

Fortunately, the letter she had obtained from King Philip now seemed to be assuring her safety, at least temporarily. When the ambassador finally had delivered the message to Alvino, the duke obviously realized that he would be held accountable should any harm befall her. It was a master stroke and should hold the duke at bay—for a while.

"The duke was gallantry personified," Diana told Tonomori and Toriko as they relaxed beneath a blue-and-white striped awning in the garden behind the de Edgemont mansion. Not far away, groundskeepers pruned the remaining shrubbery back into shape.

"I do not like his officers." Toriko shuddered as she spoke. "They touched me everywhere with their eyes, and made lewd remarks they thought I did not understand." She peeled an apple with a dainty ivory-handled knife kept for that purpose on a salver of silver-gilt. When at home and not receiving guests, Diana and Toriko returned with relief to the comfort of their loose Japanese silks.

Tonomori also seized on the opportunity to take his leisure in a short kimono, the *hakama* bunched at his knees, his calves wrapped in leggings of contrasting pattern. His two-handed sword lay on the grass beside him. The women lounged in comfortable leather-bottomed chairs, but Tonomori still preferred to sit cross-legged on the flat tiles, on guard. He adjusted the *wakazashi* thrust through his sash and continued experimenting with the flute he had bought in Goa.

"It is a pity that Alvino is such a monster. He is very handsome," Diana commented, but there was no real regret in her voice. "He seems to be able to adapt to his surroundings, suiting his words and manners to the occasion. Lucifer must have been like that, shining without and twisted within."

"Yes, and it is a fascinating story," said Toriko. "That of the angel of light who challenged the ruler of Heaven and was cast down in all his pride."

"Yes, he overreached himself, having thought he was unable to fail." Diana was finding it difficult to think. The music from Tonomori's flute was pleasant, but haunting, evoking memories of other times, other lands, of bamboo smoke and the rustle of wind through ancient trees, and of stone gods.

"That is lovely, Tonomori-san. What is it?" Diana asked softly.

"It is an air based on the legend of a samurai who loved a daimyo's daughter," Tonomori explained. "When the lord learned of the affair, he sent the samurai away and forbade his daughter to see him again. The daughter took her own life rather than marry another man her father had chosen. From her grave, a maple tree grew, tall and strong. It was in the late autumn, when the winds grew as bitter as the sorrow within his soul, that the samurai knelt at her grave. Surrounded by the gaunt beauty of the dying season, he took his life, his blood darkening the roots of the tree.

"And then his lover's spirit cried out to him, and the leaves withered and fell, gently covering the body of the fallen samurai. Now every autumn, the maples shed their leaves, red for blood and gold for the love that transcends eternity. And thus is the samurai Saemonjiro remembered for all time." He picked up the flute to resume playing.

Toriko looked up. The parallel was close to their own situation, she knew. It had to be painfully evident to both her friends. There was no need for words. Toriko had awakened once during that fateful night, had heard Diana's small cries of passion. She only hoped that the force of their love would not result in disaster for them. Toriko had been on hand to greet them when they had returned from their encounter with Alvino the next morning. Frans was overseeing repairs to the doors Tonomori had smashed; the dogs already had been buried to spare Diana additional distress. They had been fed poisoned meat.

Toriko had a strong affection for Tonomori herself. The absence of a jealous response within her was strange, she thought, because Tonomori exemplified everything she admired about a samurai.

"It is very beautiful, Tonomori-san," Toriko smiled.

"Yes, the beauty makes it difficult to think of anything else." Diana felt overcome with emotion.

The playing stopped.

"Oh, please continue!" Toriko asked.

"Later, when we have time. We have important things to discuss first," Tonomori said. "I know that you had a caller today—a Count Hoorn?"

"Yes," Diana said. "He is a man I have known for many years. I believe he wishes me well and is trying to keep me informed, so that I can avoid dangerous mistakes. I am confident that I can trust his motives. He tells me that the duke is making certain discreet inquiries, sounding out the opinion of some important nobles." As Tonomori's eyes opened in silent inquiry, she continued, "It seems that Alvino, having been stopped in one maneuver, is going to try another. I think he expects to make me his duchess!"

"Could he *force* you, Diana-san?" Toriko was aghast.

"No, but I believe he could make it unpleasant for me and for my friends if it could appear that I crossed him." Diana spoke thoughtfully. "Hoorn heads an alliance of Dutch and Flemish nobles. That is the position that my father once occupied. Normally, I would see such an alliance as advantageous to us. But even though they don't trust Alvino, they think they can't afford to insult or aggravate him."

"Stall him, then, until we can work out our plans," Tonomori suggested.

"That brings us to a second point," Diana went on. "Remember when we were wondering what Alvino would be planning next? Well, Hoorn is collecting information from all kinds of sources, and he has learned that the duke is planning a military operation."

"Where?" Tonomori was puzzled.

"That is the riddle. The count can't figure it out; the people he talks with have no logical explanations. Certainly the duke does not have the excuse of rebellion in the northern provinces or closer to home in the Brabant, because there's not even a hint of such a development. And the Holy Office seems satisfied, for the moment, that the spread of heresy has been stopped. So we have to assume that he can't be planning something in that respect, either."

"Then obviously he is planning an operation elsewhere." Tonomori applied a warrior's reasoning decisively.

"That is what occurred to me, too, but it would be impossible," Diana objected. "After all, Alvino has no authority at all outside the Netherlands."

"Perhaps he expects to?" Toriko asked.

"That is just what I want to discuss with you," Diana told them both. "I think we should plan an outing for tonight. I will have to rely on your skills. Hoorn says that Alvino maintains warehouses on the quay near the fortress, the one commanding the northern approach of the Scheldt. They are very heavily guarded, so you will have to be extraordinarily careful. Nothing has changed. I want Alvino dead. It is time *we* took the offensive."

The soldiers were grumbling. They had been posted to stand guard, not to move crates full of steel.

"All this stuff has to be moved tonight, to make room for another three wagon loads that are due in tomorrow," the man-at-arms in charge of the work party reminded his men.

"Are we starting a war, Sancho? It's a long way to the Bay of Naples," one of the guards muttered.

"Watch your mouth! Other men have had their tongues cut out for less than that," Sancho growled. . . .

A figure in the darkness slid away, unseen, unheard.

"What took you so long?" Tonomori whispered when Toriko finally emerged out of the night, her black *ninja* wrappings still wet. Her *ninja* training made her especially suited for this aspect of the night's work. Tonomori had stood a watchful guard near the warehouse, alert to any slight sound that should not be there.

"I swam out to go aboard the ships, too," Toriko told him. "Let's get moving! I'll tell you about it as we ride."

They swiftly ran the mile to where their horses were tethered, but circled that area carefully to make sure that a Spanish patrol, having stumbled onto their horses, might not be lying in wait for their owners. All was clear.

Toriko stripped off the damp wrappings before trying to put her new Dutch gown on again. Tonomori was appreciative of her slim figure, aware of the small dark triangle pointing like an arrow, but he was not stirred. The image of a fuller figure and a tangle of blond hair crowded his vision in a way that even Nobuko, the golden butterfly now long dead by her own hand, had not done. He would never forget Nobuko. The butterflies that his people considered flowers of the air would always remind him of those few summers they had shared. How much time did he and Diana have? He would not think of that—only the clear beauty of her face with its downturned mouth, and the spirit that could rise above its own mortal fear and fly at death itself. Tonomori shook his head slowly and smiled.

He picked up an object that Toriko had dropped, started to hand it to her . . . then looked more closely, and stared. There, dangling on a thin silver chain, was a sword guard, like his own though smaller, decorated with a sixteen-petaled chrysanthemum, the imperial crest. His mind was in a whirl. *Could Toriko be somehow connected to his own origins?* Was it *karma* that led him halfway around the world to find another key to unlock his life's mystery?

Toriko took the sword guard from him and fastened it around her neck before pulling on her gown. "This *tsuba* has been mine since I was a baby. I have speculated on it

244

much, but having been separated from my family, I had no one to answer my questions, and I still do not even know who my family was. Not that it matters just now. But I would like to find out some day.''

Tonomori knew that they would have to talk—later, when they had a suitable opportunity. He thrust a knee into her back as he pulled tight and tied the lacings of her cumbersome gown, silently deploring its ugly slashings and panes, so adored by European women. Tonomori yearned for the simplicity of the kimono. His own short neck ruff scraped below the chin. After helping Toriko onto her sidesaddle, he settled into the stirrups of his mount and they were off, spurring down back roads and little-used side paths to avoid any Spaniards on the prowl. They met none.

The horses were weary but eager to return to the stalls and a bucket of oats, so they made good time.

''Alvino is refitting two ships, both of them empty at the moment,'' Toriko reported as they rode. She had pulled up beside Tonomori so they could converse.

''What about the warehouses?''

''Crammed full of arms, and they are expecting even more to arrive. The ships are bound for Naples eventually, so at least we know their destination.'' Toriko's hair was loose and flying in the wind. She felt revived in body and spirit by being in action once again.

''Could you torch the lot?''

''I could destroy the ships or the warehouses—but not both, not tonight. Not if it is to look like an accident,'' Toriko said. ''The wind should be perfect, from the northwest, when the flames conceivably could jump from the ships in a straight line to the buildings. Otherwise there would be suspicion, and this is something to be avoided.''

They walked the horses the last quarter-mile to cool them down. Pieter, the groom, took the reins when they reached the stables, and Diana was there to greet them with a candle lantern.

''Were you successful? What happened?'' she demanded excitedly. In the lantern's soft light, Tonomori thought she never looked more lovely, and he felt desire stir within him as he remembered how their shadows had joined as one in the glow of another candle.

"Yes," Tonomori assured her. "We had success, and we shall have more." They had found what he wanted and more—the secret arms cache of the Duke of Alvino, and also a small piece of hammered iron that could affect his destiny.

"We had the full moon, after all," Tonomori said, returning a warm smile for Diana. "And it was very illuminating."

Chapter Eighteen

Claaack! Three weapons flashed in the lamplight. The tip of Tonomori's sword slid down the inside of the nearest blade, glanced off the guard, then flicked down farther to parry a slash to his vulnerable left leg.

Two swords against one. Tonomori almost lost his footing, shouldered into the wall of the long, narrow room, and they were on him. The swords tangled and he pushed off the wall, then spun on the slippery floor to face them again, moving to the right, always to the right, circling as widely as possible.

A feint from one of the dark figures: Tonomori blocked it but felt the other blade sing across his breastplate inside his guard. No damage, but he grew more wary.

"Eeyyyaaaaaa," Tonomori suddenly screamed, and at the same time cut with perfection, throwing the nearest swordsman off balance. A reverse cut; missed. Tonomori

swore. The air was sticky and warm, like his own breath coming in gasps. The walls were pressing him in.

He blocked another cut. *Damn*, he thought furiously. *That was too close*. The swords, painted totally a flat black, were difficult to follow in the dim light.

Tonomori knew that against two swords, he should draw the second shorter blade tucked into his sash. Such a sword might be carried, in Japan, only by a samurai. But in this contest of skills—two blades against one—his pride kept Tonomori's second weapon sheathed. Pride had been the red death of more than one samurai, he knew from experience. But it is the manner in which one falls, not defeat itself, that matters.

The swords were dangerously close. They were figuring out his rhythm, his moves, his timing. So Tonomori changed his stance, lowered his blade, and when this threw them into confusion, he backed away.

A wooden bucket was in the way. Tonomori kicked it and sent it skittering across the planked floor into the shins of the nearest opponent, heard a satisfactory yelp, and moved in. The figure lashed out blindly, trying to roll away, but Tonomori was on the attack, refusing to give the assailant time to recover.

One almost down and one to go, Tonomori thought. He circled quickly, looking for an opening against the second figure before the first could get back into position. This was the crucial moment, when one opponent had to cover for the other. Too late. Tonomori waited until their balance was just off. . . .

His sword whirled to the right, but it was a trick. A quick turn of his body, and the blade came out of nowhere from behind him. A reversal. The blade connected hard, and Tonomori, wrenching it back to attack position, stepped over the fallen form.

One down, one to go. Tonomori sidestepped a stab to the throat, leaned to the left, watched the opposing sword pull into guard position—then brought a heavily powered draw cut across the breastplate.

The blow was good. He moved back and bowed.

"Very good," Tonomori said, helping the fallen figure

247

to her feet. He was pleased. "Next, we will try it with spears."

"I couldn't! Not yet. Let me catch my breath," gasped Diana, once she was standing. When her helmet was off, Diana wiped her sweating brow with a padded sleeve. She limped over to a water jug by a bench against the wall, took a drink, and spat it into the bucket, which Tonomori had returned to its usual place. It was the same bucket that he had knocked into her shins.

"How do you expect to build stamina if you don't practice?" Tonomori asked, smiling with the assurance of a man who has satisfied himself that his physical condition is excellent.

"He is right, you know," added the other figure. Toriko had removed her helmet and was looking at Tonomori and the countess. Toriko would have welcomed a respite from their exertions and the unfamiliar weight of the European steel. Her own Japanese armor was much lighter and more flexible, and her muscles screamed for relief. But she would be damned if, in Tonomori's presence, she would suggest a rest. Toriko, as a *ninja*, could not allow him to show her as weaker.

"He may be right, but I've had enough for now," Diana objected. Her breathing was less ragged now. She rinsed out her mouth once more and spat. Diana knew better than to drink too quickly after a strenuous practice. She would end up with her head in the bucket, retching piteously, while Tonomori laughed at her discomfort and her carelessness. God, how she'd like to beat that big bastard at his own game!

Diana took a careful swallow and smiled inwardly. She almost had. Painting the practice bamboo swords black had been her idea, and she told herself that it had almost worked. She almost had been able to use the advantage to defeat Tonomori at last. On the other hand, the dimness of the training room making it so difficult to see, to move, was at Tonomori's own insistence.

"You think everyone fights at noon, with plenty of light, on level ground?" he had demanded scornfully.

"Learn to fight under the most difficult of circumstances. After that, everything will be easy!"

When Diana had trained with Toriko before encountering Tonomori, Toriko never had been the taskmaster that Tonomori proved to be. She would ease up when her pupil was sweating. Tonomori just pushed harder.

But not today, Diana told herself; *I've too much to do.*

"I'll practice harder tomorrow. Really I will," Diana assured her teachers. She paused. "What are you doing, Tonomori-san?"

She saw that Tonomori was not paying attention to her protests. Instead, he was hefting a light practice bow and examining the shaft of an arrow with a padded tip.

"Noooooo," Diana pleaded. Toriko already was retying her helmet and moving out of the way. Muttering to herself, Diana jammed on her headgear without bothering to tuck in the wisps of golden hair sticking out, and dove for the cover of a storage chest. An arrow hummed by and thudded against the end wall, adding yet another dent to a collection of many.

While Tonomori nocked a second arrow, Diana broke cover and scrambled back against the far wall. Though they were completely in the open, at the relatively long range the shafts lost much of their power and—with concentration—could be deflected by the bamboo blades of their practice swords.

The cellar held many happy memories for her. Used as an arms exercise room a hundred years before, when the mansion was built by the second Count de Edgemont, it gradually had become a storage room and wine cellar. Diana remembered the scoldings she had received when, disobeying orders, she went down to play, covering herself with dust and cobwebs.

Thwaaack! Diana stifled a cry as an arrow grazed the inside of a thigh.

"Did I awaken you, Diana-san?" Tonomori called out caustically.

I had better think about what I am doing, she decided.

Tonomori stepped closer and continued shooting. The arrows were coming in faster now, and Diana was finding it increasingly difficult to block them. Toriko hardly used the practice sword at all. She just twisted out of the way, like a cat. Diana had learned much from Toriko: to use a spear, to move silently without being seen, to throw a *shuriken*, the small deadly throwing knives favored by the *ninja*. As for Tonomori, she wanted to learn much from him, too. Diana knew she couldn't match him. But it might give her an edge in achieving her goal of personally killing the Duke of Alvino.

"Ooooow!" Diana yelled as Tonomori scored a hit on her shoulder. That one would leave a welt, she was sure. Only one door led out of the cellar, and that was past Tonomori. Diana was doubtful that she could make it.

The arrows stopped.

"That is enough for now," Tonomori told them, setting his bow into a rack pegged into the wall. He walked forward to retrieve the shafts. Several had snapped when the women stepped on them in avoiding the arrows as they flew from Tonomori's relentless bow.

"How did I do?" Diana asked. Yanking off her helmet revealed her unkempt hair; Tonomori thought it looked like a golden cloud. He wanted to reach out and touch it but refrained.

"Not bad. But you must learn to keep your balance." Tonomori took her shoulder in one hand and placed the other in the small of her back, then pushed.

"Like that. Toriko-san does it perfectly," he added.

"I will try," Diana agreed with a grimace.

"We will work together," Toriko assured her. Already out of her practice armor, she was sponging off sweat with a dripping rag from a tub of water. When she was through, Toriko would regretfully, but without complaint, allow Diana to lace her back into an uncomfortable European gown. The luxury of her kimono was only for private times and for those occasions when they wished to put on a rich face for others.

Again, Tonomori became aware of the imperial chrysanthemum dangling from the silver chain that swung between her small breasts; each time he saw the intricate design of the sword guard now was a fresh occasion to ponder briefly the mystery of the apparent connection between himself and the *ninja*. Would Toriko be sharing these thoughts when she inevitably realized that the crest was exposed to his gaze?

Once out of her own armor, Diana washed carefully, unmindful when Tonomori turned toward her. She had no secrets from Tonomori, nor did she wish any. And in Japan, in any event, she had acclimated herself to men and women bathing together as a matter of course.

She dabbed gingerly at the round welt on her shoulder and the pink streak on the inside of her right leg. Where the arrows had hit, the skin was broken and the marks were beginning to sting sharply, promising green and purple bruises by the morrow.

"I'd like to shoot at *you* next time," Diana said shortly to Tonomori.

"Certainly. If you feel you don't need the practice," he replied in a detached tone.

She had no answer to this. Diana did need the practice, and she recognized it candidly to herself.

The women took turns with their laces while Tonomori examined the last of the arrows. One of the shafts was cracked and ready to split; another had lost a fletching. These he placed in a bundle to be repaired by Yamahito and Oshabiri. Repairing arrows was something they enjoyed, a link with the past and all that had been familiar to them. They seldom complained, at least not within earshot. Their discipline was too good for that. But Tonomori knew they longed for the green mountains of Japan, the land of the gods.

"Will you join us in the garden, Tonomori-san?" Toriko inquired when they had dressed.

"Perhaps later. I have a few things to do yet."

"Please do. It would be very pleasant," Diana added.

Tonomori turned away from them, already oblivious to their departure except for the rustle of their skirts. And to the creak of the stairs' timbers; this, he knew, served as an alarm to the servants who would have been listening at the door leading to the cellar.

Almost immediately after returning, Diana had resumed

251

her training with Toriko and Tonomori. The servants were naturally overwhelmed by curiosity as to what happened in the cellar every afternoon.

This time, Diana and Toriko were met by Frans, who, as the chief steward, offered apologies for the intrusion. But he found it necessary to speak, circumstances being what they were.

"I hesitate to say anything, but a few of the servants are giving credence to the oddest rumors on what goes on in the cellar," Frans told Diana with his best effort at diplomacy. He tried to be vague, and he purposely neglected to say that because the mysterious Japanese were involved, the servants assumed that they must be up to something exotic, perhaps even immoral.

Frans had realized that the gossip had reached epidemic proportions only when he had found it necessary to break a stick across the thin shoulders of a young servingman who was overheard to say, "You don't suppose that big Jappo is popping the pair of 'em on, do you?" After tongue-lashing the ringleaders, Frans summoned the resolve to approach the mistress herself. Prudently, he omitted the more lurid details.

"I should have known they would all be curious," Diana laughed. "It is all completely harmless, I assure you. Come, you shall see for yourself."

When Tonomori heard footsteps on the steps again, he turned to see Frans descending, his thin beaky nose in the air with more gravity and dignity than even the countess herself could display. Frans could hear the whispers and giggling of the servant girls, but to have this rare privilege of being taken into his mistress's confidence was balm to his officious soul.

The cellar smelled, not unpleasantly, of oil and sweat. When his eyes became accustomed to the dimness, Frans could see pole weapons, swords, and several firearms set in racks along the walls. It was a Spartan, but effective, *salon de armes*—weapons-storage and exercise room combined in one. He noticed the Japanese lord was wearing armor.

"The samurai Tonomori is a Zen archer in his country,

252

among other things. This is very special," Diana mentioned to Frans. "When I lived in the Japans, I had occasion to see Zen archers at their practice." This was a lie. Diana had not even heard of a Zen archer until she crossed Tonomori's path. "They are very good, unbelievably accurate, and I found it beautiful to watch. I was sure to watch their practices daily. Now Lord Tonomori indulges my fancy for this sport."

Tonomori had heard many of Diana's fabrications, for the benefit of Europeans, about his odd behavior, and he felt no need to contradict her now.

Frans saw that Tonomori was holding a strange bow that reached almost to the ceiling. And the arrow was positioned a third of the way from the bottom; most curious. European bows always nocked dead center.

"Why doesn't he shoot outdoors, Your Ladyship?" Frans asked in a low voice.

"It is part of the Zen ritual to shoot indoors a good part of the time," Diana explained, sweetening the lie with a little smile.

"Uh," Tonomori grunted. "We begin."

The countess stood back and waved a hand, indicating that she was ready to watch.

While Frans looked on, incredulous, Tonomori whipped five arrows into a round target hung on a peg at the far wall. The center of the target was the size of a ducat.

"You look," Tonomori offered.

Frans was very conscious of the quiet as he walked up to the arrows. The steel heads had sunk in around the rim of the black center. Frans peered closely. The white X in the dead center was untouched. Still, at that range and with poor lighting, remarkable.

An arrow suddenly punched into the X with tremendous force and quivered just two inches from Frans's sweating nose.

"Better now. Last one for you." Tonomori growled.

Frans felt his heart drumming in alarm. The savage brute had almost killed him!

"The samurai Tonomori never misses," the countess called out. "He would deem it an honor to demonstrate for you further evidence of his skill. Snuff a candle in your hand with an arrow. Split an apple on your head, or . . ."

Frans bowed deeply, praying that he would not faint. "That will not be necessary, Your Ladyship. I am deeply honored by being offered that opportunity, but as you know I have pressing duties."

"Of course," Diana said kindly. "But if you change your mind, just let us know. And the invitation is extended to all the servants as well. Please pass the word."

"Yes," Tonomori said, playing his part. He flourished an evil-looking sword that gleamed like polished silver. "You balance grape on nose, I cut off for you. Very easy. I very honored. You say when."

Frans made a strangling noise and tottered for the stairs with the expression of a man groping his way out of purgatory.

"It is worth your life to go down into that pit!" Frans announced wildly to several stunned servants after he had closed the door thankfully behind him. Then he fled to the farthest corner of the house. The servants' curiosity in what went on in the cellar began to diminish from that moment.

Below them, Tonomori was laughing aloud, Toriko's shoulders were shaking, and Diana was grinning wickedly. "You balance grape on nose, I cut off. Ugh!" she repeated in imitation of Tonomori. "Honestly! Did you have to talk like that to the poor man? You do know how to speak somewhat better, after all."

"Your faithful steward considers me a barbarian," Tonomori answered. "I didn't want to disappoint him. And the idea—your idea—as I understand it, is to discourage active interest in our activities. I think we may have succeeded."

"Yes; well, I hope we haven't scared the faithful steward out of his wits," Diana observed with an effort at pity.

Tonomori popped a grape into his mouth from a wooden bowl on an old table holding the rest of his target arrows. He tossed a second grape into the air, and with a hiss of steel drew his sword and sliced across it, snatching the fragments before they splattered onto the floor.

"I have seen that done before, Tonomori-san. Our knights can cut a grape in half also," Diana said almost condescendingly.

"Can they?" Tonomori asked, depositing the fragments in her hand. She looked. There were four pieces.

"Well done," Diana conceded. *Show-off*, she thought.

Toriko said nothing. Tonomori had been eclipsing her of late, and her own abilities and her pride made her even more determined to reassert herself. But not now; it would be too apparent that she was competing again with Tonomori, and that might upset their mistress.

Tonomori went on eating grapes. When the women had left, he turned his full attention to a matchlock musket lying disassembled on a stout workbench. It seemed to him that anything he might learn about the European guns might prove useful in his quest for revenge against the man responsible for the death of his master.

Tonomori looked at the ceiling. "Masanori-sama, do you still live?" he asked. "Do you wonder if I still live? Do you await my return?" Not even an echo of an answer.

Tonomori had said *sama*, meaning "great." But Masanori was far from great. A spider scuttled across the edge of the bench and disappeared behind it. *Webs*, Tonomori thought. *Webs of deceit and treachery*.

He could still see Masanori's snickering smile of victory, the thin lips drawn back to expose mottled gums and rotting teeth. That Masanori still lived was a daily insult to men and gods alike.

Tonomori thought of the Christian cross attached to the Buddhist rosary beneath his armor. The cross was a concession to his mistress's welfare. He could not protect her in Europe without converting. He would have been burned as an infidel, and still might be if the Holy Office considered him an apostate, a backslider into pagan beliefs. The rosary was Tonomori's little joke. No one, except perhaps a Jesuit who had been to Japan, could possibly distinguish it from a cross, they were so much alike.

"Damn!" Tonomori swore after dropping one of the

brass pins that held the gun barrel to its wooden stock. Guns like this one finally would blow Masanori into eternity.

Shaking his head, Tonomori poked around for the pin, seized it finally, and replaced it on the bench. This matchlock, German made, incorporated a unique variation: As the trigger was pulled, a mechanism slid the priming-pan lid forward, exposing the priming powder to the descending jaws of the arm that held the smoldering fuse. The fuse touched off the priming powder, and it in turn sent a shower of sparks through the touchhole at the side of the barrel to ignite the main charge behind the bullet. Simple but effective. Many samurai were learning not to disdain the power of firearms, and thus to avoid a fatal mistake of many of their European counterparts—knights who had been toppling with alarming regularity from their saddles with odd holes in their breastplates.

Satisfied at last that he understood just how the mechanism worked, Tonomori set about putting the lock back together. At the other end of the bench was a wheel-lock pistol that he had dismantled after buying it. A mistake; the lock, still in pieces, was daring him to tackle it again. Tonomori was tired of chasing springs across the floor.

An army of men armed with wheel-lock muskets would dominate the world. But only after bankrupting it, Tonomori told himself.

The wheel lock did not depend on a burning fuse or a source of fire to light one. Its inner mechanism, wound with an external key, or spanner, rotated a steel wheel that ground against a metallic piece of pyrites. The shower of sparks from the resulting friction fired the priming powder. This was faster and more sure than the clumsy matchlock.

The wheel lock was also twenty times as expensive—and delicate. Guns frequently were used as clubs after musketeers had fired their single shots; few wheel locks were equal to that kind of pounding. In an emergency, a matchlock could be fired with the lock broken. Because the mechanism was based on the action of a timepiece, the powerful guilds, which still wielded much political clout in Europe, dictated that only a watchmaker could put one together.

But anybody could make a matchlock.

"And buy them, and transport them out of the country, and take one and stick it against Masanori's quivering belly, and pull the trigger," Tonomori said aloud.

He put the pieces of the wheel into a wooden box. Tomorrow, he would take them into Antwerp, listen impassively to the acid comments of the gunsmith about tampering with something one knows nothing about, and then watch him assemble it again. So perhaps it wasn't for nothing. Tonomori would learn something there, after all. And it was for knowledge and guns that he had come to the Netherlands, almost as strong a motivation as his mission to protect Diana, and his need to be with her.

Tucking the box under his arm, Tonomori stood and headed for the stairs. The steps groaned loudly with the added weight of his armor.

Another sigh. He wore European armor now, a necessity. His beautiful lacquered leather armor hung on a rack in his room. In Japan, it was very valuable. Each of its leather scales had been aged seven years, then carefully lacquered and laced together. It was light, waterproof, and arrowproof.

But not bulletproof. Here it was useless. And soon would be useless also in Japan. Japan had been introduced to guns only fifteen years ago, by Portuguese traders. Already, Japanese swordsmiths had learned to copy them and were turning out guns in large quantities.

His own breastplate, at least, was bulletproof. The round dent in the cuirass over his left pectoral was the "proof" mark of a bullet fired into it by the Augsburg smith who had forged the steel.

Tonomori longed for the mobility, the fluid ease that Japanese armor afforded; European armor was not as flexible. But, as even Tonomori admitted, it was stronger, smoother, less likely to catch a sword's point.

He clumped through the mansion, purposely making unnecessary noise as he went. The serving women tended to shriek an "Eeeek!" whenever Tonomori moved up silently behind them, as if he were going to ravish them on the floor. With his fierce eyes and small thin mouth set in a broad face that had a natural predatory look, Tonomori was a forbidding and seemingly dangerous presence.

As he saw Wila, a chirpy, lithe young woman polishing the wainscoting in the hall with an oily cloth, he whispered "Psssst!" in a conspiratorial tone. "Tonight I am going to take all of you women to the moon! On a flying carpet I stole from the Turks."

Wila's eyes grew wide and she dropped the cloth.

"Yaaaaaaaaa!" she was screaming all the way out the back door.

Taking the stairs leisurely, Tonomori could hear Wila's progress through the garden and a hubbub of querulous voices.

Once his door was latched, he began carefully removing his armor. First, the vambraces and upper brassards that protected his forearms and upper arms. Then the gorget covering the throat and the pauldrons over the shoulders. Tonomori pulled the breastplate and backplates over his head, as the attached tasses clacked in his ears, and began unbuckling his leg plates. He stacked all these carefully by his pallet in the far corner.

Downstairs, the uproar was subsiding. The serving women were simple peasants, quite harmless, and he could not resist the impulse to tease them. Perhaps the day was too quiet; he was bored.

Tonomori noticed that someone had placed two late-blooming roses in a vase on the single low table against the near wall. He paused to admire their beauty and wondered who had brought them. The only other pieces of furniture were two ivory inlaid chests he had bought in Goa. Tonomori preferred to squat on the floor, as he always had done in Japan.

He would change out of his arming doublet after bathing outside in an old wine tun that had been sawn in half for his use. Filled daily with fresh cold water, the tun was beneath some broad oaks, screened from prying eyes.

He heard footsteps on the stairs. Light ones. A woman? Tonomori listened carefully and smiled. The pattern was Diana's. This afternoon she was favoring her right leg.

"Tonomori-san! When you are not busy, I'd like a word

or two with you, alone." The tone of the voice through the door was even and firm, not at all the manner of a lover dropping by to exchange flowery sentiments.

Ah, thought Tonomori. *If I remember correctly the right expression, I think she is here to pluck a crow with me.*

"I still don't know whatever possessed you. The child was scared half to death," Diana greeted him that night after Tonomori had climbed into her room through a window.

By mutual arrangement, she left a candle burning in her window, its latch left open, whenever she thought it safe for Tonomori to visit.

Tonomori leaned his long sword against the wall by the headboard and tucked the short sword beneath a pillow, a Japanese custom he still observed.

"I thought you'd had enough to say on the matter this afternoon," Tonomori rejoined somewhat curtly, stepping out of the heap his *hakama* made on the floor. The *hakama* were loose bagged trousers the Japanese traditionally wore. Tonomori seldom had a chance now to wear his, except at night. He still hated the feeling of doublet and hose.

"Besides, she is not a child," Tonomori continued as he slid out of his kimono and between the linen sheets where Diana was tucked so neatly and invitingly. "She is a fully matured young woman. I was only teasing her with a farfetched suggestion. It is not my fault she is so gullible as to credit a flight of fancy. You act as if I showed her this stout weapon of mine."

It was a vision that Diana could not resist, and she giggled. "It might have been better if you had! Wila apparently doesn't care for heights, but she *does* like men, so I am told."

"In that case, I'll have to try your suggestion. Wila is very pretty," Tonomori grinned in the dark.

"Oh, no, you don't!" Diana countered. "I'm keeping you all to myself."

Tonomori's blood was thick with lust, but he held himself in check.

"Since you seem determined to discuss such mundane matters as serving wenches while I am in your bed," he

259

began, "instead of whispering endearments and encouragements . . .

" . . . I must point out to you that you still haven't decided on Alvino's three ships and the secret store of arms in the two warehouses. You remember them. They can't have slipped your mind." Tonomori intercepted a slim hand which was roving under the sheet.

Diana leaned on an elbow, her hair tumbling golden onto the pillow. "I can't think very clearly with you so near."

"You don't think very clearly when I'm not here," he countered amiably. Diana pinched his leg and he pulled her to him with a suddenness that took her breath away.

I . . . need . . . more time. We . . . must have more information before we can act," Diana gasped. "Then we can burn him out . . . like a wasp's nest. Ouch!"

Tonomori leaned back. "What is the matter now?"

"You ought to know," Diana said, rubbing the shoulder where the padded arrow had struck. A bruise had formed beneath the alabaster skin. "And there's a strawberry mark on my leg."

"Let me see. Perhaps I can make it feel better with some attention." Tonomori swept back the sheet. He thought Diana was well named. Her body was that of a goddess— long, tapering legs; swelling hips; a trim, embraceable waist; large, firm breasts. And the face of a minx, triangular with high cheekbones, an almost patrician nose, and a downswept mouth now slightly parted as if asking a question.

His gaze returned to her legs. The rosy streak he had noticed in the cellar was much redder now. The skin had been broken slightly.

"Does this hurt when I touch it?"

"*Yes!* A little." Diana crooked her knees farther apart to oblige his probing fingers.

Tonomori looked past the pinkish cleft, the thicket that crowned it, to her eyes and breasts. The former were wide open, the latter rising and falling heavily. She had bathed; he could smell the soap.

"How about this?" Tonomori pressed his lips to the

mark. He had unbound his hair and it lay across her thighs, glossy and black. "A kiss will help it heal better."

"Ah . . . yes. That does feel nice." Diana addressed the top of his head. She felt his lips moving higher.

"What are you *doing*?"

"Quiet! I'm chasing a mouse. And there it is!" came the muffled reply.

Diana, her heart pounding, felt a fluttering in her loins like pigeon wings.

"You can't . . . You aren't . . . Oh, God . . . you are! . . ."

"For the fifth time, the answer is no!" The handsome blond man behind the desk drummed his fingers impatiently on the expensive marquetry. The Duke of Alvino was annoyed.

Gutierrez, his second in command, shifted in his chair and tried another tack.

"The creditors grow wearisome. They demand payment for arms and armor received. If we do not pay soon, they will complain to the ambassador, our civilian counterpart. And, stupid as he is, even he will be able to figure out that something is up." Gutierrez waited for Alvino's reaction. The duke grew snappish late in the afternoon until he had his wine.

A servant arrived with a tray bearing a decanter—and a single goblet, a fine piece of Venetian glass on a fluted stem. When the servant had been dismissed, Alvino unlocked a drawer in the desk with an ornate bronze key and extracted a small packet of brown powder. This he emptied into the wine, then stirred it with the key.

With two gulps, Alvino's mood improved perceptibly.

"That's better," he sighed. "Now to business."

Gutierrez gave the duke his complete attention but, behind a hand, frowned at the sight of the packet. He feared Alvino was growing dependent on opium, that it was clouding his judgment. On the other hand, Gutierrez, a swordsman, used to looking for openings, could predict that Alvino might grow more pliable later. So far, his actions had been clearheaded.

261

"That clever bitch, the countess, is as slippery as a greased eel. She should be dead, but it seems that I have mostly incompetents in my pay. But no matter now. I shall take care of the wench myself." Alvino took another gulp and refilled the goblet from the decanter. Gutierrez observed that this time the duke did not add more opium.

"The king himself has taken an interest in her welfare," Alvino said after a draught. "Not content to bungle his own affairs, he has seen fit to meddle in mine. With a dispatch under the royal seal directing me to be personally responsible for her safety, I cannot afford to have her killed now."

"Then we must pay—at least something to show good faith," Gutierrez argued. "There are always your pay chests . . ."

"No! They are as inviolate as a nun's bed." Alvino saw Gutierrez's wicked grin, and responded with a thin smile. "Or as inviolate as a nun's bed should be.

"Let me remind you," he went on. "When I am appointed governor-general of Naples, the ships and arms will not be enough to back up my claim on the kingship. I can only maintain it by *force* of arms, and then the whole of southern Italy is mine.

"But you know better than I that troops do not fight on promises. Without the pay chests, they would defect to the first prince with a purse full of gold, taking *my* armor on their backs. And without troops, I suggest we take Magellan's route and find an undiscovered island somewhere. We would be in the same boat. For treason, I would kneel under the headsman's sword. You, they would draw and quarter."

Gutierrez nodded. They were playing a tight game. "What then?"

"In this coffer," Alvino told him, pointing to an enameled chest, "are two gold chains and my personal jewels. Sell them and give it all to my creditors. Tell them they will be paid in full in two months."

"And then?"

The duke leaned forward, to say quietly, "I have decided to marry. The countess will make a lovely bride. I

262

will announce it as a love match. The bishop owes me a few favors—the lady and I can be wed in a hurry. Afterward, her estates become mine and I can dispose of them. My creditors will be happy in anticipation.

"By the time they realize that payment is not to be forthcoming after all, my new duchess will be adorning my debt-ridden estates in Spain, I will be ruling Naples, and my creditors can piss up a rope for their money," Alvino said with satisfaction.

Gutierrez frowned. "And if the lady refuses? . . ."

"She won't be able to. You are my spymaster, as well as my second in command," Alvino reminded him. "How widespread lately have been the activities of the heretics?"

"Quiet. Discreet. Not worth tying up troops for."

"Wrong! The whole countryside is a sinkbed of heresy and should be put out with fire," Alvino exclaimed vigorously. "When the countess sees her friends and neighbors going up in flames, it will be only natural that she turns to me."

Gutierrez bowed. "Your Grace commands."

A servant knocked and entered with a sealed letter. Alvino slipped open the envelope with a thin dagger. Gutierrez heard marching outside: the changing of the guard.

"Ha!" the duke said with satisfaction. "Everything goes in our favor. It is an invitation from the countess for a celebration at her estate. And I am to be the guest of honor! What an occasion to plant the seeds." He looked up. "Write out a list of names, people who will be suspected of heresy. Take no action until after the celebration. And of course I want to see the list, in case I wish to add to it."

The discussion was over; Gutierrez bowed and took his leave. If only Alvino remained levelheaded, Gutierrez stood the chance of winning his own dukedom—it had been promised. The risks were tremendous, but so were the prizes if they succeeded.

The door closed. Alvino was alone. He took a second packet from his desk and stirred the contents into his wine. It took two packets now to calm his troubled mind, and another in the morning. The morning dosage was new, but Alvino was not worried. Once he had claimed his kingdom, his destiny fulfilled, the bad dreams would go away and with them the canker that gnawed at his waking hours. Of that he was certain.

Now the fly invites the spider into her parlor, the duke was thinking with a chuckle.

Chapter Nineteen

"What are you making?" Diana asked, stretching languidly on a stone beneath an elm tree in her garden. She felt guilty about stealing a few moments of precious time away from her duties, but it was a beautiful day, bright with puffy clouds, and she was savoring the smell of the lilies, the lazy drone of the bees.

Tonomori concentrated on a small piece of boxwood he was carving with a *kozuka*, the utility knife that fitted into the slot in his short-sword scabbard. "A cricket cage," he replied.

"I had forgotten about those. How pleasant! How long will you keep it in there?"

"For a week or so. Then I will catch another. They are considered good luck. There!" Tonomori was finished. All that remained was the drilling of the holes to receive the dowels that would hold the small box together, and the cage would be done.

In the distance, beyond the garden, workmen were stacking lumber and crates for the summer celebration Diana was planning. She took a deep breath. It was time to begin spinning the web that would catch a duke.

"This is all very pleasant, but . . . The day for the celebration will be here before we know it. I already have been the guest of honor at two banquets, one by the merchants and one by Alvino," Diana said. "Now it is my turn. It is the expected thing to do. And it will serve well to disguise my real aim: revenge!"

Toriko swatted at a fly—a never-ending occupation in summer. "You must be expecting a great many people."

"I am. This one will be a spectacle, lavish and gaudy, so you are both warned. In Antwerp, these things are done in grand style or not at all. Spectacular events, my father once said, accomplish two things: They help discharge your social obligations, and they demonstrate, even though blatantly, your power and the wealth that sustains it."

"In two weeks, then, we will be up to our ears in rustics, is that it?" Tonomori wanted to know.

"Be kind. Country people are usually the best. And there will be city folk as well. It will be fun. You'll see. I only wish I had said two months, but if we wait too long, the summer will be gone. And then there is the matter of the Duke of Alvino nosing around everywhere. We just don't have the time."

Before they were halfway through, Diana wished she had said a year. The list of invitations swelled from two hundred to five hundred, then almost doubled again. There were the merchants and the agents of foreign banking interests to invite—German, French, English, Spanish, Italian, and Swedish, plus their wives and offspring. Then came the ambassadors and their staffs, the many noble families with whom Diana was acquainted, her neighbors and their numerous progeny, all the city officials and, of course, *their* wives and children. When traveling into the city, Diana carried invitations in her purse in case she met someone who should have been asked.

"I have seen a night watchman on the Lieder Canal whom I think you forgot to invite," Tonomori mentioned a few days later while Diana was crossing off the items that had been accomplished. She had hired professionals for the work and masters of ceremony to oversee it. In the end, however, the responsibility was hers. The formal procession she had arranged for her presentation to King Philip in Seville was child's play compared to the extravaganza she was planning now.

"That is not very funny, Tonomori-san. Don't you have something else to do, someplace else you wish to visit?" Diana rebuked absentmindedly.

"I remain at your side, on duty," Tonomori said placidly.

"That reminds me," Diana said, finally looking up from her lists. "I think you have been stretching yourself too thin. We need some more men, reliable men." She explained that Captain de Wynte was back in port and had called on her. When she told him of their situation, de Wynte had furnished some names of possibilities, if they were in town. She understood that they probably were.

"When you can spare the time, you might look him up. You appear to be at loose ends. . . . Is something the matter?" Diana asked.

"What about your safety?" Tonomori inquired.

"I have Yamahito and Oshabiri, who stick to me like glue when you or Toriko are not around."

"If you insist." It was little more than a grunt.

"Not if you think it unwise. But I do think we could use a few extra swords. Just in case. And besides, how can you visit me at night when you spend most of your time prowling around outside, poking around in the shadows instead of in my bed, hmmmm?" Diana said, blinking.

"I will go see the men and talk to them first. Then I will make up my mind," Tonomori decided.

"Good. Good," Diana repeated almost absentmindedly, turning back to her growing lists. Then she remembered. "By the way, Tonomori-san, Yamahito and Oshabiri are very conscientious of their duty, but it is not necessary that they wait outside while I am in the privy."

Tonomori smiled. "You think not? In Japan we know the story of a daimyo who was attacked by assassins in his privy. He was surprised at the manner of his passing."

Diana raised an eyebrow at this. "Very well then, if *you* insist."

Tonomori stood outside and scrutinized the sign that proclaimed the entrance to The Fatted Calf. He had been informed it was an establishment where many prodigal sons squandered their leisure time and money.

A large wooden building, it stood near the old section of the city, the heart of Antwerp, and close enough to the main canals, where barrels of sweet dark ale could be cheaply barged in. The grounds around it were snug, but with enough room for several shade trees to provide comfort outside for the warm weather, when thirsty men could drain their leather jacks at their ease.

The sound of raucous laughter and the bubbling of cheery voices drew Tonomori inside. His eyes narrowed at the dimness, and his nose twitched at the smell of burned tallow, which was lighted at night in clay pots to provide light to drink by and so that suspicious men-at-arms could keep an eye on each other's hands.

The crowd this afternoon seemed to run to unemployed mercenaries, few of them in armor but all wearing swords, and better dressed than most of the citizens of Antwerp.

Tonomori approached a long counter, where a fleshy tun of a man stood scratching a dark beard and critically observing the turning of a beef on a spit in the huge fireplace that dominated the north wall.

"Good day to you, sir. Bicker is the name, but we don't go in for quarreling here. I am the proprietor and what will you have?" said the man, carefully assessing the quality of Tonomori's clothes, his swords, and the potential for violence in his hard features.

"A mug of your best ale first," said Tonomori, drawing out his own silver tankard, which Bicker eyed appreciatively. "And second, I am looking for a certain man."

"No fighting, please. This is a peaceful place," Bicker spoke in some alarm while handing over the foaming tankard and pocketing a copper coin in his stained leather apron.

"No sword play," Tonomori assured him. He took a sample sip. Tonomori did not care for the European wines, but he was developing a taste for Dutch beer. This was good, very cool, with a creamy texture. "The man I am seeking is a Scottish knight, a soldier of fortune, Sir Ian MacDonnell. This involves a matter that might prove mutually profitable to Sir Ian and myself."

"Ah, then you've come at the right time," Bicker told him, relieved. "We have a poetry competition among the gentlemen today. I've no taste for such things myself, but I hope MacDonnell wins because he owes me nine florins." Bicker pointed out MacDonnell's table, where Tonomori could await him at his leisure.

Tonomori carefully threaded his way through the tangle of benches and trestle tables and sat down at MacDonnell's bench.

The competition was moving along at a rapid pace, and the crowd was braying with laughter. No Hapsburg soldiers were present to take offense and start a fight, so old Wissel was spouting forth an original ditty about a near-sighted Spanish marquess and his drunken search for his wife's bedroom and what happened when he bumbled into a sheep pen instead. The refrain always ended, "Of *course* this is ma-dam."

Wissel's fringe of hair gave him an owlish look. That, coupled with a wicked leer and accompanying thrusts of his larded hips to illustrate the marquess on the horns of a dilemma, brought enthusiastic applause when he had finished.

"Hooray for Wissel! A glutton for mutton."

"Wissel, you sly dog, you pulled the wool over our eyes."

Then a man in his early thirties took the makeshift platform. Tonomori watched closely. The man's doublet was worn but clean, the silver buttons polished. The neck ruff was stiff and new, but the hose had seen better days. The hilt of his sword had a steel wire-wrapped grip, with a swept-back hilt of excellent design, the dagger on the other side of his belt matching it.

"It's MacDonnell. Lock up your daughters!"

"Hey, MacDonnell, is your poem gonna rhyme this time?"

MacDonnell paused, ran a hand over dark wavy hair,

then grabbed his sword hilt, pulled it around to his back, and ran the tan scabbard out between his legs from behind. The phallic gesture was unmistakable.

"Rhyme on that, numbnuts," MacDonnell grinned. More laughter and stomping of boots in lusty appreciation. MacDonnell knew his crowd.

He held his hand aloft for silence. The buzzing died. "What I have here is a work of poignance and sensitivity," MacDonnell announced, drawing a roll of paper from his belt.

"Just read the dirty parts," called a voice from the rear.

MacDonnell rolled his eyes in disgust, struck a classic pose with one hand splayed over his heart, and began. The poem was called "The Bowman."

"Pluck the string like an Irish harper of
the king.
A man who fought for kings now hunts
Rabbits for his dinner.
My last meal a gnawing memory and tooth sharp.
Would I could bring down a doe with white haunches.
Aye, Bess's haunches were white once, till the
Earl's men pried them apart. I killed them for
That but sweet Bess was gone and a death warrant signed
For me. Would that I could see it and spit on it.
A fine how-de-do. Well, the king's justicers
Are clumsy. They wish not to tangle with
Old Cathlan. Old at 35, I could weep. I could make
Water on King William's foot were he here,
The heartless bastard, like all those damned Normans.
I'm hungry, but not enough to shoot the king's deer.
Kill an earl and William might forgive.
Kill his deer—never.
Rabbits ain't too bad. Pigs is better.
Were William a Welshman he would understand a man's
Taste for venison. But his viciousness is exceeded
Only by his ingratitude. He wears a gold crown, the
Color of Harold's hair when my arrow cut him down.
Trust Normandy to be wary of a man who has slain a king.
Chance shot me achin' arse. Those damned shields were

Waving like the sea—brave Saxon arms by weary.
My beard was brown then when the bowstring
Went past my jaw. The arrow sang Harold's death song
And his soul rose with the groans of his housecarls,
May the saints preserve him; God won't.
But Harold is dead and I live,
If you can call this living
Not one nobleman in twenty can read,
And me a lettered man. I'd embrace the Church now,
But who'd embrace fair Winifred tonight by the
Gray oaks? That is if the fine bitch doesn't
Turn me in. Maybe an archer would fare better
In Ireland. Constant in war, unfaithful in love the
Irish are, or is it the other way around? They have
Three of John the Baptist's heads there, ye know.
That's the Irish for you, too many kings and saints.
They should have kept the snakes and chased St. Patrick
Out of the land. My own land is gone now, gobbled by
The crown I won for William. No matter—I'm better off,
Except for the justicers, and the last two now have arrows
Sprouting from their throats. I have a fine helm and
Hauberk. My sword is good German steel. My horse the
Finest ever stolen. Maybe if I gave him back to William,
He'd forgive me, but I doubt it. Anyway, it's beard on
Shoulder for a while, Winifred tonight and Ireland in
The morning. Those silver candlesticks in the village
Church will pay my passage. So I'll say my prayers
Tonight on my knees behind Winifred that the next priest
Who shrives me is a man with the heart of a Welshman
And the purse of a duke.
A poor bowman in Ireland would only bring trouble."

Tonomori thought the poem good, though he did not understand many of the references. MacDonnell's baritone voice was smooth, his manner polished. The Scot bowed amid a chorus of hoots and whistles, and made his way to the table where Tonomori sat.

"Good morning," said MacDonnell with the quizzical look of a man who had not expected company. Empty tables were all around them.

"And to you. Allow me to introduce myself. I am Tonomori, and I would like to compliment you on your reading."

Tonomori thought of what de Wynte had said over a pot of beer that morning after breakfast: MacDonnell would be perfect if he was available. "He is a better swordsman than poet, and chronically short of money," de Wynte had told him. But from one end of Europe to the other MacDonnell had fought in every major armed conflict worth being in since he was fifteen years old. De Wynte had met him several years ago while carrying a boatload of soldiers from France to one of the many forgettable Italian campaigns. They had become friends, and got drunk together whenever their paths crossed after that.

"Sir Ian has a wealth of experience that might be of help to you in your wish for revenge when you return to Japan," the captain said, adding that when he ventured a word on any new weapon or tactic, experienced captains paid attention. De Wynte went on to describe him as a soldier of fortune who would have had a major command long since except for his footloose ways.

And MacDonnell never stayed in one place long enough to flatter and worm his way into the confidence of princes and lords who might employ him as a high-ranking officer. "For reasons of his own, he won't fight for the Spanish," de Wynte said, adding that MacDonnell might bring along troubles from his past. He would be considered good-looking in a devilish sort of way, at least by women who liked to be courted by dangerous men. Tonomori looked at MacDonnell's lean face and hard gray eyes. This one was dangerous, all right. As a keen judge of fighting men, Tonomori was intrigued and eager to talk.

"Thanks for the good words, but I won't win," MacDonnell replied. "All the judges are drunk." He pointed out five ruddy-faced men who bore clear indications of beery puzzlement.

"If they are judges of poetry, I'm the king of Sweden," MacDonnell said. "A pity though, because I could use the fifty florins as prize money."

"Then maybe I could be of assistance," Tonomori said.

271

"I need a few military men. You have been described to me as an expert on the use and manufacture of weapons. Also as loyal, and reasonably honest."

MacDonnell nodded, without taking offense at hearing his honesty described as somewhat limited.

"A lot of good that does me now with the doves of peace lately nesting in my helmet," he remarked. "A few more treaties and most of the men in this room, myself included, will be sleeping in cow barns this winter. Some of them will be taking to the road, relieving passing strangers of their more valuable possessions. You know, people bitch a lot about the loss of life in battles. You can even hear it in church—if you're foolish enough to go there. I remember hearing it once from a wheezy old fuck who kept interrupting my nap when I had ducked into a pew to sleep off a little wine." He paused and scratched his head. "Where was I?"

"The tremendous loss of human life . . ."

"Oh yes. Anyway, few people seem to notice that when kings and princes aren't at each other's throats, and good fighting soldiers are out of work, the crime rate goes up." MacDonnell said it with obvious satisfaction.

"You have vision," Tonomori assured him.

"An honor without profit," MacDonnell observed laconically. Their conversation was interrupted by a scuffle between the last contestant and two hecklers in the front row. Their friends pulled them apart, and when the shouting had died down, the versifying resumed.

"I am in a position to offer you employment in the service of the Countess de Edgemont," Tonomori told him.

MacDonnell now studied more carefully Tonomori's face and clothes. He noted the curved sword with interest, and settled in to bargain.

"How much?"

"You haven't asked me what the job entails."

"Does it matter?"

"It just might," Tonomori said with some asperity. "Do I have to do your negotiating for you?"

"You've got a captive audience. Please proceed."

Tonomori leaned forward to speak quietly. "Much is involved. Guarding the countess comes first. She has enemies. Already one attempt has been made on her life."

MacDonnell's eyes narrowed to slits.

"Beyond that, we will be establishing a cannon foundry, powder mills, and arms factories later. For export," Tonomori continued. "The details are confidential for now, as is the involvement of the countess. Her name will never be mentioned in these dealings. We will be competing with the arms makers of Augsburg and Milan."

"Sounds interesting." MacDonnell was cautious. He knew there had to be a catch somewhere.

"Also, I will be needing information," Tonomori threw in now. "Some high-ranking Spaniards are among the enemies of the countess."

"That's normal enough." MacDonnell saw what the catch was. "But high-ranking Spaniards are expensive. I'll need fifteen florins a day."

"Ten," Tonomori countered.

"Twelve, plus meals and a place to sleep." MacDonnell spoke with finality.

"Agreed. However, I must tell you that you will work through me. Follow orders without question, and we will get along."

"Sounds good, but I'll need a half-month's pay in advance to settle my accounts here and elsewhere." MacDonnell did not mention that it would also get his armor out of pawn.

"I can arrange that. First, though, I also need a man who knows his way around horses," Tonomori said.

"Easily done." MacDonnell cupped his hands and yelled across the room, "Hey, Müller, haul your dead ass over here."

A big German with a round, open face ambled to the table and eased his bulk onto MacDonnell's bench. "Yah, my brave captain. Someone has clipped a donkey's ears and sold it to you as a horse? . . ."

"No, shithead, we have here a man with a job," MacDonnell told him amiably.

Müller leaned across the table, as far as his paunch

273

would allow. "I know horses," he declared proudly. "Break, train, buy, sell, doctor . . . ." He looked around to see if anyone was listening, and confided in a low tone, "Or maybe steal."

Tonomori was aghast at the casual disregard for other people's property. Thievery, in all its myriad forms, seemed to be a national industry everywhere in Europe. Nevertheless, he said wearily, "If you can start immediately, ten florins a day." Müller nodded without arguing and thumped the table for a round of ale to seal the bargain.

A stout barmaid with a lantern jaw arrived with a pitcher of ale. MacDonnell and Müller seemed to suddenly be preoccupied and Tonomori realized belatedly that they expected him to pay.

"A custom here," MacDonnell lied cheerfully. "The new man always pays."

"They be friends of yours?" the barmaid asked, looking hard at Tonomori. "I hope you have a lot of money. You'll need it."

"Agnes here is a cynic." MacDonnell patted the barmaid's ample backside. She slapped his hand with the accuracy of someone with much practice at it.

" 'Agnes here' is used to dealing with scoundrels." She said it, as though confidentially, to Tonomori, but loud enough for the others to hear.

"Let us continue to be good friends, my dear. . . ." MacDonnell continued smoothly.

"You're into me for five florins. When are you going to pay up?" Agnes asked.

"That's not all he's into her for," Müller said in an aside, and yelped when Agnes smacked him in the ear with her tray.

"Patience, my dear. I am now gainfully employed. All will be repaid today," MacDonnell told her.

"Well then, why don't you just drop around this evening after hours, when I'll be glad to collect. With interest!" She smiled sweetly and swept away to calls for more beer elsewhere.

MacDonnell looked dubious. "I don't know. My old wound has been acting up lately. . . ."

"Yah. It moves all over his body," Müller remarked. "Especially if there is hard work to be done."

"Agnes isn't hard work," MacDonnell protested. "Agnes is . . . is *formidable*. And she scratches." He brightened at a sudden memory. "There is also a story that she can cave in a musket barrel. Well, a loan must be repaid . . ."

Tonomori wondered what he had let himself in for. If these were men who were admired and respected and trusted, then what were the rest like? He began to think that, to have such misfortune piled on his shoulders, he must have committed some spectacularly evil deeds in a former life.

A sour-faced man sidled onto the bench across the table from Tonomori, next to Müller, who scowled. Another man with a heavily pocked face took a position at the head of the table between them. Two bench-lengths away, several of the strangers' companions were talking low but guffawing loudly.

"If you are having a party, MacDonnell, we'd like to join in," the sour-faced one sneered.

"It is a private party," MacDonnell growled. Tonomori slid his bench backward slightly, to give himself room.

"We just invited ourselves," the pockmarked one added.

"The Di Frisi brothers, Ugly and Uglier," MacDonnell said to Tonomori.

"We are discussing business," Tonomori told them mildly.

"We are not averse to discussing business. Our business is drinking. You seem to have plenty of coins to rub together." This from Ugly, on the bench. The brothers had been drinking. Tonomori was disgusted by the rankness of their breath. "Call it a loan," Uglier suggested heavily.

"I am not a moneylender." Tonomori shifted his weight to the right side of his body. MacDonnell could sense trouble getting ready to explode like a cannon with a cracked breech. The brothers were in a foul mood, and their drinking companions obviously had been goading them. He would have to warn his new employer about being more discreet when showing his purse.

275

"Stand us a couple of mugs, then," Uglier demanded.

"I can't stand either one of you at all," MacDonnell said pointedly.

"I never buy drink for strangers," Tonomori added.

"Fine haired, aren't we?" Ugly began. "You know, these days they'll let any foreign scum walk in here. . . ."

Ugly's head suddenly snapped back, his nose and mouth bloody pulp. MacDonnell moved out of the way. What he had seen was so deceptively simple and amazingly effective: Tonomori had raised slightly on his right leg and kicked across the table, low and rising, with his left.

With the same motion, Tonomori grabbed Uglier by the back of his neck and his belt and slammed his body twice onto the top of the table. Uglier rolled off, limp and bloody.

Tonomori heard benches skidding behind him at the table from where the Di Frisi brothers had come. He pivoted, and hurled his own bench with surprising accuracy.

One down, four to go. Müller started to leap to his assistance, but MacDonnell held him back. "If he needs help, we'll give it to him. Otherwise, stay out of it."

Ugly struggled to his feet, spitting out red slime and pieces of teeth. He fumbled for his knife and lurched toward Tonomori's back.

"No knives, asshole," MacDonnell warned, kicking his feet out from under him. Ugly tried to rise again until MacDonnell's knee connected with his jaw, and joined his brother on the floor.

The remaining four belligerents rushed Tonomori at once, trying to drag him down. Tonomori slammed the palm of one hand into the chin of the nearest man, who dropped like a poleaxed steer.

A giant of a man reached for Tonomori's throat, his teeth showing in a snarl that turned to shock when the samurai stepped in to meet the rush and broke his forearm above the wrist. A scream, and the man broke away, holding the useless arm.

The remaining pair had grabbed benches. Tonomori circled away, leaned over, and wrenched a leg off a table.

"If you insist," he muttered. He swung with incredible

power. His nearest opponent tried to block it, but the force drove the bench backward into the side of his face and he fell senseless.

Tonomori began raining heavy blows with the table leg against the last man, who was trying to back away from the relentless terror who had decked his companions. The wood was beginning to splinter when the man's scabbard tangled between his legs and he tripped. Twisting like a weasel, he scrambled toward the refuge of the open door and was helped along for several feet by a kick from Tonomori.

All that could be heard was the sound of running feet. The suddenness, the ferocity of Tonomori's attack had stunned onlookers who themselves had been veterans of many brawls.

Tonomori returned to his table.

"Couldn't have done better myself," MacDonnell told him.

"Yah. He usually loses," Müller interjected.

"Thank you for your assistance." Tonomori was barely panting.

"What assistance?" MacDonnell shrugged.

"The one with the knife. If he had drawn it, I would have been forced to kill him," Tonomori explained.

MacDonnell thought hard. The man's back had been turned. He couldn't possibly have seen the danger, unless he had eyes in the back of his skull. . . . There was far more to this one than MacDonnell had imagined.

"Do you still wish to take service under my command?" Tonomori asked.

"Oh yes. I wouldn't miss it for worlds," MacDonnell assured him.

Bicker appeared at their table, looking surly while his underlings dragged the unconscious forms over the north wall, where the proprietor could keep an eye on them. Bicker would see that at least their purses and valuables would not be rifled while they were regaining their senses. He had a reputation to uphold.

"Who is going to pay for this mess?" he demanded.

"How much?" Tonomori accepted the responsibility.

Bicker considered a moment, doubled the sum, and said, "Four florins."

"Here are two," Tonomori replied.

Bicker hesitated, then accepted the coins. He usually had trouble getting anything at all. "What started it?"

"Ugly and Uglier were insulting your paying customers again," MacDonnell told him.

"They can stay out for a while." Bicker gathered a brother under each doughy arm, and deposited them against the wall.

"Whew!" MacDonnell exhaled. "It is fortunate he didn't think *we* started it."

"Why? Do you fear him?" Tonomori was surprised.

"His method of dealing with troublemakers is simple, but it's effective," MacDonnell explained. "Bicker just picks up a full thirty-gallon keg of beer, holds it out in front of him, and charges in. He can only do it once, but it sure does break up a fight. People leave, one way or another."

"I think it is time we left, too," said Tonomori.

Chapter Twenty

Lieutenant Enrique Serrano peered blearily into his mug and hiccuped. The mug had been refilled three times and drained three times since his good friend and fellow officer Felipe Pidal had bounded upstairs with the latest addition to the shy flowers at The Bed of Rose's. She was a veritable madonna, that one, Serrano thought, and he had hotly wanted her for himself. But because it was Pidal's twenty-third birthday, Serrano had engaged her services for him in honor of the occasion.

Rose's price for any of her girls was two ducats on the bed, three ducats *in*. Serrano's three ducats nestled among the shiny pile in Rose's cashbox, which also contained florins, livres, shillings, and a few rings. Barter was permitted, but newcomers were well warned that Rose could spot a gilt-plated lump of lead at ten paces. She considered such dishonesty as no better than rape, and anyone foolhardy enough to attempt to pluck Rose was abruptly shown to the door and barred permanently thereafter.

"Another beer, sir?" The serving wench was demure, seeming to hardly dare meet Serrano's out-of-focus gaze.

"Ah . . . why not?" Serrano replied happily.

The girl was back in moments with an overflowing mug, the foam sliding tantalizingly down the outside. Serrano pushed over a few extra copper coins.

"Oh, thank you, sir," she murmured breathlessly close to his ear. "If you need *anything* else, just raise your hand, and I'll be glad to . . . take care of you. My name is Suzanne."

She averted her eyes modestly again, but the invitation in her voice was unmistakable. It needed to be: The appealing come-on was Rose's best stock in trade. Suzanne cast a wary glance toward the corner where Rose kept vigilant and sometimes vigorous tabs on her clientele and her stable. Nothing escaped her scrutiny, the girls knew from bitter experience—whether slackers on her staff or loose coins that might just happen to slip out of gentlemen's purses. Her girls might be hardened whores with years of paid practice, but when Rose had put the finishing touches on their training, a customer could only feel that they were maidens who must have just recently fallen from grace because of the need to provide a few coins for a dying mother or a crippled brother. Rose's ravaged face was heavily lined under its thick layer of powder, but her deep-set, beady eyes searched out gold and silver as greedily as a duck goes after beetles.

"I will," Serrano mumbled, though privately he doubted that he'd be up to it. For one thing, he felt too drunk to be able to do her or himself any good. Serrano really was not accustomed to so much to drink. For another, Pidal should be back soon—and where in the fucking hell was he, anyway? Serrano hoped that Pidal had remembered to take his spurs off. He wouldn't want torn sheets added to his expense for the evening.

Suzanne gave him her best version of a coquettish smile and slipped away, her brown curls bouncing along with her curvesome charms, to serve a loud group of merrymakers at a table by the stairs. Serrano, sighing, wished he had not drunk quite so much. If Suzanne was not enough reason for a degree of sobriety, the Duke of Alvino's staff meeting in the morning would be. A thorough disciplinarian and taskmaster, the duke did not look kindly on sleepy junior officers who weren't fully ready for whatever orders he might have for them. Serrano pushed away his mug. He had no desire for some such assignment as poking through barrels of herring in search of contraband, the fate of a fellow officer who had shown up with a head throbbing from a night's excess, and his clothes reeking of stale beer.

At the sound of feet on the stairs, Serrano looked up. Pidal was flushed and content, his arm around the madonna's waist. At the foot of the steps, Pidal sent her on her way with an intimate pat on the rump and then rejoined his friend.

"A wonderful idea of yours, Enrique! I owe you," Pidal exclaimed. "A fantastic lay, and so willing, so naive, so inexperienced. An angel! But I wonder what she meant when she called me her trick. I could use another pot of beer. I may have been drunk—a little—when I got up there, but now I've worked up another thirst."

"Here, take mine." Serrano hiccuped.

"Nonsense! This one's on me." Pidal snapped his fingers for service, appraised Suzanne's generous curves— first with a genial eye, then with an amiably objective hand—and ordered a round. . . .

Pidal's head was swimming, and he was hard put to

keep Serrano on his feet when they finally left Rose's, awash in beery sentiment and camaraderie. It had been a most satisfactory evening, no doubt about that. They found the street dampened from a shower, but now the moon was out and they should have a pleasant enough ride back to headquarters if they could remain on their mounts. But where was the stable where they had left the horses?

Frowning, Pidal looked around. He shook his head. They must be headed the wrong way. Despite the excellent reputation of Rose's as one of Antwerp's better licensed brothels, it was located in a seamy section of the city where footpads often made game of unwary pedestrians. Pidal shuddered slightly. *Let's find those horses!*

Serrano began to slump to the cobblestones. "No, you don't, my friend," Pidal told him. He put Serrano's arm around his shoulders and supported him at the waist.

"Where . . . going?" Serrano belched.

"Home." Pidal was reassuring.

"Don' have home. Got kicked out, heh, heh," Serrano giggled. "You don' have home, either."

"Yes, I know, but the fortress is our home away from home. . . ." Pidal hesitated, having spotted an alley that seemed familiar. He cudgeled his whirling thoughts. A shortcut to their horses, of course! He remembered now.

They lurched off the street into the alley, mushing through refuse and puddles. Pidal didn't think he could support Serrano much longer. *How much farther could that stable be?*

"Get them," a guttural voice rasped, and shadows rushed in.

Pidal's sword was out in an instant and flashing. He heard a yelp of pain and saw one of the men dart back, then join the three others closing in.

Christ, we're done for, Pidal thought frantically. He probably could save his own skin by abandoning Serrano, but Pidal's ears burned at the mere thought; he could never do that. He could only make the cutthroats pay well before they took his life. Serrano had his blade out now, but his head was muddled with liquor.

The robbers had picked their victims well; drunk, inexperienced men, hemmed in like chickens for the catching. They hit them at once, not giving them time to marshal their befuddled thoughts.

Serrano tripped over his own scabbard and felt a knife blade sear across his ribs. He struck out with a foot and connected with a leg, then held out his sword feebly, much as a blind man tapping with his cane.

Pidal, on the ground too, felt a man pinioning his arms, saw the blade plunging toward his exposed throat. He closed his eyes to utter a silent prayer for his soul.

He heard a solid blow, felt the man holding his arms suddenly release his grip and go limp, gurgling horribly. Twisting free, Pidal turned, saw the man shudder and die. Blood flooded from a gaping wound at the base of his neck. The robber with the knife, who had knelt on Pidal's groin, was also lying still, his neck at a grotesquely crooked angle.

Too weak to move, Pidal felt himself pushed down onto the ground. "Stay down, out of the way," snarled a powerfully built man, his contorted face and slanted eyes like those of a demon in the half-light. Pidal could see that the man was holding a short curved blade, low and steady, as he moved against another of the cloaked robbers. The attack was so swiftly brutal that Pidal could hardly follow it, but the bandit was down, coughing wetly and wildly, weakly clutching at his chest.

Serrano! Pidal made a motion to crawl to his aid. But a tall man already was there, forcing one more of the cutthroats backward with a long sword. Pidal saw him feint a move with his left shoulder and lunge, pinning the robber against a brick wall. A thin scream, and his body crumpled forward as the tall man's blade withdrew from it.

Eerie silence followed, except for heavy breathing and a steady drip from overhanging eaves three stories up.

The demon-faced man gestured casually to his tall companion, then turned to Pidal. "You two ought to know better. . . ."

Pidal fell back in shock as a hulking figure rose up from the shadows behind his rescuer. There had been a fifth robber! The figure whipped a garrote around Tonomori's

282

neck, and hauled back. Shaking with impotent rage, Pidal knew he could not help this man who had saved his skin. Pidal had seen by a faint gleam that the garrote was made of twisted wire; with that giant on the handles, it would rip the man's head off.

Instead, to Pidal's astonishment, the straining victim arched farther against the pull, kicked backward with each foot, and forced his assailant against the wall. His vicious short blade was out again. The demon-faced man stabbed backward between his left arm and rib cage, aiming accurately for the robber's chest. The giant gagged, tottered, then slammed against the bricks again as Tonomori whirled and drove the blade into his chest once more. The giant was dead before his body rolled onto the ground.

Pidal felt himself being helped to his feet, and heard, "I think your friend is not hurt badly. . . . Will you be able to stand now?"

"Yes . . . Yes, I'll be all right, except my *cojones* are scrambled." Pidal gingerly indicated his genitals. He doubled over as a fresh wave of pain struck. "I shall have to ride sidesaddle for a month," he groaned. Nausea, where so recently there had been ecstasy.

"I think I have only a slight scratch on the ribs, *compadre*." Serrano had limped over to Pidal's side while leaning on the tall man.

All four men caught their breath. They had been at the brink of sudden death before, and they realized that they'd need time before they could step back and look at this experience with detachment. They exchanged names and handclasps.

"Sir Ian MacDonnell? You have a reputation as a swordsman, sir, and well deserved it is," Serrano told him.

The name Tonomori rang a bell for Pidal. *Of course! The Asian lord who had come on the Dutch ship with the Portuguese license. The one who guarded the countess in whom the duke had been so interested as of late! Damn, who'd have thought a foreigner could move as fast as a Spaniard?*

"You, Lord Tonomori, have my very considerable thanks.

They'd have had my life along with my gold and my family jewels," he said.

"And mine," Serrano added. "We owe you our lives." He was sober now, but with a throbbing head.

"I thought you were a goner, m'lord, when that giant struck with the garrote," Pidal told Tonomori.

"So did he. It was his mistake." Pidal and Serrano were disquieted by his strange eyes, glinting and hooded like a bird of prey. He looked as dangerous as he had proved to be.

"Can we buy you a drink? No? Well, perhaps that's just as well," Serrano shrugged. "I guess we've had enough for one night, after all. My mouth tastes like someone did something bad in it."

MacDonnell was kneeling. "Do either of you know these birds? Have you ever seen them before?"

Pidal looked down. The light was bad. "No. Wait . . . Yes . . ." He recognized the one who had pinioned his arms.

"That one. He was in the brothel earlier. I'd swear it!"

"Well, now you don't have to," MacDonnell commented grimly. "He undoubtedly had a quick look into your purse and a look at your condition, and decided to help himself to its contents with the assistance of a few friends. Just like I told *you* earlier, eh, Lord Tonomori?"

"Yes." Tonomori faced the Spaniards. "My friend here warned me earlier today against such an indiscretion."

Pidal and Serrano felt themselves little better than green rustics.

MacDonnell was busy now, moving among the bodies. He cut their purses and lifted their weapons. Like so many other of the armed robbers who were the scourge of Europe, they seemed to be far from coarse men of low birth. MacDonnell guessed that one or more of them might be, like himself, a knight come on hard times.

"I hope you don't object," MacDonnell mentioned. It wouldn't matter if they did. He had made his polite reference merely out of form's sake. MacDonnell tucked the purses into the top of his doublet and rolled the weapons into a cloak that one of the cutthroats would no longer need.

"Be sure to take care of that cut," he admonished Serrano, who had plastered a handkerchief against the wound. The bleeding had already stopped.

Tonomori had noticed the young officers' spurs, and offered to walk with them to claim their horses at the stable.

"Ordinarily I would have been insulted by the offer to be escorted, but not tonight," Pidal conceded humbly. "My friend and I shouldn't be let out alone, I'm thinking. It was more than a pleasure to have made your acquaintance!"

When the officers had recovered their horses and paid the ostler his fee, they parted from Tonomori and MacDonnell in a good mood, sobered by their brush with death. Pidal rode sidesaddle.

"They'll learn," MacDonnell mentioned as he and Tonomori headed for their own mounts.

"They'd better!"

"Yes, there usually isn't a second chance. You just cock your toes up."

MacDonnell clucked his tongue and Tonomori laughed. "In *my* country, people cock their toes in ecstasy."

"Is that so? Well, here they cock their toes in eternity." MacDonnell thought for a moment. "Curl their toes, eh? The women?"

"Especially the women!"

"You know this from personal experience!"

"Of course. And from the *shunga* prints."

MacDonnell brightened. "You mean dirty pictures?"

"Not at all. Only men and women together doing what pleases them. No sexual acts are forbidden in my country," Tonomori informed him.

"Well, we've got some dandies here, including a couple that would get you burned at the stake, in fact. You don't have any of those pictures with you, by any chance?" MacDonnell licked his lips.

"No. I brought none."

"What a pity." MacDonnell sounded somewhat bitter. "We could have gone to a woodblock carver, had him make a master, run off a bunch of prints, and then sold them all as originals before some slimy bastard could beat us to it.''

"I am samurai. We do not indulge in such behavior." Tonomori's tone was distant.

"Well, I could have handled the details and cut you in for ha— . . . a third, to be sure," MacDonnell told him. He shifted the bundle of weapons he had slung under one arm, and cursed his aching feet. It seemed as though they had been walking for hours, from one end of the city to another and back. MacDonnell felt he had walked over each of the hundreds of canal bridges.

Tonomori seemed to have an unquenchable curiosity. They had visited armorers and foundries, provisioners and mapmakers. Müller had left them after the tavern incident, agreeing to meet later at the stable. Tonomori had stabled his horse with MacDonnell's and they had proceeded on foot.

They had stopped only for the evening meal, then had gone at it again. Tonomori wanted to know everything: Who made the big clock at the town hall, and how did it work? Who supplied the fishmongers and how far did the fishermen have to haul their catch? Why did he see so many priests but so few nuns? Why didn't everyone bathe more often? And wouldn't it be better for all concerned if the contents of chamber pots were gathered and used to dung the fields instead of being emptied into the streets, sometimes onto the heads of passing strangers?

"I only live here. I don't make the rules or set the customs," MacDonnell finally told him. "I'm a military man. That's what you wanted, isn't it?"

Tonomori limited himself to questions of a martial nature after that, but maintained the same relentless pace.

"We are almost there," Tonomori called. MacDonnell could see the lantern in front of the stable. The soles of his feet screamed for relief. "Thank God!"

Waiting for them, the stable owner had been grumbling at being kept from his bed, but he kept his shiny face split with an affable smile in hope of a tip. He had carefully brushed the horses, so he received the largesse he had expected. He also informed them that Müller had left word not to wait for him, that he would be delayed on business.

"I trust he will catch up with us later?" said Tonomori, once he was in the saddle. Müller had requested, and received, a considerable advance on his pay.

"Müller? He's trustworthy enough. If he says he's on business, then business it is." MacDonnell wondered what Müller really was up to. He and Müller made a practice of covering for each other. On the other hand, Müller might actually be earning his ten ducats a day. MacDonnell, not really believing that, dismissed the idea from his mind.

What MacDonnell really wanted to know was what kind of man would be leading him. Correction: *was* leading him . . . had already led him on a tangled journey all over Antwerp and capped it with a bloody alley brawl.

He didn't want to offend Tonomori, but he could think of many questions he wished to put to his companion.

"Where are we going?" MacDonnell asked instead. They were heading north. The direction of the de Edgemont estate was to the east.

"To a silversmith," Tonomori replied.

"Oh?"

Silence.

MacDonnell tried again. "Why?"

"To pick up some silver pieces I had cast earlier this week," Tonomori explained briefly.

MacDonnell frowned. This was going to be difficult. His new commander was employing a tactic he himself had used often. It involved answering a question only within the perimeters of the information requested, but not volunteering anything. It forced the inquisitive person to ask many questions, at the cost of becoming a nuisance.

MacDonnell decided to be direct. "Tell me, if you would, how you knew that the man behind you in the tavern had a knife or that he was even there, yet under similar circumstances back in that alley, you almost got yourself killed." MacDonnell ran his sleeve under his nose and waited for a reply.

For a long time, while Tonomori seemed to be considering an answer, there was only the sound of their horses' hooves clicking along the deserted street.

"It is difficult to explain to someone who is not samurai, even a person as accomplished as yourself," Tonomori finally said, breaking the silence.

"Can you try?"

"You would have to understand Zen, what is regarded as the *nothingness* of Zen, but which I know as *everything*," Tonomori explained.

"You are right; I don't follow you. Can you try to say it in words that even I might be able to understand?" MacDonnell was intrigued.

"Do you remember ever knowing, being absolutely positive, that someone was looking at you behind your back? And then you turned and found that this was actually so?" Tonomori asked.

"Yes . . . Yes, I have."

"To be trained in Zen takes time, understanding . . . to extend your powers of perception beyond their normal limits. Above all, genuine wisdom is needed—and someone to point the way. And it is not something that is fully understood; yet it exists; it seems to work. At least, that is my own experience. But apparently it is not for everyone."

"Then in the alley, the power failed you?" MacDonnell was stating a conclusion in his question.

"Not at all! It was I who failed."

"Then I *don't* understand!" MacDonnell thumped his forehead in exasperation.

"It is simple enough. I knew he was there. I should have killed him where he lay crouched. But logic told me that if I ignored him, he would run for his life while I came to your assistance. I think now that he was too stupid to run away and that is why he jumped me. Logically, he should have taken to his heels as I understand the custom here among thieves to be." He paused. "I will not make *that* mistake again."

MacDonnell considered for a moment. "Would it be possible for you to teach me this . . . Zen, as you call it?"

"It might be possible. You may have the ability,"

Tonomori conceded. "Whether I will do it remains to be seen. I will give it further thought."

"One more question and then I will give way. I have my own opinion as to what could have saved your neck back there. That garrote should have taken your head off."

"In Japan, we call it a *nodawa*," Tonomori said briefly.

"A *nodawa*?"

"Do you repeat everything?" Tonomori was becoming annoyed, and he wanted to concentrate on other things on his mind. He struggled to master his impatience. "In your language it would be called a throat ring."

"Like a gorget?" MacDonnell was familiar with the rather ordinary piece of armor used to protect the fighting man's throat.

"Yes, but much thinner. And stronger." Tonomori exhibited his. "As you can see, the fashion of high collars on the doublet hides the *nodawa* very well. I also take the precaution of wearing a thin shirt of mail under my doublet."

"That is wise. I do the same when I'm not in full plate armor. It has come in handy once or twice," MacDonnell agreed. He saw the teeth in Tonomori's smile. "Two or three people in the past have tried to rearrange my liver," he added.

"I see. I have had similar experiences myself." Tonomori's impatience had vanished. After all, he needed to question MacDonnell in detail about European arms and armaments. If the man was eager to acquire knowledge, an exchange of information would be only a fair bargain.

"I will answer all your questions, if I can," he told MacDonnell. "But later, if you please. Right now, I would like to collect my silver pieces and get out of Antwerp."

They stopped outside a small shop. A single candle gleamed in the window; otherwise, all was darkness.

"It is after hours. He is closed," MacDonnell objected.

"I told him I would be late. It has been arranged. You will wait here, please." Tonomori dismounted, and Mac-Donnell took the loose reins while he rapped on the door. A thin face peered through the pane. They heard the bolt being worked back, then Tonomori slipped inside as the heavy door opened slightly to admit him; the bolt was thrown home again. Hearing the slam of the bolt, which ensured that he would not also try to enter, MacDonnell was not offended. This was merely the shop of a man who took no chances.

Inside, Tonomori was led to a workbench covered by a fringed hammercloth, heavily ornamented. On it gleamed many pieces of silver.

"Thank you for being so patient," Tonomori murmured before picking up one of the pieces and examining it closely.

"Not at all. It was a pleasure, sir," the silversmith, Jan Dalbritten, assured him. The wrinkles at his eyes and mouth deepened with satisfaction. "These are castings from your original, but I am happy with the quality."

"The work is good. I also am pleased," Tonomori nodded. He returned the piece to its pile.

Dalbritten handed him a small wooden box. "This is the original. I took great pains; it has not been in any way damaged in the making of the mold, I assure you. I have never seen anything like it. The hammer work, the carving— the product of a great artist. Completely beyond my ability. What . . . what is it used for, if you care to tell me?"

Tonomori opened the box and removed the object that had excited Dalbritten from the first moment he had laid eyes on it.

"It is called a *menuki*, a hilt ornament for a sword. They are made in many shapes and themes, always in pairs," Tonomori explained. "This praying mantis was the personal badge of a lord whom I once served."

"Then it has a twin?" Dalbritten cried. "I would consider it a privilege to see that!"

Tonomori considered, then removed a thin silk brocade bag he had tucked into his sword belt. He untied the cords and withdrew a dagger. It was nearly a foot in length. Any Japanese lord would have given many times its weight in gold to own it, based on the exquisite appearance alone.

Dalbritten was speechless. The theme of the praying mantis was repeated on the fittings throughout the dagger. He hardly heard Tonomori say, "This type is called a *tanto*."

290

"The handle is covered with pearls?" the silversmith asked, incredulous.

Tonomori laughed. "No. This is called *same*. It is the strip of skin taken from the back of a . . ."—Tonomori searched for the words— ". . . a manta ray and glued to the handle, called the *tsukka*. Usually, the *menuki* would be held in place by silk or leather crossed wrappings. But this is a presentation piece, so the ornaments are held on with pitch."

Dalbritten saw where Tonomori had carefully removed the *menuki*. On the other side of the handle, the ornamentation was slightly different. Here the mantis was devouring a gold butterfly. The detail was unbelievably fine. The antennae of the butterfly were barely visible. The mantis on the guard was raised and chased in gold, as was each mantis on the rich brown lacquered scabbard.

Tonomori withdrew the blade slightly. Dalbritten hardly noticed it, so intent was he on the wonders before his unbelieving eyes. "All this work for a knife?" he whispered.

"It is signed 'Kunimitsu'," Tonomori pointed out dryly, sliding the blade back into the scabbard. Dalbritten missed the inflection in his voice and Tonomori almost laughed at the man's ignorance. The fittings were nothing compared to the blade, a treasure almost beyond price, made by the genius Kunimitsu almost three hundred years before in Sagami province.

The *tanto* had been Lord Betsuo's final gift to Tonomori. It is sad, Tonomori thought, that not a single European can completely appreciate such a work. He replaced the *menuki* and rewrapped the *tanto*.

As Dalbritten carefully sacked the dozens of cast silver pieces, Tonomori tucked the *tanto* into his belt and counted out five gold coins. "The price, as we agreed. Is it satisfactory?"

"Oh, yes. If you have any other ornaments that you would like to sell or trade, I believe I could offer you excellent terms."

"If I should ever decide to sell, I will see you first," Tonomori agreed, though he knew he would never part willingly with any of his swords or their fittings.

291

Once outside, Tonomori stowed the sack of cast *menuki* in his saddlebags, then swung into the stirrups. He had a plan forming about the *menuki*. If he could find suitable transport for them, they could reach his friend Obushi, who would need no further suggestion as to how they could be used to persuade Masanori that he still would have to deal with Tonomori.

"Is it customary in your country to mount from the right?" MacDonnell inquired as Tonomori settled into the saddle. In Japan, he was known by the horses as the Giver of Sweet Fruit and Hard Kicks.

"Usually."

"We mount from the left, as you of course have observed."

Tonomori nodded. "Which is probably why he always balks when I climb on. He'll have to get used to it."

"Turn him over to Müller for a while. When Müller gets through with him, you can use his lower jaw for a steppingstone and walk on over his head," MacDonnell suggested jocularly.

"A good idea. I am not a trainer of horses."

"Nor am I. Weapons and armor are my forte, but a good horse can save your ass."

They rode with proper caution along the quiet thoroughfare, encountering only the night watch, walking in teams of two men.

By the time they reached the outskirts of Antwerp, the watch had already cried out the hour of eleven. Otherwise, one could hear only the sound of hooves, the creak of saddle leather, and the calls of occasional night birds. Each man was considering the measure of the other. The question foremost in their minds was one of trust.

At length, Tonomori, having made a decision, broke the silence. Captain de Wynte had vouched for the man's trustworthiness, so that would have to suffice for now. Time enough yet to discover what his limits might be.

He felt that he did not yet know MacDonnell well enough, however, to entrust him with the secret involving their plans to destroy Alvino's ships and warehouses. But if he could confirm his initial positive impression of the man, then soon he must bring the Scot—and probably Müller too—into the plot. And the long-deferred plan of action would have to be carried out quickly after that, before the duke's own scheming progressed too far to be halted. The night of the thousand cannonades could not be very many sunsets away.

"I am told you are an honorable man," Tonomori said suddenly. "We face dangerous times ahead. I would like to know more about you."

"First, answer one question of mine, and I'll consider telling you." MacDonnell pulled his horse to a halt. "Who was it who told you I am honorable?"

"A fine man himself—Captain Peter de Wynte."

"If he told you that, then he must have told you a few other things about me, as I remember your comments at the tavern. So, he must consider you discreet. De Wynte's not a big talker like a lot of people I know. Go ahead, then, ask your questions. I'll answer as honestly as I can."

"De Wynte tells me that you refuse to fight for the Spanish. Why?"

"It's not for the usual reasons." MacDonnell spoke with a grimace. "You talk to anyone in this country and they all hate the Spanish. Many of them have good cause indeed. I don't hate the Spanish because they are Spanish. The people and the soldiers seem no worse or better than others I've met.

"Take your average Spanish sword-and-buckler man. Say you're in combat and he lands a mortal blow. You're down and dying. Then he moves in and cuts your throat, or stabs in under the breastbone. The idea horrifies some people, but I don't consider that an act of cruelty. One quick cut, and you're gone, rather than lying on the field and dying after two or three days of agony. The Spaniard has done you a left-handed favor, even though he hardly intended to.

"But their commanders, their leaders, their churchmen— *them* I despise!" MacDonnell exclaimed. Tonomori was not prepared for the venom deep in his voice, and kept silent.

MacDonnell reached into a pouch hanging from his

saddle housing and extracted an earthen jug. "Talking always makes me thirsty." He took two rapid swigs and offered the jug to Tonomori.

"This is vile!" Tonomori gasped as he returned the jug after a single swallow.

"It grows on you." MacDonnell shrugged, took another drink, and replaced the jug in the pouch.

"Several summers ago," he said, "more than I like to count, I rode with the French in an Italian campaign. Our commander was a good man, but the Spanish overran our position and many of us were taken prisoner. The soldiers were rough, but they treated us decently enough. Then came the priests, with the connivance of the Castilian gentlemen who commanded.

"They culled out all the prisoners from England, Germany, Scotland—anywhere the Calvinists or the Lutherans are known to have made inroads. Then they set about extracting confessions from all of us. Their methods were not gentle. Half the men died on the rack, without really knowing why. The trick was to guess what crime it was you had committed. It's difficult to say which is worse—dying under torture or confessing to an imaginary crime and burning for it afterward."

"Did you confess to anything?" Tonomori interrupted.

"I probably would have, in time. As it was, Müller and another man broke into the prisoners' area and found me. I was at least half dead. The man with Müller was killed in helping me get out. Müller carried me a long way. I don't remember much. He stole food to keep us both alive, and when I finally was able to ride, he foraged a couple of horses. And so we got away, into Germany."

"I find your point of view interesting. I will keep it in mind," Tonomori observed.

"You mean the soldier's point of view," MacDonnell laughed. "You speak to civilians, you hear one thing. Talk to the military, and you hear another. I try to listen to all sides and then sort it all out. The truth is hidden somewhere in the middle. Sometimes you will find many truths, if you listen long enough."

"What about the arrogance of the Spanish? I find them

very irksome people, and I am continually at swords' points with one or another of them.''

"If you think the Spanish are arrogant, wait until you come up against the French,'' MacDonnell snorted.

"They can be worse?''

"Let's put it this way. To hear them tell it, after God made the angels, he created the French—and improved on the design. I remember hearing a dominie back home saying that if Christ had been a Frenchman, he'd have walked on wine.''

Tonomori found himself chuckling.

"I don't know what you've learned so far, but remember,'' MacDonnell cautioned, "everybody hates somebody else. It's a matter of degree and personal or national whim or prejudice. Frenchmen and Spaniards have been fighting each other for centuries, off and on; usually on. The Germans usually are fighting each other, though they've been known to take sides against others. The Italians think they own the world—when they're not being wiped on as doormats by the Spanish or the French. And the English steal from everyone, but consider the French to be their private preserve—all others please poach elsewhere. . . .''

"And the Scottish?''

"Ahhhh!'' MacDonnell exhalted proudly. "*We* steal from the English!''

"And may I ask for your own beginnings?''

"My father is said to have cheated the hangman many times. But his luck had to end sometime. He marched off to war when I was eight years old and never came back. It was said of my father that he could steal a red hot anvil without singeing his fingertips.'' MacDonnell reflected for a moment and continued. "My mother died only a year later. That left my younger brother and me and my sister, Mary. She was fourteen. It was Mary who kept us from starving. My uncles didn't care if we lived or died.

"Some women take in wash to make ends meet; my sister took in cocks. We only had one bed, so if she was, ah, entertaining, my brother and I slept on the floor. But Mary did right by us for years. Finally, she was able to apprentice my brother to a furniture maker. I suppose he's still making tables. Me, she apprenticed to a sword maker when I was turning twelve. Then she married a good man and went away with him. I only hope she is happy somewhere.

"My master was a Frenchman who had left some bad debts and a worse wife in Paris. He taught me about swords, how to make them, and armor—and women. He also taught me his language. Before he was imprisoned in Edinburgh for his debt—my fellow Scots are more vigilant about deadbeats—he gave me his best blade, the one I carry today, then kicked me loose. He must have known, even then, that he was dying. After that, I headed for the border of England, served a Scottish chieftain for a while, and survived my first few skirmishes with the English. By the skin of my teeth, that is. I've been at it ever since. Your turn, if you please."

Tonomori considered that MacDonnell had omitted significant bits of the story, but he let it pass for the time being. He would get the Scot drunk in due time and let wine pry his tongue loose. What had he done to gain knighthood? Not every soldier of fortune was to be called Sir Someone-or-other. He decided to tell his own story equally tersely.

After he had told MacDonnell of the role of the samurai and the disgraced status of the ronin, he quickly passed over the events that had brought on Lord Betsuo's death and Masanori's succession to the title. He told of his chance meeting with de Wynte and Diana, and their voyage together to Europe. "I will return one day!" he exclaimed.

"And?" MacDonnell wanted to know.

"I will kill him! With guns! With the new knowledge I have! And then I will piss on his grave!"

Their horses picked up their pace, having scented the de Edgemont stable ahead. Water, grain, and a stall were their only goals.

"Vengeance is that important to you, then?" MacDonnell asked.

"It is my duty. If I do not avenge my master, then my life is a failure."

"But what if you return and find that this Masanori is already dead? What then?"

"I have considered that. It would be most unfortunate, but it would make no difference. When I speak of Masanori, I mean Masanori and his entire clan." Tonomori could tell by MacDonnell's expression that he did not fully understand. "The Betsuo samurai have forfeited all honor by serving such a traitor. If Masanori already is dead, then I will deal with them—all of them—in his place."

It was not the chill night air that made MacDonnell shiver. What he heard was the quietly spoken intention of wholesale slaughter, of an undying hatred. He wanted to know more about this strange man from the other side of the world, a man whose capacities he could only guess at.

A groom came out with a tallow candle, unwillingly blinking sleep from his eyes. While he unsaddled the horses and stored the riding gear, the men rubbed them dry with handfuls of fresh straw. When the mounts were watered and fed, Tonomori led the way from the stable to show MacDonnell to his new sleeping quarters.

"When will Müller be joining us?" Tonomori wondered. He took a lamp from a sconce in the hallway.

"Tomorrow at the latest. He's probably picking up my gear for me." MacDonnell omitted that much of it was in pawn. "And he is probably making some inquiries on your behalf, among friends who are in, ah, close contact with the Spanish." He hoped this would prove to be true.

MacDonnell was a firm believer in acquiring and storing information. After he had almost lost his life in only the second skirmish of his military career, thanks to his commander's stupidity, MacDonnell had realized the necessity of being alert and using all of one's faculties. It was not enough to have the skills necessary to get inside an opponent's guard. Better still was to discover early what your opponent might be up to, and lure or maneuver him into an untenable position. And then, with ease, dispatch him and his helpless forces.

"Yes, I can use such information," Tonomori acknowledged. "Since I came here, I have learned many useful things. But one puzzles me, something almost as important as my revenge. . . . Ah, here we are!''

MacDonnell was irritated by the interruption. They had arrived at his room. It was on the mansion's ground floor, far enough away from the servants' wing to be respectable quarters for a distinguished soldier. The room was sparsely furnished but looked comfortable. MacDonnell saw the stub of a candle in a pewter holder and lighted it from Tonomori's lamp. It would give enough light to get undressed by. Actually, this was a luxury; MacDonnell usually undressed in the dark, or more likely slept in the day's clothes.

"This will be fine for me. You were saying?"

"The Portuguese now trade with my country. They established an empire along the way. I can understand that,'' Tonomori told him. "The Spanish conquered the New World. They are said to have been looking for the route to China, a shortcut that people are beginning to think doesn't exist after all. But that is neither here nor there.

"I am trying to determine to my own satisfaction, how a country like Spain, with only a handful of troops, could have conquered two empires in the New World.''

With the Portuguese moving in from the east, and the Spanish pushing beyond the New World from the west, Tonomori saw Japan as a vulnerable nut being enclosed slowly by two iron pincers. Japan had suffered two invasions by the Mongols. The first had been slapped aside, but the second had come close to succeeding. The Japanese had been saved only by the intervention of the gods who sent the *kamikazi*, the divine winds that drowned the Mongol fleet.

Gods, like lightning, rarely strike twice in the same place. Could Japan withstand an invasion by the Spanish and the Portuguese? It was a question that troubled his dreams. The danger was not *immediate*. But the threat would grow with each passing year, and so long as Japan remained divided, squabbled over by feuding warlords, she would be vulnerable. Perhaps her future lay in the first strike, catching the larger, superior nations by surprise, and then making the best use of her own fleet—aided, one could always hope, by the *kamikazi*.

Chapter Twenty-one

Diana's thousand guests, including the elite of Antwerp, screamed with laughter. The acrobat on stilts seemed ready to topple over, but always recovered in time. Wobble . . . wobble . . . wobble! Suddenly, a small member of his troupe gaily ran away with one of the poles. Then, waving resignedly to the fascinated onlookers, the acrobat fell slowly, hit the grass with a roll, and ended with a back flip to his feet amid thunderous applause as the sun glittered on his resplendent purple and orange costume.

The music of jongleurs and gleemen was everywhere, merry and bubbling like the two great bronze wine fountains spouting thin ribbons of pale yellow and scarlet into ever-ready cups. And the day was not half done.

Dwarfs darted here and there, jingling bells of warning. They delighted particularly in preying on plump women and girls, whom they pinched or tickled with ribald cries. They exemplified the lusty age, with its appreciation of bold jests and jokes with double meaning.

When laughter made the crowd thirsty again, huge wooden tuns were ready to pour forth a river of pale ale. A bounty was piled on outdoor trestle tables: Mounds of bread and cheese sat alongside pickled herring, freshly caught bream, and tubs filled with crabs and lobsters. From the spits, ovens, and pans of a kitchen set up in a large green tent north of the mansion came other delicacies—meat pies, pastries filled with fruit jams, rich custards. Several dishes made with milk or cream, rarities because they spoiled so quickly, were devoured at once. Merchants, bankers, and ambassadors vied at the tables with neighbors, nobles, and nabobs.

For the Countess de Edgemont's festival, it was the best of days, bright and clear, the breeze light and cool as the ices and sherbets being handed out lavishly by the confectioner. Rumor swept the crowd to the effect that the countess had spent nearly two thousand ducats for ice alone.

And not a dark cloud was in sight, unless one counted the Duke of Alvino, dogging Diana's heels everywhere, as welcome as some assiduous hound bearing a reeking bone. Or the swarm of flatterers, handsome ne'er-do-wells, and would-be suitors with an eye to a profitable marriage or affair.

Diana adroitly avoided them all.

"It is a marvel, how you seem able to make yourself scarce," Alvino purred after Diana had shrugged off another opportunist while sacrificing none of her dignity and good manners.

"It's simply a matter of keeping my wits about me, Duke," Diana said. "I only have to see someone heading toward me with purpose and bother writ large across his puffing features, and I just duck behind the nearest large object."

"Simple but effective!"

"Such stratagems are always the best, don't you agree?" she asked.

"Of course," Alvino agreed.

"But you should be enjoying yourself, Your Grace, and not wasting your time here with me," Diana protested lightly, and tapped him on the wrist with her fan. He was trying to lead her away from the throng, and Diana had no intention of letting him get her alone—yet. She had the excuse of her duties as a hostess.

"I would enjoy myself nowhere else," Alvino countered. His manner and speech conveyed the assurance of a Castilian courtier.

Diana was annoyed by the arrogance in his tone but did

not show it. Alvino was too confident, too used to having his own way, and Diana rebelled at his idea that he could lead her like a child.

Everywhere they walked, they were watched, and their movements commented upon, their relationship a subject of speculation and suspicion. *They* were the main spectacle, not the entertainment or the decorations—not even the impressive pillars and arches that Diana had ordered gilded and garlanded as they had been for a celebration several years earlier.

Together, Diana and Alvino might have stepped out of a painting by Titian, or better yet, by Botticelli. And they had no warts, pocked skin, or stumpy teeth requiring the kindness of the artist's brush.

But Alvino had eyes only for power, not for the quietly lovely young woman who graced his side, her golden hair piled on top of her head and wreathed with cornflowers. Her gown of rich green silk brocade was trimmed with silver braid, perfectly matching her necklace of emeralds and white gold. Green was also the color of the envious ladies of fashion who totted up the cost of such an ensemble and shrieked silently in dismay. Their husbands or fathers approved; they could not possibly be expected to match such magnificence.

No less splendid was Alvino, in a brown velvet doublet, matching slops breeches slashed and paned with gold satin, and black hose, with yellow leather slippers. Seed pearls circled his buttons, which contained rubies—like drops of blood.

The duke, too, was estimating the cost. Bills for the feast alone would be staggering, and he begrudged every ducat. Diana's extravagance would mean less for his own coffers when he wedded and bedded the elegant Dutch bitch.

Her emeralds, he realized, were so astoundingly precious that the proceeds from their sale might stave off his creditors until he was clear with the ships. Alvino had not realized that the countess possessed such resources, and resolved to pry deeper into her affairs. He must see to it at once!

301

"As with everything else, you take the lead in fashion," he said, commenting on Diana's folding fan.

"This is nothing new, after all, Duke," Diana reminded.

"In Spain, no. Here, yes," Alvino corrected, but he succeeded only in irritating her further. Until only a few years before fans had been made of a single piece of thin, painted wood. The folding fan, arriving from the East via Portugal into Spain, began to catch on there, slowly, before reaching Italy, where it gained a further toehold. Then Catherine de Medici brought several with her to France upon her marriage to Henry II. Once adopted by the French, the fashion of the folding fan was taking Europe by storm.

In other words, once more we bumpkins are finally catching on, is that it? Diana merely smiled sweetly. *We Dutch will show you Spanish bastards a thing or two yet!*

"The Japanese have been using this kind of fan for the last thousand years. As I said, Duke, hardly anything new." Diana didn't have any idea whether this was true.

It was Alvino's turn to smile. He was reminded that he had plans for the surly-looking Japanese lord who was strutting arrogantly everywhere. Soon the lady's self-satisfied look would turn to fear, and she would have to look to Alvino for aid; she would have nowhere else to turn.

"I must go," Diana told him with finality. "I have to see that everything is running smoothly. Remember your promise. At one o'clock?"

"At one. I shall not disappoint you," Alvino assured her. They exchanged bows and went their separate ways, Diana glad for even temporary relief, and Alvino to change into his parade armor. He had assented to Diana's request that he star in a spectacle calculated to astonish and delight all spectators.

The efficient Gutierrez quickly sought him out in the pavilion set aside for the duke and his staff.

"I have been keeping an eye on him. The Japanese lord is going nowhere. He enjoys the sights but remains in the background. People seem to be wary of him," Gutierrez reported.

Alvino divided his attention between his second-in-command and the hapless squire who was assisting him into his armor.

"The cuisses first, idiot!" Alvino snapped. The squire returned the breastplate to its pile and returned with the cuisses, defenses for the upper leg and knee. These were ornately decorated and chased in gold.

"Let him enjoy himself. He will be feeling nothing soon, except hellfire," the duke said to Gutierrez.

"Do you wish me to fight him before the spectacle or after?" Gutierrez helped himself to a pear from a silver bowl and began peeling it.

"After. Nothing has changed. Make sure you don't fail," Alvino instructed. He turned to his squire. "*Now* the breastplate. Do I have to tell you everything?"

Gutierrez bowed and left, devouring the pear. The day promised to be an exciting one, and he looked forward to the kill. The Japanese savage would make good sport.

MacDonnell found Tonomori in heated conversation with his two *ashigaru*. The conversation was entirely in Japanese, but MacDonnell could discern that Tonomori was unhappy about something.

"In the future, keep your monkey on a leash. His manners are as bad as your own," Tonomori lectured loudly.

Oshabiri quailed. "Yes, Tonomori-sama. But it was not Saru's fault. . . ."

The object of their discussion was ensconced in a nearby tree, squealing in impotent rage while below, a white gander flapped his great wings and stretched his long neck to hiss his wrath. The gander knew an egg thief when he saw one—and a tormentor of goslings, too. Pleased at having routed an enemy, the gander settled in to preen. Saru chittered in indignation, refusing to come down to face the black beak.

"It is *always* Saru's fault. He is spoiled beyond belief. I have been too lenient. You are warned!"

Tonomori turned to Yamahito, who was standing by impassively.

"And you! Our mistress informs me that you were seen pissing against a tree by at least two hundred people."

"In Japan, sir, . . ."

"Ah, you are suffering from the delusion that you are still in Japan, where a man may piss against anything that takes his fancy?"

"No, sir!"

"A miraculous cure—see that there is no relapse! Or perhaps you were advertising for a girlfriend, Yamahito-san?" Tonomori said caustically.

"No, sir."

"If you feel the need of a woman, then proceed to the nearest whorehouse like a civilized person."

"Perhaps they will not admit a Japanese, sir. Europeans are very bigoted, I have noticed. Even more than we are."

So far, the only experience that Yamahito and Oshabiri had had with women in the Netherlands had been to satisfy their craving on the mother of a young traveling tinker who had spent a day at the estate. Her curiosity had overcome any prejudice she might have had, and so the tinker's dam had giggled the entire time they had sweated in the hayloft over her unwashed body. Kept on a short leash by Tonomori, they had been desperate.

"Your powers of observation are sadly lacking," Tonomori conceded now. "I have been remiss in your education. The whores I have encountered so far will lift their skirts for anyone with a few pieces of silver, even for a demon with two cocks. In fact," he laughed uproariously, "if you *had* two, they'd do it for nothing. Maybe even pay you for brightening their lives."

"Very well, sir."

"Your education begins at once," Tonomori said, adding, "Take Oshabiri-san with you. And see that he stays out of trouble. I hold you responsible."

"That has always been my sad *karma*, sir," Yamahito responded. Oshabiri puffed up in protest but said nothing. He was excited at the prospect of visiting a foreign brothel and inspecting all those hairy portals. To Yamahito's disgust, he would undoubtedly talk for weeks about nothing else.

Oshabiri looked anxiously at the tree where Saru languished.

"Leave the monkey," Tonomori suggested. "I don't think he will be going anywhere for a while." He was right. The gander, joined by his mate and three downy goslings, settled in to stay as passersby tossed scraps of fruit from a safe distance.

"I've been looking for you," MacDonnell began as soon as the two *ashigaru* had departed in animated conversation. "Can we talk privately?"

"Certainly," Tonomori said politely.

He located a deserted spot behind an ornate obelisk and they stood in its narrow shadow.

"I overheard Alvino's second-in-command talking to a couple of his men. He aims to pick a fight with you," MacDonnell told him in a low voice.

"I look forward to it! I was afraid this was going to be a dull afternoon."

"Take care, my friend. Something is afoot. I think, more than just a fight."

Tonomori was all concentration now. "How so?"

"Well, Gutierrez is a tough customer. He'd have to be, in order to remain as Alvino's right-hand man. He's a damned fine swordsman, I hear—I've never seen him fight—and he has a reputation for liking blood."

"I enjoy a fight myself."

"The point is: Gutierrez wouldn't be looking for a fight unless he had Alvino's approval. He'd be on his best behavior," MacDonnell said. "This doesn't sound good at all."

Tonomori considered. This foreign shogun was at work then, trying to manipulate them. *To what end? Think!*

Having slaughtered the heirs and confiscated the de Edgemont estate on behalf of the Spanish king, the duke then attempts to assassinate the countess to prevent her from regaining the property. Yes, Tonomori told himself, but the Spanish king returned it. If he had wanted to keep the lands, he could have used a dozen opportunities in Seville to have Diana killed along with her entire household. So there must be another motive, another plan, like a Chinese box within a box within a box. *Find the key before this man destroys your mistress and, along with her, your honor.*

"Gutierrez? Is that the one with the face like a brute?" Tonomori asked at last.

"Yes. Watch yourself! We're in some kind of game," MacDonnell cautioned. "I'd like to know the rules, if any, and the odds."

"Why the odds?"

"To determine if the game is worth the risk."

"And if it isn't?"

"I'll let you know. I'll tell you one thing, though: Alvino is a sly fox and a veteran of many hen houses," MacDonnell observed. "If he's risking Gutierrez in a fight, he must be exceedingly sure he's going to win." He hesitated. "Stall for time if you can. I'll try to get more information."

"Please do. And I'll try to arrange for some additional time."

"Just be careful!" MacDonnell urged, trying to appear much less apprehensive than he felt. He would prepare well for what the day might bring.

At one o'clock, Countess Diana shut her eyes in a silent prayer, crossing her fingers, and stepped into view of the hushed throng, hoping that nothing would unexpectedly go wrong.

The setting was perfect: a miniature castle whose pointed towers were complete with banners and heraldic devices; even a drawbridge over a newly dug moat. It was a scene out of an illuminated manuscript. On the castle grounds, numerous artificial trees held brightly embellished shields.

In the middle of this splendor, Diana waited. Soon, a white horse, with a gilt horn neatly strapped to its forehead, approached and took an apple from her hand. The fair virgin, with the power of her purity, demonstrably could lure the ferocious unicorn to her side at will. Diana had hoped the beast wouldn't balk at her loss of proper credentials—though it wasn't, after all, a real unicorn. She need not have worried.

Smoke from concealed smudge pots suddenly began to

306

obscure the castle, and an ogreish figure in animal pelts rushed into the clearing amid a crash of thunder. Even the unicorn fled in fright. The ogre forced Diana into the castle, then reappeared alone to announce in bad French that he had defeated all knights who had dared to tilt against him, and he now held them in thrall. He pointed to their vanquished shields hanging in the trees as a warning to any who might think of opposing him.

When Diana appeared at the castle's parapets, fluttering a handkerchief, she cried out, "Is no one valiant enough to save me and the castle from the spell of this villain?"

The crowd, waiting breathlessly, was not disappointed. Trumpets sounded a fanfare as a helmeted figure in glittering armor rode into the clearing and dismounted.

"I accept the challenge!" the armored figure shouted.

When Diana dropped the handkerchief to the ground, the armored knight ran to pick it up but found his way barred by the ogre, who sneered, "I will add your shield to the rest."

"You will be the one who will be at rest," the knight replied, drawing his sword.

They closed and fought furiously for several minutes, the sword of the knight against the ogre's huge club. Finally, the ogre was struck down amid more thunder and resounding cymbals. Diana was escorted from the castle by the vanquished "knights," who were released from the ogre's spell.

Now attendants in rich surcoats threw paper packets of sweets and candied fruit to the cheering spectators.

When the conquering hero stepped forward to receive the coveted handkerchief from Diana herself, he removed his helmet and proved to be none other than the Duke of Alvino.

The applause grew louder. Though the Dutch despised the Spanish duke, they knew better than to take a chance on antagonizing the man who commanded the foreign troops infesting their soil.

"You must be pleased to realize that you are so popular among the people," Diana said coyly.

"So I see," Alvino conceded, impressed not at all. He

had consented to take part in this charade with paid actors—
bad ones at that—only to work his way further into Diana's
confidence.

Diana sensed an edginess on Alvino's part, but speculated that it was caused by the exertion of besting the ogre.
She had originally wanted to make the spectacle larger, but
this was, after all, only a simple country festival. When
King Philip had received the crown of the Netherlands
several years before, the burghers of Antwerp had mounted
a spectacle one hundred times as vast, and *that* only half of
what they had originally envisioned. Plans had been scaled
down when it was learned that Philip had failed to obtain
the succession to the title of Holy Roman Emperor. Philip
himself had performed as a victorious knight before the
garlanded towers prepared by the Antwerp craftsmen to
mark his triumphal entry.

"You probably would like to change out of your armor,
Duke. And I hope you will join me later for a cup of
wine," Diana said.

"Only if I receive it from your hands."

"I could do no less for my rescuer, could I?" Diana
bowed.

After Alvino left, she had no time to think further of
what might be bothering him. She was occupied with the
main part of the feast, which was about to be served. The
cattle, goats, and sheep had been turning on spits during
much of the night before. Diana had to preside over the
cutting of the meats before anyone could be served. The
food that had covered the tables from early morning had
been thoroughly picked over, and the guests were ready
for more.

Tonomori had been appalled when Diana had informed
him that the festivities would go on for at least two or
three days.

"They will keep coming back until not a scrap of meat
or a drop of ale is left," she had mentioned brightly,
adding unnecessarily, "We Dutch love a party."

Tonomori was viewing the guests with a faint sense of
disgust. Many simply sprawled on the grass with wooden
bowls or trenchers and began hungrily devouring chunks

of beef, mutton, and roasted goat, swiping their faces with their sleeves, and wiping the grease from their fingers on their clothes. Some of the nobles and foreign banking agents did employ napkins, but did not throw them away. Instead, Tonomori noticed, they actually saved the pieces of soiled cloth. He was once more shocked by the inscrutable practices of these barbarians.

Tonomori wandered to the trestle tables with a bowl brought by a house servant, and picked through the wreckage until he found a brace of smoked wild ducks that somehow had been missed. In keeping with general custom in Japan, he ordinarily did not eat domestic animals or fowl. But wild game was another matter. He sliced one of the ducks and began to eat almost daintily with a pair of lacquered *hashi*. He walked as he ate, ignoring the stares and whispers of passersby. *Ignorant peasants!*

When Tonomori was finished, he handed his eating bowl to one of the serving men with instructions to wash it and return it to his room. Later, Tonomori would wash the bowl again himself, never trusting the cleanliness of Europeans, even the Dutch.

Then he saw Toriko fanning herself beneath a white canopy and decided to join her.

"You are enjoying yourself?" Tonomori asked after he sat down.

"Yes, but I find all this . . . *display* . . . extremely vulgar."

"I find it amusing, generally. Quite vulgar, but the people are enjoying themselves and that is what our mistress wishes, is it not?"

"Yes, that is why I am here. Like you, part of the spectacle," Toriko responded sharply, wondering if Tonomori was trying to rebuke her for finding fault with Diana's efforts. It was not a samurai's place to criticize the master's decision.

Tonomori accepted the rebuff. Women could be so touchy, and he did not want to quarrel with Toriko and mar the festivities.

"Did you see that actor dressed up as the god Mercury,

leading the merchants to be presented to the duke?" Tonomori asked, to change the subject.

"Yes, it was very odd. I did not understand the meaning."

"Ah, Mercury was an old god who protected merchants. It is apparent that they still feel they need protecting."

"I thought that it was the Catholics who made it a practice to throw down idols wherever they found them," Toriko remarked.

"Unless they happen to be old Roman gods that the Italians happen to dig up. These they keep and put in their gardens. The Pope has several, I understand."

"Do they still worship them?" Toriko wondered, touching the rosary beneath her kimono.

"No, but some people are willing to pay great sums of money just to possess one."

"And yet the church condemns Lutherans and Calvinists as heretics. Barbarians are incomprehensible," Toriko declared flatly.

"True; however, the actor today was just a symbol. I am told by Diana-san that in some spectacles they bring out images of Martin Luther and Mohammed, roasting side by side over eternal coals," Tonomori said. "The barbarians are a mass of contradictions."

"Why do you suppose people would want old gods who no longer have any power?"

"It is very fashionable; therefore it is the thing to do," Tonomori explained smoothly. "Actually, they can't find enough old gods to go around, so the Italians obligingly carve new ones that they age beautifully and peddle for the same price as the originals."

"No! Who would do such a thing?"

"Michelangelo, for one," Tonomori said, casting about for an artist Toriko would be likely to recognize.

"Not *the* Michelangelo! The one who still lives in Rome?"

"The very same. Artists, it seems, are excused many crimes," Tonomori observed. "Diana-san expects that it all works out, though. Someday, maybe someone will be forging some of Michelangelo's works."

Toriko was shocked, but she laughed. Tonomori was

right. Who could understand Europeans? They did not even understand themselves.

"There you are! It is fortunate that I found you so soon!" MacDonnell had approached from behind the canopy.

Tonomori noticed that in addition to the dagger he had been carrying earlier, MacDonnell was now wearing a heavy German short sword with double "S" quillons forming rings for the handguard. It was a type known as "the mangler," favored by mercenary *landsknechts*.

"You are perhaps expecting trouble?" Tonomori inquired. He did not trouble to stand.

"Gutierrez is moving this way with some of his officers. It might be better if he didn't find you," MacDonnell suggested.

"Better for whom?" Tonomori asked insolently. He could hear a babble of loud voices. Some Spanish were indeed coming.

"I've asked around. And I hear that Gutierrez intends to kill you so his master can more easily pressure the countess into marrying him," MacDonnell continued. "If she does marry him, I wouldn't bet a clipped penny on her future. People who tangle with Alvino seem to lead short lives."

"I think I'll stay," Tonomori said, finally getting to his feet.

"It's your decision, but watch him closely," MacDonnell added quickly. The Spanish were drawing near. "Gutierrez carries an *espada,* a light broadsword, double-edged. Cut or thrust! Get inside his guard if you can. Then pull his guts out." He moved out of the way but kept his hand near the short sword.

Gutierrez now approached, grinning widely. "Señor! We were just discussing your country. You must find it very lonely so far away from your own land." The three men with him stood with military rigidness, their eyes hard but smiling, as if at some private joke.

"Never . . . when among friends," Tonomori said haltingly. He wanted Gutierrez to think him backward. He could use more than just a blade to get inside someone's guard.

"You are learning our language well. Very good," Gutierrez said, winking at his officers.

Tonomori counted four men and marked their positions, deciding in an instant the order in which to kill them if need be. "You . . . kind," he responded, bowing.

"Not at all. The countess has shown us a splendid event. But I am surprised, sir. You are not properly dressed for the occasion," Gutierrez taunted.

"Something wrong . . . my clothes?" Tonomori inquired narrowly.

"Not your clothes, man," Gutierrez said with irritation. "Your weapons! You should be carrying a proper sword. We have a saying: *Spanish courage! Spanish women! Spanish steel!*"

Tonomori, moving closer, saw the officers stiffen.

"This Japanese sword. Very good." Tonomori patted the grip of his *tachi*.

"But there is nothing like a Spanish sword. Or don't you agree, sir?" Gutierrez looked affronted.

"Oh, I agree!" Tonomori dropped the sham accent. "Just keep working at it. You'll get the knack of making them before long."

"So! You understand Spanish better than you let on," Gutierrez said dangerously. "Well, understand this! You'll apologize for your insult. Or choke on it."

"I understand Spaniards. You pick a quarrel and demand that someone else apologize for it. A childish ploy . . ."

"Childish! You'll pay for this arrogance, sir," Gutierrez yelled.

"Come now," Tonomori remonstrated. "I thought arrogance was something you always gave away free of charge."

Toriko remained seated, gathering her fury. Gutierrez had deliberately slighted her. If Tonomori needed any assistance, which she doubted, she would be happy to offer it. She would rip the belly out of any one of Gutierrez's officers who might make a wrong move.

Gutierrez swore and reached for the grip of his sword. But Tonomori grasped his hand, and then Gutierrez felt his face explode. He found himself crawling on the ground, spitting blood and teeth.

Tonomori still had not drawn his sword. Gutierrez's three men made a movement toward their weapons, but stood frozen momentarily as MacDonnell made his presence known.

"Draw them and you eat them!" he warned.

The three officers realized they were caught between the Japanese lord and the tall mercenary. Still, Spanish pride had been pricked. Three Toledo blades flashed into view. MacDonnell drew his own sword, wishing he had worn a longer weapon, but he had expected that any fighting would be at close quarters, where a broadsword was less effective.

Gleaming with a light of it own, like the thin arc of a new October moon, Tonomori's *tachi* rested firmly in his hands.

"Stop this at once!"

Tonomori heard Diana's command but never took his eyes off the Spaniards. They also heard but kept their sword points up, shifting their gaze between the menace of Tonomori's sword and MacDonnell's.

Then they heard the duke's voice. "You men, put up your swords. At once!"

The officers obeyed. Tonomori and MacDonnell lowered their blades but stood at the ready.

"Please, Tonomori-sama . . ." Diana pleaded in Japanese.

Tonomori sheathed his sword in a single fluid motion. MacDonnell returned his blade to its scabbard, admiring Tonomori's movements.

Gutierrez tried to sit up. The right side of his face puffed out like a ripe melon and blood caked his beard.

"What is the meaning of this?" Alvino asked with a low menace.

"An insult! He . . . he struck me," Gutierrez tried to explain thickly. He began to get to his feet but fell back.

"Your Grace, please tell your men to stop this," Diana asked urgently.

Alvino tried to marshal coherent thoughts, but stumbled

313

on his rage. The Japanese lord was supposed to be dead. *Instead, Gutierrez is on the ground, the fool!* If no witnesses had been present, he would have received the duke's foot in the ribs.

"It was a trick! He tricked me. I'll kill him. . . ." Swaying slightly, Gutierrez finally was able to push himself to his feet.

"It is regrettable, Countess, but blood has been drawn," Alvino said, turning to Diana. "If I stop this now, my men might mutiny. The fight must continue to an honorable conclusion, or we would be encouraging other such . . . incidents."

Alvino looked at Tonomori, trying to read the thoughts behind his dark eyes. "This officer is unable to continue at present," he said to the samurai. "Do you agree to resume at a later date when he is recovered?"

"I agree," Tonomori immediately responded.

Alvino whirled on Gutierrez's three men. "Two of you take this *gallant* back to the fortress. And the other will notify the rest of my staff that we leave at once."

As the officers hurried to comply, Alvino bowed to Diana. "I regret the disturbance to your splendid party, but I must return to my duties." He lingered over her hand, enjoying what he took to be a look of apprehension clouding her face.

"If there is any way Your Grace could help to settle this matter, I would be most grateful," Diana said hurriedly.

"I am afraid I can do very little. This is a matter of honor!" Alvino strode away in a slither of armor.

The crowd now was buzzing around; Diana was at a loss for words.

MacDonnell thrust his hands above his head.

"It was just a disagreement. No one was hurt badly," he called out, hoping to avert a general panic. "Plenty of food and drink is left, and I suggest that we fall to it before someone else gets it all," he said, raising a cheer. People began to move toward the tables, but a heavy murmuring could be heard beneath the gaiety.

*　　　*　　　*

314

"Stop that chatter! I can't hear myself think," the duke demanded harshly. His two lieutenants exchanged questioning looks, but they stopped talking. Young and impulsive, they also were ambitious and knew how to take orders. The duke's irritability was one of the privileges of rank.

They rode by a pretty gooseherd as pleasingly plump as her waddling charges. Behind the duke's back, the officers tipped their velvet caps and winked. Had they been by themselves, they would have flirted shamelessly with the little wench and, were she willing to exchange her ripe body for a little silver, taken turns tupping her in the long, cool grass.

A sigh. Felipe Pidal turned in the saddle and blew her a silent kiss as the girl looked coyly over a smooth shoulder. Pidal and his friend, Enrique Serrano, tried to subdue their high spirits. He would have given much to have seen that pig Gutierrez wallowing in the grass, staring at his own bloody teeth. Pidal and Serrano could not wait to give their companions a vivid, second-hand description. Gutierrez was feared, but he also was hated. To see him humbled, and by a foreigner, was satisfying indeed. A plague on His Grace, the Duke of Alvino. They remained alert, however, to his shifting moods, and wary of his tendency to snap out quick orders that they would miss at their own peril.

Alvino now was oblivious to their presence, to even his own surroundings. His mind wandered alone down dark corridors, searching for a certain door; he would find it, he *had* to find it.

Alvino was accustomed to cutting through tangles with a sword or a hired knife. But this woman seemed to lead a charmed life. An omen?

"You have met the countess twice now; what are your impressions?" he asked suddenly.

"Worthy of a Donatello, Your Grace," Pidal exclaimed, kissing his fingertips for effect. Part of the two lieutenants' duties required hanging on the fringes of the duke's activities, constantly vigilant to any of his needs. He frequently sought their observations on people he met, so they found it prudent to be prepared.

315

"A Venus in velvet," Serrano added with genuine enthusiasm. "I am sure she is flattered by Your Grace's attention and esteem."

"You have a keen eye." Alvino fell silent again.

"A man would have to be blind not to see her glowing beauty," Pidal continued, "and deaf to defy enchantment by her voice, like tinkling silver bells. . . ."

"Enough!"

Pidal willingly turned his thoughts to the goosegirl. She might be receptive to his advances, and cheaper by far than the girls at The Winded Bull, another establishment of dubious reputation, which now enjoyed his patronage since the near-fatal encounter near The Bed of Rose's.

The thought of the Japanese lord entered his mind, and Pidal frowned. His allegiance was to Spain, but he also owed his life to this foreigner.

His emotions warred within him, so Pidal turned his thoughts to other matters. The countess! What a beauty.

Though he was a *hidalgo* by birth and of the purest blood, a countess was above Pidal's station in life and he knew it. Still, a man could dream.

Pidal and Serrano were notorious dreamers. From good families, they were second sons, packed off to the provinces for a military career where they could put to good use their wildness and penchant for brawling.

"Attend to me!" Alvino commanded.

The men were instantly alert.

"This affair of honor. There must be no slip-ups, no opportunity for malicious rumors by the enemies of His Majesty," Alvino instructed them.

"Yes, Your Grace," Serrano said complaisantly.

"Of course, Your Grace," Pidal added, straight-faced.

"When we reach headquarters, find out at once how long it will be before Gutierrez recovers. Then make arrangements with the foreign lord. Set the time and the place, and report back to me."

"Immediately, Your Grace." Pidal had come to a quick decision, one that might get rid of Gutierrez and at the same time repay the Japanese lord Tonomori. It all would depend on Tonomori's skill.

Alvino seethed. Gutierrez was incredibly stupid to get himself injured when he was needed the most. With slurred speech, though, he already had assured Alvino that he would return the blood insult with more blood.

Gutierrez is right, Alvino thought. *Fists are one thing. Swords are another.* He looked forward eagerly to the duel.

And when that was over, he would have a few more surprises in store for Diana, Countess de Edgemont. Since she had put him to an incredible amount of trouble and expense, it would be amusing after their marriage to make her life a burden to her—before he ended it.

Alvino already had his eye to an eventual alliance with an Italian family that would be better suited to further his regal ambitions. A man of vision might well be able to swallow the whole of Italy.

"Your Grace is amused," Serrano commented when Alvino laughed aloud.

"A private joke," Alvino said shortly. He had decided that when he and Diana were married and Tonomori was dead, he would give the lady Toriko to Gutierrez as a mistress, or he might even keep her himself—an entertaining thought. Alvino was also thinking of the look on Diana's face when he had informed her that the duel necessarily would have to be held.

And he was mistaking that look for one of fear.

Chapter Twenty-two

Approximately every other day, Diana found herself longing to be back on the *Schoen* at sea, free to go anywhere, to smell the fresh salt air again, hear the cry of the ocean birds and be at peace.

In her nostalgia, her thoughts turned to her adventure in Portugal and Spain, particularly her reception in Seville by Philip. In retrospect, he seemed a peculiarly pathetic figure, and for a moment she almost gave way to a feeling of pity for him.

Almost! Philip had to fight a ruinous war against the French; exert pressure on the English to help him; maintain vigilance against the heretic Lutheran princes in Germany; checkmate encroachment of the Turks in the Adriatic, in Hungary, in Austria; suppress the Barbary pirates swarming out of Tripoli; and search out the privateers preying on his ships carrying treasure from the New World.

To all this, Diana hoped to add the flames of rebellion in the Spanish Netherlands. To assure rebellion's success, she would need time and money in fanning the flames. The mere idea of pity for Philip seemed utterly preposterous.

But now events and circumstances were conspiring to drag her down like an anchor. And all of her own doing. Or had she really chosen her course?

Almost daily, gifts were arriving from the Duke of Alvino—bouquets, sweetmeats, a silver goblet, precious jewels stuck in the sealing wax of flowery notes that assured her of his desire to protect her from a violent world.

Twice he had arrived in person, at the head of a troop of his officers, to pay her court. When they walked in the garden, she pinched herself as a sharp reminder that this was the same man whose bloody hands had taken her father's life.

"He pointed out that if I were his betrothed, an attack on a member of my household would be regarded as an attack on his own person," Diana told Tonomori one evening as they sat in the garden.

"He is not as clever, then, as I had thought. His efforts to manipulate you are all too obvious."

"Don't be too sure. I have the feeling that His Grace must be holding something in reserve. I only wish I knew what!"

"If he surprises you, what will you do then?" Tonomori asked her. "Remember, Gutierrez is almost recovered. So the duel is set for Friday at dawn—little more than two days from now. There may not be much time left."

"I intend to flutter my eyes, wring my hands, and look like a helpless woman. If you lose, I would have to give in. But I can't believe you will not win. The only thing I fear is treachery."

"Actually," Tonomori told her, "the only thing you have to fear is fear itself. I expect to win. As for treachery, they won't try. Too many witnesses. At least two noblemen of Holland, Hoorn and Van Amstel, will be present, I understand. Count Hoorn saw the quarrel, and wishes to assure fair play. Van Amstel is a former soldier who enjoys a good fight. We will be fighting according to the rules that these gentlemen of Europe have created. That is all right with me, though I am not accustomed to fighting while limited by such niceties."

"I would like to be there, to see you win, but women aren't permitted," Diana said with a tinge of bitterness.

"I'll wear your favor instead, as is your people's custom. You will be present in spirit." Tonomori took her hand.

"That, I fear, might be misconstrued." Diana looked at

him archly. "However, you *could* wear my perfume. I'll make sure some of it rubs off on you. The night before . . ."

Yes, she thought, *in addition to guarding against a murderous duke, I must juggle my life with a lover, run an estate, fend off unsuitable suitors, and command a business empire more complex than anyone suspects—and vastly richer.*

Agents and caravels of the de Edgemont empire were everywhere, carrying furs, bronze and silver jewelry, and walrus ivory from Sweden, Finland, and Norway. Her herring boats swarmed across the North Sea. Diana's agents were also in Venice, fading queen but still ruler of the Adriatic, dealing in glass, textiles, enamels, and grain; in Augsburg, capital of the Austrian Hapsburgs, exporting armor, clocks, and weapons; and in London, where they skimmed some of the best of the lucrative wool trade.

In Lisbon, there was disappointment. Secret correspondence indicated the Portuguese were about to revoke licenses for the East Indies spice trade for all but their own citizens. Diana would need a naturalized resident there to circumvent this move, and would have to contact Lucas Giraldi for assistance. She had yet to complete arrangements to introduce Giraldi's representative to the key people in the Antwerp merchants' guild. This would have to be done before she would ask Giraldi for any more favors. Diana began to understand the complaints of the leading merchants and bankers on the difficulties of running international business dealings.

It was this empire, run from an unassuming office in Antwerp, that now was threatening to consume all of her time. Diana was putting off the day when she would have to move to her own town house on the Velvet Canal, so named for the luxurious homes of wealthy owners along its lush banks. She much preferred the country life; the estate was her refuge, but for how long could it be?

"Two Spanish gentlemen are here wishing speech with you, sir," Frans informed Tonomori, his voice reflecting his distaste for the callers.

Tonomori swore silently and gave up the thought of

finishing his interrupted meditations. First, two of the maidservants had been singing, off-key, while finishing their work down the hall. Then Diana barged in after knocking but without waiting for an answer, to ask if he would join her for dinner.

In reply, he tried to run his hand up her skirt, but her long legs were too fast for him. Seated on the floor in the lotus position prescribed for Zen, Tonomori was at a disadvantage.

"Dinner!" he exclaimed. "You are a feast for my eyes right now." He unhooked one of his ankles and sprang. This time Diana was not quick enough to evade him.

"You can't!" she protested.

"I am," he insisted.

"It's daylight."

"I'll close my eyes."

"The servants will hear us."

"Not if you don't make any noise." Tonomori pulled her down beside him. One hand began exploring her bosom. "We'll try the Cranes with Turned Necks."

"If that's like the Shouting Monkey, I won't do it—ah ah!"

Tonomori had already parted his kimono, rolled up her skirt, and lifted her onto his lap. Diana buried her face against his neck as Tonomori cupped his hands under her backside and pulled her into a tight embrace.

"Remember, no noise now," he cautioned teasingly, with the arrogant assurance that his women enjoyed a rough wooing on occasion.

When they had caught their breath after the explosion of physical passion, Diana disengaged quickly, smoothed the pleats of her skirt, and left humming a popular ballad, "The Soldier's Lady."

For almost an hour, Tonomori attempted to return to his meditations but visions of Diana kept interrupting them disconcertingly. The arrival of Frans dispelled his last hope.

Tonomori found the Spanish gentlemen in the refectory, where a maid was serving them a clear white Burgundy and fresh Gouda cheese.

Pidal and Serrano rose to their feet and bowed.

"Remain seated, please. I'll join you," Tonomori told them.

He declined to share the wine and cheese, and instead called for smoked eel and boiled rice with a pot of ale.

"We've come at the duke's orders to settle matters," Pidal began after extended compliments and pleasantries.

"You mean Gutierrez is offering to apologize for his insult?" Tonomori asked, surprised.

"Hardly that. Gutierrez means to fight," Serrano interjected.

Tonomori looked appropriately relieved.

"No, we are here to settle the hour and the place," Pidal continued. "At dawn, Friday, then, if that is agreeable to you, in the apple orchard below the city at the Liederstaat crossing. Do you know the place?"

Tonomori nodded. He didn't know but he would find out and be certain to visit it beforehand. Would the site have been selected for an ulterior reason?

"We should mention a few rules," Serrano said. "No armor. And you may not grab your opponent's blade. And no throwing of sand or dust in his eyes."

Tonomori had already heard a warning from MacDonnell about this practice among European swordsmen, and he had intended to mention it to Serrano if the Spaniards didn't bring it up. He hoped that the disclaimer would stand up in the stress of the duel, if they were to fight according to an elaborate code.

The rice and smoked eel arrived. Tonomori excused himself and began eating. Between bites, he asked, "Do you wish any restrictions on the type of sword used?"

"None. You each provide your own weapons." Pidal cut himself another wedge of cheese, then leaned forward conspiratorially.

"Our official business is concluded," he said in a low voice. "Now we wish to talk with you about a more personal matter."

"How personal?" Tonomori asked after swallowing a piece of the eel. He picked up another piece with his *hashi*. Pidal and Serrano were fascinated by his deft facility with the eating sticks.

"Your life could depend on it," Serrano said solemnly.

"I am, as you say, all ears."

"First, Señor Serrano and I realize that we owe you our lives. This is a debt of honor. Also, we really do not care much for our captain—for many reasons, which I would rather not describe here."

Pidal hesitated. What he was about to say was virtually betrayal of a superior officer. But he salved his conscience by recalling Gutierrez's penchant for provoking quarrels.

"He will use a broadsword." Pidal was almost whispering. "It will appear that he is trying to cut through your defenses. This is only a ruse. I have seen him fight before. Remember that when he puts his feet together and tries to cut for your left leg, you must beware! It is a feint. From that position, he will lunge, fully extended, for your heart or belly. Captain Gutierrez is very quick."

"I thank you for your advice," Tonomori remarked tersely. He finished the eel and took a long swallow of ale.

"And especially since the quarrel was over swords, Captain Gutierrez will be using the finest of Toledo blades. I trust that you have a good sword?"

Tonomori thought of his blade, with its temper line running in bright waves above the razor edge. A Soshu master, forging it more than two hundred years before, had left his work unsigned, but his genius was folded into the steel.

"Yes, I have a good enough sword," he replied.

Pidal and Serrano formally wished Tonomori the good fortune an honorable opponent deserved, and left as Hans called for their horses. After reflecting for a moment, Tonomori went to hunt up MacDonnell.

He found him in the stable, watching Müller replace a leather strap for a stirrup.

"They told you that, did they?" MacDonnell commented after Tonomori informed him of Pidal and Serrano's information. "Well, it's a good piece of advice. Thrusting is becoming the thing. A shallow stab frequently incapacitates better than a deep slash." He turned momentarily toward Müller. "Do a good job with those rivets. I want to look my best."

Müller grinned and spat. "I just might rivet your skinny ass to the saddle while I'm at it."

"Where was I? Oh yes. Gutierrez. That son of a bitch!" he said, repeating a recently coined Spanish epithet that had caught on. "Anyway, I advise caution. The Spaniards are good swordsmen, whatever anyone says."

"Yah, they have to be," Müller added. He mushroomed the head of a rivet over a copper washer and examined the result critically.

"What kind of sword do you expect to be using?" MacDonnell inquired.

Tonomori indicated the *tachi*.

"Christ! That thing? Let me see the blade."

Tonomori drew the sword from its scabbard. MacDonnell whistled at its silvery arc. "Pretty! But it looks heavy. And it's too short. The blade is only about thirty inches. Gutierrez will have at least six inches on you—a yard of steel. Blades are getting longer and thinner here."

"This will do," Tonomori said confidently.

"It's your funeral. But remember that I've got a fine blade I can let you use."

"It won't be necessary. If you would be so kind, show me the moves the Spanish gentlemen explained."

"Nothing easier," MacDonnell assured him, drawing his own blade, a bastard sword with a swept-back guard of German make, designed to be used with one hand or two. The Scottish knight whirled the blade around, displaying the techniques of a Spanish swordsman. "He'll engage you quickly, probably, and then back off, like this. I would. To test the water, so to speak. Then engage again, to disable your arm or leg. The third time, he'll try to work his best trick."

"And if that doesn't work?"

"After that, you could expect him to cheat—throw sand, grab your blade with an armored gauntlet, have one of his friends stab you in the back," MacDonnell said. "That would be difficult to try, though, under the circumstances. And I will be standing by."

"You have fought many duels, then?" Tonomori asked. "I am not familiar with the rituals that engage Europeans when they fight."

"A few. I collect sword techniques. Gutierrez is from northern Spain, so watch both hands. He might fight with a dagger in his left hand. It's legal."

"Show me the move again. This time, strike at me."

"As you will," MacDonnell agreed skeptically, lifting one shoulder. He squared off, watching Tonomori closely. After feinting a thrust to the face, which Tonomori ignored, he threw a cut to the leg. Tonomori's block and counterattack was sudden, vicious, overwhelming.

MacDonnell had all he could do to back away without tripping over his own feet. Tonomori broke off the attack abruptly, and MacDonnell was sweating in the knowledge that had the fight been real, he could easily have been killed.

"Do you never thrust with that thing?" MacDonnell asked after his breathing became less ragged. The sword was more effective than he had thought possible. His glance at Tonomori's expressionless face contained an apology.

"Oh yes, but only for the throat." Tonomori patted the *tachi* and slid it back into the scabbard.

"Why is that?"

"It is not honorable to stab a samurai any place else. The way a samurai is killed is considered important."

"And if he is stabbed elsewhere?"

"It happens. But there is less honor in the kill."

"I fail to see the significance. When a man is dead, he's dead."

"In Japan, we also consider the man who killed him. The more difficult the cut, the more honor earned."

"How do you keep track of all this?"

"A sword may take any one of eighteen paths through a body. We have a name for each cut," Tonomori explained.

"The only cut my brave captain fears is a cut in his pay," Müller interjected.

"*Jesu!*" MacDonnell exclaimed, ignoring him. "It sounds too complicated. And I suppose bullets don't count, either?"

"No. Guns are new. We haven't had time to resolve the questions they create. Samurai despise guns. But arrows are quite another matter."

"You have specific points for arrows?" MacDonnell sounded skeptical.

"Not exactly, but officers may be shot only with arrowheads of special quality, not necessarily signed, but of excellent workmanship nonetheless."

"What happens if an officer is killed with a cheap arrow?"

"It is considered an accident." Tonomori's reply seemed to be offered seriously. MacDonnell laughed.

Müller spat again. "You can pay me now for the stirrup, my brave captain."

"Put it on my account," MacDonnell told him. He had no such account, but was only returning to the standing joke between them. They owed each other their lives, debts that could not be paid in coin.

"That means I don't get paid again," Müller remarked to Tonomori.

"You're right, for once in your life," MacDonnell said.

"Müller-san, what have you learned so far among the soldiers? You were expected to report," Tonomori reminded him.

"Yah, I was coming to that," Müller said.

"What Müller means is that I was piecing everything together with what I have learned," MacDonnell explained hurriedly.

"Next time, please report at once," Tonomori instructed.

"Anyway, Alvino is covertly purchasing large amounts of cannon, guns, powder, shot. And rivets, leather, horseshoes . . ." MacDonnell was trying to divert Tonomori, who, he had discovered, was a stickler for promptness.

"Yah, but no horses," Müller observed, biting into an apple. "He go nowhere without horses."

"It's a puzzle," MacDonnell continued. "But, then, Alvino himself is a puzzle. Philip trusts him, for one riddle. Why, no one knows—Philip usually doesn't trust anyone. And you can hear talk of a streak of madness in Alvino's family, just as among Philip's."

"I've seen his son, Don Carlos," Tonomori mentioned.

"Then you know what I mean. I understand that Philip has forced the Spanish nobles to swear acceptance of Don Carlos as his heir. He seems to be hoping that the crown will force the boy to live up to his destiny.

"With Alvino, it's another matter," he continued. "No trouble finding rotten limbs in that family tree, and the closets are crammed with skeletons. Listen in the right places and you'll hear that Borgian blood contaminates Alvino's claim to impeccably pure Castilian lineage."

"Is that important?" Tonomori asked. "I don't understand what you mean."

"It might be important; it might not. The Borgias were a bad lot, but then so are the Alvinos. The old duke found pleasure in throwing a peasant to his hunting dogs every so often. Claimed it improved their performance."

"It does sound revolting, but I've known of Japanese nobles who did much worse."

"Oh? Well, this is nothing new. The Viscontis of Milan carried on like that all the time until their line came to an end that was long overdue. The badge of the Viscontis was a viper swallowing a man. An unsavory lot, the Viscontis!"

"The Borgias?" Tonomori prompted.

"The Borgias! Well, Pope Alexander the Sixth, who actually was Rodrigo Borgia, produced several children. That was sixty, seventy years ago. A daughter, Lucretia, was known for her beauty. She was used as a pawn in Italian politics by her even more renowned brother, Cesare. While he was using his mercenaries and assassins in trying to swallow up the Italian city states, Cesare made a lot of enemies and widows." MacDonnell seemed to revel in the recounting of horror and tragedy.

"In the end, though, Cesare lost. When the Pope died—and as legend has it, was carried off by six devils—Cesare was ill. Everything fell apart very shortly, and Cesare ran to Spain. That was where they originated and where they finished—Cesare was killed in battle there. Maybe he mixed in with the Alvinos; I certainly don't know. Clandestine affairs, after all, aren't a novelty with us, are they? It *could* have happened. But the important point is whether Alvino *thinks* it did.''

''Why?'' Tonomori felt the onset of a headache.

''Because the Borgias were ambitious and their name became a byword for murder carried out for gain and power politics. It was Rodrigo Borgia, by the way, who drew up the treaty that divided the New World and all undiscovered lands between the Portuguese and the Spanish.''

''He couldn't give away what he didn't own. . . .''

''Tell that to the Spanish and the Portuguese. They own it now.''

''Not my country. Not Japan!'' Tonomori bristled.

''Not yet. If those greedy bastards see a chance, they'll take it,'' MacDonnell said. ''Look out!''

''How do you know all these things? If they're true, that is.''

MacDonnell was not offended. ''Well, for one thing, the Spanish and the Portuguese argue about it all the time, and they keep badgering their present Pope to change the terms of the treaty in one way or another—for their own benefit, of course. And I'm a military man, so I find it pays to know what is going on. As for your country, it's safe—for a while. Both sides are stretched too thin to do anything about it.''

Tonomori said only, ''I see,'' and fell silent. The specter of Portugal and Spain closing in on the Floating Kingdom from both sides hung before him once more.

''At any event, you can see the type of people you are dealing with. Ruthless, greedy, ambitious! And that sums up the duke nicely.''

''And the arms?''

Müller held up the hand with the apple in it. ''He can do nothing without horses,'' he said irrelevantly. ''He start buying horses, you watch out!'' Müller fed the apple core to his horse.

''So we are back to where we started.'' Tonomori's brow creased in concentration. ''I will consult with the countess.''

''Better get some rest first,'' MacDonnell cautioned.

"You fight soon, remember! Plenty of time to worry about Alvino later."

"I am ready to fight now. But you are wrong about Alvino! I don't believe we have any time left at all."

Tonomori left them to find Diana.

Chapter Twenty-three

The turtledoves' calls were just beginning when Tonomori awoke abruptly from a deep and restful sleep. The moon was down and the room was pitch black. He dressed quickly in the gloomy darkness. His weapons and clothes always were in the same place so he would not fumble for them in an emergency.

The house was quiet, and through habit Tonomori padded softly down the stairs, along the inner edge of the treads, so the boards would not creak and announce his departure.

He found a red glow remaining in the kitchen fireplace. With the addition of a few pieces of pine kindling and an elm log, Tonomori soon had a small blaze going. He lighted two candles from it and set about preparing a cold and spare breakfast.

After munching several pickled herring that he dredged from a crock, raisins, and a few handfuls of leftover cold rice, he wrapped some more raisins in a cloth napkin to enjoy later, when the fight was done, when he had won.

Correction! If he won. Nothing in life except death and *karma* was certain. Even the tryst that Diana had promised for the night before had somehow failed to materialize amid the welter of so many comings and goings in the household. But as for the duel, he did not expect to fail.

Tonomori turned at a sound at the doorway.

"I thought you would at least say good-bye," Diana whispered. She held a lighted candle in one hand, and though it was not a cold morning, with the other she clasped her robe together tightly in front.

"Our good-byes were said last night," Tonomori responded quietly. He wiped some grains of rice from his hands with a towel.

"I wanted to say . . . I don't know *what* I wanted to say." Diana hesitated. "Oh, Tonomori-sama, I am frightened!"

"For me, or for yourself?" he asked gently. He did not move, torn between the desire to offer her comfort and the need to maintain his dignity, and hers, in the face of possible death. He hoped that she would understand—she would have to understand. Samurai was samurai. He was still that, even so far from home. Home? Where was that now? Nowhere. Everywhere.

"For myself. For us both. I wish to be brave and to be strong, like a rock, like the woman you deserve. And I find myself trying not to cry, not to imagine the most horrid things. . . ."

Seeing her struggling to maintain her composure, Tonomori searched for the right words, hoping he would not be misunderstood. *So much that she does not know about me, or I about her,* he thought.

"Some things cannot be said, can never be said. I was born to this. Would you have it any other way?" Tonomori waited for her reply, stifling his anxious desire to be saddled and on the road. Through the big windows he could see that the last stars were fading and the eastern sky was becoming pink and gold on the horizon.

"No." Her answer was in a small voice.

"Then remember this, Diana-chan. I have never been beaten. And I do not intend to fall today."

Tonomori bowed and left quickly before she lost her

330

remaining composure. As a lover, as a friend, as a samurai, he must let her save face.

When he was gone, Diana sat down in the doorway. The first sudden, silent tears quickly became the inconsolable, racking sobs of a lost child.

Yamahito and Oshabiri were waiting for Tonomori outside the house, their faces showing disappointment at not being able to attend. It was an affair of gentlemen, and foot soldiers of any nationality were not included.

Nevertheless, they wished Tonomori well. "May the gods be with you today, sir," Yamahito said, bowing deeply.

"And the Christian God also," Oshabiri added.

Tonomori returned the bow, deeper than was customary, thus giving them honor. He was pleased that his men remembered and were up to see him away.

"Thought you had decided to sleep late this morning," MacDonnell remarked good-naturedly at the stable.

Müller had the horses saddled. He was cursing the inefficiency of Diana's grooms. "I had to do everything myself. When we get back, I lump some heads together, you'll see," he grumbled.

"You are early; that is good," Tonomori said to MacDonnell. "What happened? Did the tavern catch fire?" The emerging brightness of the early morning lightened his spirit.

"Not this time," MacDonnell laughed. "Müller and me, we kept a vigil all night. Praying."

"And what did you pray for, MacDonnell-san?" Tonomori asked, swinging into the saddle.

"That we wouldn't run out of beer—what did you think?"

Tonomori grinned. "Let's ride!"

Rain had fallen during the night, just enough to settle the dust. The air was cool and sweet.

They talked as they rode.

"I have been thinking: If the duke does not plan to use those guns and cannon here, we can assume that he is thinking of using them elsewhere," Tonomori said.

"That is possible, but where?"

"In Italy! You said the Borgias hired mercenaries, employed assassins, used murder and terror to carve out a duchy. But his eye was on all of Italy. Now let me ask: Does Cesare Borgia remind you of anyone you know?"

"Christ, yes!" MacDonnell exclaimed, letting the idea sink in. On the face of it, such an idea was preposterous, but kingdoms had been stolen before. If Alvino struck suddenly and quickly consolidated his position, the tautly stretched Spanish would have one hell of a task in dislodging him. In fact, he could think of many in Europe who would welcome civil war in the Hapsburg empire. "Have you told the countess?"

"Not yet. She has enough on her mind. I will tell her today. When I return."

"And if you don't? . . ." MacDonnell left the question unfinished.

"Then you may tell her my suspicions. She must be cautious! Alvino is playing a bold game, and with the stakes as high as they appear to be, he would slaughter anyone he even suspects might know such a secret."

"Yes, I agree that he would," MacDonnell said grimly, calculating his own chances for survival.

"Yes. We must have a plan for her escape when the day to resist Alvino comes. If I fail today, my orders now are that you are to go to the Lady Toriko, tell her that I said 'ships,' and that the duke must die. She will know what to do."

"The Lady Toriko?" MacDonnell whistled. "She is pretty, but what can she do?"

"You'll be surprised," Tonomori promised him.

The sun's earliest rays were streaming through the trees and the dewy grass shone like cold diamonds. Müller led away their horses, and MacDonnell left Tonomori to join the small knot of murmuring Hollanders near the apple trees. Tonomori recognized only Count Hoorn among them. As Tonomori's referee, he looked grim, his eyes cast downward until MacDonnell approached him.

The Spaniards clustered by themselves closer to the

332

center of the clearing, their mood obviously one of barely suppressed gaiety. Only the duke remained mounted, and Tonomori saw him lean down and exchange words with an officer, smiling as if sharing a jest.

Gutierrez, bare to the waist, stood several paces away. He was wearing only the baggy pantaloons sometimes favored by Spaniards, and pale hose with plain leather shoes. His right hand held a light broadsword; with it, he was cutting as though to fragment the rays of sunshine. The captain was putting all his effort into each cut. Tonomori saw that he was also armed with a long dagger that had a metal shell guard.

MacDonnell returned to Tonomori's side.

"We're almost ready, if you are. The Hollanders are in a bad mood, by the way. If you lose, the Spanish will be lording it over them again. And even if you win, they fear reprisals. They lose, no matter what happens. But their necks are not out, as usual."

He took Tonomori's kimono and waited as Tonomori unbound a queue from atop his head and retied it as a horsetail falling behind his neck. A pure white headband, now placed across his forehead, bore in its center a blood-red disc, symbol of the rising sun. His *hakama* was tucked into leggings to aid his freedom of movement. After he handed his *tachi* scabbard to MacDonnell, Tonomori carefully wrapped the silken handle-cord around his right wrist.

MacDonnell looked from Tonomori to Gutierrez, from Gutierrez to Tonomori, and the Japanese lord's chance for survival began to increase before his shrewdly speculating eyes. Gutierrez was brawny, with a thick pelt covering his chest. Tonomori's skin was smooth and golden, his chest enormous. In his heavily muscled arms, thick veins ran down like blue-gray snakes.

If Rodrigo Gutierrez looked like a capable pit dog, Tonomori's appearance was that of a marauding lion looking for his next meal. MacDonnell remembered the brutal savagery of his counterattack when they practiced. He saw that Alvino, studying Tonomori intently, was frowning. Everyone now was watching the men with piercing interest.

The physician, standing neutral between the groups with his wooden case of instruments and a flagon of water, was particularly intent.

Alvino motioned with his hand. Serrano walked to the middle of the field, followed by Gutierrez. Hoorn too approached the center, and Tonomori strode over to meet him.

Drawing his own sword, Serrano raised it and stepped between the two combatants, then Hoorn did the same.

"My lord," Serrano said to Hoorn, "does the field seem fair to you?"

"It does, sir," Hoorn replied after clearing his throat.

Serrano addressed the swordsmen. "This is an affair of honor. Let there be no treachery or acts of a coward. The quarrel may end now with an apology. The man who struck first may speak first."

Tonomori laughed. "How is your jaw?"

"You'll see—soon," Gutierrez hissed. The thin veneer of gentility had cracked. Spymaster, thug, butcher for the Duke of Alvino, this man was like so many others in every country in Europe—polished flatterers and killers, climbing their way to success over many bodies.

Serrano nodded to Hoorn.

"When I lower my sword, you may begin," the count said. "This duel is to the death, unless quarter is asked. The man defeated is considered to have apologized with his blood." Hoorn lowered his blade, and Serrano did likewise. Both men backed hurriedly away across the damp grass.

For a short moment, Tonomori and Gutierrez stood, taking each other's measure, while the officers and nobles held their breaths.

Then Gutierrez began moving, first pacing to the right, then to the left. Tonomori held his position only briefly, and edged forward steadily.

Gutierrez lashed out with his *espada*. Once. Twice. Three times. His blade was a silvery blur, but Tonomori picked off all three cuts.

Gutierrez was breathing hard already, his concentration tremendous, but he knew he had the advantage of the longer reach, at least half a foot, more than enough. He needed only to stay slightly out of range, and he could strike with impunity.

Tonomori attacked without warning. The shock of the blows nearly tore Gutierrez's sword from his grip. He fell back, slashing furiously with the *espada*, the handle now wet with his blood.

When Tonomori broke off the onslaught, Gutierrez had a fraction of a moment to see that his top quillon had been sheared off, and along with it part of his right thumb. Stung to rage, Gutierrez cut again at the circling Japanese, trying to set him up for a thrust to the body. And nearly lost a leg.

The *whick* of the *tachi* through Gutierrez's pantaloons jarred through the stillness. The Hollanders gasped, and the Spaniards stared in disbelief. A red stain began spreading at the captain's left knee and soaking his hose.

Gutierrez, beginning to panic, tried to force himself to think clearly. He had never lost. He was being too rash. *Slow down!* he told himself.

But Tonomori would not let him change his pace, much less rest. The short, murderous attacks were wearing him down. His left foot was awash in blood inside the shoe. He tried to bring his feet together in his feint. It was futile.

In desperation, Gutierrez made the move Tonomori had been waiting for, the one Pidal and MacDonnell had warned about. His lunge would stretch him to his utmost and leave him the most vulnerable for a counter move.

As it came, Tonomori swept his *tachi* under the broadsword, forcing the point up. At the same time, he stepped in. Gutierrez tried to scramble back, to retain his footing on the treacherously wet grass. Tonomori disengaged and struck in a furious, slashing motion.

For a heartbeat, it appeared, incredibly, that he had missed. Then a scream of agony tore from Gutierrez's throat. It was cut short as he began falling to earth, with a curiously twisting motion, in two distinct pieces.

Before he turned away, Tonomori saw a look of white wrath on Alvino's face. Behind him, pandemonium reigned.

The distressed cries of the Spanish clashed with the Hollanders' astonished gasps.

MacDonnell was at his side. "It was unbelievable! What did you do?"

"As I told you, it was one of the many paths of a sword through the body." Tonomori was wishing his friend away, to experience in solitude the moment of victory. But he knew MacDonnell would not understand, so he added, "It was the eighteenth path, the most difficult, through the hip bones. It is called the Cut of the Carriage Wheels."

"I'd better go see what is happening!" MacDonnell exclaimed irrelevantly, and rushed away, continuing to clutch Tonomori's kimono and scabbard.

Tonomori turned, now alone. He still held the *tachi* with its crimson smear along nearly half its length. The Hollanders were watching him in silence, considering, evaluating. Alvino had dashed away at once, quirting his mount into a gallop, with the other Spaniards rushing for their horses to follow him. The virulent henchman was taken care of, Tonomori reflected, but the source of the evil still lived.

Serrano, now joined by his friend Pidal in the center of the field, announced over the fallen captain's body, "The affair has been settled honorably. It is now over." Hardly anyone heard.

Hoorn approached, returning his sword to its sheath. "You have acted with distinction, sir," he said sincerely to Serrano. "Be sure that I will not forget it."

"Thank you, Your Lordship."

"If I can be of assistance? . . ."

"Ah . . . yes." Serrano looked embarrassed. He gestured at the spymaster's body. The count then saw that the overconfident Spanish had made no arrangements to remove a corpse. He scratched his beard. "My men can assist you in loading the gentleman on a horse. The surgeon can sew the pieces back together first," he said, brightening somewhat despite the macabre idea.

Pidal assented, glad for a solution to the grisly problem.

Across the field, Tonomori finally had reclaimed his kimono. "And here's your *tachi* case," MacDonnell said, handing him the scabbard. He was waving his hands

336

excitedly. "The Spanish were in a rage, but they can't say that it wasn't a fair fight. Anyway, Gutierrez seems to have had no more allies than a spy could be expected to have. So I don't think we'll have any trouble from that particular quarter. The duke, of course, is another matter. This may force him into moving sooner than he had planned. Whatever we are going to do for the countess, I suggest we do it very soon."

Tonomori tucked his kimono inside the *hakama*. "I agree completely." He tossed some raisins into his mouth from the small supply wrapped in the napkin. Gutierrez quick or Gutierrez dead—both were forgotten.

Müller stepped forward with the horses and handed Tonomori a jug of ale. He gulped it thirstily, and to his thanks Müller beamed, "You are welcome. My captain, he always lead us safely through the valley of death. But me," he added, thumping his expansive chest, "I think of the *important* things!"

"She is very lovely, isn't she?" Toriko remarked, appearing at MacDonnell's elbow from out of nowhere as he rested in the shade, watching Tonomori and the Countess de Edgemont strolling in the garden.

"Eh? Oh, yes. It is you, Lady Toriko," MacDonnell said, almost choking on his ale. The woman amazed him with her ability to come or go silently, at will. "Please join me."

Toriko unrolled the straw mat she had been carrying and sat on it. MacDonnell was now very much aware of her presence, even of the soft rustle of her dress. Her hair, black and glossy, bound at the neck with red ribbon, nearly brushed her waist.

"Lord Tonomori is very strong, isn't he?" she asked, trying to guide MacDonnell onto the subject of the duel. She did not want to show bad manners by prying the information out of him, and she was eager to know what happened, how Tonomori had won. She wished she could have been there.

"Yes, he was magnificent against the Spanish officer this morning," MacDonnell replied briefly. He lapsed into silence, not wishing to offend the lady with the bloody details.

Toriko waited impatiently, wanting to throttle the information out of him. Finally, she smiled sweetly. "I have been privileged to see samurai fight before. I had wondered how they compare to the European swordsmen."

"Very favorably, if Tonomori is my yardstick," MacDonnell said. "It reminded me of a fight I saw in France. These two cavaliers had been arguing over the same lady and . . ."

With an ample supply of good ale to lubricate his throat, a captive audience, and nothing else to occupy his time, MacDonnell rambled on without pause. An hour later, Toriko wished she had bitten her tongue. She knew far more than she wanted to about estocs, harquebuses, fortifications, the latest siege techniques, the new cast-iron cannon, fluted armor versus plain, the conditions of camp life, lice, admonitions against dicing for large sums of money with strangers, how to steal chickens quietly, the proper way to cook them in a helmet, and on and on.

He was beginning to pour out his life's story, still without mention of the duel between Tonomori and Gutierrez, when MacDonnell noticed his large mug of ale was almost empty.

"Let *me* get it for you," Toriko said urgently, seizing on a polite way of escape. Before he could reply, she had vanished with the mug. Several minutes passed before a serving woman returned with the mug, brimming to the top. "The Lady Toriko asks to be excused, but she has a headache," the woman said. MacDonnell shrugged. "Care to join me?" he offered.

At the other end of the house, Toriko finally succeeded in cornering Tonomori. "I tried to find out from MacDonnell-san what happened. Never again! The man is incapable of civilized conversation."

Tonomori pursed his lips. "That is their way. European knights believe in sheltering their women." He saw Toriko bristle at his use of "their," and added, "*All* the women."

"I am samurai. I need no protection," she said assertively.

"But he thinks you do, not knowing any better."

Tonomori looked amused, and Toriko was becoming annoyed, but curiosity won out over pride.

"I would consider it an honor, Tonomori-san, if you would kindly tell me what happened this morning."

"Very well. But before I do, I would ask a favor of you. I wish to know the circumstances of your birth, and your upbringing."

Toriko looked puzzled, and so he added, "It is a harmless request. I will tell you the same about myself. I have a reason."

Santa Maria, am I to be the only human being in the province who has not heard about the duel? Toriko thought in frustration.

"I was born in Kyoto . . ." she began slowly. As it turned out, Toriko could tell him little enough about her background. She was of high birth but illegitimate, therefore useless for a political marriage when she came of age, and too well born to sell into prostitution. Many of the great clans subsidized and employed their own *ninja,* so it was decided when she was at an early age that she was to be developed into a weapon to repay the Hoju clan for the expense of her upbringing.

"But I was told practically nothing about my parents. Though I have repaid my benefactors many times over, Lord Hoju would tell me nothing."

"From what I heard, I judge that Lord Hoju is as difficult to crack as a Sukemitsu blade," Tonomori observed.

"Yes, and as tough," Toriko amended.

Tonomori took a small cloth bag from inside his kimono and extracted a *tsuba,* the iron sword guard with the secret imperial crest that had come to him from his father. "What do you know of this?" he asked without elaboration.

Toriko's hands flew to her throat. "How did you know?"

"On the night you scouted the duke's ships and warehouses, I saw it in the moonlight, hanging around your neck. Yours is the smaller mate to this one, which belonged to my father."

"*Your* father?" Toriko gasped. She fought for control and regained her composure.

"Yes. Possibly *our* father, I have been thinking,"

Tonomori said. "Or, it could all be a coincidence. But I doubt that it could be coincidence. I was not sent halfway around the world for nothing."

"Nor I."

"I am also beginning to find it curious, if not incredible, that I should possess a *tachi* with the crest of the Hosokawa family, and with secondary cherry blossom *mon* all over its fittings. It is a sword that even the emperor would not be ashamed to wear. A gift from Lord Betsuo. I was greatly honored."

Toriko had seen the *tachi*, and was impressed. It was made for use in war. Not a mere court ornament, its scabbard and fittings were covered in purple leather. Even the handle wrappings were leather, dyed dark blue and carved with the basket-weave design. The *menuki*, usually made of metal, were leather and covered with the gold *mon*, the famed family crest of the Hosokawa. A solid gold ball, surrounded by eight smaller balls, signified the constellations of Ursa Major. The Hosokawa crest with a secondary cherry blossom *mon* was repeated in gold lacquer throughout the sword. It was the weapon of a wealthy man.

"You mean, given to you by someone else *through* Lord Betsuo," Toriko corrected shrewdly.

"Precisely! My foster father, Shijame-sama, maintained residence in Kyoto near the imperial palace, as the Hosokawa have done since the dawn of time. Shijame-sama had many friends among the Hosokawa, including the lord himself. And both of them were friendly with the emperor after he abdicated in favor of his son."

"I have often wondered myself about certain things. . . ." Toriko murmured, lost in her own thoughts.

"What things?" Tonomori asked narrowly.

"You must let me think. I need time to think!"

"Certainly. But when we return to Japan—if we return to Japan—will you go to Kyoto with me?"

"I would consider it an honor." Toriko bowed. "Now, Tonomori-san, would you *please* tell me what happened this morning."

Tonomori smiled and began, omitting only the details

that he chose to censor. When he finished, Toriko was visibly excited. "Ohhh, if only I could have been there. A perfect cut. I could have written a poem."

"And been completely misunderstood. The Europeans are different. Like MacDonnell-san. They are all southern barbarians, *nambanjin*, but among them are some good men, men who command respect."

Toriko considered Tonomori's words, but they were difficult to comprehend. Lately she had felt restless, out of things, with events seeming to pass her by, beyond her control. Perhaps in time she would come to understand the barbarians.

"Command respect? Not the Scottish warrior," she exclaimed.

"You will see."

"Never. He smells," Toriko protested.

"They all smell, but MacDonnell-san bathes more often than most. So does Müller-san. I thought him a pig at first, but I was surprised. I think they smell because they eat too much meat," Tonomori added. "That must be it."

"It makes no difference. They are barbarians," Toriko insisted.

"Talk to MacDonnell-san. You will see," Tonomori countered.

"Never. Did you notice? His eyes are gray, like an old sword. They give me the shivers."

"Have it your own way," Tonomori told her, and gave up.

Toriko left with much to ponder. She dismissed MacDonnell from her mind, and was thinking about the matching sword guards and their significance later when she unexpectedly encountered MacDonnell again in the practice room beneath the mansion.

Dressed for practice in an old kimono and baggy *hakama,* she was surprised by MacDonnell, and the *naginata* she had been reaching for clattered to the floor.

"Here, let me get it for you," MacDonnell promptly said.

"No, it is not necessary," Toriko told him.

"I insist." MacDonnell quickly stooped to grasp the

341

haft of the spear—and found himself suddenly sailing through the air, landing flat on his back. He pulled himself up and looked about him. Toriko had vanished like a ghost.

His scalp prickled. It was impossible! She could not have reached the stairs. He had not been knocked unconscious. He would have heard her go. Then where the hell was she?

"I am over here," a voice said behind him.

MacDonnell whirled and found Toriko standing calmly several feet away in the center of the room. He was stunned.

"How did you do that?" he demanded, not without admiration. His backside was bruised only less than his pride, but he believed in learning from his mistakes.

"It is considered bad manners among my people to touch a person's weapon without asking permission first," Toriko explained coldly.

"Then I must apologize. I did not intend to offend you," MacDonnell said. "I had only intended to help, but I've put my foot in it. How can I make amends?"

Toriko was totally disarmed by the apology. And from a man!

"Your apology is accepted," she assured him. "You have no need to make amends." She lowered the *naginata* with feline grace.

"But perhaps I can. Tonomori told me a while ago that you had wanted to hear about the duel. I would be very happy if you would hear the tale from me."

"Again, there is no need. Tonomori-san told me himself this afternoon."

"Ah, but you only heard *his* version. Tonomori is an effacing man. I'll wager he left out the good parts."

"The good parts?"

"Yes, the slippery grass. Blades flashing in the rising sun. The Cut of the Carriage Wheels. His enemy falling in two pieces . . ."

Toriko caught his excitement. "He did not tell me that," she conceded.

"Always modest, is Tonomori," MacDonnell agreed.

"I will hear your version," Toriko told him, firmly caught.

MacDonnell proceeded to embroider a scene as bloody as a French hunting tapestry, embellishing many of the details, inventing others.

"Oooooh, it sounds wonderful, MacDonnell-san!" Toriko said, her lips parted, when MacDonnell finished. He was surprised at her reaction, but also pleased. Never had he encountered such a bloodthirsty woman, ready to hear the last murderous detail. Or a woman who could knock him on his ass.

"It was exciting, all right," he said. *But not nearly as exciting as yourself,* he thought, viewing her, for the first time, from another vantage point.

"Why are you looking at me so strangely, MacDonnell-san?" Toriko's voice was a mixture of curiosity, intrigue, and mild alarm.

"I have never met anyone like you. Do I offend you?"

He did, but Toriko had decided that she should become accustomed to all the *nambanjin*. She decided to end the conversation nonetheless. "No, you have not, but it is time for me to practice."

"May I watch you?"

"This time, no. Perhaps another day. I will consider it." She hoped that she did not sound overly harsh.

"I look forward to it, then." MacDonnell turned to leave, paused. "Are there many like you in your country?"

"Like me?" Toriko asked thoughtfully, almost sadly. "No, very few." *No, most exist only to please men, walking a few paces behind, experiencing little joy and many hardships, the only fate I really fear.*

"That is too bad," MacDonnell remarked as he left.

Toriko watched him go. When the door latch had fallen, she looked at the *naginata*. It seemed dead in her hands. She tried a few passes but gave it up and sat down on the floor.

Why has the barbarian troubled you so? Is it because he has reminded you of what you are, an object to serve, like a good knife, or a pillow? Remember your training. For-

get what you have seen among the barbarians. Forget everything.

But she could not. Diana had shown her a whole new world, strange and dangerous. People took chances, defied *karma*, rebelled constantly, showed their feelings openly and without shame. How could she exist among such people?

Tonomori, like her, was different. A known quantity, samurai, proud and strangely wise. A bond had formed between them. Was it a common blood, the same heritage? What did Tonomori know that he was not yet telling her?

Toriko's thoughts returned to MacDonnell again and again, and she became increasingly irritable. Was it his kindness and gentleness, so unexpectedly coming from a warrior with many wars behind him? Was it the engaging smile, the gray eyes that warmed her with open admiration?

With grim determination, Toriko decided to keep busy, to practice, to learn all she could of the new culture. And to put Scottish knights as far from her mind as was humanly possible.

Chapter Twenty-four

Tonomori knocked an arrow to his war bow, while MacDonnell pulled back the jaws of the wheel-lock pistol he had drawn from a saddle holster. Müller gripped his musket tightly. Their horses were thundering down a narrow dirt road, several miles from Diana's mansion, toward another estate that now was a mass of flames. Even from a

344

great distance, the fire had illuminated the early-morning sky below clouds of dense smoke. In curiosity mixed with alarm, they had quickly decided to investigate.

As they neared the main house, they could see that many of the buildings were burning, and already glossy black crows were flying overhead in ever-narrowing circles. Their harsh cries mocked the last bitter screams of the dying for whose final gasps the birds impatiently were waiting before launching their triumphant swoops.

By the time MacDonnell, in the lead, called for his companions to rein in, the gouts of gray smoke were obscuring almost all the buildings, though orange flames were licking out of every opening. Müller went into a coughing fit, and their horses began shying at their greatest fear: fire.

"Move them back or blindfold them, or we lose them," Müller hacked. The horses were wide-eyed and muttering. Neither Tonomori nor MacDonnell was listening. Müller swore under his breath.

Tonomori studied the hoofprints dug into the earth. The droppings were fresh, too.

"They're not far ahead of us, maybe five minutes, not much more," Tonomori said, swiveling in the saddle.

"It doesn't make much difference," MacDonnell shouted over the crackling roar of the fire. "They're on a murder raid. Looks like thirty, maybe forty riders. We could never stop them."

The three moved their stamping mounts out of the smoke. A roof noisily caved in somewhere. The bodies of what seemed to be all those who had lived on the estate littered the ground. The homely elements of their life had fallen around them—baskets of laundry kicked aside in fright, freshly gathered eggs dropped beside a path.

The estate's smith apparently had put up a good fight with a bar of iron, but he, too, finally had been cut down. MacDonnell read the signs. "He bloodied two of them before they got him from behind. The others tried to run, but what good did it do them?"

A gust of wind cleared the smoke in a sudden swirl, and they could see a woman hanging by her neck in her

345

doorway. At that moment, her clothing and hair burst into flames.

"Spaniards?" Tonomori said, though he intuitively knew the answer only too well.

"Who else? That tears it!" MacDonnell snarled.

A Spaniard ran swiftly out of one of the surrounding buildings. His sword belt slung over a shoulder, he was frantically tying the drawstrings of his slops breeches.

Before MacDonnell could turn, Tonomori killed the soldier with an arrow through his right eye.

"Good shot," MacDonnell said, as he quickly inspected the body while they dismounted. Müller held the skittish horses.

The Spaniard had fired the building, and as Tonomori and MacDonnell entered the smoke made their eyes water bitterly. They saw the reason for the soldier's haste. The heat was beginning to build quickly. The building was a tinderbox. On the charring floor lay a woman who had been raped and stabbed in the breast.

"The bastards!" MacDonnell swore. He spun at the sound of a thin wail from inside a pile of sacking, and poked at it. "Goddam! A brat," he said. The howling infant, perhaps six months old, clung to MacDonnell's forefinger in a grip of instinctive survival. They heard a shot as they rushed outside before the building could collapse with them in it.

Müller was reloading his musket.

"Got one! He come out of the smokehouse. With an armload of bacon," Müller said with satisfaction. "Sent him off to hell to cure his hams for good."

With one hand, MacDonnell jerked the arrow from the soldier Tonomori had killed, and returned it to him, commenting, "Now when they're found, there's no way of telling who did it. Fucking scavengers! They won't be missed."

Tonomori grunted approval. No other sign of the enemy appeared, and he readily assumed that the pair had dropped off from the main body of troops in order to do some private raiding. No use, then, in wasting time looking for others, because there hardly could be a place for a Spaniard to hide as building after building collapsed in flames.

"I found this, my captain," Müller called. He handed over a torn booklet. MacDonnell examined its cover, which depicted a pope and several cardinals dancing on a hellfire fed by papal proclamations. He sent it flying through the smoke.

"Lutherans! Their books are strictly forbidden on pain of death. Religion can turn people to foolhardy, dangerous, or cruel practices. And this is what can happen when the Spaniards find the evidence of foolhardiness." He scratched his beard as he raised his voice to be heard; the baby was in full scream. "Easy, brat; I won't let them get you," he said softly.

"Now what?" Tonomori asked.

"They'll be burning farms throughout the province, damn them. The rumors were right for once. Your Duke of Alvino is said to have reinstituted what they're calling the Council of Blood. And what an apt name! Here you see its results. The danger and the cruelty."

"Then we fight!"

"It's not that simple," MacDonnell rejoined. "They have too many men. We'd be killed at the next farm, and for nothing. We should try to sound the alarm if we can get ahead of them."

"Diana-san!" Tonomori exclaimed.

"She's safe," MacDonnell assured him. "If she were a target, they'd have hit her first. Her land is ten miles back. Due south as the crow flies, the way we came. They rode out of the fortress directly west to take out this small farm, and now they've hooked north. The man who owned this place had powerful enemies, or lacked powerful friends. . . ."

"Or was just in the way."

"Something like that. If Alvino's men are running true to form, they'll be riding in small groups in widening circles. Unless they have certain specific targets, it'll just be hit and miss." As he spoke, smoke began to billow on the horizon a mile or two to the northeast.

"See what I mean?" MacDonnell said, pointing. "If

347

you're still worried, we can ride back and alert the countess. But I'd guess that somebody probably has done that already."

Tonomori thought of the men he had seen as they were approaching this farm, scythed down like the wheat they had been tending. What would his mistress want? He gave it consideration, putting aside his own inclination to ambush the marauding troops. Diana would want him to warn others, he decided.

"We ride. To warn others," Tonomori said. "Give the child to Müller-san."

"Me!" Müller was aghast.

"Is anyone else named Müller around here?" Tonomori wanted to know drily. MacDonnell looked grateful as he handed over the wailing bundle.

Trying to back away, Müller finally took it gingerly. "What am I supposed to do with it?" He looked at it dubiously.

"If you had tits, you could feed it, Müller-san. It sounds hungry," Tonomori said. "Lacking those, take it back to the countess at once. The women will know what to do with it. And hurry. The sooner you get there, the sooner it will stop screaming. Tell the countess what happened. And tell her I don't know when we will be able to return."

Müller stared at him.

"Move!" Tonomori commanded.

Müller swung into the saddle with the infant and spurred.

"Time for us to do the same," Tonomori said. "We must swing around these Spaniards in order to get ahead of them."

The alarm was already spreading with urgency, with the billowing pillars of smoke sending out warnings even before fleeing families and outriders could. But at least three families owed their lives to Tonomori and MacDonnell. Grabbing what they needed most for survival, they fled, on foot, on horse, by rowboat. One young couple and their small daughter headed across the River Scheldt by grasping inflated animal skins. They had lost everything except their lives, but were thankful for the opportunity to escape.

Tonomori and MacDonnell overtook hundreds of Hollanders already on the run, but kept moving to speed the word of approaching peril.

"They aren't taking any chances. If Alvino's men don't find any evidence, they'll plant it," MacDonnell explained at one point. "Once the Holy Office of the Inquisition has you, your family and friends mourn you as already dead."

Fire had consumed dozens of farm buildings and fields. The sun sank redly into the haze, like a dark blot hanging over the day. The stench of burned flesh greeted them frequently. They found several victims tied to road markers, where soldiers had piled anything that would ignite—dead limbs, sheaves of straw, staved-in wagons—and left them to die in fiery agony. MacDonnell, who had witnessed the horrors of war many times, was sickened by the senseless butchery. Tonomori, saying nothing, had seen worse. His people had studied cruelty under the Chinese—and learned it very well. In Tonomori's opinion, if a man was to be killed, it should be accomplished quickly.

"I'd like to ride farther west. I'm ready, but the horses won't make it," Tonomori said. It had been a killing pace, covering fifty miles or more, and they had changed mounts twice. On their way back, they needed to pick up their horses and return those they had requisitioned.

"And no more to be found, either. We were fortunate to get those that we did," MacDonnell added. He was weary but game, and very angry. They were six miles from home. Home and a bed. Both were very tempting.

"I am surprised that we have encountered no patrols," Tonomori mentioned.

"All moving north, ahead of the main force probably. Alvino is pushing his luck, this time. The Dutch are different from anyone else. They'll turn on the Spanish in time, wait and see!" MacDonnell predicted.

"I hope I don't have to wait much longer."

The horses were well lathered, so they walked them the last three miles to the de Edgemont mansion. A rider galloped by at one point, giving them a wide berth, and still concealing his face. The house was ablaze in light, with servants bustling in all directions.

"Someone has stirred up an anthill," MacDonnell observed.

"Or a hornets' nest," Tonomori amended.

They left their weary mounts with a groom and sought out Diana. She was, as Tonomori expected, in a cold fury.

"I'm glad you're safe," Diana said, looking relieved. "Half of the Seventeen Provinces, from Zeeland to the French frontier, seem to have been hit."

She sat down, urged them to join her, and called for pots of ale, with cold chicken, bread, and goat cheese. They waited until it had been brought and the servants dismissed before speaking of the urgent situation. The Spanish were masters at extracting from nosy underlings conversations they might have overheard.

"The counts of Holland are said to be meeting tonight. As many as can be gathered. In secret, of course. The duke's troops have killed hundreds of people, according to what I am hearing from word sent by Count Hoorn. Alvino must be mad! This . . . this slaughter. And so many homeless little ones like that baby Müller brought in today. And how many more perished in the flames?" Her rage flared in a new direction. "King Philip is not the man his father was. King Charles never would have allowed this. He left us to our own devices and we prospered. We are not fools. We always have been willing to compromise. My people have been discreet."

"What makes you think that Philip can even know what is happening?" Tonomori inquired.

"He must know!" Diana insisted harshly.

"Not must. Might," MacDonnell corrected. "The Spanish courier service is fast. The duke could have sent a dispatch to the king, advising him of the action he was about to initiate."

"Yes," Tonomori said, "and Alvino can assume that the king will endorse any action he takes against the Protestants. And at the same time, the duke hems you in with a ring of fire."

"Not yet he hasn't!" Diana objected vigorously.

"But he will try to, even more than today. Count on it," MacDonnell warned. "And the Holy Office of the

Inquisition will sanction any atrocity, any measures. The priests of that order have much influence with the king.''

"Yes, I know." Diana's voice was bitter. "The king would consign his own children to the flames if he caught one of them humming a Protestant hymn!"

MacDonnell interrupted her. "How many troops has Alvino diverted for this, ah, punitive action, as I believe it's being called?"

"I gather they number at least three thousand. He has divided them into small groups, not expecting much opposition." She turned back to Tonomori. "The duke can't be doing all this just to pressure me. If he did force me to wed him and got my properties, what then? With rebellion fomenting under his aristocratic nose, he would be recalled in disgrace by the king."

"But Alvino won't be here to suffer the consequences," Tonomori said. "He will be the new governor-general in Naples, and putting his next scheme into action. Paid for in part by your money."

Diana licked her lips. "Of course. Then . . ."

". . . his successor will inherit all the problems. Duke Alvino will have all the glory," Tonomori went on. "And then all will be exactly to his design. MacDonnell-san tells me the people of Spain are weary from fighting France. The Low Countries in rebellion would give them something else to occupy their energies." He paused. "The duke as the newly appointed governor-general of Naples and commander of all the Spanish forces in southern Italy surely could think of a way to provoke the Turks into taking on the Spaniards. And with all of King Philip's troops then engaged on every front, the duke would have a golden opportunity to consolidate into an unassailable position. It all means that we must put all our plans into action, and soon!"

Diana rose quickly. "I will see Toriko-san immediately. She will be the key to success. You stay—rest and eat well. This may be your last opportunity for such luxuries for a while."

"What does the Lady Toriko have to do with carrying this off?" MacDonnell asked after she had left. If he was going to play the game well, he wanted to know what cards they were holding. Toriko already had surprised him once, and he did not want something like that happening again.

"She's a woman of many resources," Tonomori said briefly.

"You're telling me! She knocked me on my ass the other day." MacDonnell explained the circumstances, and Tonomori laughed uproariously.

"She is dangerous, never what she seems," Tonomori said, suddenly serious once more. "If I am killed, as I said before, and if it seems that Diana-san is in greater danger, send Toriko to kill the duke. I would suggest it to her myself now, but she has her own pride. If you must tell her after I am dead, it won't matter—at least not to me."

"I will deliver the message if it ever becomes necessary," MacDonnell promised. "I'm still curious as to how she could disappear like that. Do you know how she did it?"

"Yes, but I think Toriko-san would be angry if I betrayed her secrets." Tonomori began to eat hungrily from a bowl of fish soup.

MacDonnell had been served a cold joint of beef. The servants were becoming accustomed to their individual preferences.

"Could you have done what she did?" MacDonnell asked after washing down a mouthful of meat with a gulp of watered wine.

Tonomori thought for a moment. "Probably. But you might have seen me. I am too big to be good at the Art of Invisibility."

"Then it is an art?"

"Oh, yes, very much so. It has been so for centuries in my country. But the people who employ such arts are the enemy of samurai." Still hungry after finishing the soup, he overcame his distaste for bread and broke off a chunk from a round loaf.

"Then the Lady Toriko is your enemy?"

"Once, yes. But we have agreed to maintain a peace between us." Tonomori went on eating. He did not care

352

for the wine, but because he was thirsty he sipped at it sparingly.

"I sure would like to know how she can do that," MacDonnell grumbled, recounting again how Toriko had simply vanished, and then reappeared as if by magic several feet away in the opposite direction.

Tonomori said nothing. He knew what MacDonnell had not seen. It was all so easy: MacDonnell was right-handed. When he had landed, undoubtedly the first thing he'd done was to look over his right shoulder—while Toriko ducked down and to the left.

With her *ninja* training, Toriko knew that he would quickly look over his left shoulder next, so she then ducked to the right. When he regained his feet, MacDonnell would have pivoted to the right, and Toriko would remain low, turning with him as he did. She would reappear or not, depending on what the circumstances called for. She had been there all the time. MacDonnell had not known where to look.

MacDonnell's curiosity was intense. If he had been an enemy, he realized, he would have been dead. "Does the countess know about all this?"

"Yes, she knows. Why don't you ask her?" Tonomori asked genially.

MacDonnell was stopped, and he knew it. One did not pry into the affairs of nobility—not and remain employed. Or, perhaps, even in one piece.

When Tonomori went to find Diana, MacDonnell sought out Müller. He found him in the kitchen, enjoying the attention of a half-dozen women.

"Welcome, my captain! Have some ale," Müller shouted.

"Well, Müller, you certainly look fit. I've always thought you belong in the kitchen," MacDonnell said.

"Yah, I learn to cook good. Put some meat on your bones," Müller rejoined. In front of him was a half-empty plate of sweet cakes.

"Where's the brat?"

"Sleeping like a baby. In the pantry. The countess, she fix up a leather bag for him. Tie some string around the bottom to make a nipple and poke holes in it. He guzzle a

353

bellyful of goat milk, belch like a good German, and go to sleep," Müller said happily.

"*He?* Then the brat is a boy?"

"Yah, hung like a Flemish dray horse. He make some little girl very happy when they grow up."

"You said 'good German.' That's something that cannot be," MacDonnell said in a thoroughly good mood. He and Müller often abused each other heartily to pass the time and to make reality seem more distant.

"And 'bad German,' my captain?"

"A redundancy, my fine dunderhead."

"Like 'thieving Scot,' eh?"

"You are catching on, Müller. Very soon you'll be a true Scot like me, pinching pennies and eating haggis."

"No stuffed sheep's belly for me," Müller retorted, making a face at the thought of haggis. He leered at the rounded forms of two of the women bustling near at hand. "I want a warm belly, I stuff it myself—personally, heh heh."

The women looked knowingly over their shoulders at Müller, who bore watching. They had been tittering at his rough humor, but they kept out of arm's reach. They could see little future in bedding a mercenary who plainly lived so close to the edge.

"Müller is a hero, saving the baby and all," one said within MacDonnell's hearing.

"A hero, is it? Well, Müller, my friend, you can have the glory. I'll settle for the ale."

"Anything you say, my captain," Müller beamed. Nothing could disturb his good humor.

The duke's armor glowed hellishly, rippling from the intense light of the inferno that had been a home. His men were everywhere, yelling, poking weapons into haystacks, trying to ferret out any elusive heretic who had escaped their scourge.

A sergeant wearing a crested morion helmet with jaw flaps rode up to Alvino and saluted. "The vermin have escaped, Your Grace. Someone must have warned them," the sergeant said. Gunshots echoed far away in the darkness.

"Anyone with half his wits will be gone, Sergeant. Our activities hardly can have escaped their attention." Alvino adjusted the white silk sash that marked him as the commander, then rested a hand on the ivory grip of his long sword.

"We have nothing more to be done here, Sergeant. Pass the word. Prepare to move out in five minutes," Alvino ordered. The sergeant saluted and spurred away.

Alvino was exhilarated, glad to be in fighting armor once again, not that garish Pisan "pots and mops" suit in which he had pranced around at Diana's festival. The white plume of his helmet was drooping—but not his spirits, and Alvino was sure that this time opium had nothing to do with his feeling of well-being. The fires seemed to have cleansed his mind as they had purified the land of Protestants.

If all this didn't bring the countess groveling to kiss his signet ring, then perhaps even sterner measures would be needed. Alvino was completely sure of himself and felt ready for whatever developed. The Dutch were stubborn, but they could be taught manners and, by God, this time they had better learn whose was the whip hand. The countess herself could profit from a few vicious lashings.

Alvino gazed into the blaze, fascinated. The stairs to the second floor, about to give way, jolted, and a rack of old armor at the top of the stairwell began to topple, rolling along the railing amid the snapping flames. It collapsed at the bottom; the leathers inside were being consumed, tightening and curling. One arm was outstretched, as if pointing. To the duke, it seemed as if the gauntlet was beckoning him toward the inferno.

The dream! It was like his father in the dream, the dream that steadily was getting worse. He shuddered at the thought of the hideous nights. . . .

Alvino was all at once very much afraid again. If he dreaded one prospect above all others it was hellfire. And with all the crimes staining his soul, crimes that he could not confess, not all the priests in the church could grant him absolution, and the release he craved.

"Ensign, sound the call for assembly!" Alvino shouted

to the youth carrying the double-eagle standard of the Hapsburgs.

Their hoofbeats soon faded into the night, leaving the house to collapse on itself in the demon dance of the flames. Alvino knew that soon the cellar would be a pit brimming with glowing ash, and he did not want to be there to see it.

Diana paced in her dining hall. MacDonnell and Müller rocked back in carved chairs at the table. Tonomori and Toriko remained standing, waiting for the storm to blow itself out before trying to appeal to her reason.

"The Council of Troubles is convening again today! My people do not call it the Council of Blood for nothing," Diana raged. "They are expected to approve all the duke's actions, and sanction even more. Several of our nobles are refusing to serve in the council. Not that it matters. His Grace has enough flunkies there to assure that he gets what he wants. The senile fools who have agreed to sit with them are just painting a stinking lily."

She paused, out of breath, then sat down, ready to weep in frustration and anger. *So many deaths, and so useless.* Diana had sent food and medicines north through her business agents to help the refugees escaping persecution. Nothing would repair their shattered lives, but Diana felt she had to try to help somehow.

Tonomori broke the silence. "Diana-san, the time has come to kill him. Before this, you held back for fear of reprisals. What difference does it make now?"

MacDonnell, startled, suddenly sat forward. He couldn't believe what he had just heard. "But Alvino will be doubly guarded now. They will be expecting revenge—attempts on his life. We can't just walk in and cut his throat."

"Oh, but we can, MacDonnell-san, we can." It was Toriko, who knew that at last the time for her to speak had come. MacDonnell looked at her, wondering.

"But I do not think that it is enough to destroy this man. First, we must destroy his hopes, his ambitions," said Diana, wanting her revenge complete.

"I agree," Tonomori said. "We should begin immediately. You are too vulnerable. The Spanish daimyo has grown reckless. He is making such a big gamble that the stakes must be exceedingly high."

Diana put her palms flat on the table and spoke decisively. "I have made up my mind. All that I feared has come to pass. I only hope we have not waited too long. Sir Ian? . . . ."

"Yes, Countess?"

"Can you help Toriko get past the Spanish patrols and close to the shadow of the fortress?"

"It may be difficult, but yes."

"Then the duke dies!" Diana snapped.

Müller and MacDonnell were breathing fast with excitement. Tonomori looked as impassive and predatory as ever. Toriko would remain an enigma.

"But first, before he does, I must know a few things about his ships," Diana added.

Walking with Tonomori in the garden, it was an hour of double sorrow for Diana.

"I am sorry, Tonomori-san, but you must not come to my bed any longer," she said softly but with finality. "This saddens me greatly, but I must say it."

Tonomori felt his heart begin to pound, but he mastered his emotions.

"That is your decision, Diana-chan," he said at last. "I must ask you why. Have I done something to offend you?"

"It is difficult to put into words. These are dangerous times. I am afraid."

"But it is in times of danger when you need me the most," Tonomori objected. "It is then, when we might be torn from each other at any moment, that we should count precious what few hours we are together."

"I agree, but I am resolved, despite all the sentiment. I am different from you, Tonomori-san, in an important way. I cannot lie happily in your arms while my people are being put to the torch, and dying by the hundreds." Diana's voice was little more than a husky whisper.

"It will not help them to worry yourself into unhappiness."

357

"I know that, but their situation affects me just the same. Don't ask me to explain. I have no words. What I have said to you is difficult enough." She looked at him, the feeling of wanting him, needing him so badly, surging within her as she turned him away.

How *could* she explain? True, the murder of her people had upset her. But that was not the whole reason.

With every thrust and gasp on her rumpled bed, they were courting potential disaster. People would suspect that Diana was entertaining Tonomori in her bedchamber even if she weren't. No, that wasn't really the problem. The world might find out their affair, might wink and snicker, but the Countess de Edgemont would not be condemned or shunned so long as she remained discreet. Every man, of position, it seemed, had his mistress, from the pope on down. So it followed that women, even countesses, would take lovers.

To Diana, the problem lay in the ever-present danger of a child, Tonomori's child.

True, many a bride went to the altar already pregnant. In parts of the Low Countries, people even considered this a sign of good fortune: The woman would be fecund enough to provide many children to help run a farm or a business.

If Diana had a child by Tonomori, a scandal of the highest order would result. She could never marry him, a foreigner. The same would be true of him. Any son or daughter she might bear would never be accepted in either of their countries. Such an unfortunate child would be an outcast everywhere.

Diana was not thinking entirely of herself. She did not want to bring ruin to an innocent child, like the infant who had been brought in late that morning, screaming in fear and in hunger, and triggering a forceful renewal of the caution that she had been pushing out of her consciousness. It had been there all along, like a crossbow bolt waiting to be released, and piercing her just as bitterly. To keep Tonomori at arm's length would be difficult. He had kindled a fierce physical desire within her, and she recognized the passion that he expressed each time he came to her.

But, after all, they had known from the outset that the affair could not last indefinitely.

"May we not at least remain friends, Diana-chan?"

"I must have that! You must know it. Let us always be friends, no matter what."

"You are aware of how difficult this is going to be?" Tonomori began.

"I know it very well. More than perhaps you realize."

They parted without touching. One spark would fan the smoldering embers and consume both of them. Diana tearfully stumbled off to her bed, to weep alone.

Tonomori remained in the garden, his thoughts steeped in sorrow. Night birds in the trees called to each other, and he shared their solitariness.

At last, he took from his sash the flute he had intended to play for Diana. Tonight, he would play for the spirits of the garden, and for himself.

A poem welled in his soul like tears. It wrenched free as would a lover falling from a precipice.

> My sleeping love sighs in solitude,
> while my flute weeps sad songs,
> empty echoes on the lonely rocks.

Then silently but with deep fervor, he swore, "Bugger it all with poxied lepers!" and felt better. For that he was indebted to this barbaric race. To be able to curse fluently was a joy. Japanese possessed no equivalents to European profanity, though it was otherwise a rich tongue. Diana deplored at times his rough language, but MacDonnell laughed in amused delight. It was MacDonnell who collected bad habits the way a pig snorts after truffles. But in time, with practice, he predicted, Tonomori would be able to curse as well as himself or any Scottish bishop.

"To hell with it," Tonomori said at last. He sought his own bed. With dangers looming ahead, he needed the rest. Despite his worries, sleep came quickly.

Outside, Yamahito and Oshabiri remained at their vantage point in the garden, conversing in low tones. They had seen Diana talking with their master but could not hear what was said.

"Why is everyone so unhappy?" Oshabiri wondered.

"Not everyone. Just the daimyo."

"But they should be the happiest of all. They have everything."

"Ah, but that is the point! The higher the rank, the more you have to lose," Yamahito philosophized.

"Then we should be delirious with joy because we have so little," Oshabiri said. "I don't feel particularly happy."

"But you are not really sad, either."

Saru stirred fitfully in Oshabiri's arms as he slept, and the little archer scratched his ear fondly.

"That is true. So long as I can visit a girl I've met at Rose's who has strange copper hair, I am reasonably content. And she charges only me half price," Oshabiri said proudly.

"She charges by the length perhaps, and your jade stalk is only half what she is used to," Yamahito offered.

"Not true. She moaned fearfully at the moment her peony was sprinkled with dew," Oshabiri said.

"In disappointment, no doubt." Yamahito decided to change the subject. "It would be better for all concerned if our master took both women to bed, both Diana-san and Toriko-san."

"At the same time! What a happy thought."

"No, idiot. At different times. Then everyone would be joyous, especially us," Yamahito said.

"Why especially us?"

"Well," Yamahito said, clearing his throat, "I do not enjoy being awakened in the middle of the night to run five miles, engage in a mock attack, and run back, all because our master is restless. You remember what he is like, when he has not had a woman in a while."

"How could I ever forget?"

"Then you'd better hope something happens soon. Otherwise, we are going to get a lot of exercise before you know it," Yamahito declared with finality.

Behind them, Toriko slipped away into the darkness, unheard.

Chapter Twenty-five

"My captain, I look all over for you. Where you been?" Müller, not used to hoofing it about town, was flushed and puffing.

"I'm surprised you made it past the first tavern, my friend," MacDonnell said.

"Better yet, I went to Rose's instead."

"Müller! This isn't the time for that sort of thing."

Müller waved his hands. "No, no. It is not what you are thinking. I *talk* to Rose. The secretary of the bishop—he go to drink there and to play, all the time. I see him before. Anyway, last night he got drunk . . ."

"The *bishop* drunk in a whorehouse?"

"No, the secretary," Müller said, exasperated. "He only a monsignor. He let it slip that the duke plans to get married. Very soon."

"How soon?"

"Within a week. He get permission from the bishop to cut through formalities."

"You did good work, Müller."

"Yah, but Rose, she charge me two ducats for the information. I need to get repaid."

"Don't look at me, friend. Apply to Tonomori. What you should have done is go upstairs with your two ducats and one of Rose's girls. The girls always know what's going on. She'd have thrown in the information," Mac-Donnell said. "It looks like you got screwed twice, depending on which way you look at it. If you want to recoup, tell Tonomori it cost you four ducats."

"Nothing doing! The last time I try that, Tonomori grab me by the throat, lift me off the floor with one hand, tell me that if I ever lie to him again he will tie my tongue in a knot. I believe him."

"So do I." MacDonnell whistled.

"He say that if I want to learn how to lie real good, I should come to Japan and take lessons."

MacDonnell laughed. "They must be a lively bunch. Tonomori is as crafty as a room full of cardinals. Also, he probably is well acquainted with Rose's rates."

"I think we should tell the countess. Do you know where to find her?"

"At her town house on the Velvet Canal. Come on, we can ride there. Things are beginning to move. Tonomori escorted her over to Hoorn's mansion during the night, with me riding behind in case anyone decided to follow," MacDonnell said. "A lot of very important people were there. I don't know what they talked about, but the look on their faces afterwards told me it wasn't pleasant. The Spanish can box us up in this city very easy. So be ready to bust out of here at any time."

"I'm ready now," Müller told him.

The street traffic was lighter than usual for a market day. An air of gloom prevailed among the people on the street, and they started at the sound of shod hooves.

"See what I mean?" MacDonnell asked pointedly.

At Diana's town house, they had to wait until a servant could be found to identify them through a grilled peephole in the heavy door. Once they were approved, the thick bar behind the door was removed. Diana wisely was not taking any chances.

Tonomori and Toriko were in conference with her in an airy room that served as a study. It was well furnished with books, and with many candlesticks to read by. An expensive globe of the known world stood by a large chair. Several excellent ship models were on shelves. One was a design MacDonnell had never seen; built full size, it would be as large as a galleon, but with the quarterdeck set low, and the forecastle missing entirely.

"Sir Ian, Herr Müller, would you come over here, please?" Diana asked, looking up only briefly from a map she was studying.

"A Spanish column was ambushed near Utrecht last night. Fifteen soldiers were killed. Whoever did it got clean away. But the result is reprisals, more hangings. We must move soon to give the duke something else to think about," she informed them.

"The sooner the better, else we'll be dancing at your wedding, countess," MacDonnell said in abrupt response.

Diana looked up sharply.

"Tell her, Müller."

Müller took off his floppy velvet cap, old fashioned and a faded bilious green. He repeated the story he'd told MacDonnell, leaving out where he had obtained the information, but remembering later to ask Tonomori for his two ducats.

"I'm to dine with the duke three days from now," Diana murmured, almost to herself. "He has hinted bluntly that he plans to ask for my hand in marriage. The duke is timing this very well."

"Can you refuse him, Diana-san?" Tonomori wondered.

"Yes, and be thought a lunatic! The merchants and peasants would think I am mad to turn down the opportunity to become a duchess, even a Spanish one. My friends would see the marriage as an opportunity to end the carnage. With the governor-general married to a Dutch countess, he might become more amenable to Dutch ways, and call off his dogs."

"Then tonight is more important than ever," said Toriko.

"Whatever you can find to use against the duke will be vital," Diana said in response. "If there *is* anything. I have the eerie feeling that if I sign the marriage agreement, I sign my own death warrant." She looked glum.

"What is the plan?" MacDonnell inquired.

"As before. Nothing is changed. You will go with Toriko-san as close to the fortress as you can get without being seen," Diana told him. "Wait for her until dawn,

363

then leave without her if she hasn't returned. If Toriko-san is found out, she will not let herself be taken alive."

MacDonnell looked at Toriko admiringly. "You are taking a big risk."

"We are all taking risks," she replied. "We have no other choice."

Toward the end of the first night watch, Toriko took the direct approach and went into the fortress through the main gate.

Crossing his fingers for luck, MacDonnell had watched her go. The skill and technique involved, he thought, must have required untold training. MacDonnell had brought a supply wagon to a halt a hundred yards from the gate by throwing a smooth stone into the rump of the lead horse. While the teamster swore and fought to get the beast under control, Toriko had slipped beneath the wagon and attached herself to its supporting center beam by digging in with the curved steel hooks sewn into her black leather gloves, and the metal prongs strapped to her ankles.

Then MacDonnell settled in to wait for what promised to seem an eternity. For Toriko, he knew, it could come to just that, if she were captured. He shook his head. MacDonnell could not imagine Toriko cutting her own throat, but the countess had stressed that Toriko would do just that if necessary. And he wondered at the kind of courage she needed—with virtually no weapons—to pierce this stronghold of their enemies.

Inside the fortress, Toriko had time only for concentrating on her goal, digging the hooks in more securely with every jolt and sway of the ancient wagon. At last it stopped, and Toriko twisted for a quick survey of her surroundings. They were outside a storage building.

She knew the details of the fortress well. More than a hundred years old, it had numerous additions, many of them built by civilian labor from the city. The ever-cautious Dutch had kept notes and drawings. Diana had obtained these from resourceful friends, and Toriko had memorized each detail.

She dropped to the packed earth and rolled free from the

wagon before the driver even jumped down. Then she was away, into the shadows, black on black, like a cat coursing along familiar fences in pursuit of a favorite rat hole.

Twice she approached groups of soldiers and stiffened. She was not noticed. They were not expecting trouble— and if it came, they assumed it would have to arrive over the reinforced walls into the murderous crossfire of their well-placed guns.

Few lights were burning anywhere. The hour was late, and the quartermaster did not condone the waste of oil or candles.

The pair of sentries in front of Alvino's personal lodgings were for show only. They were leaning on their halberds and talking in low tones.

Toriko ascended quickly up an outside wall, using her steel hooks, reached the roof, and then swung silently down onto a balcony. She was two rooms away from success.

The servants would be in their beds, except for a doorman downstairs, who could be expected to be asleep in a chair by the front door, snoring softly. So far, Diana's information had proven accurate. The door latches and hinges opened without a sound. She slid into the nearest room and passed through unlocked doors to the duke's study.

Toriko paused until her heartbeat slowed back to normal before attempting to pick the lock on Alvino's desk.

The lock proved stubborn. She stopped again to think, and tugged on a silver drawer pull. It slid open smoothly. The drawer had not even been locked.

Her brow wrinkled in disappointment: a dagger, a few packets of powder—Toriko sniffed and found them to contain opium—and a rosary with a crucifix attached. Nothing of any importance. She tried another drawer. This time a leather folder rewarded her efforts.

Quickly, she took a round tube from the folds of her clothing. A narrow spike was soldered onto its side. This she jammed into the wood lining the desk's kneehole. Toriko inserted a slim candle into the tube; the soft scrape of a flint and steel, and the tinder from a waterproof cylinder sparked into a soft yellow flame. When the wick was burning, Toriko put away her implements and curled inside the kneehole to read.

The handwriting, in Spanish, was the duke's own. She recognized it from the notes Diana had received. As Toriko read carefully, the training of her *ninja* masters steadied her nerves.

The lists of arms and ammunition were impressive. So was the amount of gold and silver coins stored in strongboxes aboard Alvino's ships—a king's ransom. A few drawings puzzled her—a bull's head. They were sketches of a bronze at the other end of the room, dark and heavy in the banked glow of the fireplace. The other was a hat, which seemed ridiculous in appearance until Toriko realized it was a crown, heavily studded with pearls and gems. "Henricus Rex," the legend beneath it said.

Henricus Rex—Latin for Enrique the King. *So Tonomori was right, after all*, Toriko thought. *The duke indeed has visions of grandeur.*

She heard a sound not far away and snuffed the candle, carefully replacing the folder in the desk. She tucked the candle inside her clothes, but grasped the holder tightly; its poisoned spike protruded from between her fingers.

Had it been a shifting log? An ember? Toriko crept from behind the massive desk.

She could hear no other sounds, but Toriko had to make sure. All her senses, shrieking danger, urged her to fly. Instead, she crawled farther into the room. Rising up over the end of a long couch that faced the glowing fireplace, Toriko looked directly into the glittering eyes of the Duke of Alvino.

The duke had been feeling the strain. In the saddle for two days running, he was able to maintain his usual self-control. The lightning raids had presented one immediately beneficial effect—smoothing the rumblings of his creditors, when two of them were stabbed to death in their homes after Protestant literature, planted there by the duke's men, was thrust under their protesting faces.

Other such details remained to be dealt with. Festering

366

under the loss of the luckless Gutierrez and needing to replace his second-in-command, Alvino chose Captain Hernan Nunez, whose ruthlessness matched his zeal for gold. Then Alvino ordered Tonomori's murder by five cavalrymen eager for promotion and favor.

"Do it soon, and kill him where you find him. Make it look like a street brawl. It shouldn't be difficult," he had told them before riding out of the fortress on the second day of bloodshed. Alvino had no qualms about shedding blood, except when it came to women. He always would remember his mother's splattered body. When women had to die in the course of his ambition, he preferred that it be by strangulation, or smothering, or by fire.

The killing stopped on the third day, and Alvino chose to ride at the head of his troops on a showy parade through the provinces surrounding Antwerp, banners and honors flying, ready to strike dread into any Dutchman ill-advised enough to harbor ideas of insurrection.

The Dutch, especially the Countess de Edgemont, now had their warning. Alvino calculated that the provinces would bow their heads tamely as usual. It was important to him that they did, and promptly. The most recent dispatch by the efficient courier service from Seville had brought the alarming message that the king himself intended to visit his subjects in the Netherlands.

Alvino damned the man's penchant for meddling. He wanted to have the Naples appointment—unaccountably delayed for months now—in his hands and be gone before his successor had a chance to begin picking through the wreckage. King Philip was notoriously dilatory and suspicious, and Alvino could no longer afford any of his foot-dragging.

Once the countess had capitulated to his persuasions, he would have her money in his own coffers the hour after the vows were exchanged. Next, he would have her hustled out of the Netherlands for his lands in Spain before the marriage bed was even warm. It all required the most delicate timing, and the strain was beginning to shorten Alvino's notoriously bad temper.

And despite the frenetic activity, the duke had been

sleeping badly as usual, whether on a bedroll in the field or in his canopied bed in his lavish quarters within the fortress. His nights were full of terrors. Opium, and only opium, could dull the torment, and lately not even it could hold back the dreams that were becoming increasingly more hideous.

His bedchamber was stifling with its tapestries and velvet drapes, and even the lovely harlot lying in wait did not lessen the gloom. Alvino had sent her away. Instead, he had chosen to take his rest on the couch in his study. Here, where he spun out his webs of intrigue and formulated his grandiose plans, Alvino felt more in charge, ready to take whatever action the situation might call for.

This night, the wine and the opium helped him achieve only a half sleep. He dozed fitfully after staring at the bronze bull of the Borgias for what seemed like hours.

The dream was almost always the same.

A young Alvino stood at the head of the grand staircase in the ducal palace, holding the same bronze bull, his most cherished possession and the symbol of his unspoken ambition and pride. But his father did not understand. The old duke shouted at him, "This obsession of yours must stop. The story of the Borgias is all nonsense," and grabbed at the statue. A look of bewilderment came over the old duke's face as young Alvino struck him in the head with the bronze. The body tumbled slowly to the foot of the stairs. In the dream, young Alvino padded softly to his father, now a rotting corpse staring with silent accusing eyes. "Patricide," the eyes screamed from the sunken sockets. Then the arms unfolded, and the bony fingers beckoned. . . .

And this night, a demonic form was waiting for him, small and dark, and reeking of death. Alvino screamed and reached for the sword lying on the floor beside the couch. When he turned back, the figure had vanished.

Alvino's breath came in rasps. The sword grip was slippery in his hand and of little comfort. The muffled sounds of approaching servants did nothing to allay his fears. The sword dropped to the floor with a metallic clatter, and the duke continued to tremble.

*   *   *

What was stirring? MacDonnell was suddenly alert. Sentries were closing the main gate. Why—or, perhaps, why not? He strained to detect sounds of alarm from within. Nothing. Then, the sound of a horn. *Damn, there it is,* he thought. He wanted to give her a few more minutes, but their horses were tethered in a thicket a half mile away and MacDonnell had no desire to try outrunning a mounted search party for the entire distance.

"Move quickly but stay low!" MacDonnell's heart leaped at the sound of Toriko's voice, but he plunged into the wake of her fleeing shadow. Now was not the time to ask questions.

The horses whickered softly in recognition. "Thank God," MacDonnell said in a loud whisper. Horses were treacherous beasts that could bolt on the slightest provocation. Now was also not the time to be cast afoot. They must be off to the town house as quickly as possible.

If MacDonnell didn't miss his guess, Spanish troopers would be beating the bushes for them, and very soon. His heart was suddenly in his mouth again as Toriko stripped out of her black wrappings, revealing a tiny naked figure, perfectly proportioned. She stuffed the wrappings into a saddlebag, then began to pull on simple hose and doublet like those worn by young page boys and beginning squires, leaning all the while against MacDonnell for support. He found it difficult to swallow and was becoming aroused in spite of himself.

Not now, he thought. MacDonnell's chagrin was adding to his embarrassment. *Maybe she won't notice.* But Toriko, even occupied as she was, could not help but notice. She brushed against MacDonnell to be sure, and felt him stiffen even more.

Toriko felt oddly flattered, but only momentarily. Men were so strange, to think of lovemaking at such a time. Then she was in the saddle, looking down at MacDonnell with an amused expression.

"If you can ride in that condition, we had better get moving."

MacDonnell almost choked, but he mounted his stamping horse and followed her into the gloom.

369

* * *

No one had slept well, and fatigue showed on them all. While Yamahito and Oshabiri stood guard outside to discourage snooping, Diana tried to maintain her composure at the breakfast table at the town house with a patter of small talk about the rescued baby's progress. Since no one knew his name, he was called Jan. Word came from the staff at the estate that he was gaining well—a lusty little fellow with a large appetite and a voice to match.

Toriko picked at her food with little interest beyond replenishing her strength. MacDonnell drummed his long fingers on the tabletop after an enormous meal of sausages, flatcakes, boiled eggs, fresh bread with butter and honey, and a few pickled herring. Tonomori stared ahead at a wall tapestry depicting a court dancing scene. His appetite was only for Diana, and the famine that had been his lonely bed only sharpened the aching.

Since Toriko's return with MacDonnell, and her astounding revelations of the full extent of Alvino's perfidy and the recounting of her brush with the duke, they had been waiting anxiously for Müller to return.

He had ridden out at dawn, to search for off-duty friends from the fortress, hoping to obtain information without prying—and to return. That was the big question. Would Müller return alone, or under arrest, followed by a column of the duke's troops? And if that were the case, should they fight, or flee, or perhaps try to brazen it out?

Tonomori was spoiling for a fight, but MacDonnell opted for getting out of the country—to Germany or France, even to England, while they still could, before the roads were choked with soldiers and all rivers and canals blockaded.

Diana was inclined to be brazen. After all, Toriko's face had been muffled, the light was poor, and Alvino had screamed in fright. Even the duke, who had the most suspicious of minds, could not suspect that a small Japanese woman could penetrate the defenses of his headquarters and slip away undetected. Or could he?

MacDonnell had been furious when he found out that

Toriko had thrown away an opportunity to cut Alvino's throat. However, Diana's plan for revenge was more sophisticated than simple murder. Dead men did not feel any pain, and Diana wanted the duke to suffer as she and others had suffered. Toriko had been ordered not to harm Alvino or anyone else if she could avoid it.

"Women are going to be the death of me yet," MacDonnell mumbled. Impatient with the waiting, he went to the window that commanded a street paralleling the Velvet Canal. He could see no suspicious or hostile movement down there. True, the street seemed more quiet than usual, but the recent raids had the citizens of Antwerp in such a grip of fear that few people budged out of doors unless they had to.

"He's here," MacDonnell said quietly at last.

All heads turned and Diana went to the window. "He's whistling," she said with relief.

Concern still showed in MacDonnell's face. "That means nothing. Müller will be whistling when he weds the widow," he grumbled.

"What?" Diana asked, not understanding.

"Wed the widow! That's gutter talk for going to the gallows. You'll have to excuse me; I wasn't thinking."

Müller barged into the breakfast room. "We are safe! They suspect nothing. I buy breakfast for two of my acquaintances who had guard duty last night. They say the duke had another bad dream and had the place turned inside out. He has been acting strangely, too, but they did not think anything was amiss. The duke has trouble sleeping and so he takes drugs, it is said, and he sees things. That's all."

Diana could have dropped with relief, but she was still in a furor over what Toriko had discovered. She was distressed, too, by how some of her friends now were reacting to the latest Spanish infamy. They were beginning to attach blame for the reprisals to Tonomori's defeat of the Spanish captain. And they blamed Diana for not having prevented the duel with its bloody result. Everyone knew how touchy the Spanish were about their honor;

couldn't she and the Japanese lord leave well enough alone?

The counts of Holland and other noble houses knew differently. And eventually, Diana thought, others would learn how mistaken they were. But for now, her temper was boiling. People insisted on being so blind; they could not accept what was in front of their very noses.

Müller surveyed the table with pleasure at the prospect of a second breakfast, and began piling food onto his plate.

"Anything else?" Diana inquired.

"Is there any more of that currant jam?"

"No, meathead!" MacDonnell corrected impatiently. "The countess wants to know what more your friends may have told you of importance."

Müller chewed for a moment, beamed, and swallowed. "Yes. I forgot. One of my friends has a friend in the clerk's office. It is supposed to be a secret, but the King of Spain will be touring the Netherlands in a month or so."

"King Philip? Here?" Diana exclaimed incredulously.

"The very same. Spain is about to conclude a treaty with the French. When the war is done, the king intends to mend his fences. So they talk now."

"Then we must begin planning now! I am going to the duke's house tomorrow night. Alone. Because of the heat, it will be a late supper, at ten o'clock. I will be expected to exchange vows then. We may finish eating at midnight. Whether we do or not doesn't matter. The watch changes at eleven o'clock. Launch the attack then," Diana instructed.

Müller continued to eat, unperturbed, as if the countess had announced a boating expedition. For the next day and a half, he was the only one who showed much self-restraint. MacDonnell worried about the numerous things that could go wrong with the plan; he did not care for it. It could literally blow up in their faces. It would succeed, or fail, spectacularly. Toriko, with her equipment assembled and checked, rested to conserve her strength. Diana, with her own many duties, avoided Tonomori, who paced like a caged tiger, chafing at his enforced confinement. Public sentiment was overwhelmingly against him, a surprising reaction that he never had encountered before, and he remained within the town house. Tonomori was accustomed to acclaim for acts of bravery and valor.

Diana's Nuremberg timepiece had only the hour hand—just as the clockmaker had crafted it many years before. The hand seemed to move with agonizing slowness.

Finally, the time for action arrived. Diana was nervous, but encouraged by the relief shining in her companions' faces. They had gone over the plan dozens of times. If they each did their jobs, they should not fail—but there was always the prospect that the wholly unexpected would intervene fatally.

Diana was beautiful as she descended the steps to the waiting litter and the twenty horsemen sent by the duke as her honor guard. They saluted with precision, envious of their master. The gown of red silk with gold trim would cost them two years' wages alone, and the sapphires that winked at her neck were beyond their comprehension, as was the emerald that bulged through the slit in her gloved hand.

A dainty crown of gold, set with rubies, emeralds, and diamonds was the mark of her rank, although several thought her blond hair alone was a true crown.

Diana closed the curtains of the litter, and the procession began for the march of nearly an hour to the forbidding fortress commanding the Scheldt.

What lay ahead of her tonight she could not foresee—but she knew her own iron determination: The duke would die. Or she would. How would the evening progress meanwhile? She could expect a prolonged series of irritating events and conversations. The duke would be at his devilish best while on public display, taunting her, subtly challenging her to resist anything he might malevolently choose to say or do. Would he be leading up, during the dinner, to some long-delayed effort at a tryst with his newly betrothed after the guests had departed? At least, she had been spared so far any attempt by the duke to get her into bed. The public nature of their relationship had taken care of that possible problem.

But whatever his expectations tonight, the Duke of Alvino was in for a surprise.

MacDonnell had left with Toriko hours before, and had returned alone once she had taken position somewhat downriver from the ships. Yamahito and Oshabiri, to their disgust, were ordered by Tonomori to remain behind. They were still in bad odor with their master, ever since Toriko had told him of their intemperate remarks about their superiors; the Western civilization was ruining their discipline. Tonomori had rudely awakened them in the middle of the night, run their legs off, and ominously suggested that they use their spare time in more constructive pursuits.

As they watched Tonomori ride off with MacDonnell and Müller, Yamahito colorfully blamed Oshabiri, who in turn cursed all the evil spirits that had dogged his footsteps ever since they left Japan.

Sundown had come and gone. The streets were cooling pleasantly, the foot traffic light in the twilight. When Tonomori, Müller, and MacDonnell turned onto the Niederstrasse, three horsemen were blocking their path.

The leader, a curly-haired man with missing front teeth, had unsheathed his sword.

"We have gone to a lot of trouble for what should have been so simple an errand," they heard the leader say.

"Perhaps the duke should send some smarter errand boys," MacDonnell observed, looking around for a way out. Two more horsemen slid in from behind. They were trapped.

"Stay out of it, friend. Our business is with the Jappo. Stay out and you won't get hurt," the rider with the missing teeth warned in a menacing tone. When he saw Tonomori and his two companions draw their own blades and prepare to fight, he sought to cut down the odds.

"We spotted you two streets over. We have picked the position well. You are outnumbered, and we are not novices at this game. Leave the Japanese man to us, and you can ride clear. This is a personal fight, none of yours."

MacDonnell turned to Tonomori. "Slash your way clear and keep on going," he said in an urgent undertone.

"I'm not afraid to fight," Tonomori replied calmly.

"Don't be a fool! We haven't the time for that. If they hold us up now, we risk everything. Is that what you want?"

Furious at being put into a position of running while others fought, Tonomori knew MacDonnell was right. "I will do what you say."

MacDonnell wheeled his horse around, drawing his pistol at the same time. "Hit them now!" he shouted, and fired. All the horses jumped, but one saddle now was empty.

Müller fired straight ahead and saw a soldier double up over the saddlebow and drop his blade, then charged into the confusion.

Tonomori slashed a third rider down as he galloped clear, and then spurred without looking back.

MacDonnell and Müller now had no time to think. The score was three men down and two left, but they were deadly opponents who knew their trade. The man with the missing teeth was pressing home a violent attack. MacDonnell could only parry, and when his horse slipped on the cobblestones, he had to scramble to get clear. His sword was lost in the tangle. The toothless man was bringing his blade around in a deadly arc. MacDonnell twisted the barrels of his pistol, rearmed its striker, aimed at the gaping grimace above, and desperately pulled the trigger. It blasted off the top of the man's head.

By the time MacDonnell found his sword and remounted, Müller had opened his sweating opponent's sword arm from the elbow to the wrist. The man howled, dragged on the reins with his one good hand, and raked his mount's flanks with sharp rowels. The hoofbeats receded into the deepening grayness of dusk.

Powder smoke hung heavily in the air, reeking of sulfur. "You are bleeding, my captain," Müller observed calmly.

MacDonnell felt a warm trickle from a stinging scalp wound.

"It will have to wait. We're out of time. The watch will

375

be on us if we don't haul ass out of here," he warned. "This pinprick will dry up quick enough."

Soon only barking dogs and the distant howl of a startled baby could be heard on the Niederstrasse. And the running footsteps of the watch.

Chapter Twenty-six

The horns of the moon were rising, and already the plan was going awry. Toriko knew she could wait no longer. MacDonnell and Müller, who should have begun their diversionary tactics by now, were not in position, though the watch had just changed. It could not be helped; she must move to carry out her assignment on the duke's three ships lying offshore in the Scheldt.

The loose-limbed boy in rags and floppy hat who had been scavenging the riverbank all afternoon, poking through the decaying mud and the flotsam, had disappeared—and Toriko was relieved to be rid of the disguise. Now, wrapped in black cotton, she worked her way carefully through the ribs and debris of dead ships and barges that had long since been dragged ashore to await salvage. The wind was in the right quarter and rising. The sky had been pink and milky with thin clouds, so they were due for some gusts that would aid the devastation that was about to erupt.

The evening breeze brought Toriko the scent of meat roasting on the quay. She could hear soldiers and sailors there laughing and joking together. Good! At least that part of the plan was working. With a fistful of Diana's money, MacDonnell had ordered a delivery to the quay of five wagonloads of wine, fresh beef, port, Gouda cheeses, round loaves still warm from the ovens, golden onions, and a barrel of mottled olives. It all, supposedly, was with the compliments of the Duke of Alvino on the occasion of his betrothal. The seamen and troopers were to share equally, but the guards who accepted the windfall were cautioned to say nothing to outsiders, lest the duke be accused of favoritism. The garrison at the fortress might try to horn in, they were told. And if the men felt like drinking to the health of the duke and his betrothed, His Grace certainly would wink at a slacking of duty.

Judging from the lilt of the merrymaking, the guards and sailors had taken the deliveryman at his word. Why shouldn't they? A hundred soldiers and half again as many seamen from the three ships were on hand, with enough food and drink for double their number. Already, plans were heard for continuing the celebration the next day.

"Cheers for His Grace," someone yelled lustily, and those within hearing range bellowed with enthusiasm. Toriko was buoyed by the noise. Perhaps the guards would be drunk enough, and she would not need MacDonnell and Müller's diversion.

The night was warm, and the frogs along the banks were croaking joyously. Toriko slipped into the wet coolness with hardly a ripple, as much at home in the water as an otter. The current was steady and not too strong. She swam steadily, alert for sound or movement that would signal danger. The wind was still rising, but Toriko was between the quay and the bow of the first ship in line, a towering carrack named the *Bonaventure*. Too many soldiers and sailors were near the lip of the quay, so Toriko decided to go around the windward side. The swim would be slightly longer, but she had less chance of being seen. She would swim past the carrack and the second ship, and strike first at the last of the three.

A figure plunged into the water almost beside her with a startled cry. Before he could make another sound, Toriko pulled the man under the dark surface. She killed him quickly with a stab of her *wakizashi* under the breastbone.

377

Then she wedged his foot between two pilings to keep him from floating to the surface.

Now she could not risk coming up for air. The only chance was to dive under the carrack's hull. Toriko kicked off into the deep, swimming down, down, down, her lungs screaming. *Too late to turn back. Can only keep going! Keep going! Keep going!*

The hull flattened out, began to curve up. She had to have air. . . . Her discipline superb as ever, Toriko broke the surface quietly, filling her lungs. She tried not to gasp, listened for sounds of alarm. The voices from the deck above were slurred and complacent, far from alarmed or suspicious.

"Juan! Where are you, Juan?"

"He's down there. I heard him fall in."

"Juan, answer us, or we drink your share of the wine."

"Juan already drank his share."

"No more for Juan."

"Juan, where are you?"

"Forget him. He got drunk. He fell in. It's his own fault."

"The bastard owes me money."

"You want him, *you* go in after him. Me, I'm getting some more to drink before those goddam guards drain the barrel."

"Me, too."

Toriko heard the voices fade away. *Blessed Jesus, but her karma was good!*

Behind her, a light was growing. Fire in the salvage yard. MacDonnell and Müller were finally in position—better late than never. The wind was whipping the flames, spreading them quickly. The port side of the second ship, the *Santa Barbara,* slid by. Boarding the third ship first would take longer to get into position while swimming against the river's current, but once she started her attack, the current would lend her speed from ship to ship.

Toriko swam along on her back, with an eye to the railings, hoping that no one would choose this moment to relieve himself over the side—much less tumble overboard. She reached the rudder chain of the last vessel, a galleon named the *Perrera,* flagship of the Duke of Alvino. *So far, so good*, she thought as she rested briefly. The wine and the food were keeping the crewmen in good spirits and diverted from the thought of danger.

Pulling herself up the rudder chain, Toriko climbed onto the *Perrera's* stern and scrambled across the ornate grille. She worked her way along the side, below the quarterdeck. She saw an open port on the windward side, and slipped silently in. The layout of the ship was etched in her mind. Again, Diana, whom she had sworn to protect with her own life, had successfully provided the necessary plans. Toriko was samurai and she was *ninja*, the white and the black combined. The ships would be destroyed and Diana would live. Toriko did not hesitate. The ship's powder magazine was only seconds away.

"Here now, what're you? . . ." The quartermaster's words gagged in his throat as Toriko crushed his trachea with the heel of her hand. The man died hard, rattling his bare feet on the deck. Toriko cut the ring of keys from his belt. She could avoid taking time to pick the heavy padlock. She worked without undue haste. On the fifth key, the lock unsnapped, and Toriko dragged the body inside. She closed the hatch and prayed nobody would notice the lock was not closed.

The waterproof container had not failed; she had a candle lighted in seconds and went to work. With a pry bar taken from the wall, Toriko levered open a keg of gunpowder and attached a slow-burning fuse. It would detonate in about thirty minutes. Plenty of time, if all went well. The corridor was clear when she emerged. She inserted a thin file into the keyhole of the padlock, and snapped it off. Even if she were discovered now, they'd need more than thirty minutes to unjam the lock. The duke's flagship was doomed.

Toriko retraced her steps and slid down the rudder chain into the current, letting it carry her along to the next ship, the *Santa Barbara*.

On the quay, men were laughing and yelling even more raucously. The party was a success. Few parties would end so riotously as this one.

An open gunport yawned an invitation, and Toriko went in with the aid of a knotted line and a small grapling hook. They certainly were careless tonight, she thought. An open gunport was a serious breach of discipline, a flogging offense if the ship's captain saw it. Toriko was counting to herself. Five minutes gone, twenty-five to go—maybe. Fuses could be tricky. She hoped Tonomori was as fortunate as she had been so far, but she had no time to spare him much thought. She must concentrate totally on the mission. Good *karma* or bad, they were completely committed.

Voices were coming through the corridor. Three of them.

"So the mate wants to visit his girlfriend and we're stuck here."

"Yeah, but at least we got that wine and the food. A feast! And the mate didn't get any of that."

"Piss on 'em all!"

"You piss on 'em. I'm tired of the lash."

They were almost on her, the shadows from their swinging lantern bobbing closer. Toriko lifted the latch of the pilot's cabin and rushed in, pressing herself breathlessly against the door as it slid shut.

The men clumped past.

"You'll have to wait your turn outside," a man snarled from a cot in one corner. A female voice giggled drunkenly. A sailor and his harlot, taking advantage of the pilot's absence, were fornicating in his quarters.

Toriko kept her voice low, in imitation of a man's. "Sorry, mate. Thought you were through."

"I paid for the hour. Get out. Find yourself a woman somewhere else."

They were too drunk for her to waste time by killing them. They would go on coupling and fumbling with the bottle until the ship blew apart around them.

The danger passed; Toriko was out in the corridor again, racing for the powder magazine. She found it unguarded. The lock, well oiled, flew open with a few twists of the lockpick. Including the delay, she had perhaps eight minutes left before the *Perrera* went up. The fuse was burning nicely when Toriko closed the hatch, then jammed the padlock with another file. She headed for the gunport, retrieved her grappling hook, and dove out headfirst, knifing cleanly and soundlessly into the river.

The *Bonaventure* loomed high out of the water, and Toriko's heart sank. The rudder chains were too high to reach. And even with the grappling hook, the quarterdeck and stern jutted some thirty feet above the rippling waters. It meant the carrack had not been fully loaded, else it would have sat several feet lower in the water. Toriko pushed off from the rudder and swam the length of the ship on the river side. No open gunport this time. Nothing. Not even a bowline trailing. She worked back around between the ship and the quay to the spot where she had killed Juan, the sailor. His outstretched arms were waving with the current; the white hands, just below the surface, looked like dead crabs.

Toriko looked up again. Nothing. Wait!—the ship was secured to the quay by taut hawsers, and the bow anchor was lashed to the side beneath the forecastle. The anchor cable drooped invitingly just a yard from the water. Taking a deep breath, Toriko dove and kicked her way back up, shooting from the surface like a fish after a fly. She grabbed the end of the cable, but her hands were wet, the cable slippery with moss; a fingernail peeled back. Toriko, ignoring the pain, pulled herself farther up, and hooked a leg over the cable to keep from falling back. She had lost precious time. Now the eye of the anchor gave her a handhold, and from it she reached the tackle lines of the foresail mast.

No one had noticed her. The men were still reveling. If sailors were on duty, Toriko could not see them. Perhaps they were below decks. She would have to eliminate them if they stumbled into her way. They would die in the explosion anyway, and the resulting fire would obliterate any trace of Toriko's ever having been there.

She padded through the forecastle and down a ladder onto the gundeck. The powder magazine would be below and amidships. It must be her goal, even though the carrack did not carry the full load of the other ships. The hatch cover had not been replaced and the opening gaped like an open tomb. With the grappling hook jammed firmly in the wood, Toriko descended into the darkness.

The magazine door was open and a dim light was shining yellow from inside. Voices argued; again, three men. Toriko edged closer. No retreat now!

"I don't care if the captain did sign them off, goddamit, the pay chests are my responsibility as officer of the watch. If a single gold ducat is missing, it's my cock that goes on the chopping block, along with everything else."

So some of the duke's money was aboard this ship; further good reason to send it to the bottom, Toriko thought. A lucky strike! The voices resumed.

"We're missing the fun."

"Fuck 'em! I'll just check the locks, if you don't mind."

"Suit yourself. No need in being hard-nosed about it. Look for yourself."

"I intend to."

"Martin is just being careful, that's all, aren't you Martin? No offense meant, is there?"

"Piss off, the pair of you."

Toriko heard chains rattling. The pay chests were being opened.

She froze again. Nearby, someone cleared his throat, then he sneezed and loudly wiped his nose on his sleeve. Toriko, counting the seconds, rushed him in the dark. The point of her *wakizashi* bit through his body and dug into the beam he had been leaning against. He died with a gurgle as she withdrew the blade, covering his gaping mouth with her free hand.

"What the hell was that?"

"What was that? It was nothing."

"I heard something."

"So what? The guard caught a chill. He's been sneezing."

"He should stay away from us. We might catch whatever he has."

"Do you both mind? I'm trying to count these coins."

Toriko was through the door, and the nearest officer dead with his throat cut before the other two realized their peril.

The man kneeling in front of the pay chest drew a pistol, but Toriko took off his arm at the shoulder. The last man tried to draw his sword as Toriko stabbed him through the heart. The officer kneeling came out of his shock and began to scream for his arm. The *wakizashi* slashed deeply across his forehead, and he fell without a sound.

Toriko's ears were thudding heavily. She laid out her tools—file, fuse, pry bar.

The goal was so close! And then the duke's flagship erupted in a red thunder of splintering death. Another explosion, and the carrack rocked violently. The fuse in the magazine of the *Santa Barbara* had burned through prematurely. Toriko was thrown into a post, and pain exploded in her temple. Her mind swirled into nothingness.

Tonomori refused to believe his eyes. Could it be a trap? The watch had just changed on the quay, so it was time for him to move, yet they had posted no guards at the warehouse, first of the two that he was to torch. MacDonnell and Müller *had* to be behind him, so their diversionary fire in the salvage yard couldn't have been set yet. He had crept swiftly across open ground to the rear wall of the warehouse, the one closest to the ships but still some two hundred yards from them. As the plans provided by the Hollanders showed, the building had no door here at the sheltered rear, except for one at the second story, and it would be barred from the inside.

As he crouched there, his back to the wall, raucous laughter assailed his ears.

"Izzy! No sad songs, please. Give us a saraband—something to lighten the feet. The ladies here want to dance, to show off their long legs."

Ladies? Tonomori wanted to laugh. The idiots had not only deserted their posts, but they had invited in whores to spice up their feasting. He could not easily envision such foolhardiness, but here it was, blatantly before him. With all the noise, Tonomori speculated, he could shinny up the building in a suit of armor, and they wouldn't notice.

Taking a coil of rope from his shoulder, he twirled the padded grappling hook at its end, and sent the hook flying

383

onto the roof with its gradual slope from front to back. He tested the rope; the grapple had stuck fast above. Sweat had plastered the dark blue doublet to his back. His trousers were baggy and bunched at the knees, but were not so loose as to get in his way by snagging. He wore thin leather shoes but no hose, just as an average Spanish soldier would. Tonomori climbed quickly up, but had unexpected difficulty getting over onto the roof. The wooden shakes, old and rotten, crunched with each movement he made.

Hands were clapping in the distance below him, and a fiery staccato erupted from the gut strings of a gittern.

"*Hola*, Izzy. That's the way!"

Tonomori pulled the rope up beside him. When he pried at the shingles, they came up easily. The thin boards beneath were dry with age and dusty. He levered them up with a pry bar, wincing with each creak. But the dancers were lost to their own delights as the music and cheering enveloped them and lent wings to their feet. A voice came through clearly.

"Bella, when you're done dancing with Sanchez, come on over to my tent. I've got a bone I want to share with you."

Tonomori could imagine Bella showing her teeth in the firelight. "A bone, Hector? From what I've heard, it's a scrawny chicken neck that you wring by hand every day."

With ears undoubtedly burning at the rude laughter, Hector shouted angrily in reply, but Tonomori missed it as he disappeared down the rope into the inky well of the warehouse. The grappling hook held fast in the shingles.

Once on his feet inside, he lighted tinder with a flint and steel and soon had a candle burning. No light was visible from outside except through the hole in the roof. Muffled sounds came through, and Tonomori was able to make out a few words. The salvage yard, he gathered, was starting to burn, so MacDonnell and Müller were now at work. That was good, but it also meant that Tonomori might more easily be seen on the roof when he made his way across to the next building.

The smell suggested the presence of barrels of grease for

axles and tallow for candles. He also remembered Müller's reference to casks of olive oil. Taking into account that the building itself was dry as kindling, it would burn like a beacon in the night with a little help and the combustibles within.

The candle penetrated the gloom only slightly, but Tonomori knew from information turned up by Müller that at least a thousand pounds of gunpowder were stacked somewhere within the building. He found some piles of cordage he could use to start a real blaze, emptied a bottle of lamp oil onto the base of the stack, and touched it with the candle flame. The oil burned with a flare, and the fire immediately started to spread.

When he was sure that the flames had taken hold, Tonomori made his exit quickly, hand over hand, up the rope. Once on the roof again, he could feel the heat building up, pouring through the hole like a natural chimney. He crawled to the roof's edge. He would have an eight-foot jump across to the top of the next warehouse—and, if he slipped, a long drop to the ground, very likely with fatal results. The fall might not kill him, but the soldiers surely would.

With a running start, Tonomori leaped across the abyss. He landed, rolling, in a spray of splinters, and realized that if he didn't halt his momentum he was going to spin off into the void. He drew his *tanto* and plunged it into the wood, hoping that it would brake his gathering speed.

It held—two feet from the edge. No time to lose in blessing his *karma*. The center of the roof was spongy, and the thin supporting timbers groaned under his weight. The wood pried up easily, though, and again Tonomori slid quickly down his rope. In this warehouse, there was no upper story, and he descended nearly fifty feet to the earthen floor, landing amid barrels of sulfur and tar.

Once the candle was lighted, he looked around. No cordage was on hand, but he found many crates, all of wood, and containing muskets. Once the tar and sulfur started to burn, nothing would extinguish their hellish flames.

Having touched the candle to the oil he had splashed,

Tonomori had just stepped back from the suddenly boiling blaze when the *Perrera* exploded.

The voices outside changed from merriment to alarm, and Tonomori heard the sound made by hundreds of hobnailed boots moving in panicky haste.

His own fire was burning with urgency. Tonomori dodged among the barrels and crates for the dangling lifeline. The smoke already was thick, the dancing light intense. He was a perfect target for any soldier who might come barging in at that instant.

A sharp crack echoed overhead, and the escape rope sagged. Tonomori looked above him. The timber holding the grappling hook was giving way to age and dry rot. He kept climbing. Another *pop!* and the rope dropped a few more inches.

The grappling hook tore through the brittle wood with a crash when Tonomori was not yet halfway up, and he plunged backward, twisting toward the crackling glare.

Consciousness returned to Toriko in a flood. Her head ached unmercifully, but she pushed herself unsteadily to her feet. Two decks above her, panic reigned. Hundreds of voices all over the harbor were yelling and bellowing over the thunderclap of secondary explosions and the creak and groan of crashing timbers.

That she hadn't been discovered and killed was a miracle. Now, nothing was left but to finish it all. Toriko dumped the last bottle of incendiary oil over a roll of fuses and kicked it among the stack of brown kegs filled with gunpowder. Then: through the door, jam the lock forever, get out now, any way possible.

In the hatchway, a seaman started at the sight of her, muffled in black, bleeding from the side of her head, eyes piercing like the holes in gun barrels.

"What are you? . . ."

He choked and clawed at the double-bladed *shuriken*, the throwing knife Toriko whipped into his throat. He tumbled past her as she scrambled upward, upward toward a night now incandescent with the heat of a funeral pyre.

The burning foremast of the *Santa Barbara* had pitched

forward onto the stern of the *Bonaventure*. Sailors were trying to free the carrack with axes while others were poling the vessel clear of the fire. No one saw Toriko as she dived over the side. The river was flecked with burning debris, and Toriko looked back with satisfaction. The flagship and the *Santa Barbara* were fully engulfed, and the wind was fanning the flames to an even higher pitch. Seven of the duke's men had died by her hand, and now dozens of others were frying if they hadn't already been blown to bits.

The ships' heavy guns, now heated red-hot, were falling backward, crunching through the blackened decks and the inferno below, to tear out the bottom of the hull. Masts tilted drunkenly, and the rigging was a cobweb of liquid fire.

Beyond the smoke and lambent radiance, the roof of the nearest warehouse erupted with the fury of a blast furnace.

Toriko turned back and put all her remaining strength into increasing the distance between herself and the carrack, where molten worms were squirming in its belly, ready to devour everything.

Then the world shattered: Huge splinters of wood, jagged pieces of metal, and burning rubble were boiling the water. Toriko was struck on the back of her head by a falling timber, but fought to remain afloat. She had been so close, so close! Now her last reserves of strength were draining, her head buzzing with a thousand angry bees. She lost her grip on a chunk of driftwood. The water was pulling her down into a darkness more vast than the night, yet with the tranquility of pure peace.

The surface and dappled firelight were receding. Toriko closed her eyes as if to sleep. . . .

Pain crowded into her mind. She fought it, struggled, and convulsed to get away.

"Got you! Ooooowww! Goddamit, she bit me."

Toriko coughed and retched. And all resistance was gone. She could not even muster the strength to find her dagger and cut her throat. The shame of capture . . .

"Hold still and keep down. We're not out of this mess yet." Dimly, Toriko recognized the voice of MacDonnell.

She was, all at once, safe and alive. Relief began to warm her. MacDonnell pulled Toriko to his chest and clasped her there.

"I saw you come into the water and then go down. We took a chance on coming out with the skiff. After what you've done, I couldn't let you drown. You were . . . magnificent. No one else could destroy three ships like that. No one!"

MacDonnell spoke softly, occasionally sucking on his wounded hand and cheerfully cursing Müller for not rowing faster.

"It would help, my captain, if you got out and pushed," Müller puffed, tugging on the oars.

They beached the skiff at a landmark two miles below the spectacular blaze that was all now remaining of the Duke of Alvino's dream of empire. Müller left the boat to the river current. MacDonnell carried Toriko, who was too weak to stand.

Their horses were snugly tethered inside a thicket of brush, their rendezvous point a hundred yards from the river. Müller's horse whinnied at them in recognition. A spare mount was on hand for Toriko, but MacDonnell lifted her onto his own horse, holding her for support. Müller led the third horse as they started off.

"The bleeding has stopped, and you'll be sore for a couple of days, but you'll live," MacDonnell told Toriko in a gentle voice. "Just grit your teeth. We'll be home soon."

Toriko nodded vaguely. She was dozing off. A pack with a change of clothing for her was on the horse's back, but she was much too weary to think of pulling off the soaking *ninja* garb and dressing more suitably for any encounter with the Spanish. They would just have to chance it.

"What about Tonomori?" Müller asked.

"We can't go back there," MacDonnell said, jerking a thumb at the conflagrations behind them. "And we can't stay here. Tonomori will take care of himself."

*　　　*　　　*

Trapped! Tonomori thought. The fire would be streaming through the hole in the roof before he could try with the grappling hook again. The building was windowless; the door would be securely fastened. An impossible gap of fifty feet between him and escape over the roof.

That a pile of sailcloth had cushioned his fall cheered him not at all. It only meant that he would bake without the added pain of two broken legs.

At least, he had the satisfaction of completing his duty to Diana. The explosions reverberating outside meant that Toriko had completed hers. The rest would be up to Diana in making complete the revenge against the Duke of Alvino.

The heat was driving him back. It would all be over soon enough. His eyes were watering, and he was coughing violently from the smoke. He dropped to the floor, intent on trying to find the door, knowing that reaching it and forcing it open would be hopeless.

But as he crawled, the door burst inward. Four soldiers rushed several feet inside before they halted, appalled.

"Get that powder out before everything blows! Christ!" said the one in command.

The other three were terrified by the fire. "Let's get out of here," one of them yelped.

"Stay at your post. Get the powder first!" the commander snarled.

Tonomori unsheathed the sword slung across his back. He had to get to the entrance and he could not afford to leave any witnesses. The open door brought in a bellows of fresh air, adding impetus to the fire.

The nearest soldier died quickly, without ever knowing what had struck him down. Tonomori killed the second while he was trying to draw his sword.

The third tried to cut his way past Tonomori, to reach the door and flee. A single stroke split his skull, and he sprawled at Tonomori's feet.

The commander lowered his pike. He had range on the sword and the experience to make the most of his advantage. Tonomori would have to get past the point of the pike.

He tried a feint. Another feint. The pikeman stabbed at Tonomori's lower belly, but the *tachi* brushed it away harmlessly and Tonomori stepped inside, pressing the commander, who backed away toward the blaze.

Intent on the driving blade and his own frantic need to break clear in order to bring his weapon into play, the pikeman tripped, fell backward, and instantly was engulfed by flames. His shrieks rose with the smoke. The roof was caving in. Tonomori stumbled to his knees. The smoke was confusing him. *Where is the door?*

"What is happening here? Get out! Now!" A voice dead ahead.

Tonomori answered it. "The roof went. Where are you? I can't see." Tonomori wiped blood from one soldier's body onto his face and clapped on a helmet, a large morion with jaw flaps.

"Over here! Quickly!"

Tonomori crawled toward the voice. He was painfully at the doorway and into fresh air.

"Good God, man, your face!"

Tonomori looked up through the blood, unrecognizable. "I'm better off than the four men cooking in there," he muttered, and staggered away from the warehouse, calling back, "Warn everybody to get away! The powder is going to blow. You can't stop it." It was necessary that the dead soldiers' wounds not be discovered before the fire made them unrecognizable.

His benefactor ran to spread the alarm. Tonomori continued to play the part of a dazed man. No one even bothered to notice. Too many others were staggering just as he was.

The darkness soon swallowed him up completely. From within the glaring circle of light, no one could possibly see more than a few feet into the gloom.

Tonomori turned away from the dazzle to regain his night vision, then circled back to find his horse in the copse where he had tethered it.

It was gone. Probably shied away at the first explosion, he thought. *Son of a bitch!*

He had no intention of trying to find MacDonnell and Müller in the dark. Or Toriko. That wasn't in the plan. He couldn't help them now and could only hope that all had successfully made their escape. They were to rendezvous at the town house. By starting now, he knew, he could be there in an hour. If he ran.

Tonomori began to run to the northeast. Directly north, five miles away, Diana would be lifting a glass with her unsuspecting host.

They could do no more for her tonight. Like them, Diana was now completely on her own.

Chapter Twenty-seven

The honor guard executed a smart salute, pivoted sharply, and marched away in cadence. Two rows of heavy cavalry stretched across the parade ground, their armor burnished to a pale silver. Helmet plumes and the hammercloths beneath the black saddles were cardinal edged with gold, the ducal colors. On command, they dipped their lances in honor of the Countess Diana de Edgemont, to whom great favor was being shown this night.

Not all this pageantry was in Diana's honor. It was a demonstration of the might of Spain, a reminder of the precision with which she tamed nations and brought others to heel in fear.

The lances rose back into parade-rest position. Diana's chin went up. Her light hair was reddened by the glare of the scores of torches, but her face was pale. She felt very small in the center of what seemed to be at least twenty acres of exquisite landscaping. Her chin went up higher: She was a countess, by the grace of God, with a proud lineage from a great people. For further reassurance, she patted a slight bulge in her full left sleeve.

Now came a rumble of drums and a heraldic fanfare of trumpets. The Duke of Alvino rode onto the grounds, resplendent in his favorite black velvet and silver. He raised his extended sword in salute to the horsemen. As he approached Diana, Alvino slowed his mount to a prancing walk. The black stallion was a war-horse and temperamental, but Alvino kept him under control with spur and a reminder from the thin whip that trailed from his wrist. Even Diana was impressed with his mastery of the animal.

The duke raised his velvet cap, and at his command the horse knelt on its forelegs before her. Alvino dismounted, and Diana clapped politely.

Three liveried grooms at once sprang to the horse's head as it pawed the ground and whinnied its annoyance. Alvino did not bother to turn around; his men were expected to know how to deal with such a horse.

"You are even more lovely than at our last encounter," Alvino purred, bending over Diana's gloved hand. The emerald caught his experienced eye as he kissed her fingertips. It would buy several cannon or a mountain of powder.

"You are a kind host," she murmured.

"Please," the duke laughed. "Don't call me that. We are to be more to each other than that."

"Yes, I suppose I had better get used to it."

"It will be easy for you. Come," Alvino said smoothly, mentally evaluating the rest of her attire. The tiara alone would pay for two companies of *landsknechts* for a month. "I have gone to great pains to make your evening here an enjoyable one."

"If not memorable?" Diana teased.

"Of course. I realize that the martial air might be a trifle stifling, but this is a military establishment, not an assembly of dancing masters."

"We are all in your protection, Your Grace." Diana stopped and giggled. "Oh, look!" A harassed servant had been running around behind the cavalry horses with a shovel and a burlap sack. Now he climbed the stairs to the

392

east wall, and, in full view, leaned through an embrasure and emptied the sack's malodorous contents.

The duke's jaw tightened, and he snapped his fingers. A young aide appeared at his side. "See to the jackass on the wall," he ordered.

"Yes, Your Grace."

Diana touched Alvino's hand, at once cloying and entreating. "Please, Duke, for my sake. I was not offended, and I am certain the man would have meant no slight."

Alvino frowned and snapped his fingers once more. The aide stopped in his tracks and turned. "Let him off with a warning," the duke countermanded.

He was again affability personified. "See how eager I am to please you, Countess?"

Diana was not impressed this time. She had heard graphic tales of Alvino's cruelty. Had she not intervened, the servant surely would have been whipped or, worse, sewn up in the offending sack and thrown over the wall to his death. Thank God she did not really have to marry this man. Her bleak future would consist of interceding with a pitiless master on behalf of her servants, who probably would be scourged anyway. Alvino had his best face on tonight, but the fangs even now were jutting through.

He extended his arm. "Allow me to personally escort you to my headquarters. There we will contrive to make you comfortable for the occasion."

"I am honored, Duke." Resting her hand on his forearm, she was repelled by the touch but made certain that her face did not show it. His quarters were in the heart of the fortress. It was whitewashed stucco, with arched colonnades along the bottom floor and cast-iron fretwork around the balconies above. A walkway on the roof, decorated with blue tiles carried all the way from Toledo, was the only place in the fortress where it was possible to see over the walls. It had been added for strategic purposes, to direct defenses against besieging troops. But commanders traditionally found it a pleasant place to relax. Flowers flourished there in wooden boxes, and fish swam in a shallow pool. In times of extreme heat, a canopy was erected to provide shade.

Only a small portion of the building was used by the military commanders for daily operations. The rest comprised the duke's personal apartments.

This night, the residence was ablaze with light. Thousands of candles burned everywhere, in wall sconces, on tables, in chandeliers, in floor-length candelabra. At every doorway, servants bowed and scraped, as if minutely inspecting the polish on their boots.

Diana smiled at the lavish display, but thought to herself that the place seemed shabby and disorganized. Each preceding governor-general had left his mark—a black marble fireplace brought from Italy, French walnut panels carved with grape clusters and leaves, marquetry floors. One entire hallway was of carved Spanish leather, dyed red and gilded, that portrayed a field of lilies. Well, at least she wouldn't have to live there.

Diana made an effort to cover her nervousness with charm and gaiety. She had walked into this lion's den of her own choosing. *Be calm, and think of the task at hand,* she told herself. While the lion in his den is busy eating out of your hand, his enemies are destroying his pride beyond the gates.

"How splendid, Duke. I did not know that generals live in houses like this. I thought you all huddled in tents or some such," Diana gushed. She was trying to make small talk successfully. Her thoughts were on the several options she had given herself as to when she would strike.

Alvino smiled at her naiveté. Such a child in so many ways; he anticipated a vicious pleasure in schooling her to the realities of life. With her look of a lovely statue but seemingly as cold as one, she probably was still a virgin, he guessed. He did not care if she wasn't. But if she was, he would find a certain added spice in their wedding night. A set of erotic etchings he had procured while serving in France would serve as an inspiration for the little mare when he put her through her paces.

"Not so, Countess. I insist on some of the finer things. A stout roof is one of them. Good cooking is another. I think you will be pleased. Come!" Alvino waved his arm toward the stairs leading to the balconies and the rooms beyond where the other guests awaited.

Alvino stopped midway up the steps. "Before we go in, I want to be sure of one thing."

"And that is?"

"Once through that door, there will be no turning back," the duke said. A group of musicians was beginning to play a galliard.

"It is not for me to turn back," Diana said, looking back at him directly without fear. "Do I have your assurance that the killing will stop?"

"It has stopped, Countess. The bloodshed was unpleasant but necessary."

Diana stood firm. "You have not answered my question, Duke. Do I have your word that there will be no more raids?"

"I think the Protestants have had enough lessons for now. They are well chastened. So, unless my country goes to war again, the answer is—yes," the duke said, suppressing a wave of irritation. She was in no position to make demands.

"Very well. I will do my part," Diana said.

They entered the hall together, a magnificent pair, facing some thirty guests of rank and power, each as proud as a peacock, and some dressed even more gaudily. The music stopped, and the guests bowed in deference to the ducal rank and in honor of the event.

"Play on," Alvino ordered. The musicians struck up where they had left off, with horns and violas. During the meal itself, lute, recorder, and flute would be played in gentle song to aid digestion.

For now, the note was festive. Alvino made the formal introductions. Diana had already met or knew of most of the guests, except for a few officers invited because of military protocol.

"Countess Diana, may I present the Bishop of Utrecht? . . ." Diana bobbed with a courtesy she did not feel. The bishop's diocese included Antwerp. The income from his benefices was enormous and he spent half of it yearly on jewels and art, though it was said the most brilliant of his prizes was his mistress. He kept her, the incomparable Claire Moreau, in a rich setting of a mansion along the Velvet Canal.

The old satyr's face was heavy and blotchy. His experienced eyes strayed from Diana's emeralds to her breasts. He seemed to be pondering which he admired more.

"I am enchanted, Countess," he said with feeling.

Diana swept along through the glitter. Soft candlelight winked from ten thousand facets, the bright surfaces of Venetian glass, silver plates delicately edged with orange and red enamel, hammered silver candlesticks, and gold saltcellars in the shape of reptiles and birds. No opportunity in such a setting for her to make her move. It must come later.

"May I present to you Doña Beloti? . . ."

Diana checked her temper. The nerve of Alvino! Doña Beloti, smiling back so archly at her, was the duke's most recent plaything. The affair had been broken without animosity. In his present circumstances, Alvino found her habits too expensive, and had passed her on to the bishop, who had popped her into his collection.

"Ambassador Maldonado and Lady Maldonado, the Countess Diana . . ."

She had met them before, on her arrival from Japan and at her festivities at the de Edgemont estate. The ambassador was a genuinely friendly man, and Diana was glad to see him. Maldonado was also a rarity, a Spanish ambassador who loathed politics. In a variety of assignments, many an unruly faction had been soothed by his superb hospitality and congeniality. Dissidents never obtained any real satisfaction from him, but they generally were so charmed that they forgot their complaints or didn't realize that conditions hadn't really improved.

"I wish you much happiness, Countess," Maldonado boomed heartily. He disliked the Duke of Alvino and his arrogant methods. In a highly secret letter to the king, he had recently suggested that the governor-general be removed from command and sent to a less volatile post, in order to forestall a revolt in the provinces.

"Countess Diana, may I present my second-in-command, Señor Nunez? . . ."

Diana looked into the dark, steady eyes, and remembered that he was called Snakeface. Behind his back. MacDonnell had cautioned her, "That one is an adder, totally ruthless, and strikes without warning. He'd steal the pennies off a dead man's eyes—after killing him. I wonder that Alvino trusts him."

"Your servant, ma'am," Nunez said. His attempt at obsequious friendliness was an effigy, ending in a smirk.

It seemed to Diana that the introductions and greetings would never end. She could feel a headache coming on. The room grew warmer, and menacingly enclosing. At last, the majordomo announced the serving of dinner. The duke gave Diana his arm to lead the procession to the dining hall.

The tables, covered with fine dusty-pink damask, were set up in a long T. The duke escorted Diana to the place of honor, on his right at the head table. Servants in conspicuously new uniforms stood behind each chair to ensure prompt attention to every whim. Would this be the spot where the duke would die?

Diana, looking down while the bishop pronounced the invocation, glanced along the table. All places but two were set with silver plates; she and the duke would sup from golden ones. The sight further diminished her appetite. In such large establishments where kitchens were maintained outside the dwelling—because of the danger of fire—food could be expected to arrive at a banquet table congealed and cold. Chafing dishes such as those she had noted on side tables could help; even so, the best that Diana had hoped for was an unappetizingly lukewarm meal. The massive gold plate would promptly absorb any remaining shred of warmth.

The duke himself seated Diana in a chair of carved black oak that must have been designed to cause supreme discomfort. The bishop wedged his bulk into a chair to Diana's right. It threatened to be the longest evening of her life. *How were Toriko and Tonomori faring? Would they succeed? Would they live?*

397

Food began to arrive in a never-ending stream. First came the fresh fruits—berries, peaches, melons. Slices of pork, fish, beef, and venison were laid on large platters in symmetrical patterns. Whole roasted piglets, kids, lambs, and large fish were carried around the room with ceremonial pomp before being deposited on the carving tables.

Diana picked at the morsels lying leaden on her plate, while the bishop, a noted trencherman, elbowed her steadily. At least, she thought, his elbows were easier to contend with than his hands would have been. He was so intent on his successive massive helpings that he paused only to briefly dip his greasy and gravy-spattered hands in rose water before digging into the next course. Forks were not in general use, and the bishop, like most others, ate with his hands and a knife, and licked the scraps from his fingers noisily.

It was the plate itself that interested Diana most. It was of German make, with a hunting scene carved around the wide rim, a doe at bay, surrounded by dogs. *How appropriate*, she thought, wondering where the duke had pillaged it.

"You are hardly eating, Countess," Alvino observed as his hand moved to cover hers, then dropped to her thigh.

"I am hardly hungry, Your Grace. The heat . . . Fatigue . . ." In turning to speak to him, she moved in her chair sufficiently to remove his warm palm from her lap. She let her words trail off, and gave him her best wan look, with a slight plea for compassion thrown in. The irony in her looking to the duke for any degree of mercy did not escape her.

"Of course. I understand completely." *Let her squirm some more. The best is yet to come.* But he did not replace his hand.

The duke was deliberately ignoring her otherwise. Instead, he chatted with Lady Maldonado at his left. The wife of the ambassador was acting as his hostess because as yet Alvino had no wife.

When Diana leaned forward once to survey the head table, she thought that Lady Maldonado gave the appearance of wishing herself at some more congenial gathering, such as, perhaps, supervising the construction of a cesspit. A woman who shared her husband's likes and dislikes, she pitied Diana.

Alvino flirted occasionally with his former mistress, sitting two places away at the lower table, and she winked back. The event was going to his satisfaction.

Across from Doña Beloti sat Nunez, impassive, polished, and repulsive. In giving him her attention so obviously, Doña Beloti was wasting her time. Even if he were a jealous man, Alvino would not have worried about Beloti; Nunez had eyes only for the duke's youngest page. The duke considered this tidbit as a potentially useful lever, for use someday in pressuring his major. Despite his satisfaction, however, Alvino could feel himself becoming irritable. The drug he had been taking these recent months was requiring stronger and more frequent doses. Wishing he had a small glass of it now, the duke weighed the risk involved. He did not want to dangerously dull his senses, but neither did he desire to have his guests see his hands shaking like those of a palsied old man, as they soon might be.

Alvino lifted a finger for his house physician, Doctor Delacruz, standing by in a blue velvet doublet, somberly surveying the diners. His violent purgatives and extensive bleedings had finished off more patients than a pie full of green meat, yet Delacruz was generally held in high esteem. The *maxima medica* of the day was, "The stronger the medicine, the more effective the cure." Patients who survived his treatments tended to speak well of him, but they guarded their health better than they ever had before.

Delacruz leaned over as the duke whispered in his ear. He was back shortly with a small cordial glass of wine. Alvino drained it with a swallow and returned the glass to the physician. He felt relaxed and confident almost immediately.

Now castles made of marchpane were paraded about the room, just before a pie baked in the shape of the upright Hapsburg eagles was sliced open. Out flew a flock of white turtledoves.

Nuts, sweetmeats, preserves, wafers, and more fresh fruit arrived to tantalize tired palates.

It was time! He gestured to the majordomo.

Ring bearers stepped forward and kneeled beside him with gold cushions. The majordomo pounded his staff of office for attention.

"Pray silence," he bellowed.

"Most noble lords and ladies," the duke began after arising. "On this occasion, I call upon you happily to act as witnesses to the betrothal of my house to the ancient lineage of the de Edgemonts."

As if to verify the church's approval of the betrothal ritual, the bishop took his place beside Alvino, jostling Diana as she tried to stand up.

Radiant despite the wan appearance that she feared the tension was creating in her features, she barely reached to the duke's shoulder. From one of the gold cushions she lifted a velvet case, took out a yellow gold ring shaped in entwined hands, and put it onto a slim finger of Alvino's outstretched hand. The touch made her skin crawl.

"I, Diana, Countess de Edgemont, hereby pledge . . ." she began.

From the other cushion, Alvino took a second ring, also worked into the shape of entwined hands, but made of white gold. The white symbolized silver, the traditional lesser metal worn by brides; the woman was the lesser vessel in matrimony, after all. Over the centuries, however, so many brides had complained of the silver that tradition finally had been modified. Gold they wanted, and gold they got, though still with the subtle reminder of inferiority.

"I, Enrique, Duke of Alvino, also pledge my honor . . ."

A tight band seemed to constrict Diana's heart, as cold and hard as the circle of metal now placed on her ring finger.

The bishop wheezed the church's blessing, made the sign of the cross, and beamed expansively at the couple, to convey his personal sanction. Diana sensed that beneath the smile was a leer. Insisting to herself that she would not let it affect her, she slipped demurely into her chair, to sit half-turned away from the bishop's.

But Alvino was not through. He remained standing, and again turned to Diana. "Now that we have exchanged promises, it will give me great pleasure to be able to lift the burdens that have been weighing heavily on your shoulders these past months," he said with a show of solicitude. "But first, I wish to present you, my affianced, with yet another ring as a token of my love and my esteem."

A ring bearer once more extended a cushion. Alvino opened a velvet case, extracting an impressively large and striking ring. The entire assemblage *ooh*ed and *aah*ed at the dramatic play of candlelight on three massive pigeon's blood rubies set in carved gold flowers. Doña Beloti frowned; the ring was twice as large as the one the duke had given her as a consolation present when he told her that she was being displaced.

"I am deeply touched," Diana said, accepting the ring with a slight bow. As she slipped it on a finger of her right hand, she noticed that one stone was flawed and the other two cleverly cut to disguise impurities. A shabby bit of trumpery. And no doubt he would expect to take it back soon on the pretext of having it fitted to her finger—and then sell it.

"And further, to free you from the cares of mundane affairs, I have taken it upon myself to select a suitable duenna, a guardian who will be guided in all things by myself until we are united in marriage. Until that time, I count the days," Alvino said, barely concealing the sardonic note in his voice.

"A duenna, Your Grace?" Diana's anger was rising. She could not choke down the question with all its obvious irritation. The public display of a private dialogue seemed shockingly out of place.

"Yes. You met this evening. The Lady Suzanne."

Lady Suzanne Candillo, elegant beauty with an oval face, a piled mane of chestnut locks, cultured, fluent in five languages, with the morals and scrapping ability of an alley cat. In short, an intriguer and known instrument of the Duke of Alvino. The guests were mutely shocked at such an open insult. The silence was palpable.

Her temper immediately at the boiling point, Diana kept the lid on if only to avoid giving satisfaction to Doña Beloti, who was scrutinizing her with amused interest, and Nunez, who was openly enjoying what he assumed would be her discomfort.

Diana could read nothing in Lady Suzanne's patrician features. *She is cleverer than she looks*, Diana thought. *She sees no need to make an enemy of someone whose charge will be her responsibility. I had better watch my step here.*

"You see, my dear, I try to think of everything," Alvino continued. "Lady Suzanne speaks many languages. Since you also are somewhat of a scholar of languages, Countess, you both should get along well."

An ominous peal of what sounded like ragged thunder interrupted the duke and startled the gathering.

"It had not looked like rain when we left. And me without my cloak," Lady Maldonado murmured in dismay. She was also thinking of the ride home in their uncomfortable coach. The slightest rain would churn the roads into a quagmire.

"You may have mine; I don't mind a little dampness," the ambassador assured his wife, stroking her hand. To Alvino, he added, "Please excuse the interruption, Your Grace. We are grateful to be safe and dry under your roof."

"Thank you, Your Excellency." Alvino turned back to Diana. "Perhaps you would like to say a few words now to our guests."

Diana's heart was beating like a trip-hammer. *Was it indeed a storm, or had Toriko actually wreaked destruction upon the duke's ships?*

"I . . . I am speechless," Diana stammered. To the guests, she said, apologetic for her awkwardness, "Thank you all for your sincere wishes and for your company on this night. I shall never forget it."

The guests applauded politely. But their heads turned and they looked at each other at the violent clap of another thunderbolt.

Diana's chin was lifting up, hope growing stronger with

every heartbeat. The duke's hour was nearing. Further delay would be impossible.

Lady Suzanne, seated two places down from Doña Beloti, leaned forward to speak to Diana. "I understand that you speak Japanese. I would consider it an honor if you would teach it to me." Her voice was husky and thick, her address smooth as a butterfly's wing. "I have traveled extensively, though nothing compared to your voyages, and I find that one never knows when another language will prove useful."

"Yes, don't I know it," Doña Beloti interrupted with a coquettishness that annoyed Diana. "I have found that an ability with *tongues* is a passport to almost anywhere."

Red faces disappeared behind the ladies' fluttering fans, and several gentlemen coughed abruptly in embarrassment.

Because the duke had made no gesture to stop her, Doña Beloti was not to be put off. "The Japanese lord and lady in your household have been very diverting. They have such odd names. Tomo-something? . . ."

"Tonomori-sama," Diana corrected, adding the personal ending. She felt better to be able to speak publicly of him.

"How *beautifully* she says it," Doña Beloti remarked at large. "*Such* a wonderful name. Tell me, Countess, what would be *my* name in Japanese, hmmm?"

A guard had entered the room, unnoticed by most of the guests. Diana saw the duke's mouth drop open slightly as the guard whispered in his ear. Diana turned back to Doña Beloti buoyed by a sense of triumph.

"With the greatest pleasure, Doña Beloti. *'Anata wa shiri-ana no kao desu,'* " she said with a tinge of venom, repeating one of Tonomori's ruder insults: *anus face*.

Alvino's face was troubled and drawn. "Excuse me," he said in an undertone, and strode from the room quickly.

Lady Maldonado spoke up when he had gone. "I think he mentioned something about a fire."

"Fire?" One of the lords took up the cry. It was a great fear. Once started, fires could quickly get out of control and blacken half a city before burning themselves out. And this one might be on their very doorstep tonight, for all

403

they knew. Two men excused themselves and followed in the duke's wake. Other chairs were scraping back.

Diana fought for self-control. She wanted to leap up, to join the burgeoning exodus. The time was narrowing when she would be able to take the action for which she had come. She must review her plans.

Doña Beloti looked around, then back to Diana. "And pray, what does that mean, Countess?"

"It means 'woman with the face of a russet flower,' " Diana said with mock sweetness, "but that's only a rough translation."

Of the servant behind her, Diana asked, "Where are the men going?"

"To the roof garden, Your Ladyship, in order to see where the fire is."

Half the men had left, and could be heard rapidly ascending to the roof.

Amid the confusion, Diana still was able to note that Lady Suzanne was watching with amusement her exchange with Doña Beloti. Doubtless assuming that the countess had said something rude and well deserved, Suzanne would be speculating on how her chaperoning assignment could be made to prove useful to her.

A servant slid Diana's chair back. She stood and bowed to those who remained on hand. "When in Rome . . ." she remarked to no one, and went to find those already watching the blaze. Once on the stairs, she crossed her fingers, then lifted her skirt so she could take the steps two at a time. *Now!*

Diana had to jostle and push her way past a score of sturdy male bodies in order to get a view of the waterfront and the vivid destruction there.

The entire south anchorage of the Scheldt was a sheet of fire crowned with pinpoints that resembled shooting stars. Light-filled explosions blinked, but on the rooftop they could not hear the accompanying crackle for several seconds. More flames gouted out in fiery arcs.

"Jesus; I am thankful that was not in the main harbor! It would be ruin," a man remarked in a subdued voice.

"Yes. I wonder what could have happened." At the five-mile distance, discerning details was difficult.

"I heard that a detachment was sent out to determine what caused it."

Diana drew back from the edge, disappearing among the throng. She saw now exactly how to strike; she would need to come to grips directly with the duke. She saw his face in profile, his features shining redly, sunk deeply within his own thoughts.

Alvino had immediately identified the location and identity of the explosions' victims. His eyes narrowed as the holocaust witch consumed the instruments of his ambition. He had lied, he had cheated, he had murdered—only to come to this place at this moment in time, rooted like a heretic chained to the stake with the flames of destruction licking at his feet. He had shown no mercy, and he could expect none.

So many days he had walked proud in the sun, the mere shadow of his banner striking fear into his foes. He had shaken the Earth, but his enemies had toppled him all the same. It was like a waking nightmare. Who had done this thing, had gotten past his guard, had blinded him to the peril that ultimately had engulfed him? The duke had nowhere to go. His enemies would only turn him over to the king's men.

So be it. I can walk to the scaffold, or I can drink the cup of hemlock, Alvino thought, *but before I do either, the one who did this will taste the bitter pain of death before me.*

Who?

As if sensing Diana's darkling gaze, Alvino turned slowly and met her eyes. His lips drew back in a chilling smile. Diana darted for the stairs as if to flee; she had to let him seize her. Alvino was there before her. He grabbed her arm in strong fingers. She tried to pull away.

"Not so fast," he commanded. "I need to have a few words—and to get answers."

"Let me go," Diana replied lowly.

"Not yet. The drama is not complete. It occurs to me that I have been underestimating your talents."

"I don't know what you are talking about," Diana said, still appearing to struggle against his strength. The moment had arrived.

"But I think you do, and you are going to tell me all about it . . . *ahhh!*"

Diana had seemed to pluck at his wrist, meantime pressing the catch of a large gold signet ring on the forefinger of her right hand. A thin, short blade popped up and locked into place, its polished gleam dulled with a smear of the most virulent poison. She aimed for where the muscles swelled below the elbow, and delivered a stinging punch. Her action seemed almost inadvertent in her fleeting contact with the duke. He fell back, clutching his right forearm where a droplet of blood glistened, black on black.

The triangular blade folded back within the ring as Diana pressed the catch, her breasts heaving. She spun away and plunged down the stairs as Doña Beloti and Lady Suzanne were rustling upward. Lady Suzanne gave her an inquiring look, but Diana hardly noticed. She couldn't remain with the duke, but she must not try to leave, either.

A moment later, Alvino brushed past both women brusquely. He found Diana in the banquet room, otherwise abandoned now except for the bewildered servants, who fell back apprehensively. The countess had a small smile on her face.

"Get out! All of you get out," he screamed.

"Certainly. Nothing would give me greater pleasure," Diana said as the servants scurried to obey.

"Not you! Not yet," he commanded, approaching her.

"Me, Your Grace? Why, whatever could be wrong?"

"Don't act the innocent with me," Alvino shouted savagely. With his left hand, which bore her ring, he was clutching his wounded arm. "I have clever people in my pay. You escaped them all. Your Japanese lord killed my second-in-command—I think at your instigation."

"You must be jesting."

"Oh, very serious, Countess, as you will see," Alvino continued. Spittle was forming at his lips. His arm hurt, his limbs were tingling, and the bitch was still standing in front of him, mocking him.

"I am leaving, Duke. I am breaking the betrothal."

Alvino made a lunge for her. Diana darted around the table, pulling the tablecloth with her. Glass and pottery shattered on the floor, and Alvino slipped on the shards.

"You are leaving for an appointment with my rackmaster," he called after her. "We will talk about the matter of the intruder here a few nights ago, which I think now you can shed some light on." He felt increasingly strange, weak, and leaned against the back of his massive chair. Breathing was becoming difficult.

The countess stopped and turned to watch him, but Alvino was finding difficulty in focusing his eyes.

Sure now of her victory and of the potency of the poison smeared on the blade, Diana gave voice to her malice.

"Yes! I am better served than you. Your people failed where mine succeeded. Those Jappos, as you so laughingly call them, have destroyed your dreams. Lord Tonomori has burned the guns in your warehouses, and Lady Toriko has sunk your ships."

They had succeeded—but were they safe, too?

"Goddam you!" Alvino exclaimed hoarsely. He fumbled at his side for a dagger, brought it out in front of him. Diana raised her skirt and nimbly kicked it away. The blade clattered into a corner, out of reach. Alvino was sinking to the floor.

"Maybe so, but you'll burn in hell before me," Diana said through clenched teeth.

Alvino had difficulty keeping his head up.

"The new Cesare Borgia. I know about that, too. How odd that you die poisoned by one of your intended victims," Diana told him triumphantly.

"P-p-poison? Y-y-you can't . . ."

"I have! The wound in your arm. And there is no antidote. You have no hope. Die, knowing that it is my doing. You and the Borgias have much in common. You'll be talking to them soon," Diana said in no more than a whisper.

The duke opened his eyes again, but Diana was gone. Hardly any feeling was left in his limbs except creeping cold. He was so cold!

Outside the banquet room, Diana sought out the duke's physician, Doctor Delacruz.

"Quickly!" she urged. "The duke has suffered some kind of attack."

"My God." Delacruz rushed to Alvino's side. The duke was stretched out behind the head table, the scene only minutes before of what had seemed his proudest hour.

Alvino tried to scream. *Father has come for me at last, his rotting fingers prying at the waxed winding-sheet that enfolds his corpse.*

The duke's vision cleared enough for him to see Doctor Delacruz, and he felt a stirring of hope.

"Diana . . . she . . ." Alvino's tongue refused to work further.

"She is at your side, Your Grace," Delacruz assured him soothingly. The most important thing was to keep the patient calm. "Everything that can be done will be done."

The physician looked around him in sudden panic. "My instrument case! He must be bled at once. A fever of the brain. Send the servants for it quickly."

"There is no time. Here, use this," Diana offered, drawing her dagger. "It is very sharp."

Delacruz tested the keen edge with his thumb, taking care, Diana saw with relief, not to cut himself. The blade was smeared with the same poison as her ring. "This will do," the physician nodded.

With mounting horror, the duke saw the knife jabbing toward his arm, but he was powerless to speak. Diana wondered if he knew—hoped he knew—that the blade was poisoned. It was her one trump if the ring had failed. Eternal night was enfolding him, and the duke's last vision was that of the Countess de Edgemont, holding his nerveless hand and soothing his brow while Delacruz cut into him further with the assassin's knife.

The duke died an hour later without regaining consciousness.

Doctor Delacruz made the announcement in sepulchral tones. "Despite all our efforts, His Grace, the Duke of Alvino, governor-general of His Majesty's provinces, died after suffering an attack of apoplexy. Spain has lost a great champion and defender of the faith.''

The physician then hastily absolved himself from all blame. ''God's will is done.''

Diana, sobbing in relief, was given comfort by Ambassador Maldonado and his wife.

''There, there, child. Have a good cry. We will take you home. You will feel better when you are home,'' Lady Maldonado said. ''Here, look at me!'' Diana's eyes were streaming. Her tears were for her father, her brother, the hundreds of people martyred by one man's bloody ambition.

''That's better. Listen to me,'' Lady Maldonado said kindly but insistently. ''You are young; you are pretty. You have your freedom yet, no small thing, believe me; and I am more fortunate than most, with the husband I got, a man who does not beat me, nor scold me, nor expect me to perform miracles and cater to his every whim. You will have your happiness.''

''Do you think so?'' Diana asked, continuing to play her part as a grieving woman. She blew her nose in a linen handkerchief and whispered to Lady Maldonado. ''You know, I didn't really want to be a duchess. It's just . . . just that I didn't have any choice and . . . the duke was *so* handsome. . . . ''

''I know, I know,'' Lady Maldonado said, thinking, *How fortunate she is to be rid of the son of a bitch!* With the duke's reputation for cruelty, it would have been such a pity to see this little flower trampled. She wondered where her own husband could be. Just like him to be gone when she needed him the most. *Men!*

With the duke dead, the ambassador found the fortress plunged into uncharacteristic chaos. All he wanted was an honor guard, but he could find no one to order it out.

Finally, he turned to a harassed-looking officer. ''Señor, a moment please.''

''Excellency!'' The officer snapped to attention.

''I need an honor guard for my coach. The guards can also escort the Countess de Edgemont to her home.''

''That, at least, can be arranged.''

"Señor? . . ."

"Pidal, sir."

"Señor Pidal, what in God's name is going on?"

"Sir?"

"Don't 'sir' me! This command is a shambles. Why are the officers not doing their jobs?"

"Most of them have left, sir," Pidal told him.

"What about Major Nunez?"

"He left first, sir, shortly after the duke died. Riding like the hounds of hell were after him."

"I suppose that when a dog dies, the fleas leap to another cur," Maldonado mumbled.

"Sir?"

"It doesn't matter. However, I am concerned about the lack of order."

"We all are, sir."

"Well, I have certain powers in time of great emergency, and I am assuming them now." Maldonado stroked his beard. "Order the call for assembly at once and have all officers report to me in front of the command building in five minutes. After you have done that, send my regrets to my wife, and escort her home, along with the countess."

"What about the other lords, Excellency?"

"They're on their own."

"Yes, sir."

"And I want a complete report on that fire. Within an hour."

Pidal remained stationary, not knowing whether to salute a civilian. "Yes, sir."

"Well, don't just stand there, goddamit, get moving!"

Pidal departed, on the double.

For a while, it seemed to Diana that she would never be able to leave, and the strain began to tell on her. The same guests who had come to congratulate her also felt they had to pay their condolences, one by one. Even Doña Beloti seemed genuinely saddened, if only for herself and for whatever largesse she could have pried out of the duke had he lived.

Diana had been considered a trifle overwrought when

410

she had insisted on being taken to Doctor Delacruz to retrieve the little dagger he had absentmindedly pocketed. With the blade safely back in its scabbard, Diana could rest more easily. She wanted no other deaths that could not be readily explained. But her mind was miles away for much of the time, trying to focus sanely on the fate of her loyal companions.

Finally, when Diana was close to exhaustion, the ambassador himself, his round face showing concern, led her to his own coach.

"I will take care of everything here," he promised with assurance.

The carriage ride was jarring. They apparently were being driven by a man who knew every rock and pothole in the road and positioned the gilded vehicle's red wheels squarely over each one. And Lady Maldonado, though a kindhearted woman, never stopped talking. "When you have had time to recover from your loss, my dear, I would like to pay you a long visit."

Diana smiled weakly at the gesture and barely refrained from rolling her eyes toward heaven in supplication. The carriage wheels were grinding along on cobblestones, now. Familiar streets were sliding past. Diana counted three short bridges. One more and she was home—if the town house on the Velvet Canal could be called home, but it would be enough on such a night as this.

The officer in charge of the mounted detail guarding the coach assisted Diana to the street personally. Lady Maldonado poked her anxious face from the curtained window, determined to get one last word of advice in.

"Do you think it might be wise if you called for a physician? A sleeping potion, perhaps?"

"No, no; but thank you for your concern, Lady Maldonado," Diana said, all thin smiles. "I think that for now, under the circumstances, I should be alone." *Alone with hopes for her friends!*

Diana also thanked the officer and his men for their assistance.

"Lieutenant Moraga, at your service," the officer said, bowing. He hesitated. "May I say from myself and my men that we grieve with you at your loss. It is a hard blow for all of us and for Spain.''

Diana saw sympathy written across the rough faces of the men. Their existence was tough, with few comforts, but they had feelings, too. To come so close to becoming a peer of the highest rank, as she had, with riches beyond their wildest dreams—and then to lose it all to cruel fate was an irony that stirred them deeply. She realized that she herself was totally unmoved, not only by Alvino's death but by her part in it.

A whip's crack started the coach forward. The honor guard jangled and clattered into the darkness. Before she approached the house, Diana tossed the duke's rings deep into a thorn hedge.

Her servants were waiting on the steps. With foreboding and anxiety, she allowed Frans to lead her inside. That her plans had succeeded, she already knew. But at what price? Since the hour of the duke's death, her thoughts had been mainly for Tonomori and Toriko and for the other two men, Sir Ian and the horsemaster, Müller, whom she had come to like and respect. Had this night's work cost any of them their life's blood?

Frans looked haggard, fatigued with overwork. Diana knew that she was going to need separate staffs for the town house and the country mansion. Frans could simply not oversee the necessary work at both; Diana jotted this down mentally on a long list of things still to be accomplished.

The steward turned to her hesitantly. ''Ah, the Scottish knight and the Lady Toriko were out riding earlier this evening, and their horses stumbled. They were both slightly hurt with only a few scratches. You needn't worry. They decided to stay up and await your return.'' Frans did not add that if Lady Toriko had been his daughter he would not have let her out galloping all over the countryside with a rogue like Sir Ian MacDonnell.

Diana found them in the study, sitting comfortably together. Toriko was writing a poem with fine brush strokes on a piece of paper. MacDonnell was watching her efforts with interest. Müller was absorbed in the large world globe on the large desk there, painstakingly sounding out the names he found.

"Diana-san, we heard the sad news about the duke. We are sorry," Toriko said, for the benefit of Frans and any other servants who might be listening.

"Yes, our condolences. Is there any way we can help?" MacDonnell inquired.

"No, I will be perfectly all right," Diana said, but the large knot that had been in her stomach earlier had returned. *Tonomori was not here!*

"Thank you, Frans, for everything. We can take care of ourselves now. You can send everyone to bed," Diana instructed.

"Good night to you then, Your Ladyship." Frans closed the door.

"What happened? Where is Tonomori?" Diana demanded eagerly.

"Everything went more or less according to plan," MacDonnell told her. His terse report left something to be desired.

"Yah, the ships blow, the buildings burn, so we know he was there, too," Müller added.

"After that, we don't know what happened," MacDonnell went on. "It was too dark to see anything, and we had our hands full. Toriko took a bad rap on the head."

"It is nothing, Diana-san," Toriko insisted. "But I wanted to see that you were safe. You now have what you have been wanting for a long time."

"Only when I know that *all* of you are safe," Diana replied in a hushed voice. The Nuremberg clock on the mantel ticked loudly.

They talked avidly of the attack. Toriko listened with professional interest to the recounting of the passing of the duke. She retrieved Diana's dagger and tucked it inside her kimono. "I will clean the blade for you and get you another sheath, lest some of the poison remain inside."

"What kind of poison was it?" MacDonnell asked. He did not approve of its use, being strictly a military man, but his curiosity was overwhelming.

"It is from the *fugu* fish," Toriko informed him. She

413

explained that the poison, culled from the innards of the Japanese blowfish, was always fatal, with no cure possible. The Japanese prized the delicate flavor of the fish's flesh, even though it occasionally caused a tingling sensation in the fingertips and lips. Toriko had tried some of the *fugu* meat herself, but found its taste negligible and not worth the risk. Despite care in its preparation, many people died each year from eating *fugu* fish.

"Then why eat it at all? What's the point?" MacDonnell wanted to know.

"Danger can be an attractive spice, MacDonnell-san," Toriko said quietly. *Else why do famous swordsmen, even the homeliest, attract women like moths to a flame?*

"I suppose so," MacDonnell conceded.

Diana was listening only halfheartedly, keeping an anxious eye on the slow progress of the single hand of the clock. Her new status as a murderer fleetingly entered her mind, and just as swiftly she dismissed the thought. It must not trouble her! What had to be done was done; she had been only an instrument of mercy and justice.

An hour crept by; the clock's hand was pointing to two.

A short scream of fright came from the other end of the house, in the servant quarters or the kitchen. Diana went immediately to investigate. She met the ever-reliable Amalia, swooping down the hall in a voluminous nightshift.

"Your Ladyship! Such a night. After all you have gone through," she sobbed.

"What happened? Is something wrong?"

"That *man*. It is a disgrace."

"Amalia, tell me what happened," Diana demanded firmly, looking beyond Amalia's bulk as if expecting to see a ghost. Amalia twisted the strands of her long, gray-streaked hair. Unable to sleep, she had gone to the kitchen for a bite to eat. And suddenly, the Japanese lord had appeared, giving her such a scare with his bloody face. He was roaring drunk, and dripping wet, and making a soggy mess everywhere.

"And . . . and so I told him so," Amalia sniffed. "And then he yelled at me." She began crying again.

414

"Amalia, I will take care of everything. I will speak to Tonomori about this. Now go to bed," Diana ordered.

"Thank you, Your Ladyship," Amalia began, but Diana was gone.

"My God!" Diana exclaimed when she reached the kitchen.

Tonomori turned to her fully. "You are the second person who has said that to me tonight, Diana-san. Are we to have religious services in here? If so, I am leaving."

"Your face?"

"I thought it had washed off. The blood is someone else's." Tonomori swayed slightly. He was holding the large mug of ale he had tapped from a cask in the pantry. "I thought it best that I enter through your kitchen, and spare everyone the need to see me so."

Diana didn't know whether to hug him or hit him. She decided on neither course of action. Tonomori would only hit her back, and he was damp and smelly.

"Is it possible to get a bath, Diana-san?"

"I'll awaken the servants."

"Don't bother. They will ask too many questions. The horse trough will do."

"Did you fall into the canal?"

"No, I jumped in to avoid the watch. I happened upon a large tavern brawl along the way, and I thought it a good idea to avoid being noticed. I came across a couple of German *landsknechts,* though, and we shared a few flagons. I enjoyed their company."

"And they didn't ask any questions about your appearance?" Diana tapped her foot, impatience mingling now with her concern and relief.

"No. They thought it none of their business, and they were drunk anyway. A good thing, too. I was very thirsty, having run all the way back to the city. My horse disappeared. That reminds me—the horse trough."

"I'll get you some clothes." Diana ran to find a change for him.

When he had bathed and was back into dry clothing, Tonomori felt better. He ate some leftover cold chicken before joining the company.

"I was beginning to wonder if you had made it," MacDonnell remarked casually.

"It was warm for a while. I thought I had built my own funeral fire," Tonomori said. He bowed to Toriko. "The ships were beautiful in their death, Toriko-san. Very well done."

She returned the bow.

Slowly, bit by bit, they began to recount exactly what had happened. Some of it already had been told, but for Tonomori the adventures of Toriko and Diana were new, and these, retold meticulously, were heard avidly again by all. Bone-weary as they were, and with nicks and bruises that were beginning to sting and throb in earnest, they were too excited to think of sleep. It was time instead to think about the future. And belatedly they began to become aware of the continuing peril in their situation. Their murderous deeds might still be uncovered and traced to them—with attendant horrors awaiting. Mere suspicion, much less proven guilt, could be enough to mean torture and death for all. Mutually, they found themselves seeking out bits of reassurance for each other, and they gradually turned back from apprehension to fullest appreciation of what they had accomplished. The talk went on until dawn, when servants began to stir.

The smells of breakfast cooking reminded them how hungry they all were. The table was prepared, and Diana went to it with a sharp appetite.

Tonomori piled his plate with poached eggs, sausage, hot buns, and strawberry jam, and dug in.

Diana watched him eat for a while, surprised. "I thought you didn't like eggs and sausage."

"This morning, everything smells good. And tastes good. Would someone pass the buns, please?"

After breakfast, they began to yawn. MacDonnell and Müller dragged off to their beds. Toriko excused herself and went to her room. Tonomori left to brew himself a cup of green tea from a jar he had been hoarding. Diana instructed that even if the world came to an end, she was not to be disturbed.

Alone in her bedchamber at last, Diana undressed by

herself. Usually, she would have had assistance, but she wanted no servants tut-tutting around her.

Diana pulled back the covers. And almost screamed. Tonomori already was in bed, waiting for her, almost hidden in the deep feather mattress.

"What *are* you doing in my bed?"

"Isn't it obvious?" He smiled.

Diana was beginning to get that odd feeling again, the one that came over her whenever Tonomori was near. She put a hand over her breast. "I can't! I'm exhausted. And we discussed this before. I will not sleep with you."

"Get into bed and we'll discuss it some more."

"Noooooo!"

Tonomori reached out and took her by the hand. Gently, he brought her down beside him and pulled the covers up.

"You can't have any strength left," Diana murmured.

"There is always strength left for pillowing, like there is always room for dessert," Tonomori assured her.

"This is dangerous. You know that." Diana felt her shift being pulled higher.

"This is delightful. I do know that."

"You must leave at once."

"I want you."

"No!"

"I need you."

"No!"

"I love you for always."

A small "Oh!"

Diana put her arms around Tonomori. And kissed him hungrily.

Chapter Twenty-eight

Rays of frozen light pierced the stained glass portrayal of the Virgin Mary and the Christ child in rich golds, reds, and blues over the altar of the cathedral. Sweet incense filtered upward through the chanting of the requiem high mass.

The body of the Duke of Alvino lay on a catafalque before the high altar beneath the arched ceiling of gray stone.

Spanish and Dutch nobles alike grew restless with the Latin droning of the Bishop of Utrecht, who was as dull as his vestments were splendid.

In the front pew, kneeling on a cushion of black velvet, the Countess Diana de Edgemont, her blondness accentuating her pallor, pressed her face into clenched hands, which held a silver crucifix and jet rosary beads. In complete mourning for her late betrothed, Diana wore black silk.

It was being whispered that the white robe of the Japanese woman, the Lady Toriko, was worn out of respect. In her country, it was the symbol for death. And the less pious left off counting their prayer beads to watch the Japanese lord, Tonomori, in the rich robes of the imperial court. It was noted appreciatively that he crossed himself like a gentleman.

Ah yes, the almond-eyed madonna and the warrior from the legendary Japans. The Countess Diana was fortunate in her retinue. They enhanced her prestige immensely, and in

Tonomori she had a champion, something of practical value in these unfortunately troubled times. Not even a bride, and already in mourning. Sympathetic tongues clucked.

"Half the people present are here only to make sure the duke is dead," Tonomori whispered to Diana.

"Be quiet! People will hear you," Diana whispered back.

It was true. Only good manners kept the Dutch from gloating openly. Alvino had been hated fiercely and many considered his end long overdue.

Ambassador Maldonado kneeled stoically, but his eyes burned into the corpse. He hoped the traitorous duke would howl in hell for all eternity. Maldonado had only just learned of Alvino's plot, and he was shaken at the man's perfidy. It was dreadful news, and he rightly feared that worse was to come.

The countess, appearing to grow faint, was escorted from the cathedral by her two companions. The ambassador thought that she was fortunate to have had so narrow an escape from the fate of being married to Alvino, but would not, of course, dream of telling her so. Let her grieve over an illusion; it would do her no harm.

Outside, MacDonnell and Müller were waiting with Tonomori's horse. Diana and the Lady Toriko took their seats in an enclosed sedan chair carried by four men and went their way.

The talk among the crowds gathered near the entrance to St. Mary's Cathedral was that the countess would retire to her country estate.

Inside the sedan chair, Diana and Toriko were in high spirits but they conversed in low tones to avoid being overheard.

"What do you do today, Diana-san?" Toriko asked, leaning back against the cushions. The pew had given her a backache.

"Well, I'd like to kick up my heels but I won't. I have proper appearances to maintain. But it is going to be so hard. To be back in the country again, not to have to put on a long face for everyone, to have some time to myself.

It's wonderful . . . You know, they say that revenge turns to ashes in the mouth. That is not so. I feel good, the best in a long time."

"But you should rest, Diana-san."

"And I will. I promise. And then it's back to work. I have so much left undone."

"How so? The duke is dead, his ships destroyed."

"Yes, but mine are still unbuilt."

"You have not spoken of this before, Diana-san."

"I could not. Not when I was fighting for my life. But when we were in Goa, I began thinking about an empire. I still have a grudge against the king for appointing men like Alvino," Diana informed her. "This week, I will have the plans drawn for two more galleons and five caravels to add to my fleet."

"So much expense. Can you afford it?"

"Oh, yes. My father left me a very wealthy woman. But his dealings were very quiet. I wish it to remain that way. Money is power but so is knowledge. I have learned a lot. The fewer people who know, the better off I will be."

Diana tried to relax but could not. She was once more at peace with Tonomori. The danger to which she had given way was still there, but now she found it exhilarating rather than prohibiting.

She also hoped that Tonomori would someday find his destiny, even though it might mean losing him. He could not be caged, except by duty. In this, at least, Diana had been able to help. His share of the cargo from Goa had been fifteen thousand ducats. She had saved the money for him. It would buy some of the guns he wanted for the bloody revenge of his own. He would need a ship. Why not one of hers—perhaps even the *Schoen*? She would have to find a way past the Portuguese monopoly of the route to the East.

"I also need a man of business," Diana remarked after a brief silence.

"How so? Do you not wish to remain in control?"

"Control, yes. I can order ships built and buy cargoes. But I need someone who knows the marketplace. I want to take trade away from Spain, and make money in the process.

"We will have a rebellion here, but the people are not yet prepared. We need to supply our own arms. So Sir Ian soon will be going north among the Zeelanders, to settle a location for a cannon foundry and a place to manufacture muskets. And a powder mill to supply the ammunition."

Toriko considered. "What will Tonomori-san do in the meantime?"

"He is going with Sir Ian. I will miss him, but he has never seen a cannon foundry or a musket factory. He wants to know all about them."

"It sounds perfect for him." Toriko was pleased.

As he rode with Tonomori behind the women, MacDonnell explained the latest developments in the field of cannon.

"The breechloaders are out, or at least will be eventually. They lack power and range. And the damned breechblock corrodes. After that, you have to melt it down and cast it over again. Very expensive."

"The alternative?" Tonomori asked.

"Muzzle loaders. The Dutch make the best bronze guns, you'll see. I've heard that the English are casting iron guns, with longer range and more power than the bronze. If iron becomes the fashion, then maybe we'll hear some more pretty church bells."

"I do not understand. Please explain?"

"When an army captures a city or any town, the first thing the mercenaries do is steal all the church bells for the metal to make cannon. When the guns wear out, the bronze goes back into the melting pot and out come the bells. A cheerful thought, that! A bronze gun blows you out of this life and, upon conversion into a bell, rings you on to the next." MacDonnell looked surprised at his profundity. "I will have to turn that thought into a poem."

Tonomori, who regarded MacDonnell's most recent efforts in poetry as less than mediocre, did not encourage him. "What about the Spanish?" he asked, tactfully changing the subject.

"They usually are lousy poets." MacDonnell seemed at least half-serious.

421

"No, I am wondering about the offical investigation into our destruction of the ships and the supplies."

"Müller says their inquiry is going nowhere. And Müller knows about these matters. If I were worried about it, ah, I would have advised our riding clear of here the moment we got back."

"Then you think Diana-san is in no danger?"

"No more than we, and I have no cares in the world as of the moment."

Diana paused at the town house only long enough for the servants to pack and load her trunks into a wagon. She made arrangements to have many candles lighted for the duke's soul, certain however that it was already burning in the lower regions like a wick. Except for a caretaker, the house was empty by midafternoon when Maldonado came to call.

He regretted having missed her, but he had enough troubles of his own and dismissed her from his mind.

The duke's ships were a total loss, but the pay chests of gold coins were recoverable from the smoldering holds. The ambassador ordered a salvage crew to begin work immediately.

The storehouses were another matter. Nothing remained of the structures but ashes and scorched brick. Underneath were stiff pools of bronze that once had been cannon. Thousands of muskets were turned into so much blackened and twisted pipe. All supplies and powder were burned. Everything had been paid for with money embezzled from the crown.

Adding to the ambassador's dilemma, troop morale was at an all-time low, especially among the officers who already had come to consider the Netherlands as a tomb for their careers.

Ignoring his responsibilities as second-in-command, Nunez had slipped through the patrols, which had been dispatched belatedly. Numerous other subordinates had vanished with him. Those whom Maldonado managed to find and arrest were quietly strangled in their cells or drowned in slopping tubs dragged in by the jailers. But first they were questioned with the help of hot iron and thumbscrews. Listening to the confessions, Maldonado grew more appalled with each scream and fresh revelation. The consequences for Spain of the duke's heinous crimes were enormous. Meanwhile, the investigation into the cause of the fires petered out quickly as soon as the implications of Alvino's treasonable plot became evident.

Only one course was open to Maldonado, lacking instructions from the crown: a complete cover-up. Disasters happened; one could only shrug and say, "It was the will of God."

With the duke in his grave, the citizens of Holland seemed less unruly, and Maldonado could breathe easier in that quarter. If a rebellion were to occur now, Spain's weakened forces might be swept out of the Netherlands.

For Diana, the passing of each new day lessened the anxiety that she and her companions would be caught. She knew her apprehension was unreasonable—all evidence had gone up in smoke—but she feared the possibility of an unknown witness or some overlooked clue. And she missed Tonomori; her nights were lonesome.

Then, on an afternoon in early October, her worst dread seemed to be realized. A servant rushed in to tell her that the Spanish ambassador and armed troops were in the entryway, that she was to come at once.

On seeing Maldonado's drawn face, Diana's heart pounded and her stomach grew leaden.

"I bring you grave tidings, Countess. . . ." The ambassador's manner was melancholy.

Diana's mind raced. Tonomori dead? . . . A witness had informed? . . . *What could have happened, a month after the disasters?*

But she maintained her bearing in the face of this newest stress. If she was going to the headsman, she would do it with grace. She had always known the risks.

"I regret that I must inform you that His Most Gracious Majesty, Charles, once ruler of the Holy Roman Empire, King of Spain, Naples, and the Netherlands, is dead," Maldonado now informed her, referring to King Philip's father, who had abdicated.

"I am so sorry to hear that, Excellency," Diana responded, relief flooding her like cool water. She gratified the ambassador with a prompt show of evident concern on her pretty face. *That sensuous downturned mouth!* Though not a philanderer, Maldonado had an eye for attractive women. If he only were not so busy—and his wife so near—the countess would be a tempting prospect.

"It happened just two weeks ago, on the twenty-first of September, at Yuste," Maldonado went on after a pause. "A funeral procession is being planned in Antwerp in honor of his memory."

"Of course; I will be there. The king was a great man, and certainly well remembered by his subjects here." Diana spoke with difficulty, having almost collapsed. The ambassador construed her emotion as grief.

"I am pleased to hear you say that, Countess. I had occasion to dine with the old king and liked him very much. He knew how to set a table," Maldonado said reminiscently. His own round form was a testament to his cook.

Part of Diana's reference to Netherlanders' esteem for the late King Charles was true, she reflected. Before his abdication, he was known as a robber, one as efficient as ever wore a crown. But he was ready to compromise with the Dutch in permitting them to maintain the ancient rights and privileges of the chartered cities—if only they would pay lip service to his placards, the edicts against heresy. So long as heretics sang their hymns, read their damned books in private, and caused no trouble, Charles had offered tolerance of a sort. Though he occasionally tried to renege on the deal, the burghers cynically had expected as much. On the other hand, his son, King Philip, who did not know the meaning of the word *compromise*, demanded the strictest adherence to the placards, and extorted taxes for Spanish foreign wars that had nothing to do with Holland's interests.

Diana put her hands to her face. "Please forgive me, Excellency! I should have realized that your men must be in want of something to eat and to drink." She raised her voice. "Matilda, bring the gentlemen wine. And some

424

cheese and olives, fresh bread, the ham, and the mustard pot. And bring a tray out to the garden for His Excellency.''

"You are kind. I *was* feeling a bit peckish. I trust that we didn't startle you, but we were riding this way and I thought to give you the sad news myself,'' Maldonado explained. He found the garden refreshing and his own chair a comfort.

"How might this affect King Philip's plans to visit here?'' Diana wondered.

"That's off until spring. His Majesty is in mourning, of course. He has also put off choosing a successor to the late duke, so I am stuck to the saddle,'' Maldonado told her. The tray arrived bearing a flagon of burgundy, a plate of sliced pork and beef, fresh buns, pickles, apples, a wedge of goat cheese, and a pile of honeycakes covered with crushed almonds. The ambassador ate with gusto, and between mouthfuls exchanged gossip with Diana, such details as he thought suitable for a lady—the rising prices of silk and wool, the success of the year's crop of grain, the difficulty in finding dependable servants.

After her initial flutterings of fright, Diana enjoyed the ambassador's visit and encouraged him to return—with Lady Maldonado. When he departed with his troops, she sank back down to the garden bench, weak with relief.

MacDonnell and Tonomori returned at the end of the month during the first cold storm. After they had stabled their horses and stowed their gear, the men sought out the company of Diana and Toriko in the study, before a cozy blaze in the fireplace.

"The news is good,'' MacDonnell reported. "The sites have been purchased and the wages agreed upon with the necessary guilds, who will provide the craftsmen when the buildings are completed. That should be by late spring or early summer.'' He sipped a cup of wine gratefully. It was hot, deliciously spiced with cinnamon and nutmeg.

"What about you, Tonomori-san? Have you made arrangements for your guns yet?'' Diana asked impersonally. She was eagerly impatient to be alone with him.

Tonomori, with a wooden bowl of walnuts in his lap,

was cracking them between thumb and forefinger. "No, Diana-san. The duke created a shortage in the market. All we saw were obsolete guns, and at high prices. Perhaps next spring. I may be your first customer."

"Was your journey worthwhile, then?"

"Yes. I saw a cannon barrel being poured. An incredible sight! The mold was made in the ground. The pour was made from four large cauldrons, ten men on each, all at the same time." The event was fresh in Tonomori's mind, and he made full use of his hands in giving graphic shape to his words. "It was a sight to behold: A ton and a half of metal, like a river of gold, flowing into the earch, with steam and smoke blowing out of the vents to the mold."

He described the foundry, an unassuming structure located by a river that turned a water wheel to produce the power for many of the tools, such as trip-hammers, polishing wheels, and grinders. He had never heard of anything like it in Japan, but one day there would be, he added. He had made careful notes and supplemented them with minutely explicit drawings, which the women examined with fascination.

Toriko listened with particular interest to his account. Feeling restless again, she had promised herself that in the spring, when the roads were good enough to travel, she would go with Tonomori wherever he went. They had not discussed the prospect of a return voyage to Japan. At least a year would be needed before Tonomori would be able to accumulate the weapons he sought. Beyond that, a voyage of two years would lie ahead of them.

When Diana inquired why Müller had not joined them, MacDonnell explained that he had decided to remain behind on business. Actually, Müller had found an opportunity of wintering with a robust widow whose buxom charms and ample pantry seemed much more appealing than loafing around Diana's estate, swapping old and familiar war stories with MacDonnell.

MacDonnell had been mildly relieved when Müller had made his preference known. The Lady Toriko was beginning to intrigue him as no other woman had. He now would have four months or more to become better

426

acquainted. Few things could improve relations like close daily contact, plus cold nights with nothing to do. Müller, he admitted to himself, would have been a drag in such a situation.

By now, he had surmised that Tonomori and the Countess Diana were playing the age-old game of slap-and-tickle, as troops were rudely fond of describing nocturnal sport. Even the densest of servants were aware that their mistress had taken a lover, and a foreign devil at that. Diana ignored the whispering and the sidelong looks. She was going to have to become hardened to the gossip so long as Tonomori was slipping into her bed.

The days went on pleasantly, the nights even more so. Except for MacDonnell: Toriko was consistently polite to him, but that was all his overtures produced.

Then, on one cold, wet morning, after Diana and Toriko had gone into the city on a day-long shopping expedition, MacDonnell sought out Tonomori and laid out the problem.

Tonomori, listening with sympathy, put down his ink brush. He had been working on a scroll.

"I'm telling you, I can't sleep well. And I'm off my feed," MacDonnell complained.

"It sounds like a trip to The Bed of Rose's would set you straight," Tonomori advised.

"That's off. Besides, it's too far. And I'm really smitten."

Tonomori pursed his lips, and looked wise.

"Maybe you don't approve?" MacDonnell suggested.

"I have no authority over Toriko-san," Tonomori told him. "But I will help you. Send her a poem."

"I already did."

"And what did she say?"

"She said, 'Very interesting.' "

"Hmmm. It means she was too polite to say it stank."

MacDonnell appeared to be agitated, his lean face creased with worry.

"Do you happen to have the poem with you?" Tonomori asked.

MacDonnell extracted a folded paper from the wallet at his belt and handed it over without a word.

Tonomori read carefully, his lips moving with the letters.

> *When the dove of the morning doth spring*
> * to the sky*
> *Then springs forth my love like a nightingale's*
> * cry.*
> *Their wings beat so gently, so gently*
> * together,*
> *The dance in the clouds of two birds*
> * of a feather.*

Tonomori laughed out loud.

"Is it that bad?" MacDonnell demanded, aghast.

"Worse!" Still laughing, Tonomori could hardly speak.

"I had not thought so ill of my efforts." MacDonnell's pride had been pricked, and he was almost pouting.

"Nor do I," Tonomori added quickly, to assuage his friend's feelings. "Nothing is really wrong with the poem. You just sent it to the wrong person."

"I did?"

"Yes. Some women I've known would eat a sweetmeat like this for breakfast," Tonomori said. "But Toriko does not consider herself a tender dove."

"She doesn't?" MacDonnell repeated.

"No. You will have noticed on occasion that she possesses a certain . . . fire."

"Yes. Yes, I have."

"And she has a taste for beauty and for words. Try for a different comparison. Say a falcon. It doesn't have to be a bird, though."

MacDonnell brightened. "I'll get to work on it right away."

Tonomori refolded the poem and kept it to read to Diana later. She appreciated that sort of froth, and it would put her in a receptive frame of mind later in the evening.

The women returned earlier than expected. Diana, excited and breathless, burst in on Tonomori. "We have just heard the news. Queen Mary is dead."

"The English queen?"

"Yes, and the wife of King Philip. *Our* Philip! She died less than a week ago, on the seventeenth of November,

428

and her half sister, Elizabeth, has taken the throne already. The Spanish are in an uproar!''

To Tonomori, the death meant nothing, and his face reflected his unconcern. His thoughts were turning to the *manuki* that the silversmith had made for him—and how he could send them to Obushi, who could employ them to haunt Masanori.

Diana was undaunted. ''What it means is that the Spanish have lost an ally. Philip's tie with England has been cut, some say for good. The impression that Elizabeth has given is that she is her own person, known for her tolerance, something rare among royalty these days!''

''Then why are you excited? What good is this going to bring to you in the Netherlands?''

''In time of war, the aid of an enlightened ruler would mean much to my people in a struggle to go our own way,'' she explained.

''Don't be too sure,'' Tonomori warned. ''In my country, daimyo do not encourage rebellion anywhere. It is rather like setting a fire near your own house and then fanning the flame.''

''Well, we'll see. The Spanish, at least, no longer can count on England's help.''

''But you haven't necessarily gained a friend,'' Tonomori pointed out. Diana did not answer. Sometimes she could find nothing but frustration in even trying to talk with him.

A woman who ruled a nation! Diana was fascinated by the thought. A woman in a world usually governed by men, and making her own way. Eager for more news, Diana kept her ears open and sought sources of information. One of her best was Ambassador Maldonado, privy as he was to so many confidences of the diplomatic pouch. Isolated as the de Edgemont mansion was, she found herself making more journeys into Antwerp whenever the winter weather permitted.

By January, Diana grew weary enough of the isolation to move her household back to the town house. The task was monumental, but the servants did not complain. They, too, were bored, and the attractions of the city were many. They looked ahead to the prospect of skating on the frozen canals and to the parties and festivities that always seemed to be going on in one place or another.

When she was settled in, Diana paid a call on Lady Maldonado and the ambassador, who could be counted upon to divulge the latest news from all over the continent.

Maldonado needed no encouragement. Elizabeth Tudor, Queen of England, was the richest matrimonial prize in Europe. On the first day of the new year, as was the custom, gifts from her subjects and from opportunistic unattached princes throughout Christendom had poured, in bejeweled profusion, into her new residence, Whitehall Palace. Her formal coronation in mid-month completed her ascendancy.

"The French, of course, are enraged, little good it will do them," Maldonado chuckled. Queen Mary's death had appeared to provide renewed opportunity for France's aspirations, as everyone had recognized, but the war with Spain had left her weakened and unable to make an overt move. France claimed the throne of England belonged to another Mary, one who was descended in an unblemished line from Margaret, sister of Henry the Eighth. This Mary, "Queen of Scots," had been raised in the French court, though her mother, Mary of Guise, ruled Scotland in her stead as regent.

Elizabeth, on the other hand, had been declared a bastard by her own father after he had beheaded her mother, Ann Boleyn. Her claim therefore was invalid, according to French thinking.

". . . which is slightly muddled at best," Maldonado continued. "And here Spain shows herself to be a true friend of England." King Philip already had sent out feelers through his diplomats, along with suitable gifts.

"After all, he knew Elizabeth when he was married to her older half sister, and liked her. I hope that the new queen will show good sense, like the late queen, and take our king for her husband. Best to let a man steer the ship of state, don't you agree, Countess?"

Diana felt like kicking him. "Of course," she murmured.

Two officers stood discreetly in the doorway, waiting for the ambassador to finish. He waved them in.

"Countess Diana, I would like to introduce my two newest captains, Señors Enrique Serrano and Felipe Pidal. Fine men, both of them." Maldonado obviously was proud of them.

"Charmed to meet you, Your Ladyship," Pidal said, bowing.

"Your servant, ma'am," Serrano said with a graceful sweep of his arm.

"Your errand, gentlemen?" Maldonado asked.

"You are needed at the citadel, Excellency," Pidal told him. "The replacement officers have arrived with the supply ship. The vessel is shortweighted and the alleged officers are totally unfit."

"Mother of God!" Maldonado exclaimed. "A penance for past transgressions."

He sat back heavily in his chair, stroking his beard. "Very well. Await me in the next room, and I will be along shortly."

He nodded as they made their bows and left.

"I predict fine careers for them both. They proved steadfast during the recent, er, difficulties."

Maldonado thought that, with another year of seasoning, they would be ready for a rougher tour of duty, perhaps at one of His Majesty's naval bases in Italy, where they could put their eager swords to good use against the constant encroachment of the infidel Turks.

Then he remembered his manners and his distinguished guest, and startled Diana by mentioning a strong rumor that the French might be planning an invasion of England through Scotland. "But I doubt they've the resources. The Guises are on shaky footing in Scotland. With the Calvinists ready to stab them in the back, they have enough troubles without French intervention."

In other words, Diana inferred from Maldonado's words, the Spanish dogs were growling the frogs away from a meaty bone they had come to regard as their own.

She left the ambassador's residence in high spirits, and with a plan forming.

"England in the spring. So you still have *that* bee in your bonnet," Tonomori remarked after she had returned, so excited that she was practically skipping about the house.

"No bees about it! *You* may come if you wish. Or stay, if you wish, but *I* am going," she announced breezily.

"If you go, I go. You will be in need of my protection," Tonomori retorted.

"Oh, I am sure many handsome English lords will be ready to come leaping to my aid." Diana's sugary tone was calculated to annoy Tonomori. Expecting a more enthusiastic response, she now was irritated.

"Then they'll look like a great lot of fleas," Tonomori said. "You have a penchant for trouble, Diana-san."

"Spoken like a true hero, my champion."

"It is my duty to save you from yourself," Tonomori bluntly told her. When she was in one of her fractious moods, nothing he could say would be satisfactory.

"Well, as far as I'm concerned then, it is settled," she declared imperiously. "And, I might add, I am going to employ someone immediately to tutor us in English. I speak none, and MacDonnell's accent carries too much of a Scottish burr to be of any use."

"Son of a bitch!" was Tonomori's comment. He had heard Englishmen speaking, and thought they sounded like barking dogs, almost as bad as Germans. Or the Dutch.

"Your choice of language seems to have declined since Sir Ian joined our ranks," Diana chastised. "Speaking of which, I wish you would talk to him."

"About what?"

"Toriko. He has been courting her constantly, making a pest of himself."

"Has she said this to you?"

"No, but I think . . ."

"Then let whatever happens run its course. Think, Diana-chan, would you have listened to anyone who warned you against me?"

"Nooo."

"There, you see?"

Diana wasn't through. "Well, if there's any trouble, don't say I didn't warn you." She left the room in a huff.

Tonomori was puzzled. "Why should she warn me?"

he wondered aloud. "Why should there be any trouble? It makes no difference to me if there is. Why isn't she making any sense?" He wished MacDonnell and Toriko well. If their lives were to be linked, that was *karma*, and nothing he could say or do would change it.

Toriko had been carefully turning the matter over in her mind in recent weeks. She tried to occupy herself with *ninja* training but could not summon the usual enthusiasm and verve. Her efforts in writing were hopelessly inane. A winter landscape she undertook in stark blacks and whites turned out to be not even as bleak as her existence. MacDonnell kept popping up in her thoughts, like the mechanical figures in those magical Augsburg clocks. And as startling.

At first, she had haughtily dismissed him as a barbarian, uncouth and unwashed. But he seemed to have taken to the tub readily enough, and she had discovered that his manners were not so bad, using the behavior of Europeans as a measuring stick. And, when the spirit moved him, he could even write. He had helped, after all, save Diana's honor. And Toriko owed him her own life.

Gratitude and a growing affection—potent ingredients for two people living in such close togetherness.

Toriko reread his latest poem.

Winter snows, like the white salt
of many tears, melt into the earth,
stirring the sleeping life within.
From this cold death does life peep out
green and struggling, richer than princes,
timid as a bird's first song.
Then quick to blossom—a lifetime
in a summer's day.
So goes my life.
Spring was yesterday; summer today.
Tomorrow, the shade thins beneath
empty trees, winter piling ahead.
Do our shadows join in the afternoon sun,
in flickering candlelight warm as blood?
Or do our footsteps crackle alone
among the brittle leaves borne by the winds?

Toriko rolled the paper into a tube and tied it with blue ribbon. She would think about what he had written, what he had implied. Her life was lonely, but that had been her decision long ago. MacDonnell was to walk with her this afternoon in the garden, such as it was, with plants and stems covered with burlap against the·cold. What was he likely to say? And how should she reply?

Diana's announcement that they would be going to England had swept everything from Toriko's mind. She was delighted by the prospect of travel.

"I would like to see the English barbarians," Toriko told Tonomori shortly before she prepared to bundle up and stroll with MacDonnell.

"Yes, I understand that it is an island kingdom that is able to withstand the wolves howling across the channel," Tonomori replied. "A lesson for ourselves?"

"A pertinent thought, Tonomori-san," Toriko agreed. The winter's peace contrarily had put them both on edge, and they had been short with each other recently. They tried not to snarl when Diana was near, but even this restraint proved difficult, because she usually was with them.

Toriko found Tonomori overbearing and callous at times. Tonomori thought Toriko could use a good pillowing to mellow her moodiness. He wished MacDonnell luck with the lovely bitch. He was going to need it.

The *ashigaru* reacted with alarm to the news of the forthcoming adventure. Were they never going home? Why must they learn yet another barbarous tongue? And did it rain there all the time, as they had heard?

"You won't melt. You are going. That's an order," Tonomori snapped.

Yamahito said nothing in response. Arguing with a samurai was unthinkable, like pissing into the wind. Oshabiri cradled his pet monkey, Saru. As if he needed·any more troubles! Saru had only just acquired another enemy, latest on a long list—this time a cat named Bad Alice, Diana's favorite. As a kitten, Bad Alice had been bullied by Saru at every opportunity. Now fully grown, with two extra toes on each front paw and one extra on her hind feet, Bad

434

Alice considered Saru to be fair game. Her favorite ploy was to stare at him until he fled the room. And she really terrorized him at mealtimes. Oshabiri, certain that Saru was losing weight, considered dropping Bad Alice down the nearest well. He refrained because of the realization that if Tonomori found out, Oshabiri would be joining her.

The servants were in a dither. Who was to go with the countess? Who was to remain behind, denied this treat of a lifetime?

Diana, postponing any such decisions, left with Tonomori for a quiet walk. Outside, she wrapped her cloak tightly around her.

"I cannot cope with all this now. All the servants are talking to me at once," Diana said. She could see that MacDonnell already was walking with Toriko in the far corner. "Shall we join them?"

"I think not, Diana-san. It is something they must work out for themselves." Tonomori's feet were cold, and he wished he had the bearskin shoes that samurai, by tradition, wore in summer or winter campaigns.

"Have you thought some more about the voyage?" she asked.

"Yes. My country is an island. England is an island. I would like to study the similarities. Why are England's knights and men-at-arms so feared? What gives such a small kingdom its strength?"

"I had not thought of that, but yes, you are right," Diana said. "I was more concerned that you might be anxious to return to Japan."

"I *am* anxious, Diana-san, but leaving too soon would be worse than not leaving at all. So long as I live, Masanori must worry about my return one day. And I will. Masanori and Lord Atsuhira will die, and their treachery will be no more. My master's spirit will be avenged."

A sharp wind came up and sent them hurrying indoors. To be overly chilled was to risk a fever.

That evening, they sat down to a quiet dinner. Diana did most of the talking. MacDonnell hardly talked at all and merely picked at his food even more than he had been lately.

"This week I will send a dispatch to my agents in London to find a house and make all the necessary arrangements for an indefinite stay," Diana announced merrily. She noticed that Toriko was saying nothing; MacDonnell's suit apparently was not prospering. Diana felt relieved, thinking this probably was for the best. What she did not know was that MacDonnell's foot was creeping softly sideways to play with Toriko's.

"I am looking forward to it, Diana-san," Tonomori said, correctly interpreting Toriko's manner and MacDonnell's sidelong glances. "In fact, in time, we all will."

"I'm happy to hear you say that, Tonomori-san," Diana told him.

"We should drink to it, then?" Tonomori asked with smug satisfaction. *This will teach you to meddle, Diana-san.*

"To the meeting of East and West," Diana toasted, raising her goblet.

They all joined her.

Toriko left for bed early, complaining of a headache. MacDonnell, finding his conversation lagging, bade Diana and Tonomori a good-night a half hour later.

Diana found herself getting sleepy. "I think it's bedtime for me, too."

Tonomori whispered in her ear, "Care for a little company?"

The corners of Diana's mouth turned up in a mischievous smile. "*Mmmmm.* I'd like that. You're better than a warming pan."

Two rooms away from Diana's bedchamber, Toriko undressed slowly by candlelight, her every careful movement a silken rustle. Sir Ian MacDonnell sat on the bed and untied the drawstrings of his doublet, his fingers fumbling. A lump had swelled in his throat ever since her soft answer that afternoon. The blood was humming in his ears—an old song that had no words, and needed none to sing.

"Do you think he'll get over it?" Diana asked as Tonomori joined her beneath the covers.

"I'm sure he will find consolation somewhere," Tonomori predicted with accuracy.

436

"Oh, good. I dislike seeing anyone unhappy." Diana snuggled against Tonomori's side, and they were still for a while.

"What are you thinking?" Diana wondered aloud.

"A poem. Many things. And you."

Diana leaned against him. "Can you tell me?"

"When it is written, I will tell," he promised.

The brush strokes took shape in his mind. Forms floated and drifted across each other. A sandy beach stretching into a morning fog, white sea birds swirling through like rice boiling in a pot . . .

Pale wings stretching on the wind,
Free, free, follow me.
To the sacred mountains of a thousand gods,
Rising green from the deep blue waters.
Golden people in the rising sun,
Are beyond the horizon,
A fair wind sighs
To the sea, to the sea . . .

Diana moved against his side, and Tonomori pulled her closer to him with great tenderness, her hair spilling across his breast where stirred his heart. He would finish it tomorrow.

Japanese is *yasashii*!

That is, the Japanese words that appear in this book are relatively simple to understand, both in the context of their use and with occasional reference to the definitions in this glossary.

In addition, the reader will find that pronunciation often tends to follow that of similar constructions of English-language words. Thus, for example, such words as *mempo*, *ninja*, *ko-cha*, *karma* can be read exactly as they would be in English. Other simple guidelines to approximate pronunciation would include these: *a* as in father; *e* as in pet; *i* as in machine; *o* as in horse; and *u* as in book. The diphthong *ai* has an *i* sound, as in time. Some phonetic spellings are indicated below.

The dozen words that the reader will encounter most frequently in *Daimyo* (or which have the greatest significance) are shown first: other words used in the book (ordinarily in *italics*) follow.

ashigaru (ah-she-gah-roo)	Footsoldiers.
daimyo (dime-yo)	Feudal lord.
hachimaki	Cloth headband, originally worn under a helmet.
hakama (ha-kah-ma)	Loose, baggy trousers.
mon	Family crest.
naginata	Long slashing spear with curved blade; of many styles.
ninja	Assassin, renowned and feared.
ronin (roe-nin)	Masterless samurai, held in disgrace.
samurai (sah-moo-rye)	Privileged warrior caste, the equivalent of European knights.
tachi	Two-handed fighting sword, worn slung at the waist, edge down. Used in combat until early 1600s, later worn only at court.

tanto	A dagger less than 11.9 inches in length, carried by people of all ranks, occasionally by samurai as second sword.
tsuba	Sword guard.

* * *

aikuchi	Dagger without a hilt, frequently with elaborate fittings.
bo-ken	Fencing sword of hardwood.
cha	Tea; a generic term.
daikon	Large white radish.
do	Breastplate or breast armor.
dojo	School.
eboshi	Curved felt cap worn by samurai to cushion the helmet, later (after helmet liners) only as a decoration.
geta	Wooden platform shoes, like clogs.
hai	Yes.
ko-cha	Chinese tea.
kanji	Japanese writing, the complicated style borrowed wholesale from the Chinese.
ken	Ancient sword with straight blade; also a generic term for sword.
kami	Spirit.
karma	Fate, destiny.
konban-wa	Good evening; a greeting.
mempo	Mask of armor covering half the face; usually grotesque, to frighten an adversary.
mekugi-ana	A hole in sword's handle end where a peg holds the handle in place.
namban tetsu	Foreign iron used by Japanese.
nambanjin	Literally, "southern barbarians," but referring to Europeans; a derogatory term.
Noh	Sophisticated dramatic theater with rigidly stylized performances.

o-cha	Japanese green tea.
obi	Wide sash of silk brocade, tied in large bow at the back.
odoshi	Armor lacings; many forms and colors.
shoji	Sliding panel used as a door.
sukashi	Ornamental pierced iron sword guard.
shuriken	Throwing knives of several shapes.
sumo	Wrestling.
sushi	A delicacy, usually pickled rice with fish or vegetables, rolled, wrapped in seaweed, and sliced. Of many varieties.
Taira	Once a powerful clan, obliterated in battle in 1185.
taiko	Drums.
taisho	General (military).
tatami	Floor mat; also, sleeping mat.
tang	End portion of blade to which handle is fastened.
torii	Gate.
wakizashi	Short sword more than 11.9 inches but less than 24. Worn by all ranks; frequently worn by samurai as second sword.
wako	Chinese epithet meaning "dwarf," used to describe Japanese pirates in Asian waters.
yamabushi	Mountain warriors, usually in reference to militant Buddhist monks.
yoroi	Armor.
yumi-yari	Socketed spear tip fastened to end of a war bow.